THE
CHANGELING
WAR

THE CHANGELING SAGA

THE CHANGELING WAR

Peter Garrison

ACE BOOKS, NEW YORK

This book is an Ace original edition,
and has never been previously published.

THE CHANGELING WAR

An Ace Book / published by arrangement with
the author

PRINTING HISTORY
Ace trade paperback edition / April 1999

The Penguin Putnam Inc. World Wide Web site address is
http://www.penguinputnam.com

ISBN: 0-441-00552-7

ACE®
Ace Books are published by The Berkley Publishing Group,
a member of Penguin Putnam Inc.,
375 Hudson Street, New York, New York 10014.
ACE and the ''A'' design are trademarks
belonging to Charter Communications, Inc.

PRINTED IN THE UNITED STATES OF AMERICA

10 9 8 7 6 5 4 3 2 1

THE CHANGELING WAR

Disputed territories
(formerly
Kingdom of Orange)

To Kingdom
of Green

Palace
of
Gray

Aubric enters
tunnel here

Hidden treasure
of Orange

The
Room
of Choice

The Great Abyss

Aubric's
escape

The Palace
of Light

Tunnels of
THE CASTLE
(partial view)

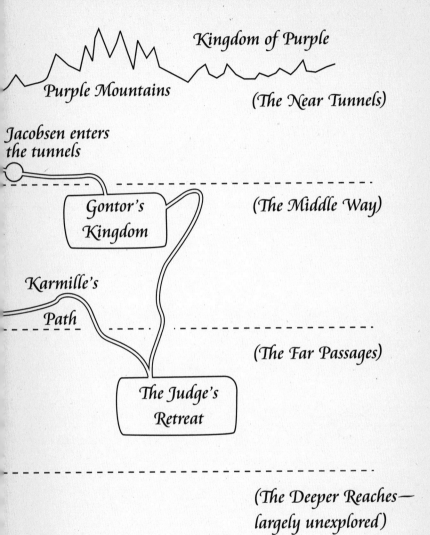

Kingdom of Purple

Purple Mountains

(The Near Tunnels)

Jacobsen enters
the tunnels

Gontor's
Kingdom

(The Middle Way)

Karmille's

Path

(The Far Passages)

The Judge's
Retreat

(The Deeper Reaches—
largely unexplored)

Prologue

H E WAS KNOWN AS THE
Pale Man. For those who dared to get close enough to in-
spect the features beneath the broad-brimmed hat that often
left his face in shadow, his skin appeared to be a very light
grey, more the color of pallid stone than the color of flesh;
the same color as the irises in his unblinking eyes, the same
color as the gums around his chilling smile; a color that
was hardly any color at all.

Few wished to get involved with someone with the Pale
Man's talents. You came to him only when you were desperate, if the need for money or dope or the latest experi-
mental wonder drug mattered so much you didn't care what
he asked of you. For the Pale Man always asked for favors
in return, favors that might haunt you for the rest of your
life. That is, of course, if you managed to live through to
the end of what you had been asked to do.

You could find the Pale Man anywhere and everywhere,
from the most sparkling boardroom to the darkest back
alley. You simply had to know how to look. He would be
waiting for you with his death grin and those eyes that

could look inside your head, your heart and your soul. And
he would get you what you thought you wanted, then ask
for so much more in return.

Eric Jacobsen, the latest of those who sought the Pale
Man's help, was ushered into the room by a pair of men
he had never seen before. The room had nothing to distin-
guish it: pale green institutional walls, with curtains of a
slightly darker hue that looked like they could use a good
cleaning. They were the kind of colors that were supposed
to inspire calm, but there was something about the lighting
here, harsh at the room's center, nonexistent in the corners,
that was anything but calming. At the far end of the room,
the Pale Man stepped from the shadows. Jacobsen was
pushed into a plastic cafeteria chair under the light. He saw
a scratched coffee table off to his right. The room had no
other furniture.

The words rushed out of Jacobsen as soon as the two
men released their grip. "They're going to kill me if I don't
do something. I don't have the money. There's no way I
could get that kind of money—"

The Pale Man brushed away Jacobsen's explanation
with a flick of his colorless hand.

"Do you have the address?" the Pale Man asked in a
tone more rasp than voice. Hearing that voice shut Jacobsen's mouth. It was the kind of voice that sounded gruff
like an animal, cold like a machine, anything but human;
the kind of voice that didn't even belong in this world.

Jacobsen realized the Pale Man expected an answer.

"Uh, yeah. They handed me the address outside, but
how—?"

"On the table in front of you," the Pale Man replied.

Jacobsen looked down and saw the gun; a short, stocky,
silver thing. He could have sworn it wasn't there a minute
before.

He had never handled a gun before, always scared he'd
do something stupid or clumsy. He touched it tentatively,

as if the metal might burn his fingers, but the gun was cool to the touch. There was nothing to do but pick it up.

The Pale Man's rasp made Eric look up. "Don't shoot until you get quite close. Less chance of a mistake."

"But I don't—"

The Pale Man frowned. "The men outside can give you any instruction you need." His hand flicked out again, a wave of dismissal.

Jacobsen didn't move.

"I don't know—"

"You will finish this, or you will answer to me." The Pale Man stepped back, and was lost in shadow.

Eric Jacobsen hadn't said all he wanted to say. But the Pale Man was gone, and the others still waited outside. The gun sat in his hand. It was very heavy for something so small. Jacobsen wanted to call out, to demand some answers, but he knew he would get no response.

He was very much alone.

Book One

Skirmishes

"At the beginning of Our Year of Triumph 15,007, it appeared that the war would never end. The current battle had raged for well over a hundred years, and each small victory seemed to breed more new factions rather than alliances, as if the never-ending warfare were causing the very fabric of society to unravel. For the first time, our Glorious and Ancient Civilization seemed on the verge of collapse without any source of strength to unify the whole.

"Ah, but a civilization as diverse and multifaceted as our own will often harbor hidden sources of strength and rebirth. So it was that a certain, unheeded corner of our own societal structure—a group ignored, even belittled by those around them, a subset of our culture kept alive almost entirely by an unthinking tradition— would step forward to lead our world toward a new era; an era that, despite certain skeptics, may hold more promise than any period since that of the Great Cruelty..."

—from *The Castle; Its Unfolding History* (a work in progress).

.1.

The World

"GET DOWN HERE THIS MIN-
ute, young man!"

Brian Clark winced. The voice sliced through him like
the sound of chalk on blackboard, stopping his phone conversation midsentence.

"Gotta go," he whispered into the receiver, to Karen,
the only girl who would ever understand.

"Your mother?" Karen shot back. "On your case again,
huh?" That was Karen. She just knew.

"Yeah," he replied. "Something's up."

"Brian?" His mother's shrill voice echoed up the stairs.
"I'm warning you!"

"Parents." Karen laughed. "They're terminally screwed,
aren't they?"

Brian chuckled, more to laugh along with Karen than in
response to what she said. He hated to think what his parents would do if he used words like that.

"Call you later," he said instead. He hung up the phone
and walked out into the hall, careful not to get tripped up
by his slightly too-long jeans. His mother always bought

them that way; she claimed he was growing too fast for her to buy him pants that fit.

"Mom?" he called down the stairs. "I'm right here!"

"Don't talk back to me, young man!" His mother was waiting for him at the foot of the stairs, her hands on her hips. "Get down here this instant! When your father gets done outside, we're going to have a little talk."

That didn't sound good, but then it hardly ever did. Brian came down the stairs carefully, one step at a time. He didn't want to rush or trip or make extra noise. His mother paced at the foot of the stairs like a hungry lion waiting for Christians.

"About time!" she announced the instant his foot hit the hardwood floor at the base of the stairs. She waved across the foyer to the family room. "Look at this place!"

Brian looked quickly at everything included in the wave; the coatrack, the front door, the front hall table with its basket for mail, the small mirror above the table—and his reflection in the mirror, pale, frowning face topped by short dark hair—the doorway into the family room, and the family room beyond. As usual, he didn't know what was wrong. Sure, there were a couple magazines on the table. And he had left an empty glass by the couch when he ran upstairs to answer his phone. But, besides that, the place looked no different from when he'd walked in from school two hours ago. Maybe it was because he'd left the TV on.

He looked back at his mother. He hoped she would give him a hint. But she just stood there and glowered.

"Sorry," he mumbled. That word alone would protect him for a minute.

"Brian, Brian, Brian," his mother sadly replied, like his name was some kind of a mantra holding back her anger, or maybe an explanation for everything that was wrong in the world. His mother still stared, the hawk ready to pounce, the judge about to pass sentence, unless Brian could instantly make things right.

Something clicked inside him. How many times had he

wilted under that stare? He didn't have to stand here like this. He was almost sixteen. Most of the kids at school—just about everybody but Karen, he guessed—thought he was some kind of wimp, and this was where it all started every day. Nobody else would put up with this kind of shit. He sometimes wondered why he hadn't left this place years ago. His fingers curled into fists at his sides.

He took a step back toward the stairs. "Mom, I've got things—"

He was stopped by a single look. His mother's gaze, cold and distant before, now burned him as if she might turn him to ash with a glance. Her lips barely moved as she spoke. "You know what happens to boys who talk back."

No. He wouldn't be pushed around. He had to make his mother understand. "Mom, I'm not a boy anymore."

"Not a boy?" His mother made a sputtering noise. "I don't see that you've made any money around here. What do you do for the family, anyway, besides eat and take up space—?"

He'd heard this all before. He couldn't stand to hear it again.

"Shut up!" he yelled. "Shut up! Shut up! Shut up!" The furniture rattled as he stamped his feet.

His mother's voice was soft, almost a whisper. "Temper tantrums are for little boys."

Brian wanted to destroy something. He slammed the flat of his hand against the wall. The whole room shook with the force of the blow.

"I've warned you about that anger," his mother continued in that same soft tone. Her tight lips had curled into the slightest of smiles. "You're going to kill somebody someday."

Brian stopped breathing. He wasn't a boy anymore! He had to get angry sometimes. Didn't he? He would destroy everything with his anger. His whole life was impossible.

He let out a single, high-pitched wail.

"You're just totally out of control, aren't you?" His mother turned her head sharply away to stare at the front door. "What could be keeping your father? I swear I can't depend on any male around here."

In the silence that followed, Brian heard faint noises coming from outside; voices raised in anger, and someone revving a car engine.

His mother frowned and walked toward the front door. Brian felt the tightness in his chest loosen just the slightest little bit. Anything for a distraction.

His mother jumped as they heard three quick bursts outside, like somebody rapping at a door, only ten times louder.

"What was that?" she demanded.

Brian thought they were gunshots.

His mother rushed to the window and pushed aside the miniblinds. She opened her mouth and made a noise unlike any Brian had ever heard, a shriek that seemed to go on forever.

PEOPLE WERE SCREAMING.

Joe Beast jumped into the car. His cousin Ernie stared at him openmouthed.

"Jeez, Joe—"

Joe stared hard at his cousin. He'd had enough back talk for one day.

"Drive," he ordered.

Ernie couldn't handle complications. His head twitched as if he was using all his willpower not to look at the man bleeding on the lawn behind them.

"You hear me?" Joe asked.

Ernie stomped on the accelerator, shifting the Buick quickly from first to third, the LeSabre's tires squealing as it jumped away from the curb. Ernie knew enough not to mess with Joe when he used that tone of voice.

Joe wiped off the gun. They'd have to find a place to

dump it. That asshole had made him shoot. Didn't anybody ever tell him not to mess with a man holding a gun?

Joe stared out at the suburban streets as Ernie quickly left the mess behind, block after block of neat ranch houses, their lawns sprouting new spring grass, tiny flowers showing here and there. All perfect little bits of suburban paradise. All except one, behind them, the new shoots brown with blood; the fat man spread across the lawn, his arms splayed out like a puppet, blood still pumping from his throat.

Joe had thought he was beyond this sort of thing. He was the college man, after all, the guy who knew how to talk his way through anything. Shooting the guy—that was the sort of thing Ernie would do; the sort of thing Ernie had done a few times too many. Roman and the boys thought that way, too. That's why they had put Joe in charge.

He was just supposed to make sure that Mr. Alan Clark gave them what they wanted, or would get delivered to a prearranged location, probably to see Joe's uncle. Uncle Roman didn't burden Joe with the exact details—it had always seemed simpler and safer that way. But Joe had never expected this kind of resistance.

He could still see the fat guy grabbing for the gun in his hand, and he could still feel his own finger squeeze the trigger almost before he could think of it, the gunshots impossibly loud in the still suburban air.

"Fucked," Ernie moaned as he stared straight ahead, talking more to himself than to Joe. "It's all fucked, isn't it? But, hey, if everything's fucked, maybe we can leave this part of it behind. If everything's fucked, what difference does it make?"

Joe shook his head. Joe never tried to decipher Ernie's logic. They might be cousins, but their brains didn't bear the slightest family resemblance.

After all, Joe had gone to college, maybe more to play football and pick up girls than anything to do with learning, at least at first. But then he blew his knee out in the first game they put him in. With football out of the question, and the draft waiting for anybody who didn't have a student deferment, he'd finally been forced to become a student.

College and a business degree had allowed him to pass some clever moves on to his uncle and his late father. They'd rewarded him with a more-or-less legitimate job at the edge of their operation. He'd bided his time, twenty years now of running a business for his uncle, with the occasional job like this on the side. Roman Petranova had praised his patience, told him it was all about to pay off. He just had to run this one little errand with Ernie, and then they'd talk.

Joe sighed. Until maybe five minutes ago, he had been destined for great things.

Ernie started to mutter again, "Maybe it'll be all right. It's fucked, but it's all right. Look at it around here. It's more deserted than midtown at midnight. Nobody even walks down these streets in the middle of the day."

Now that his cousin mentioned it, Joe realized they'd hardly seen anybody. He turned in his seat to look behind him. They were the only car on the street. Maybe they could get away from all this after all.

"Fuck it!" Ernie started to laugh. "This whole place is empty. Nobody's home! Who's gonna find us? Who's gonna know?"

For once, Joe hoped Ernie was right.

The sirens started in the distance.

· 2 ·

The Castle

AUBRIC STOPPED BREATHING for a moment, listening for sounds of pursuit. There was nothing, only the sound of the wind high up in the trees and the distant chatter of birds. Somehow, he had lost them.

Everything seemed a jumble since the Grey prince's men had surprised them. The three of them, Aubric and his fellow lieutenants, had been sitting at the edge of a clearing in the sun, far away, they thought, from enemy lines. They had been sharing stories from their childhood, in those long-ago days when they had been protected from the war. Aubric had told a joke and the others were laughing when Lepp had fallen forward, an arrow in his back. Savignon had leapt up as half a dozen men with swords had stepped from the silent woods. By the time Aubric had retrieved his own weapon, Sav was lost in the enemy's midst. But the swordsmen had been so intent on subduing his friend, no one was paying much attention to Aubric. He had seen an opening, and he had run.

Someone shouted as he ran across the clearing, away

from the fight. An arrow flew close by his ear. But then he
was in the trees, rushing down one hill and up the next, the
thickness of the forest protecting him from errant missiles.
If they wanted to catch him, they would have to chase him.

In running, he had spared barely a thought for his companions. Lepp had lain still on the ground, Sav overwhelmed by superior forces. Surely, Sav was a dead man,
too, hacked apart by the surrounding swords. Even if Aubric had lent his sword to the fight, the results would have
been the same. Worse, for they would have all been dead.
But Aubric had seen a way to escape.

He had run. His friends had died, and he had run.

He couldn't stop running, or he would die as well.

He had thought he heard sounds of pursuit at first, but
they were gone. What would they sound like, after all? He
had heard nothing before he and his friends were attacked.
Perhaps they didn't have to crash through the forest after
him, but could fly through the air, or simply vanish from
one corner of the forest and reappear in another. Perhaps
the sorcerers employed by the enemy had come up with
some magic aid that would give their troops an edge, some
twist that the sorcerers working for Aubric's side had not
yet found a way to counter.

Perhaps. Aubric only knew he had no more strength to
run. He had to stop, to think, to consider his options based
on what he really knew rather than what he might suspect.
If the others were going to catch him, they would catch
him now.

He sat on a large rock and sighed. He listened to the
noise of birds and the small creatures of the wood. The
enemy was nowhere about. His friends were gone as well.
Whether he had deserted them or saved himself, he was all
alone.

A sudden clatter overwhelmed the quiet forest sounds.
Aubric placed his hand on the hilt of his sword, quickly
scanning the surrounding forest for danger. The noise was
in front of him, in the direction he had been traveling. It

was the last sort of noise he'd expect in the middle of the
forest—a heavy, mechanical sound—the groan of hinges,
the whir of gears.

A bush shook half a dozen feet before him, then rose
from the ground. Aubric leapt from the rock and took a
couple of steps away, his exhausted muscles complaining
at even that movement. Earth and leaves shivered as the
bush swung away to reveal a trapdoor covered by six inches
of dirt. The groans grew louder as the trapdoor inched upward, as if the machine was seldom used and needed to
complain every inch of the way. It groaned to a stop at last,
revealing an opening maybe three feet wide. Aubric saw
light flicker from the dimness of the hole. He heard the
distant music of a flute.

Aubric decided he should be cautious. Still, no one had
attacked. He took a careful step forward.

A large, wrinkled face peered out of the new opening.
"About time you got here!"

"Pardon?" Aubric replied, quite startled. Still, something about all this kept him from drawing his sword. "Do
we know each other?"

The very wrinkled face—two hundred years' worth at
least—considered this. "Not at all in the past. In the future
we know each other very well."

"I have stumbled upon a madman," Aubric said aloud.

"One of the many problems with this modern world,"
the head said with a sorry shake, "is that people call mad
that which they cannot understand. Hey, that's pretty
catchy, isn't it? I always could turn a phrase."

"I suppose." Aubric decided that the owner of the face
probably wasn't dangerous. Annoying, perhaps, but not
dangerous. "Now, if you'll excuse me—"

"I certainly will not!" the face replied indignantly.
"You've got to climb in here!"

"I have to what?"

"Do you think I opened this door for my health? You

heard the way the thing complained. I barely got it opened at all!''

"It did make a bit of noise," Aubric agreed.

"Enough to alert your pursuers, I'm afraid. Oh, they are still after you. That's why I'm here, after all.''

Aubric looked quickly at the surrounding woods. There was no one nearby, but did he hear the distant sound of someone crashing through the underbrush?

"They'll catch you for certain if you're in the forest,'' the wrinkled face continued. "But what if you simply— disappear?''

"What?" Aubric asked, looking back to the opening.

"Get down here—now!''

Aubric glanced once more at the forest. He did hear the sound of voices shouting in the distance, voices he no longer had the strength to outrun. He was a dead man or a prisoner if he stayed where he was. He could do no worse by humoring this strange creature.

The face had disappeared from the opening, but Aubric heard the voice.

"Hurry!''

He dropped to his knees and peered inside. It was too dark to see much of anything.

"They'll see you in a minute! Inside!'' A hand grabbed his shirt and pulled. Aubric found himself tumbling forward. He landed in something soft as the hinges and gears began complaining all over again.

Aubric found a lantern thrust in his face.

"Going to lie about all day, are you? You certainly don't make a very good first impression, Sir Aubric. If I couldn't see the future, I might doubt my instincts.''

Aubric pushed himself to his feet as the light was pulled away. The fellow with the wrinkled face was short, perhaps four feet in height, and shuffled as he walked. He looked like nothing so much as one of the gnarlymen who performed many of the most menial tasks around Aubric's father's estate. But the gnarlymen were barely bright enough to string two words together. Or so Aubric had always thought.

The short man gave a little bow as he saw Aubric studying him. "Summitch is the name—well, at least for the moment." He pointed at his shirtfront. "This is, of course, not my true aspect. I only use it for convenience."

Summitch waved the lantern at their surroundings. "And what do you think of my kingdom?"

Aubric looked beyond the little man to see that they stood in a dimly lit passageway, brightened only by the occasional torch, that seemed to stretch in a straight line forever in either direction.

"If you'll pardon my asking," Aubric asked, "where are we—exactly?"

"Why, the castle, of course," Summitch replied in a tone that said the answer was beyond obvious. "But then, we're never out of the castle, are we?"

As far as Aubric was concerned, the answer was only beyond him. "The castle? Which castle?"

"Battle fatigue," Summitch said. "That would explain it, I suppose. We won't have a conversation of any substance until you've rested. Unless, of course, you were never taught—but that would be unthinkable. But enough talk. We have business."

The small man turned and marched down the never-ending hall. Aubric decided that, for now, he had better follow. And if he couldn't get his first question answered, perhaps he could ask another.

"Then, Summitch," he called to his rapidly moving guide, "perhaps you can tell me where we are going?"

"Elsewhere in the castle, of course." He glanced back at Aubric and grinned. When he smiled, the small man looked no more than a hundred and fifty. "I may seem evasive, but I think it best to hold off on explanations until I can show you a thing or two."

Fair enough. Aubric guessed his pursuers would never find him here, wherever he was. But the surprise and ex-

citement of finding this place was wearing off, leaving only
the ache in his legs and his chest.

"I may need to rest!" he called ahead to Summitch, who
was pulling away with his steady pace.

"No doubt!" the small man called over his shoulder.
"We all do from time to time."

Was this small man being obtuse on purpose? Aubric
felt anger mix with his fatigue. "Enough!" he shouted.

Summitch actually paused and turned back to look at
him.

"I don't understand the nature of this place, or our re-
lationship." Aubric spoke slowly and clearly, so he would
not be misunderstood. "While I appreciate the rescue,
you've really given me no reason to follow you. I have just
had a very difficult experience, and I don't need any more
surprises."

"Really?" Summitch smiled politely. "And what exactly would you like, Sir Aubric?"

"Just now?" Aubric sighed. "Probably to be left
alone."

Summitch nodded. "If that's the way you want it."

Aubric glanced at the packed earth floor. "Not that I
wouldn't appreciate an explanation—"

He glanced back up at the small man. But the small man
was gone. Aubric walked quickly forward to the last place
he had seen his guide. It looked just the same as the rest
of the passage, dirt floor, walls and ceiling of mud and
stone and brick. There were no side passageways, no doors
or windows, nowhere for the small man to have gone.

"Summitch!" Aubric called. He was answered only by
the echo of his own voice.

Aubric had gotten his wish. He sagged against the wall.
Perhaps, if he got some sleep, he could make some sense
of it. Or perhaps Summitch was mad after all and Aubric
was lost forever.

At the moment, he simply didn't care.

. 3 .

The World

Ernie was a miracle worker.

Joe's cousin had smiled the instant he heard the sirens. He'd turned the LeSabre off the main road, down one of the innumerable side streets that wound their way through the suburban hills. His smile only broadened as he maneuvered around a curve, then sped down the straightaway that followed. He beat out a rhythm on the steering wheel to a song only he could hear.

And Joe was lost. He frowned over at his cousin. "Where are we going?"

"Relax, Joe. This I can handle." Ernie chuckled. "They have no idea where we are. Place like this—all these little connecting streets—is hopeless for roadblocks; and the local police don't have any copters. No fuckin' way they're gonna find us."

Ernie took an abrupt left. He was driving quickly, though not so fast as to draw attention, just an impatient suburbanite eager to get home. "I always take a look at the maps before I come out on this kind of job. Better fuckin' safe than fuckin' sorry." He laughed again.

Joe's frown stayed on his face as he listened to the world
outside the car. The sirens were still there, but they weren't
getting any closer.

"We got some distance already," Ernie went on. The
only other time Joe had heard him talk this much was when
he bragged how good he was with women. "Two minutes,
and we're in the next town. Five more, we're in a different
fuckin' county." He laughed again. Ernie was having a fine
old time. "Usually, it's my ass that needs saving. You owe
me one this time, Joe."

"Yeah," Joe replied. The gun felt very heavy in his
hands, like it was gaining weight with every minute he held
on to it. It wouldn't do him any good to let his cousin know
how shaken he was. He smiled back at Ernie. "What? Another dozen of these chases, we'll be even?"

Ernie laughed again. Joe had never seen his cousin in
such a good mood.

Ernie slammed on the brakes. They squealed as the car
slid to a halt. Joe looked around, ready for trouble.

"Gotta watch where I'm goin', don't I?" Ernie waved
out the window. "Toss it here."

They were on a bridge, one of those old, two-lane
bridges with heavy steel beams, green with age, that met
overhead. The window rolled down with a hum on the passenger's side. Ernie had flicked a switch; this LeSabre was
loaded with all the options. Joe stuck his head out. There
was no sidewalk on this side of the bridge, only a rusting
guardrail half-covered with chipped white paint. If he
craned his neck a bit, he could see past the rail, down to
white water rushing between huge boulders.

"River's real fast here," Ernie explained. "And it gets
deep just down below. Current will carry your fuckin'
piece, lose it at the bottom of the river. Police won't find
it in a hundred years."

It occurred to Joe that Ernie might have done this sort
of thing before. He wondered how many of Ernie's guns
had already taken a ride on the river.

"Wait for it," Ernie cautioned. Joe looked back toward his cousin, and saw a Jeep Cherokee approaching them across the bridge. The driver of the other car only glanced at them as he drove on by, as if he saw people parked in the middle of the bridge every day. In this town, even the drivers kept to themselves.

Ernie watched the Jeep drive away in the rearview mirror. "In a minute," he instructed. "Lean far enough out of the car so you drop it in the water."

Joe did as he was told. First he got into this to watch over his dumb-ass cousin, now he was taking orders from him. If he pushed with his feet on the floor of the car, he could half stand, getting his head and shoulders out of the window, giving him a clear view of the river below. He let go of the piece and watched the gun fall into the swirling water, then watched the rushing current wash away his dreams.

What was he doing here, anyway?

He never planned to get this involved with the business. He remembered twenty years back, just out of high school, with a full athletic scholarship to the college of his choice; Joe Bisotti, quarterback of the future. His mother had wanted him to steer clear of his uncle's operations, and this seemed like the perfect out.

Not that he'd had much of a chance to be a football hero. Oh, he had had the moves, all right, and a knee that fell apart the second time he was tackled in a game. After the football scholarship had gone bust, he decided he was going to stay in college one way or another. But the easy money was too close, and too good. He'd supplemented his income by selling TVs, stereos, toaster ovens; things "that fell off the truck," as his father was so fond of saying. Small-time stuff, mostly supplied by his uncle—the family scholarship, as his father put it.

He swore he was only going to stay with the small-time stuff. But here he was, twenty some years later, and he'd

never put the small stuff behind him. And now he'd just
graduated into the big leagues.

"You gonna get back in the car," Ernie called, "or you
working on your fucking tan?"

The gun was long gone. Joe squirmed back through the
window and into his seat.

"About time," Ernie called as he hit the button to roll
up Joe's window. "I had to turn off the air-conditioning."

Now that his cousin mentioned it, Joe was still feeling
cold. It was only the middle of May, after all.

"Do we need it?" Joe asked.

"This car got fucking climate control, we're gonna use
it!" His cousin punched a button on the brightly lit dashboard. "We're outta here."

Ernie pushed his foot down on the gas, and the Buick
crossed the river into another town, just like he'd said. In
fact, it seemed like Ernie was doing all of the talking lately.
Something had shifted between them these last few
minutes, something Joe would have to correct as soon as
possible. He needed to bring Ernie down a notch or two.

"I'm still in charge here," Joe remarked. He watched
Ernie out of the corner of his eye, like he wasn't watching
him at all. With Ernie, Joe had to be ready for anything.

"Did I say different?" Ernie smiled at his cousin like
the world was a never-ending series of possibilities.
"Where now?"

There was only one possibility. "We gotta see Uncle
Roman."

All traces of a smile fell from Ernie's face. "Yeah. My
father. I always gotta see my father."

"We've got to tell him what happened," Joe explained,
even though Ernie knew that as well as he did. "What does
he always say? 'Face the music.' "

"The fuckin' music," Ernie agreed forlornly. "At least
I'm not the one on the carpet this time." The corner of his
mouth twitched toward a smile for an instant before he

glanced over at Joe. "I wouldn't be in your fuckin' shoes for a fuckin' million dollars."

Joe nodded his head. He and Ernie could always agree on something.

BRIAN'S MOTHER STOOD in the doorway, as if getting any closer to her wounded husband would be more than she could bear. She had stopped screaming by now, but her hands still covered her mouth, muffling her sobs.

At first, Brian watched through the living room window. There were sirens everywhere. A fire truck, an ambulance, and a police cruiser pulled up, one right after another.

The men from the ambulance and the fire truck rushed to his father. The police, one man, one woman, walked to the door.

Both officers approached slowly, looking to either side, as if they expected the gunman to pop out of the bushes or shoot at them through the hedge.

"Ma'am?" The policewoman spoke first. "Can you tell us what happened here?"

His mother only stood there and sobbed. Brian decided he'd better do something. He ran from the window to the front door, edging past his mother's side. He expected her to push him away, like she always did when she was upset, but she moved numbly to one side to let him through.

"They're gone," he called to the policewoman. "They got into their car and left."

Both officers visibly relaxed. He looked past the police at the men huddled around his fallen father. He saw four of them slide his father onto a pallet of some sort, then lift the pallet to the top of a cart. His father moved. He was still alive. They wheeled him toward the ambulance. Between the rapidly moving medics, Brian thought he saw a bloody bandage pressed against his father's throat.

Both cops started to talk at once. "They? There was more than one? Did you get a good look at the car?"

Brian told them he had only heard the car speed off almost immediately after the gunshots. His mother was the one who had gone to the window.

The woman took over the questioning again. "Ma'am? Did you get a look at whoever shot your husband?"

His mother shook her head violently. "I only saw the back of one of them. Dark hair. He wore a suit."

After it became obvious that this was all his mother was going to say, the female officer tried again. "Did you get a look at the car?"

His mother shook her head more slowly. "It was black, I think. What do I know about cars?" His mother whipped her head around to stare at Brian through her tears. "Why didn't you look out the window?"

Even the police officers glanced at each other at that.

"Maybe the neighbors saw something," the female officer added quickly. "We'll check around." Brian was glad she had taken the pressure off of him. She had a nametag above her badge. "Porter."

Officer Porter asked his mother a few more questions. Had there been any strange phone calls? Had her husband spoken about anyone whom he might be seeing? Mostly, his mother just shook her head and cried.

The medics slammed the doors of the ambulance. The large red light began its whirl.

"Excuse me," the other officer, whose nametag read "D'Ammassa," broke in. "Would you like to ride with your husband?"

His mother shook her head one more time. "I don't know. Where are you taking him?"

"From here, we usually take people to Memorial. Fred?"

The last of the medics confirmed they were indeed taking him to Memorial Hospital.

His mother hesitated, unsure of what to do. "Perhaps I'd better." She frowned at Brian. "What about the boy?"

"We'll get someone to drive him up," Officer Porter

cut in. D'Ammassa frowned at that. He took a step back, as if he didn't want to get involved in what to do with Brian.

His mother nodded and looked away, glad to have that problem out of the way.

"A couple of other teams will be down here shortly to look at the yard," Porter continued. "We may need to ask some other questions later."

His mother was already back inside the house. Brian looked around to see her grab her purse and keys. She was at his side again in an instant.

"You stay here until they're ready for you," she ordered, forcing him back inside the house with a single glance. "And don't bother the police."

The cops stepped back as she pushed her way between them. She slammed the door behind her.

Brian stood there for a long moment, aware of nothing more than his own breathing. The siren started up as the ambulance pulled away. Things had happened so quickly. One minute, his mother was yelling at him like usual, the next his father was shot. It seemed like he should feel something that wasn't quite there. Should he be afraid? Angry? All Brian felt was numb. That, and an odd sense of relief, that the house was quiet, and he was all alone.

The phone rang.

He rushed to get it, happy for something to do. Maybe his mother forgot something. But he was hoping it was Karen. She always knew when he needed to talk. He walked quickly to the hall table and picked up the receiver.

"Hello?"

"Brian?" a man's voice replied. "Sorry about your father."

"What?" Brian didn't recognize the voice at all. "Who is this?"

"He was protecting you, wasn't he?" the voice on the phone continued. "So foolish, really."

Was this some kind of crank call? Brian didn't know what to say.

"No one else needs to be hurt," the voice continued. "Just do what we say, and everything will be fine."

It sounded like this person was threatening him. Brian looked back toward the front door. The cops were just outside on the lawn. Should he get the police in here?

"Can't talk more now," the voice added cheerfully. "Just wanted to make sure you were staying put. We'll see you soon."

The owner of the voice hung up. Brian listened to the dial tone for a moment before he made his decision. He called Karen. She'd know what to do. Maybe they both had to get out of this place once and for all.

. 4 .

The Castle

THE JAGGED STONE DUG IN-
to Aubric's back, painfully pressing his chain mail against
his shoulder blades. He needed to find a place to rest. With
that strange Summitch out of sight, he felt exhaustion overwhelm him. He saw a slight indentation in the wall a few
feet along the never-ending passageway, sort of a tiny alcove. Perhaps, if he curled up there, he wouldn't be too
uncomfortable.

He stepped forward, and found that he could barely
maintain his balance. Aubric half walked, half stumbled to
the alcove. His armor was too heavy, his arms and legs too
tired. He fell to his knees. He put a hand out to catch himself on one of the outcroppings of the rough-hewn wall,
mostly so that he would not fall flat on his face.

The wall seemed to jerk beneath his hand. He yanked
his hand away, more from reflex than conscious thought.
At first Aubric thought the feeling of movement beneath
his fingers was brought on by his exhaustion, his sense of
balance following his tired muscles. Rising, he placed his
hand on the wall a second time. A panel swung away to

the left of his palm, a panel perhaps three feet wide and four feet high, large enough to admit a warrior.

Aubric pulled back from the hidden panel, half- expecting an attack from the other side of the wall. But the opening was as quiet and deserted as the surrounding hall. He drew his sword and cautiously placed his head before the new opening, slowly moving forward until he could see something of the other side. There appeared to be another passageway beyond the door, a corridor with the same rough-hewn walls and dim torchlight as the hall in which he stood. This was, no doubt, where Summitch had disappeared. He wished he had the energy to follow the small fellow.

"I knew you had hidden talents!"

The voice came from behind him. Fear and surprise gave Aubric a burst of strength. He spun about, ready to defend himself.

Summitch smiled and waved. "If you would delay your killing stroke for a moment, I might begin to explain."

Aubric slowly let his sword drop. The small man held no weapons that Aubric could see, and they seemed to be alone in the tunnel. He shifted the weight of the sword from both hands to one, and let the point brush against the dirt floor, his stance slightly more relaxed, but ready to defend himself in an instant.

"You have nothing to fear from me," the small man continued. "I know you might have some problem accepting that. It is so difficult to trust these days." Summitch chuckled, as if he found the whole situation highly amusing. "I hope you'll excuse my temporary disappearance. Even though you have come highly recommended, I still feel safer running a test or two."

"Highly recommended?" Aubric asked. "Might I ask by whom?"

Summitch let his left foot shuffle in the dirt for a moment before answering. "I don't think you will be entirely pleased with the answer. Suffice it to say that at the moment we need each other."

Aubric thought he'd had quite enough of this presumptive stranger. He was too tired for never-ending riddles. "Need each other? For what precisely? Why don't I just run you through?"

The small fellow shrugged. "Because then you would be lost underground, behind enemy lines, with no way to save yourself. There are other reasons, of course, but they are far too complicated for the moment. Why don't you just take a nap?"

Summitch made a fist and slammed the wall at his side. Another door opened behind them, this one tall enough to admit Aubric without crouching. Aubric got a glimpse of multicolored cushions surrounded by bright metal, glowing golden beneath the torchlight.

"Your accommodations for the night," Summitch said. "No one will bother you. No one besides me even knows you are here." He waved toward the opening. "Come, why don't you lie down before you fall?"

Aubric could find no fault with that argument. If the small man or someone he was working for meant to kill him, well, at least Aubric would have a little peace.

He took three steps forward, turned around, and fell back into the cushions. Never had he felt anything so soft, so comforting.

"Sleep," Summitch suggested from somewhere above.

On this, at least, they were in total agreement.

IN HIS DREAMS, Aubric never stopped fighting. He whirled about with his sword, delivering great strokes that gashed through armor, skin, and bone. But still the enemy came, so quickly he could not see their faces, but only their weapons, sword and mace, knife and arrow, all intent on destroying him. Somehow, he parried every blow, turning aside every knife point and arrowhead, but his attackers were everywhere. For every man he killed, two would take his place. He could not defend himself forever. He would be overwhelmed in an instant. He was surrounded, defeated, beyond all hope—

He opened his eyes to total darkness, and a feeling that the battle was all around him. But all was still; no cries of rage and pain, no running feet or clash of metal on metal; the place was as silent as the dead.

Totally dark, totally still, but Aubric breathed in and out, and while his muscles were sore, he was in no great pain. He lay on something soft, perhaps the same soft cushions he had fallen on.

He felt the hilt of his sword with his palm, then let his hand brush across the sheath that held his knife. So they hadn't taken his weapons. Perhaps the battle had been only a dream after all.

"Ah, you're back," Summitch spoke from somewhere nearby. "Well, so am I."

Summitch shouted a single word, and the room was filled with light. Aubric had to shield his eyes from the glare.

"A little overwhelming, isn't it?" Summitch cheered.

Aubric wished the small fellow was a little less exuberant. And there was another problem. There was only one explanation for so much light instantly filling a room. Aubric squinted up at Summitch. "You're a sorcerer."

The small man waved away the accusation. "Only a little magic. Who's to know? Ah, but you would no doubt say even a tiny spell is certainly forbidden by the High Court—for all but the Judges. And I am as far away from a Judge as one can get, may I assure you. And I will also assure you that, at this moment, we are also very far away from the High Courts."

Aubric let the small fellow prattle. He opened his eyes as he became accustomed to the glare. And what a glare.

"The room is filled with gold," he said softly. All manner of metal objects surrounded them, goblets and mirrors, crowns and scepters, swords and arrows and shields, all formed from gold.

"Ah," Summitch grunted agreeably. "Then you finally *are* awake. But you haven't mentioned the jewels."

He was referring, of course, to the numerous great stones of every conceivable color that were set within the hilts and points of the golden hoard around them.

"So we are in a treasure house," Aubric replied.

"A lost treasure house," Summitch agreed, "that once belonged to the Orange."

"The Orange?" Aubric frowned as he tried to recall his history lessons. "They haven't existed for five hundred years!"

Summitch nodded. "Long enough for this place to be truly lost."

Aubric pushed himself from the floor to get a better view of his surroundings. The heaps of gold he could see from his cushions were only a small part, perhaps one-quarter, of the place's total holdings. In one corner of the room he saw a great elephant carved from the precious metal; in another corner sat a heavily jeweled throne. "So who does this treasure belong to?"

"No one." Summitch whirled about to include the whole room in one great wave of his arms. "Or it could belong to you or me."

"You mean we could just carry it out of this place?" Aubric laughed. With wealth like this, his family could buy enough armaments to become virtually invincible. Aubric thought of his stepfather. The old man would be overjoyed with the riches, but, considering Aubric's background, how much control would his stepfather allow him to have? Aubric pushed at a stack of golden candelabra with the toe of his boot. With this much gold, he could found a house of his own.

He stopped his flight of fancy to look back at the little man. "So why am I here? Why haven't you simply taken this treasure for yourself?"

Summitch sighed. "There is another reason, besides

death and forgetfulness, that the gold is here. Pick something from one of the piles around you.''

Aubric frowned. "Is this a trick?''

Summitch waved away that notion with both his small,
dancing hands. "It is nothing that can hurt you, be assured.
Pick up something, anything. Anything that you can take
from this room will be yours to do with as you like.''

The small fellow was playing games again, but this time
the games held a prize. Aubric picked a golden shield from
a nearby pile, something large and flat and round, something without sharp points or the possibility of hidden com-
partments. Something as simple as a shield should keep
surprises to a minimum.

"A worthy choice," Summitch agreed. "A large
amount of gold, easily transportable. Take it to the hall.''

Aubric did precisely that, moving with slow, measured
steps, waiting for some attack from without.

But when he reached the door, a voice came from the
shield.

"This is the gold of Orange," the shield whispered.

Aubric frowned, and pushed the shield into the hall.

"This is the gold of Orange," the shield whispered
again. Was the voice a little louder than before? "It has
been taken from its rightful place. It is the stolen gold of
Orange! A thief has taken—''

Aubric pulled the shield back into the room. The whispering stopped.

Summitch nodded at Aubric's glance. "The gold is
beautiful. The gold is virtually limitless. But the gold is
also very noisy.''

Aubric looked at the shield in his hands. "This is some
sort of spell. Couldn't you counter it?''

"With my meager magicks?'' Summitch's hands flut-
tered to his sides. "Alas, no. What skills I have developed
are self-taught. I have nowhere near the wisdom or experience of the lowliest of Judges.''

"Then why show this to me?" Aubric felt like flinging the shield across the room.

"I have a plan that requires your assistance. There is no way we might be able to sell this gold in this world; not while the spell still holds."

Aubric still didn't understand. "So, with my help, we will somehow break this spell?"

"Oh, no." Summitch's smile reappeared full-blown. "With your help, we will sell this gold on another world entirely."

Aubric dropped the shield with a groan. What good was gold if its keeper was crazy?

"Ah, there are secrets within secrets to this place," Summitch said with a chuckle. "And I have only begun to tell you about them."

That, Aubric thought, was exactly what he was afraid of.

.5.

The World

JACKIE PORTER FELT LIKE IT was her first day on the force all over again; the first female officer with the Parkdale Police, the outsider, always looking in. She saw it in the faces of the other guys, the way they frowned at her or walked past without even looking. Even her partner didn't seem to want her asking any questions. This was an investigation for attempted murder, after all; the sort of things cops were supposed to do, not break up domestic disputes or write out speeding tickets. This was no place for a woman. This was for *real* cops.

She watched the injured man's wife march past the six other officers present—one third of the total Parkdale Police force—and climb into the back of the ambulance. Mrs. Clark's face was set in a perpetual frown. She seemed to be a very bitter woman, bitter and controlled. If there was grief present, she hid it well under the anger. Jackie felt a little sorry for the son, Brian. Always identifying with the underdog, she guessed.

Her partner had wandered over to talk to the guys. The rest of the cops stood in a semicircle at the edge of the driveway. A couple of them were drinking coffee; her partner lit up a cigarette. The staties would show up in the next few minutes to do the real work here. The best the rest of them could do was not mess up the crime scene.

There hadn't been a shooting in Parkdale for seven years, a murder for eleven. There wasn't much to see here, either; half a muddy boot print at the edge of the lawn, and a patch of grass matted brown with blood.

Jackie scratched at the short-cropped hair under her police cap, impatient to get going. She still felt she could be of use here, maybe more use than any of those coffee-drinking career officers who still looked down on her. She was a specialist, after all. She had been brought to Parkdale to fill a state-mandated position, hired because of her extensive education in accident reconstruction, trained to determine exactly where Johnny drove his car off the road after the junior prom, how fast he was going, and how many beers were still in his crippled bloodstream. Her training helped the courts, the insurance companies, and the brass upstairs. Everybody liked what she did, except for the uniforms, who thought she was nosing into their business.

But she wasn't about to shut down her curiosity. And she didn't see that much difference between a speeding car and a speeding bullet. There had to be something about this shooting, maybe even something the staties would miss, that would put everything together, and get everybody's attention. Jackie grinned at the cluster of men on the far side of the driveway. She'd like that a lot.

But where to start? If there were no clues to be found at the scene, maybe she'd have better luck with a reluctant witness.

She called to the driveway full of police, "I'll drive the kid to the hospital."

D'Ammassa said something about sticking around in case he was needed. It was almost the end of their shift. Someone else would give him a lift back to the station. Nobody else wanted to leave the crime scene. Let the girl drive the kid to the hospital. The others thought it was a fine idea.

Jackie turned and knocked on the door. It opened instantly, as if Brian had just been waiting for an excuse to come outside.

He looked really spooked. Jackie wondered if he was scared of the cops. Maybe, she realized, he was expecting to see his mother.

She smiled at the teenager. "Hey, Brian. I thought I'd drive you to the hospital. Maybe ask you a couple questions."

Brian looked beyond her at the semicircle of policemen. He flinched as if he expected them to attack. "Maybe in the car," he said, his voice so quiet Jackie could barely hear him.

"Well, let's go," she said, maybe a bit too brightly, as if her good spirits could overcome the boy's fear.

She turned and started toward the cruiser. Brian slammed the door and ran to follow. She let him into the backseat, then opened the driver's door for herself. She slid behind the wheel and looked at her passenger in the rearview mirror. Brian had positioned himself in the middle of the rear seat. She had the feeling that he'd put himself there to be as far away as he could from either door, again trying to protect himself from attack.

She started the car. "We'll be at the hospital in no time," she said, mostly to start a conversation.

"It feels good to be outside," he admitted.

She searched for the right thing to say next. Maybe something about Brian looking scared? His father had just been shot. Why wouldn't he look scared?

She pulled the cruiser out onto the street, past the handful of neighbors who had gathered to see if anything else would happen. Of course no one had heard or seen anything; hardly anyone had been home. A midweek afternoon in Parkdale seemed the ideal time to shoot someone and get away with it.

Unless, she thought again, Brian or his mother could shed some light on the identity of the would-be killers. The teenager seemed much more open without his mother around. She decided to try to ease him into conversation.

"That shooting must be pretty upsetting."

She looked in the mirror to see Brian staring at her back. "It's more than that."

"What do you mean?" she asked.

"Uh—someone called."

"For your father?" Could Brian have spoken to the gunman? She looked in the rearview mirror again.

"No. It was for me."

For him? "About the shooting?" she asked sharply.

"Uh." Brian looked down at the seat by his side. "Never mind. It's nothing."

But she had seen him looking straight at her reflection in the rearview mirror. For an instant, she had seen that fear back in his eyes.

She tried to get him to talk again, asking questions about the call, his parents, other things that had happened that day, but Brian only stared out the window, as if he couldn't hear a thing. Somehow, Jackie realized, she'd scared him. The way she'd seen his mother jump on him, Brian probably thought twice before he breathed.

She pulled the cruiser into the emergency entrance of Parkdale Memorial Hospital, stopped and got out to let Brian out of the backseat.

"They'll know where your father is at the desk inside," she said as Brian climbed from the car. "And Brian. If you want to talk to me, you can always call me at the station. You don't have to be alone with this."

Brian paused and glanced at her for the merest of instants before he strode past her, heading for the emergency room doors.

Jackie sighed and got back in the car. The boy knew something. She hoped she had gotten through.

.   .   .

DELVECCHIO'S, JOE THOUGHT.

The city blocks went by in a blur. He barely even noticed the landmarks that they passed. The Civil War Statue,
Lilac Park, the glaring red neon of Robbie's Roast Beef—
"Open All Night"—all made fleeting impressions before
he thought again about where they were going.

Delvecchio's, and Uncle Roman.

How many times had Joe been there? A hundred? A
thousand? His parents used to bring him to the restaurant
for Sunday dinners, his father always disappearing for a
minute to talk to his uncle. Later on, when Joe was a teenager, he and Ernie were shown for the first time to the
Banquet Room, with its red carpet and chandeliers, the floor
empty save for one table in the corner. And sitting at the
table, Uncle Roman and a couple of his cronies. Uncle Roman always took a seat where he could watch the door.
The cronies varied, never less than two, or more than four,
all men close to his uncle's age, some Joe knew well, others
he would see once and then never again. The routine never
varied. Uncle Roman would smile at both of them, and Joe
and Ernie would be given errands and odd jobs to make a
little money. Nothing obviously illegal, but you soon
learned not to ask any questions. Joe sometimes wondered
if they ever actually held banquets in the Banquet Room.
He never asked about that either.

"Here we are," Ernie announced, but Joe was already
staring at the brightly lit sign. DELVECCHIO'S—Steaks—
Chops—Italian Specialties.

His cousin parked by the side door so that they could
get to the Banquet Room without having to walk through
the main restaurant.

"Let's go see Uncle," Ernie said with a little grin. Joe
decided his cousin was enjoying himself a little too much.
He'd have to have a little talk with Ernie later on, if his
mouth was still working.

For now, he let Ernie lead him down the corridor that separated the kitchen from the restaurant proper, across the worn green carpet, past the pay phone and the restrooms, toward a doorway that read DELVECCHIO'S—The Banquet Room.

For an instant, Joe wondered who the original Delvecchio was. He'd been coming here for years and had never met anybody with that name. Probably the original owner, some poor sap who'd gotten on the wrong side of his uncle.

Ernie stopped and pulled open the door. He waved Joe to walk ahead.

"After you."

The room was even emptier than usual. The table was there, but it was vacant.

"There you are." The door to the kitchen opened, and out strode Johnny T, one of Uncle Roman's two main musclemen. The guy looked like he worked out constantly, his back and shoulders so well-developed that the muscles hid his neck. Joe thought that was why he was called Johnny T, because his body looked a lot like a big, capital T with a tiny little head on top.

"Yeah," Ernie called to the muscle. "So, Uncle Roman around?"

Johnny T shook his head. "He had other business."

Joe let out a long breath. Maybe he could get some maneuvering room here. "Yeah. Well, he wasn't expecting us. We could leave a message—"

The big guy shook his head again. "Oh no. He's expecting you all right. Especially after what happened."

So Uncle Roman already knew about it? Joe felt a stone growing in the pit of his stomach. Still, it wasn't like he was surprised. Uncle Roman seemed to know about everything.

"But your uncle's got other things on his mind. He said to me, 'Johnny, the minute those two show up, I want to see them right away.' " He gave the two of them a hard

look, like they should be turning around and rushing to
Joe's uncle this second.

"Uh, Johnny," Joe asked gently. "Do you know where
my uncle's gone?"

"Oh, yeah." Johnny allowed himself the slightest of
grins. "Your uncle's gone down to Funland."

Ernie suddenly didn't look so sure of himself. "Funland? Uh, Johnny T, my father knows I didn't have anything to do with this one, right?"

The muscle grinned at Ernie. "Roman didn't say nothing about that one way or another. He just said he needed
an explanation from both of you."

Now Ernie was sweating, too. Joe just wished he could
enjoy it. They both knew what happened in the back room
of Funland, the amusement arcade with the machines and
music turned up so loud that you couldn't hear a thing,
especially people's screams.

"Funland," Johnny T repeated, like it was an order direct from Uncle Roman himself.

"Yeah," Ernie said, trying to smile, then biting his lip
instead. "I guess we'd better go over there, huh?"

Johnny nodded once. "I'll call Roman and tell him
you're on your way."

"Yeah. You do that." Joe had had enough of his uncle's
mouthpiece. He turned around and marched out of the banquet room. Ernie was right behind him.

Ernie looked at Joe, then glanced quickly up and down
the hall, looking for cooks, waiters, busboys, cleaning
women—all of them Roman's spies. "Maybe we shouldn't
go to Funland," he said in a voice barely above a whisper.
"Maybe we could drive somewhere else."

Joe almost laughed. "Yeah, as long as we kept on driving. As soon as we stop, you know what would happen."

Ernie nodded his head miserably. "My father would call
on his connections. End of story." He grabbed at Joe's
jacket. "But you think he'd do that? I'm his son. You're
his nephew. We're family!"

"Uncle Luigi," was all Joe had to say.

"Oh, yeah," Ernie agreed, even more dejected than before. Luigi, the brother to Roman and Joe's mother, Antonia, who got caught in the cement scandal and blabbed to the feds. They'd promised to get him into the witness protection program, except, when they found him, there wasn't enough left to protect.

"Uncle Luigi," Ernie repeated, the name sounding half like a moan.

Joe shook his head. They'd reached the door that led outside. "Let's get in the car and get this over with."

Ernie went over to the driver's side again. "Maybe we can stop somewhere, you know, get a little something to help us through."

"Like what?" Joe asked, confused once again by Ernie's plans.

"Uh, well, a double Scotch sounds good."

"No. Roman knows when we were here, and how long it takes to get over to Funland. Any big delays, he'd get suspicious." And, Joe thought but didn't say, the stone in his stomach could get so big he couldn't move. Might as well get it over with now, while he still had the guts.

Joe got in the car. A moment later, Ernie got in the other side.

Ernie started up the LeSabre, then turned to his cousin. "What's my father going to do if we're late? Tear us into smaller pieces?"

"I tell you, Ernie, that's one thing I don't really want to find out. We got to drive to Funland. That's that."

"Funland," Ernie repeated as he backed the car away from the restaurant. That was the last word either of them said until they reached the arcade.

"Should we go in the front way?" Ernie asked as he pulled up across from the brightly lit storefront. "That way other people will see us. It'll be harder for them to kill us in the back."

"So instead they march us back out through the front and kill us someplace else? No, let's go straight to Uncle Roman."

Joe got out of the car. A moment later, Ernie followed. Together, the two of them walked down the alley to Funland's back door.

Joe rapped sharply on the steel door, three quick knocks. The door opened a crack, then swung wide.

"Ah. Joe and Ernie," Larry the Louse, Roman's other muscle, announced. He ran a grimy hand through his greasy hair. "About time."

"Bring them in here!" Uncle Roman called from a room at the end of a short hallway. Larry jerked his head toward the room, then turned and led the way.

Joe followed Larry in. The back room was full of smoke and so dimly lit it took Joe a minute to see what was going on. Uncle Roman was sitting in one chair; in his mid-sixties, his bulk was still impressive, massive rather than fat. A much thinner person sat, shaking, in a chair across the room. Joe realized his hands were tied to the arms of the chair. There were some ugly marks on his arms. Joe thought they might be cigarette burns.

"Joe, Ernie, come in. I don't know if you've met Mr. Diamond. He's helped us with our dry cleaning operation— until recently, that is. I believe he's about to start helping us again. But Mr. Diamond was just leaving. Larry?"

Larry the Louse pulled a knife from his pocket and walked quickly to the quaking Mr. Diamond. Diamond looked like he wanted to say something, but all that came out of his mouth were small cries of pain.

With two quick strokes, Larry cut Diamond free.

"You're lucky, Mr. Diamond," Uncle Roman said from his chair. "I've got business. Don't disappoint me again."

Larry helped Mr. Diamond to his feet. The thin man looked like he could barely stand. Somehow, though, he made it out of the room.

"I'd seek medical attention for those arms!" Roman called after him. "Some of those burns might leave nasty scars." He turned back to the others. "I'm sorry you had to see that. Sometimes, doing business isn't very pleasant. But, I suppose it's good to know that, too." He coughed, a sharp noise that sounded none too healthy, then took a deep breath of the smoke-laden air. "So come over here, both of you."

While Larry watched from the other side of the room, Joe and Ernie both went to stand in front of Uncle Roman.

Roman smiled. Even now, it made his face look deceptively gentle. "Joe. Joe Bisotti."

Joe swallowed. Nobody in his family ever used his real name. It sounded ceremonial, like they were about to kiss him on both cheeks and shoot him.

Uncle Roman shook his head. "And Ernie, my own flesh and blood."

Ernie shuffled his feet. "Yeah, Dad, you see—"

"Quiet, Ernie, I'm not done."

Ernie was instantly still.

Uncle Roman turned back to Joe. "I understand you had a little accident."

Joe opened his mouth to speak, but Roman held up a hand. "Accidents happen. It's what we do after the accidents that matters." He nodded his head. "Joe, You're going to have to see somebody, tell him what happened, figure out a way to get the job done. You square it with him, you got no problem with me."

Joe blinked. He hadn't expected this at all. Maybe things were going to be all right.

"Sure, Uncle Roman. Whatever you say."

Roman nodded. "Guy's name is Mr. Smith. I'll set up an appointment, give Ernie directions how to get there."

"Smith?" Ernie laughed much too loudly, overjoyed, no doubt, to still be among the living. "Dad, you think his name is really Mr. Smith?"

"I doubt it, Ernie." Roman grinned back at his son. "I doubt his name is anything like Smith. Sometimes"—it was Roman's turn to laugh—"I don't even think this guy is human."

· 6 ·

The Castle

Summitch strode by Aubric purposefully, his short legs carrying him from the treasure room to the doorway to the corridor beyond. "You are rested?" he called over his shoulder. "Come. I have no food, and my conjuring talents run in other directions. We'll have to get a bit closer to the actual castle before we can find you breakfast."

Apparently, Aubric wasn't allowed to disagree. This wasn't all that different from the army, after all. He followed the small man now striding from the room into the hall. Aubric paused at the door to take a final look at all the gold around him. The whole room shone as though they were standing inside the sun.

As he stepped from the room to the hallway beyond, the corridor seemed lost in shadow, the waiting Summitch one more dark smudge in a world of greys and browns, no match for the treasure they'd left behind. The wall closed behind him with a thump.

"More magic," Summitch remarked before Aubric could frame a question. "The Orange were once strong,

and had access to the strongest of spells. But no dynasty is
strong forever.''

Aubric felt a flash of anger. Certainly, the small man
couldn't be talking about the House of Green. Aubric's
Household was one of the oldest continuing lines among
the Twelve Kingdoms.

But why should he let words upset him? The little man
was half crazy. Aubric took a deep breath as he tried to let
his eyes adjust to the relatively dim corridor. It wasn't as
if the Green hadn't suffered some setbacks. They had lost
close to a third of their men-at-arms, and even one of their
Judgeships went unfilled. The war had gone on for so long
that it had diminished everyone. Aubric and his fellows had
been talking about the very problem, moments ago in the
forest—just before his friends were killed.

Images flashed in Aubric's head: Sav, screaming for
help as the Grey came out of nowhere; Lepp taking the
killing arrow in his back, dead before he knew they were
attacked. Only Aubric had been lucky enough to have a
moment to react, only he had been able to escape. And he
couldn't run forever. What was he going to do?

"Are you coming?" Summitch demanded.

Aubric nodded. One thing he wasn't going to do was
disagree with his savior of the moment. Aubric humbly
followed the small man, matching his pace as they both
marched down the corridor. Summitch's very existence
might contradict what Aubric knew about the place of gnarlymen in society, but at least the wrinkled fellow didn't
seem eager to kill his guest. For the moment, Aubric decided, that was enough.

That, and the thought of taking all that gold.

"Ah," Summitch suddenly announced, waving his arms
before him. "We are making some progress." He darted
left, disappearing behind a wall.

Aubric didn't want to lose him again. He sprinted forward. The hallway, which seemed to have led straight for-

ever, turned abruptly, revealing a flight of stairs carved from rock. The stairs led up into darkness.

Summitch snapped his fingers three times, and three torches sputtered to life along one side of the stair.

"I do love magic," he added with the slightest of giggles. "There is a joy in simple spells." He flashed his wrinkle-shrouded grin once more in Aubric's direction. "Perhaps we can even teach you a trick or two."

Now the small creature would have him performing magic? It wasn't enough that they were sneaking about enemy territory; Summitch would make Aubric an outcast from his own family. Among the Green, the punishments for the unauthorized use of sorcery began with chopping off the hands that cast the spells.

"But I'm getting ahead of myself, which could be dangerous on a stairway." Summitch chuckled. He seemed very pleased with his own sense of humor. "Hurry up, now," he called as he trotted up the steps. "These stairs lead straight to the Grey—and breakfast!"

Aubric felt another moment of panic. "I thought you understood. If the Grey find me—"

"You're dead, or possibly worse," Summitch replied in the same carefree tone, as if being murdered by one's enemies was something you'd expect every day. This time, the small fellow laughed out loud, a great booming sound that echoed up the stairway. "I won't begin to describe what the Grey want to do to me." He spun about on the step above Aubric, almost falling down on top of him. "Not to worry!" he called, his arms waving less wildly as he regained his balance. "The Grey know nothing of these passageways. They won't even know we're in the neighborhood." He spun about again and quickly resumed his climb. He had a great deal of energy for someone with so many wrinkles.

The steps led upward for quite some time. Aubric lost track of their number around one hundred and twenty, when Summitch began to whistle. At first Aubric thought the whistling might be a tune, but then he realized the small fellow was repeating the same five notes over and over.

"Excuse me," Aubric called up to his guide. "Is there a reason—"

"Not yet!" Summitch called over his shoulder. "But soon." The whistling resumed, echoing up the stairway in much the same fashion as Summitch's laugh had previously, so that it sounded like three or four whistlers not quite in sync. Oddly, each of the additional whistles came from a very distinct direction, one ahead to the left, another behind to the right, the third seemingly directly overhead; some trick of the stairs' acoustics no doubt, unless—Aubric realized—it was more magic. He wondered if another Summitch or two might spring forth from the bare stone walls to either side of the never-ending stair.

Instead, the whistles were answered by the sound of a horn, followed by a distant scream. Aubric placed a hand on the hilt of his sword.

"Ah." Summitch nodded. "I see." He paused for a moment, but was met by nothing but silence. "Exactly what I was waiting for," he added hastily. From the tone of his voice, the gnarlyman was almost as surprised by the sounds as Aubric.

"This is the place," Summitch added with no more conviction. He stomped three times on the step on which he now stood, a stone platform that sounded oddly hollow.

The horn sounded again as a door opened in the ceiling. A rope ladder fell from the hole to land between him and Aubric.

"It begins to grow interesting." The smile reappeared on Summitch's face. "We will have to be a little quieter once we climb up."

Aubric followed the small man up the rope ladder. They climbed to a new hallway, torchlit and waiting. Now that the fear had left him again, Aubric was actually feeling hungry.

"Can you—" he began.

Summitch put a cautioning finger to his lips. "Whisper," he said softly.

Aubric obliged. "Can you tell me where we are?"

"Deep within the palace of the Grey," Summitch whispered back. "If my information is correct, we should be almost immediately behind the throne room."

They would simply march around the throne room of the Grey? As long as they remained hidden, Aubric supposed there was no reason to panic. He still felt far from reassured. "So you've never been here before?"

"No," the other replied with his usual assurance, "but my information is usually very accurate."

Usually? It occurred to Aubric that the use of this word implied that Summitch's information occasionally wasn't accurate at all.

"Come." Summitch abruptly turned about and started down the hall. "I think this way leads to breakfast."

The small man stopped just as suddenly. "Ah, yes. If I can get my bearings, I promised you a throne room."

Aubric recalled no such promise, but Summitch had already snapped his fingers again. A section of the wall before them turned from the color of stone to a milky whiteness. The white faded in turn to transparency, so they were looking through a window into a large and sumptuous hall.

Aubric froze, staring at the splendor before him. Their vantage point was perhaps ten feet above the floor beyond, on the far side of the room from the throne, giving them a clear view of all corners of the hall. Hundreds were crammed into the room, mostly High Ones, although Aubric saw a half dozen other types of creature, including a couple that looked like himself, and from the babble of voices that erupted the moment the panel before Aubric had grown transparent, all the hundreds were speaking at once. Every Lord and Judge and Lesser in the hall was dressed in grey, but their clothes and armor were far from drab. Everything in the great room, from drapes to shields, hel-

mets to the throne itself, all were trimmed in gold. And
many of the finer clothes, along with those tapestries to
either side of the throne, sparkled with tiny points of light,
the fabrics inlaid with diamonds to catch the torchlight. The
place appeared even grander than that of Aubric's stepfather, High Lord of the Green.

The sound of a horn, three ascending notes, each held a
beat, silenced the crowd in an instant.

A voice boomed over the gathering, so loud and close
that Aubric might swear the speaker stood by his side.

"Kedrik approaches, rightful ruler of all and left hand
of the sun. All his servants show their due."

The hundreds in attendance knelt in a quick rustle of
cloth, a clank of sword and armor. Summitch brushed Aubric's arm and pointed to the edge of the crowd, afraid, no
doubt, to even whisper in this sudden silence. The drapes
were pulled aside, and two guards in full battle armor strode
forth, followed by Kedrik, the High Lord of the Grey. His
features were typical for one of the highest of the high;
chalklike flesh, high cheekbones, almost colorless eyes. But
Kedrik also sported a deep blue scar that ran from cheek
to chin, a scar, as family legend had it, that was given to
him by the High Lord of the Green.

Two more guards followed, then half a dozen others, all
well dressed, of various ages and sexes.

"The royal family," Summitch ventured, sure his whispered voice would be masked by the marching feet.

Aubric's gaze had been taken by the last of those to
emerge from the curtain, a young woman close to his own
age. There were hundreds in the room, but the minute she
entered, he realized that only she mattered. Her skin was
wondrously pale, her hair a mass of dark curls, her smile
a flash of lightning in a summer storm. She looked away
from the others in her procession, straight up at Summitch
and Aubric, as if, of all those in the room, only she could
see into their hiding place. She was the light of the moon,
as coldly beautiful as a winter's night.

The High Lord Kedrik had taken the throne, and waved to a group by his right. "Our brave captains!" he called, and four men in armor stepped forward.

Smiling, he called to each of them by name, but paused before he addressed the last of the four.

"I was separated from the others," the last captain quickly replied. Separated from his troops? In another throne room, that could have been Aubric.

Kedrik continued to smile. "Certainly no reason to be ashamed." He waved away the captain's explanation with a single elegant gesture, then nodded in turn to all four before him. "We celebrate your victory against the Green."

Aubric frowned at the words. So the battle had gone totally against his forces. He had suspected as much, but there had been no way to know. He wondered how many more of his fellows were dead.

The High Lord continued: "My daughter, Karmille, will give you your rewards."

The beauty from the back of the procession stepped forward, a female servant at her side. The four captains stood stiffly, a bit nervous perhaps, unused to this sort of attention, as the beauty, Karmille, stopped before each of them. The ceremony was repeated for each of the officers: Karmille held up her hand, and the servant gave her a garland of flowers, which she would bestow on the captain before her. Each garland gleamed in the torchlight as well, as if the flowers were strung upon a rope of diamonds.

"For your services," Karmille would say, her voice surprisingly deep, as she placed the garland over the bowed head of the captain before her. And that officer would bow even more deeply and take a step away.

The same offering was made to the first three captains, and Karmille held up her hand for the final garland. "For your services," she murmured.

Aubric, unable to take his gaze from the woman, watched as she placed her other hand behind her back and drew what appeared to be a ceremonial dagger from her belt.

The last captain screamed briefly. Apparently, the dagger was quite functional. The beauty had plunged it into the officer's heart.

Servants stepped forward to catch the dead man before he could hit the floor. Karmille withdrew the dagger and raised it to her lips, licking the blood from the blade.

She laughed, and the rest of the court laughed with her, but none more loudly than her father, High Lord Kedrik.

"Quite enough," Summitch murmured. He placed his hand upon the wall and the window grew opaque, stone once again.

"A clear demonstration of honor among the Grey," Summitch continued. "Nice of them to give you a lesson in their manners."

Aubric found he was having trouble catching his breath. At the very least, he vowed he would never court anyone from the House of Grey.

"Now that we have had our lesson, I think it is doubly time for a meal. There is a passage into the High Lord's kitchen just a bit farther along the way."

So, after watching the bloodletting, they would simply step out and get something to eat? Shouldn't they get away from the throne room? Aubric whispered to Summitch, "Is it wise to steal from right under the High Lord's nose?"

Summitch smiled. "Nothing could be wiser. In a Lesser kitchen, there is far less food for far more mouths, and they keep track of every morsel. With the High Lords, all is excess. They would not notice if we took an entire cow."

The small fellow banged on the wall by his side, and a doorway sprang open. "Won't be a moment," he remarked, darting through the door. After the demonstration they had just seen, Aubric was glad to stay behind.

The gnarlyman returned in under a minute, large shanks of meat in either hand. "No problem at all. No one ever looks at gnarlymen." He handed Aubric one of his two prizes. Aubric proceeded to tear the meat apart with his teeth, doing his best not to think of the captain and the blood. The High Lords could be cruel, but a person had to eat.

Summitch frowned mid-chew. "I was going to go back to the kitchen to fetch water, but I think I had better not."

Aubric looked up from his own meal. "Why? I thought you said that gnarlymen—"

The small fellow gestured with the remains of the leg in his hand. "Look down the hall."

Aubric followed his gesture, glancing down the corridor where they had recently watched the royal court. There seemed to be some sort of lights dancing in the distance.

Aubric turned back to Summitch questioningly. "Judge's work," the small fellow informed him. "They suspect someone is near to the throne. So they send these things out to look in every nook of the palace." He took another bite as he watched the lights. "They are their beacons. They examine everything—very thorough, but very shortsighted. If you let one get within arm's length of you, you're through."

The lights appeared to be getting brighter. Aubric imagined he could hear them hiss as they bounced about the corridor. "I thought you said we were safe in these passageways."

"I had thought we were." The gnarlyman sighed. "Sometimes even Summitch is wrong." He shook his head. "Someone, somehow, must have sensed us."

Aubric remembered how the High Lord's daughter seemed to have looked right at them. Perhaps she was the one who had sent these things.

Summitch stood abruptly, throwing the remains of his meal to the floor. "I cannot counter Judges. Best we were on our way." He started down the hall, away from the dancing, hissing beacons.

Aubric had to trot after him to keep up. "Where are we going now?"

"To our destiny, of course," Summitch said in a tone that implied Aubric should know all of this. "Yours and mine, quite intertwined. I did mention that I had seen our futures?"

Aubric was getting a bit tired of the way the gnarlyman could talk his way around a question. "Well, yes you did. But I'm not sure I can trust everything you say."

"Most prudent," the small fellow agreed. "I wouldn't trust a Lord or Judge for an instant. Would have trouble trusting most anyone associated with the High Ones."

"But I'm in one of the High Ones' armies! Why would you trust me?"

Summitch chuckled at that. "Isn't it obvious? You're a human."

A human? What, Aubric wondered, was that?

. 7 .

IN AND OUT, JACOBSEN thought. In and out. He had a job to do or he was dead.

The gun was heavy in the pocket of his sport coat. The piece felt like it weighed twenty pounds. His mouth was dry. He was sweating far too much for the crisp autumn weather. But no one looked twice at him as he walked down the street. Fat guys were always sweating. And one advantage of carrying an extra hundred pounds around your waist: the gun was just one more bulge.

He recognized the building from across the street. The men who worked for the Pale Man had given him very specific directions. It was an older apartment building, its grey façade cracked and spotted by the passing years, but the detail work above the door spoke of a grander past. A great bunch of fruit and leaves was carved in the stone, maybe meant to be a sign of welcome. To either side of this centerpiece were a pair of ornamental gargoyles, real Notre Dame–type beasties. Gargoyles were supposed to keep away the evil spirits. Jacobsen wondered if they worked on men with guns. If only life were that simple.

He wasn't supposed to walk beneath the gargoyles anyway. He circled around to the back of the place.

The basement door had been left wide open, just like the men had promised. He looked again at the photo in his hand.

She wasn't even full grown. He could shoot a woman, maybe, but a teenaged girl? Karen was her name. The men had told him that, but not much more. Karen Eggleton. How could he kill somebody who wasn't even fully grown?

He thought of the Pale Man's eyes. You might be able to convince yourself the Pale Man was human, if not for the eyes. Jacobsen's gaze had locked onto that of the Pale Man for an instant, and in that instant Jacobsen felt something beyond hatred, something beyond cruelty; as if the Pale Man's slightest glance could take Eric Jacobsen to places he could never imagine, and places he could never escape. The Pale Man had blinked. The image was gone. Jacobsen quickly looked away.

If he didn't kill the teenager, he would have to look in those eyes again. If he didn't obey the Pale Man, he was worse than dead.

Jacobsen walked quickly down the dimly lit hallway that cut through the basement, laundry room on one side, furnace room on the other. The corridor ended at a metal door painted a faded, flaking green: the elevator. Jacobsen pressed the dirty brass button at the side of the door, heard the clunk and grind of machinery far above him. The elevator was on its way. He looked at the piece of flat black metal that was now in his hand. The murder weapon. They had shown him how to use it, and given him a picture and a few facts about the victim. More than that, he didn't want to know.

The elevator door opened. The cage was empty, a good thing, since Jacobsen still held the gun. He slipped the heavy metal back into his pocket and stepped inside the box. He pressed the button for the third floor. The door closed with a groan; a sigh of gears, and the elevator jerked upwards. It would be over soon.

He tucked the girl's picture in his shirt pocket. Her mother and father both worked. Karen always came straight home from school to do her homework. This time of day, the girl would be alone.

Basement, lobby, second floor—the lights climbed the strip to the side of the door. The number for the third floor had been punched out, showing a tiny light behind the display. The light blinked on, the door groaned open.

Jacobsen stepped into the hall. Karen's apartment was the second door to the left. A quick knock on the door, a quick bullet if she opened the door, two or three shots through the wood if she refused. Karen would be dead, one way or the other, and Jacobsen would be out of here, his debt paid, with no way to connect him to the crime.

He walked quickly across the worn carpet, away from the elevator, toward the job he had to do. The door on the right side of the hall opposite Karen's apartment swung open.

Jacobsen stopped mid-step, looking first at the door to Karen's apartment, then at the short, elderly woman who stood in the now open doorway.

There weren't supposed to be any complications. But the gun was still in his pocket. Maybe he could bluff his way through this.

"'Can I help you?" the woman called out.

Jacobsen nodded in what he hoped was a pleasant way. "I have a delivery. For the apartment across the hall."

"Oh, I could take it!" the woman said brightly. She took a step out into the hallway.

Jacobsen wasn't ready for this. Why did he say he was making a delivery? He wasn't dressed in a uniform. He held no package, nor any clipboard or any of those other things delivery people always used.

But better to stick with a bad story than to have no story

at all. "I'm sorry," he added, his voice growing softer with every word. "I have to make the delivery in person."

"Are you sure?" the woman persisted. The old bag wouldn't let him alone! "Your delivery is—"

He turned away, hoping against hope that the woman would take the hint. Otherwise he'd have to kill them both. He was facing the door to Karen's apartment. He raised his hand to knock, but heard a clunk and a rattle, the sound of a lock turning. The door opened a crack before him.

"Mrs. Mendeck?" a girl's voice said from the crack.

"Delivery!" Jacobsen shouted much too forcefully. "You'll have to open the door. I'll need your signature." He reached in his pocket and put his hand around the gun.

The door opened wider. A sixteen-year-old girl frowned up at him, the same age as Mary, his wife-to-be, the first day he'd laid eyes on her; only a couple of years older than Jane, the daughter his wife would no longer let him see. The sixteen-year-old Karen looked him straight in the eye; Karen, the girl he had to kill.

Jacobsen yanked the gun from his pocket. He had to do it now.

The old lady stepped between him and the girl. She poked a finger at his belly.

"He sent you, didn't he?"

"What?" Jacobsen asked. The old lady knew?

"You know who I'm talking about," Mrs. Mendeck insisted.

No, Jacobsen thought. He couldn't let this rattle him.

His hand was shaking so much, the gun would fall to the floor.

"Mrs. Mendeck?" Karen asked. "What's happening?"

The old lady smiled at Jacobsen. "Why don't you give me the gun?"

You will do this thing.

Jacobsen's hand stopped shaking. A voice had spoken to him, inside his head, a voice that overwhelmed all the thoughts and doubts that froze him in place.

You have made a promise. There is no other way.

Jacobsen knew the owner of that voice would not be denied.

The gun no longer felt heavy in his hand. Now it felt like it belonged there. The metal was an extension of his fingers. The bullets were power that was his alone.

Something possessed him. He was the gun. The gun must be used. All emotion was gone save for a cold need to shoot. His hand would pull the trigger, and the girl would die.

Somewhere, deep in the back of his brain, he was aware that someone was screaming.

Jacobsen focused on the three of them in the hall. Both the old woman and the girl were silent. The screams came from him.

"You can fight it!" the old lady called. "It's only in your head."

"Only?" Jacobsen opened his mouth again, but his voice was barely there. "In my head?"

Mrs. Mendeck nodded. "If it was in your heart, you'd be dead."

He couldn't understand. He couldn't think. All he could see were the old lady's eyes. The gun slipped from his sweat-soaked fingers.

A pit opened before him. Light flickered, heat seemed to rise from far below. He would be swallowed by the fires of Hell.

"Who are you?" he demanded of the old woman.

She smiled. "Maybe, just maybe, I'm an alternative."

That was no answer. There were no answers. There was only the pit, and the flickering light. But then the light was gone.

Eric Jacobsen was covered by darkness.

KAREN FROWNED. WHY had she opened the door?

"Mrs. Mendeck?" she called out to the neighbor lady who stood in the hall. "Did you knock?"

Mrs. Mendeck smiled. "I was about to, dear. I need to ask you a question." She took a couple of steps closer. "Are you going to see that—Brian Clark anytime soon?"

"Brian?" Karen was a little surprised Mrs. Mendeck even knew about the boy. "Uh—I guess. He might even come over later today."

The old lady clapped her hands. "Splendid! If it's not too much trouble, Karen, I would very much like to meet the young man."

Mrs. Mendeck was full of surprises today. Karen would have to ask Brian if that was all right with him, but she couldn't see any harm in introducing the two of them. "Uh—sure," she answered with a little smile. "We could do that sometime."

Mrs. Mendeck smiled back. "I have something, well, let me just say that the two of you might be very pleasantly surprised. So do bring him by!" She waved as she turned back toward her apartment door. "I have things to do now, dear. Toodles!"

Karen almost laughed. The old lady was always so happy. Her mother called Mrs. Mendeck "dotty," but Karen thought she was sweet.

Mrs. Mendeck closed her apartment door. Karen stood there for another moment, staring out into the empty hallway. Why did she feel that she was forgetting something?

· 8 ·

First, Aubric thought, Sum-
mitch told him he was a human. Whatever that was. And then
the gnarlyman refused to talk, instead leading the soldier of the
Green through a further maze of corridors.

They started up a sharp incline, the walls changing from
rough-hewn rock and dirt to large stones carefully fitted
with mortar. The handiwork here was not that different
from a farmer's wall in the village where Aubric was raised.
This part of the labyrinth was crowded with cross-corridors.
They took two rights, a left, another right, then proceeded
down a set of mortared steps that led them into the more
cavelike passages Aubric had seen before. The tunnels were
so different that Aubric wondered if they had been made
at different times. As cities crumbled and new buildings
were constructed on the ruins of the old, perhaps the builders supplied new tunnels as well. There was a whole secret
world down here, and a world that, aside from the intrusion
of Summitch and Aubric and those strange hissing things
they were trying to avoid, seemed totally unused.

"Watch your step here!" Summitch called. The gnarlyman's footsteps produced a hollow, echoing sound as he walked forward. Aubric looked down at his own feet and realized he was at the beginning of a rickety bridge, the dirt floor giving way to a long line of ill-fitting wooden slats. A rope ran waist high to either side, no doubt to help Aubric keep his balance.

"Hurry!" Summitch urged from a dozen paces ahead, his voice a hoarse whisper. Aubric grabbed the ropes and followed the gnarlyman. Their boot heels rang against the wooden slats, the chamber amplifying every sound. Aubric risked a glance beyond the ropes, but the chasm they crossed was lost in darkness. The darkness deepened around them as well. A bridge of rope and wood was no place for a torch, magical or not.

Summitch was no more than a grey shape before him. He saw a point of light beyond the gnarlyman's shoulder. It was the torch at the far end of the bridge. Beyond the clatter, Aubric thought he heard another distant sound, a moaning, like the wind in the chasm far below. Why would the wind blow beneath them? Maybe the yawning pit below reached all the way to the other side of the world. He wondered if these tunnels might reach to the other side of the world as well.

The distant torch was becoming larger, the bridge brighter. Aubric stepped off the wooden slats and back to the packed earth and rock.

The air in his lungs left him in a whoosh. He had barely been breathing.

There was no time to rest. Summitch disappeared around a bend in the passageway a dozen paces ahead.

The tunnel turned left, then quickly twisted right. Aubric wondered why he even tried to keep track of their path. Perhaps it was to put some sort of order into their crazy flight. If he could spend all his time concerned with the mechanics of their escape, he'd have no time to wonder what he was running from, or running to.

"Wait!" Summitch announced abruptly as he stopped

fifty paces down a new corridor that seemed to be forever twisting to the right. "We have some options here. It is important to know if we have outdistanced the beacons."

The gnarlyman's voice echoed in this strangely curving hallway. Aubric did his best to quiet his breathing. His rapid heartbeat pounded in his ears. But the odd hissing that followed them before seemed to be gone.

"Good," Summitch said. "It appears my plan has worked. The beacons do not like to travel this far afield." But there was no joy on the gnarlyman's face, only a bit of relief mixed with—what? Summitch studied the corridor before them. Aubric noticed that the ever-present torches along the walls were smaller than before and spaced farther apart, causing short stretches of the hall before them to be plunged into near total darkness.

"I usually do not choose to go this deep beneath the common levels of the castle." Summitch's voice had fallen to a near whisper.

That was the sort of statement that demanded a question, even though Aubric didn't particularly feel like hearing the answer. Aubric thought of the chasm they had crossed, and his vision of tunnels stretching down forever. "Is there a reason you don't come down here?"

Summitch shrugged. "There are rumors about the place." He glanced at the dirt floor, the ceiling hewn from solid rock, the constantly curving wall, as if any one of them might hold the true answer. He frowned at Aubric and shrugged a second time. "There are always rumors about unknown places. This way." He turned and marched down the hallway.

A hundred or so paces farther along, a second corridor branched off from the first, as if rebelling against the constant curve. Summitch stopped, seemingly frozen by the choice.

There was a long moment of silence. Aubric couldn't bear it. He asked another of those questions for which he didn't necessarily want to know the answer.

"Do you know where you're going?"

The gnarlyman looked sharply back at Aubric. "Summitch always knows where he's going." He frowned, peering down one branch of the corridor, then the other. "Except when he doesn't."

He closed his eyes, his hand waving from left to right and back again. The hand stopped at the left-hand way. Summitch opened his eyes.

"We go this way."

But doubt, never far from Aubric's thoughts, had crept back in and seemed to be erecting a permanent camp.

"Why?" Aubric asked.

Summitch nodded sagely. His many-wrinkled face gave his every movement an air of wisdom; an air, Aubric realized, the gnarlyman might not have fully earned.

"I have an instinct about these things," Summitch announced.

"Really?" Aubric asked. "And where has that gotten you?"

The little man smiled at last. "I'm still alive, aren't I?"

Aubric had to at least grant him that.

"And my instinct led me to you." Summitch waved a bony finger about to emphasize the logic of it all. "That should prove something."

Aubric supposed it did, although exactly what was still quite beyond him. "Let's hope your instinct can keep us both alive."

Summitch nodded again. "More than anything, my instinct tells me not to stand still." He motioned for Aubric to follow him into the corridor leading left. Aubric noticed that this way led steadily downwards, too.

The tunnel changed again. It had become wider and higher, the walls now of deep red brick with great arched ceilings.

"There was a time when they depended more on engineering than magic to support these tunnels." Summitch waved at the ornate brickwork. "These passageways must be very old."

They walked in silence for a while, until the tunnel they marched down crossed with another, giving them three new choices. Summitch stopped again. Aubric hoped they wouldn't be there all day. He wondered, as he always did when there was a pause in the action, if he should ask about something else.

Summitch's loud yelp put an end to any further questions. It didn't seem the sort of noise one should make when one was trying to quietly escape.

"This way!" Summitch tugged on Aubric's sleeve as he stared past the soldier's shoulder. The gnarlyman turned abruptly and trotted down the corridor at a right angle from their current tunnel. Aubric hurried to follow.

"Is it the beacons again?" Aubric had hoped that they'd left the hissing magic far behind them.

"If it were only the beacons!" Summitch exclaimed. "We need to hurry." He sped up, his trot turning to a full-scale run. For a small man, he could certainly move quickly.

"How could this happen?" the gnarlyman wailed. "Perhaps the beacons were a diversion, to lead us into tripping an alarm. An alarm that would lead to this!" He glanced apologetically at Aubric while continuing to hurry forward.

"I may not know every spell that crosses these corridors." Summitch shook his head. "Oh, I know most of them, for sure. I've traveled these pathways often enough. But there are plots within plots within this castle, layers beyond layers of secrets and spells."

Much, Aubric thought, as there were tunnels beyond tunnels; a never-ending maze he would never understand. The immensity of this place overwhelmed him. On the surface, his death would have been quick and clean. Here, he might avoid death, but he might also be lost forever.

They came to another place where the tunnel split in

two directions. One tunnel was made of brick, the other, stone and dirt.

"We have—to stop," Summitch managed, gasping for air. "I need—to listen for—a moment."

Aubric was glad for a moment's rest. He guessed he was far more used to physical exercise than the gnarlyman, but even his lungs were feeling the strain.

"There!" Summitch called triumphantly, pointing back the way they had come. "And there as well!" He pointed up the right-hand way. "You hear it, don't you lad?"

Aubric frowned, concentrating on the near silence. The noise was far away. At first it sounded like the distant wind he had heard in the chasm. But this new wind grew until it had a dozen voices, all of them howling.

Summitch nodded. "You hear them, don't you?"

Aubric nodded as well. "Them?"

"M'lady's creatures."

So they were being pursued again. "Worse than the beacons?"

"The beacons will only trap you. With m'lady's playthings, there are no prisoners." The small fellow looked up and down the corridor, then at the ceiling and the floor. For the first time since he had met the gnarlyman, Aubric thought, Summitch appeared truly overwhelmed.

Summitch took a deep breath. "I thought I'd heard them before, once or twice, in the far distance. I was sure it was my imagination. I wanted it to be my imagination." He shook his head sharply. "They say if you hear them close, you hear no more. The Grey can call off their beacons. These things are only satisfied with blood."

Now Aubric understood. Before, he was merely going to die. Now he was going to die horribly.

"So close to a life of wealth," the gnarlyman said softly. He shook his head a second time and looked at Aubric. "They aren't on top of us yet. If we move quickly, perhaps we can escape."

They moved more hastily then, so rapidly in fact that

Aubric gave up any hope of making sense of their route. The tunnel changed from brick to stone to packed earth supported by great wooden beams, then back to stone again. At one point they turned left seven times, but seemed not to go in a circle. At another, Summitch began to climb up what looked like a sheer stone wall. It was only after Aubric brought his face to within a few inches of the rock that he could see the shallow cuts that would serve as hand- and footholds.

He followed Summitch up the wall.

Even climbing didn't seem to help. The howling behind them slowly grew louder. And as it grew louder, the howls overlapped each other, rising and falling endlessly, as if there were a great many things rushing toward them. Aubric wished he could shut out the sound. The tenor of the cries was chilling. The howls spoke of loneliness, and cold, and a longing that could never be fulfilled. And there was a second noise, far deeper than the howls, so deep that it was barely at the edge of hearing, a low growl so constant it seemed not to come from animals, magic or not, but rather from some great rumbling engine of destruction that would annihilate everything in its path.

"Perhaps we should quit these tunnels," Summitch called from above Aubric, "and try our luck above."

Maybe there was some hope for them after all. "Can these things not stand the surface?"

"Oh no." Summitch's voice drifted down a moment later. "From my understanding, m'lady's creatures prefer to stay clear of sunlight, but they will rush across an open field at noon if their quarry is near."

"Then why above?" Aubric called up to Summitch's feet. He could see no sense in this at all.

"More living things. These horrors are not fussy. They'll tear apart the first warm-blooded creature they see. They will be satisfied, and we will be free."

"So we'll sacrifice someone else in our stead?" Aubric

thought to challenge Summitch's sense of honor. But why would he have a sense of honor? He was a gnarlyman.

"Of course!" Summitch called back. "It may be unfortunate, but with the minions of m'lady, there is no other way. I certainly don't intend to be torn apart by those things, and I need you for my plan to succeed."

It was as simple as that. Aubric was good for transporting the gold. He looked up and saw by the light thrown by the torches that even graced this cliff face that Summitch had put some distance between them and their pursuers. Aubric would have to concentrate on climbing.

The gnarlyman's voice drifted down a moment later. "The upper tunnel is just above us. We're close to deliverance."

Despite himself, Aubric felt a bit of hope stirring within. The more he heard of the creatures behind them, the less he wished to meet them. "Will this rock-climb slow the things?" He looked up to see Summitch squatting on a ledge, his hand extended to help Aubric join him.

"Come!" Summitch barked. "Join me quickly! Nothing slows down these things until they partake of blood and souls."

As soon as Aubric was safely on level ground, the gnarlyman turned and ran.

"Come on!" he called. "The sooner we are out of here, the better our chances!"

Aubric followed. As they ran, the tunnel widened, and the roof of the passage grew ever higher until they were in a great chamber that appeared to be made not of simple stone but of marble. A dozen stone heads stared down at them from on high, some representing High Ones, others beasts of the forest, a couple of them no manner of creature Aubric had ever seen before. Beneath the dozen carvings, were a dozen different doors leading from the chamber.

Summitch stopped abruptly, his gaze darting from one door to the next. "A common area of some sort. I'm surprised I haven't stumbled on it before."

This seemed like far more than a common area. At some

point, someone had conducted the business of a kingdom
far underground.

Aubric was all too aware of their ever-approaching pursuers. "Don't we have to make a choice?"

"And quickly." Summitch nodded. "Perhaps, with a
dozen choices, it might make it a bit more difficult for
m'lady's pets to follow. At least we can hope, hey?" He
turned to the door to the right of the tunnel they had just
left. "What's this?"

Aubric saw them at the same time as Summitch: hundreds of small dancing lights before the door, lights that
bobbed and swirled and rang ever-so-faintly like the tiniest
of bells. They formed a great cloud before them, a thousand
bright pinpricks that whirled about in a silent, glowing
waltz.

Were these a sign that this was the passage to use, or a
warning to stay away? Aubric's gaze was drawn into the
swirling pattern. Maybe the lights were here to enchant
them, to keep them here for their pursuers.

Summitch tugged at Aubric's sleeve. "Whatever they
are, we must move from this open space." He frowned at
the nearby lights. "I say we avoid them."

"That might be more difficult than you think," Aubric
replied, nodding at the doors around the circle. Half a dozen
of them were masked by smaller groups of the dancing,
ringing lights. So many of the delicate chimes now sounded
that their music almost hid the ever-growing howls.

"Wait!" Aubric called.

He heard a different music: the sound of a distant flute,
the same music he'd heard when Summitch had first opened
the tunnel to him.

But Summitch seemed lost in his own agitation. He
hopped from one foot to the other and back to the first
without making a single step forward.

"Decide," he muttered to himself, little more than a
whisper at first, but louder with every repetition. "Decide!
Decide! *Decide!*"

"Listen!" Aubric insisted.

The gnarlyman looked wildly about. "What, are they coming from somewhere else?"

"Don't you hear that?" The flute played a melody, low and mournful and quite compelling. The sound cut through the bells, rose above the unearthly howls of whatever pursued them. It sounded like a greeting and a welcome. Aubric wanted to pursue it. After all, how could things get any worse?

"Which?" Summitch demanded, eager to be out of this place. "These damn bell lights, or m'lady's creatures smelling our blood?"

"No, someone is playing a flute." Aubric pointed at the farthest door on the right. "Over there, I think."

"A flute?" Summitch shook his head, his panic tempered by a look of pity. "You aren't the first to go mad from this sort of stress."

"But—"

"Who knows these tunnels?" the gnarlyman demanded.

Aubric had to admit it. "You do."

Summitch grabbed Aubric's sleeve again. "Then let us make a choice before it is made for us!" Dragging Aubric behind him, he ran for the third door on the right of those still free of the lights.

The door swung away without effort, and the two of them started down a new tunnel no different from a dozen before.

Mere seconds passed before Aubric heard a great commotion behind them. The howling was much louder than before. Even the growling was more apparent. And the ringing music was replaced by a high-pitched screeching, as if thousands of tiny creatures were being torn to shreds.

"I think our pursuers have reached the chamber," Summitch remarked as he started to run. Aubric had reached the same conclusion.

Aubric felt a warm wind behind him. It blew out the torches to either side. The air carried a sulfurous, unpleasant smell. The howling redoubled again, filling the space around them.

"It is the breath of the creatures!" Summitch shouted. "They are close now."

The tunnel they now ran through was long and straight. Aubric risked a look behind. He wanted to see what was going to kill him. The torches were out behind him as well, the passageway plunged into darkness. He thought he saw a dozen glowing red orbs in the dark, bouncing up and down in pairs. Were they the glowing eyes of their killers?

"I recognize this symbol!" Summitch yelled from just ahead, waving at something Aubric had taken for a blemish in the rock wall. "There is a passageway here to the outer castle! Follow me!"

Maybe they could save themselves yet. Aubric watched as Summitch pressed a hidden switch in the wall. A door swung away. Both Aubric and Summitch jumped through.

Aubric saw a moment of brightness. Daylight, he thought, after being trapped in the tunnels' endless night. But with the light came an instant's dizziness. The light shifted, blurred, and dimmed. Summitch made a sound that wasn't quite a word but sounded quite alarmed nonetheless.

The bright light was gone, but so was the darkness of the tunnels. The light here—barely enough to see by—had a distinctly greenish tinge.

"Where are we?" he called to the gnarlyman.

"Nowhere that makes any sense," Summitch whispered. He shook his head, as if all this, including the place in which they found themselves, was completely beyond him. "According to the sign in the tunnel, we should have come out upon a public way, surrounded by others. I think we were bound there, too, until—I don't know what." He shook his head again. "This feels very wrong."

The space they now stood in was barely large enough for the both of them. Aubric could see no sign of a door behind them, only a featureless stone wall. Before them was a heavy drapery of some sort. Aubric thought he heard muf-

fled voices somewhere nearby. Perhaps Summitch was
wrong, and the public way was just beyond this heavy
hanging. If they were to go any farther, the drapery had to
be moved.

"I sense magic," Summitch whispered. "Surely this is
a trap."

A trap? Aubric frowned. Even a trap might be preferable
to what had been chasing them. "Is there any other way
out of here?"

"Not that I can see," the small man admitted.

Well, Summitch was the expert. The trap it would be.

Summitch squawked again as Aubric pulled the drapery
aside.

They were in a large, well-appointed bedroom, as far
removed from a public way as Aubric could imagine. Fine
tapestries lined the walls, showing scenes of noble knights,
fine ladies, and the occasional fantastic beast—as unfamil-
iar to Aubric as those stone carvings in the tunnel. Curtains
of golden silk were drawn around a large bed in the center
of the room. This was most likely some part of a palace,
then, but whose palace?

The curtains of the bed opened. The lady Karmille
stepped out, wearing a dressing gown of gold and grey.
She smiled. "It took you two long enough to get here. And
what have you done with my pets?"

Aubric could hear the muffled howling on the other side
of the wall.

The lady clapped her hands. Four of the palace guards
stepped out of hiding places in the corners of the room.
The howling grew even worse on the other side of the hidden door.

She nodded to one of her guards. "Oh, let them in. We
can't deprive them of seeing their mistress, now can we?"

Aubric took a deep breath. "So they will kill us after
all?"

Karmille smiled again. "Oh, I think not. At least not
yet." She pointed to another guard. "You. It is time."

The second guard paused for an instant before he marched stiffly toward Aubric and Summitch.

The lady smiled at them again. "Now stand out of the way, you two. Over here by the bed."

Aubric and the gnarlyman did as they were told, moving within half a dozen paces of the lady.

She turned from them and nodded to the first guard. "Let in my lovelies now."

The first guard stood well to the right of the draperies that had first hidden Aubric and Summitch. He pulled a golden rope by his side, and the drapes rose from the floor.

Aubric saw a blur of motion rush into the room. The blur moved about the guard who stood in the spot where Aubric had been a moment before, surrounding m'lady's man so that he, too, was lost within the chaotic motion. Aubric could not get a clear look at it. It seemed to be a dozen different things, all moving close together. He thought he saw a bloodred eye here, a snapping jaw there, the glistening coil of a striking serpent, razor claws drenched in flowing crimson, an obsidian coat covered with sweat. He could hear a dozen angry sounds as well. The howling, growling, hissing mass was so loud it might deafen him, yet through it all he could still hear the guardsman scream.

"You have your price!" Karmille shouted. "Now begone!"

In an instant, the creatures were gone. Where the guardsman had stood, there was only half a torn boot and a deep red smear on the rich carpet.

Karmille turned back to Aubric. "If your answers displease me, you will be next."

"I don't know what answers you want," Aubric replied. "I know far less than my companion."

Karmille tossed her head back and laughed.

"Our soldier has courage. He makes his little jest. So you know far less than a gnarlyman?"

"I have never seen the tunnels before today," Aubric insisted. "This fellow—" He looked down at Summitch, and stopped. Summitch looked at the floor, shifting his weight from one foot to the other, mumbling in a language only he could understand.

For the first time, Summitch was acting like a gnarly-man.

Karmille waved to one of the remaining guards. "The gnarlyman amuses me no longer. Have him taken away and whipped." She smiled at Aubric. "I have more interesting uses for this one, although whipping would not be out of the question."

Summitch did not object as he was led away. He only appeared confused. Again, just like a gnarlyman.

"Soldier of the Green." The lady Karmille stepped quite close to Aubric. She smiled again. Aubric had never seen whiter teeth. "Let me put it to you simply. You will find I am always direct."

She raised a lace-encircled hand to Aubric's cheek. Her touch was cold. "I discovered through my sources that someone in the tunnels was using magic. Who could it be? The Judges, at least the Judges of the Grey, shun the tunnels usually. I had to know, even though it meant I used my own source of magic, outside the Judges. I do not use that magic lightly." She paused to stare at Aubric. The irises of her eyes were as grey as her robes. "We scoured the tunnels and could find only two—you and the gnarlyman. Well?"

She paused, waiting for an answer. Aubric knew no answer he had would satisfy her.

She ran one delicate finger along his jaw and down the side of his neck. "We will get you to use your magic, soldier, unless of course you would rather die."

She smiled at the two guards, then looked back at Aubric, her mouth shrinking to the slightest of pouts.

"Whatever you have, brave warrior, I'll get it out of you."

Aubric had no doubt that she would.

. 9 .

BRIAN COULDN'T BELIEVE what was happening outside his bedroom window. It was zoo time. The police had used hundreds of feet of yellow tape to keep out the crowd. Where had all those people come from? He hardly recognized any of them. The Channel 9 News van had parked down the street. Brian saw a scruffy guy with a camera and an overdressed woman with a microphone marching toward the house. The crowd parted for the newcomers, then closed tightly behind them, surging forward like a pack of animals gathering for the kill.

Still, they were all outside, far below Brian's second-story window. For the moment, he was safe. With his mother out of the house, he had time to think.

Brian was sure this all had something to do with that stranger. It had been obvious, once it had occurred to him. He had even mentioned it to his father, telling him about the creepy guy who had waited for him outside of school. The dark glasses and the hat had only made the man's skin seem paler. He had followed Brian across the street, called out Brian's name, told Brian he had a deal that couldn't be beat.

Brian knew better than to talk to strangers. The man with
the glasses had called out to Brian one final time, told Brian
he'd be sorry. Is this what the stranger meant? Was Brian's
father shot, almost dead, because of him?

Brian didn't want to go back to the hospital. He didn't
want to see his father surrounded by monitors, or to hear
his mother complain about how no one was paying attention to her. *How could her husband leave her like this? Her
trials were more than a woman could bear. All this, after
having to deal with her ungrateful son day after day—*

Not that she would say anything about Brian in public.
That wouldn't be at all proper. But she would look at him
and he would know; there would be plenty in store for him
when they got back home.

Four hours ago, his mother had taken one look at him
and sent him right back home. His father was still in a
coma. Brian was too much of a bother . . .

Brian started. A woman had called his name. No, not
his mother. It would be Officer Porter, the lady cop who
had offered to see that he got a ride. Brian sighed. There
was no way around it. No way out of going to the hospital,
and no way out of coming back home again.

His mother always had been critical, but the last year or
so she had been far worse, lighting into his father or Brian
for the smallest things, sometimes for nothing at all. Her
husband was late from work. He had forgotten to pick up
milk. Brian wasn't fast enough, or polite enough with a
reply. It was a rainy day when she had wanted sunshine.

It could be anything.

His father tried fighting back once or twice, reminding
her, maybe, that he had run the errand after all, or that she
was reminding him of something she had never mentioned
before. His objections only made things worse. The whole
house became a battle zone. Even his room wasn't safe.
His mother could burst in any time of the day or night and
start in all over again.

He thought of Karen. He wished he had called her again

when he had had the chance. But he didn't want to go near the telephone again; as if, when he next picked up the phone, that strange, threatening caller would still be there, waiting for him.

"Brian!" the woman called again.

Time to move. He pushed himself away from the window, grabbed his jacket, and headed for the stairs.

She smiled up at him as he came into view. "I can take you back over to the hospital now." She was trying too hard to be cheerful. When you had a mother like Brian's you learned to read the emotions going on behind the words. Behind the officer's friendly words, she seemed nervous, and almost as upset as Brian.

"You can tell all your friends you rode in a police cruiser," she urged. "Twice!"

Brian managed a smile, too, as he reached the bottom of the stairs, but not for any reason the officer would understand. According to his mother, the police should have come for him long ago.

Officer Porter opened the front door, letting in a rush of noise; voices and cars, mostly. There was a siren in the distance. Brian wondered if that was another police car, coming here, too.

"Stick close to me!" she called, guiding him out onto the front steps with a gentle hand between the shoulder blades.

More TV people had shown up in the last few minutes. They had pushed their lights and microphones to the front of the crowd. They tried to scream over each other, surging forward to break past the police. They sounded angry to Brian, demanding answers just like his mother.

Four policemen stood side by side, holding the media back for a moment, creating just enough room behind them to get to the cruiser. Officer Porter hustled him into the backseat of the police car. The reporters surrounded the car, rapping on the windows, demanding his attention. Just like his mother, like he was the one who had done something wrong. Brian the freak. That's what Brian thought of himself. It was the message he always got from his mother.

Officer Porter climbed behind the steering wheel and started the car. She reached down to the dashboard and picked up a small, hand-held microphone, just like the kind you saw on TV. Brian knew she was going to press a button on the side. "Unit sixteen en route to Memorial."

"Copy sixteen," a woman's voice crackled from the speaker on the dashboard. "The Chief is hot to see if anyone can identify the perps. He wants you to take some mug books with you to the hospital."

The lady cop said something under her breath. She pushed the button again. "Not now, Claire. I'm taking the victim's son over to the hospital."

A moment passed before the voice on the radio replied, "Okay, Jackie. But the Chief really wants this." After a moment's silence, the voice added, "I think he's gonna bring the stuff over himself."

Officer Porter muttered something else before she signed off. She slammed the microphone back in its cradle.

"Well," she said over her shoulder to Brian, "you're one important guy. The Chief doesn't take special trips for just anybody. In fact, I can't think of anything that would get the Chief out of his office!" Brian saw her look at him in the rearview mirror. She sighed and shook her head. "You've got enough problems without hearing about mine. Let's get you to the hospital."

Officer Porter tried to start a conversation a couple of times, asking questions about Brian's father. Did anybody dislike him? Did Brian know of any problems his parents were having lately? As if Brian's parents would tell him anything like that.

Brian's answers were short and noncommittal. He simply didn't feel like talking.

People turned their heads as the police car drove by. Who was that in the backseat of the cruiser? A burglar, a murderer, a freak? Brian slumped down in his seat, the scourge of the city.

Not that this was much of a city in the first place. Brian couldn't wait to get out of the place. In a year or two he could go to college. His mother would never pay for it. Maybe he could get a scholarship. Karen and he could finally find a new life.

Karen. Now that he was away from his house, he wanted to talk with her more than ever.

Maybe he could call her from the hospital.

They turned another corner. The hospital was just ahead, set up at the top of the hill above a bright green expanse of lawn. Whenever he passed the place with his parents, his father would mention that this was where Brian had been born.

He hoped his father would be all right. He half felt like he was going to cry.

The stab of emotion surprised him. His mother had always been prone to flashes of anger, but in the last year or so it had gotten almost impossible to be around her. He'd learned to cover up anger, laughter, any kind of emotional display that would draw attention his way. Sometimes, he'd forgotten he could even feel.

Right now, in the back of a police car, where his mother couldn't see him, he wanted to let it all come out.

"Whoa," the policewoman called from the front seat. "Looks like we've got company."

Brian looked up, expecting to see more TV news vans and a new crowd of reporters. Instead, he saw another cop car parked in front of them, up close to the hospital. Two individuals walked away from the car, a stout man in a police uniform and a tall, thin man in a trench coat and hat. They were so deeply engaged in conversation that they hadn't noticed Officer Porter's cruiser pull into the parking lot.

"The big boss is here already." The policewoman glanced at Brian in the rearview mirror. "Brian, you must be something special. I never saw the Chief move so fast in my life."

The two men paused before the automatic door that led into the building.

"Who the heck's with him?" Officer Porter said, more to herself than Brian. "The Chief's got connections everywhere. Could be federal, I suppose."

The tall man turned to look at the Chief, and Brian could see half of his pale face.

Brian knew exactly who it was.

"That's him!" He spoke in a hoarse whisper, even though they were still inside the car. "That's the man!"

Officer Porter glanced back at Brian and frowned. "Which man?"

Brian pointed at the tall man talking to the Chief, just as the two of them disappeared inside. "The man who stopped me outside of school. The man who wanted me to go with him."

"Wait a moment. When did this happen?"

Brian quickly explained what had happened the other day, how his father had reacted, and how he felt it all fit in.

Officer Porter stared into space with a frown. She glanced back at Brian. "I think I might need to have a little talk with the Chief." Brian heard the locks pop open on the cruiser's rear doors as she opened the driver's door. "Come on."

Brian didn't move. "You're going to take me inside?"

Porter got out of the car, then opened the rear door. "He doesn't know the connection. The Chief would never harbor a known felon. I'll explain everything to him. It'll be fine."

From the frown still on her face, Brian got the feeling she was trying to reassure herself as well as him.

"Look," Porter continued. "We're walking into the county hospital in the middle of the day. There will be too many people inside for this character to risk anything."

Brian got out of the car at last. Officer Porter nodded to him. "Nothing's going to happen to you while I'm here."

Brian nodded back, and found himself walking at the officer's side. After his father's excuses and his mother's anger, it felt so strange to find an adult he could actually depend on.

She brought Brian in through the emergency entrance, asking at the desk for the whereabouts of his father. The receptionist told her to step into the nurses' station, where the nurse on duty checked a chart, then a computer monitor. Porter and the nurse talked quietly. Even though Brian stood only a dozen feet away, he couldn't make out anything they were saying. This place was built for privacy.

Maybe a dozen men and women, most of them dressed in white, rushed back and forth through a honeycomb of corridors on the far side of the nurse's station. Brian couldn't figure out what any of them were doing, but they sure looked busy. There was no sign of the strange, tall man or Porter's boss anywhere around here. Brian imagined they had to be upstairs somewhere, closer to his father.

Officer Porter walked back to her charge. "They've transferred him to ICU—Intensive Care. That's one floor up. According to the nurse, he's still unconscious but he's stable. They say they're 'cautiously optimistic.'" She shook her head at Brian's frown. "I have no idea what that means, either. I imagine your mother's up there, too. Do you want to go see them?"

Brian didn't know what he wanted to do. "Do I have a choice?"

The policewoman smiled. "Well, here's the way I see things going. Originally, I was going to sit you down and ask you some questions. I think the Chief wanted to be in on that, too." Brian must have looked pretty upset at this, because Officer Porter made a flapping motion with her hand like she wanted to wave away his problems. "Don't worry. I think you've already told me a lot of what I need to know. You don't have to talk to anybody you don't want to."

He liked her direct approach. He thought again how dif-

ferent it was from his too-quiet father and too-intense
mother; she was an adult who explained things and actually
followed through on them.

Brian thought of his father, unconscious, helpless in a
bed upstairs. What if the stranger wasn't here for Brian?
What if the stranger wanted to do something else to his
father? It was important for both Brian and the policewoman to get up there.

"Let's go," he said.

They took the elevator to the second floor, a large cage
with padding on the walls so that the hospital staff could
easily move stretchers in and out. Brian's father had probably come in on one of those stretchers.

It would be good to see him alive.

The doors opened to show a sign, white letters on a
brown background, that read Intensive Care Unit; Immediate Family Members Only, with an arrow pointing right.

"Easy enough," Porter said, stepping out of the elevator
first and looking either way down the corridor before mo-
tioning Brian to follow. "Let's go."

There was a door about twenty feet up the hallway with
the same Intensive Care sign, this time without the arrow.
The policewoman pushed it open.

They walked into a large, open space with a dozen cubicles separated from each other by windows or curtains.
Each of the cubicles opened toward a central nursing station, empty at the moment. Brian wondered where the
nurses had gone. A dozen monitors hung above the station,
screens showing a dozen different heart rates, green lines
bouncing across a black background, bright rows of numbers on the screen's right-hand side, numbers constantly
shifting up and down.

Brian had no idea what any of them meant. They certainly looked impressive. He wondered which one of the
monitors belonged to his father. There was something hyp-
notic about the way the green lines jumped across the

screens. Brian could stand here all day, watching the patterns of a dozen hearts.

Officer Porter touched Brian on the shoulder and pointed ahead. There, standing by himself to one side of the nursing station, was the Chief of Police.

"Porter!" the Chief called. And the tall man stepped out from behind a pale green curtain at the far end of the room, as if he had been waiting for the police chief's signal. He made no move to come forward. His pale skin looked like wax in the harsh hospital light.

The Chief smiled at Brian and Porter. "I'm glad you got over here so quickly. We've got a few questions for the boy."

Porter stepped forward so that she stood between Brian and the Chief. "Who's 'we,' Chief?"

The stout man frowned. "I don't think that need concern you." He waved toward the man at the back of the room. "Mr. Smith here is on loan; he's very busy. I've asked the nursing staff—there's a conference room at the end of the hall where we can have some privacy. Thank you for bringing the boy, Porter."

Porter didn't budge. "On loan? From whom?"

"I'm afraid you don't need to know, Porter." He looked away from her, straight at Brian. The smile was fading from his face. "I'm sure you have other things to do."

"I promised Brian he wouldn't have to do anything he didn't want to. Why don't we give him a little time, talk to him somewhere where he's more comfortable?"

The Chief shifted his substantial weight from one foot to the other. "Mr. Smith doesn't have time to waste."

Mr. Smith spoke then, with a voice like sandpaper over stone, "I think it's time for Brian to grow up."

Officer Porter shook her head. She stared hard at her superior. "I'm afraid I have something to discuss with you. In private. Something with a real bearing on this case."

Porter looked very unhappy. It seemed to Brian that Smith was controlling things here. He wondered if the policewoman felt the same way. Maybe now she would believe Brian's story.

The Chief was turning a very peculiar shade of red. "I've just about reached the end of my patience here," he said, his voice, oddly, becoming quieter with every word. "Can I make it any plainer? Get back to work."

Porter didn't move. The waxy-faced man took a step forward, but the Chief gestured for him to stay back. Everyone stood there, frozen for an instant, the only sound the faint beeping of a dozen monitors.

The silence was broken by a cry from the far end of the room.

"You!" Brian's mother called from where she had just stepped out of a curtained alcove. "What have you done to him?

"This is unthinkable!" His mother strode forward. "I would never, ever, have agreed to anything like this!"

It took Brian a second to realize she was talking to the tall, pale man.

His mother knew the stranger? Whoa! This could change everything. Maybe what happened with the gunmen had more to do with his parents than it had to do with Brian.

Mr. Smith raised one pale eyebrow at the woman's approach. "We have nothing more to discuss."

His mother was so angry she was shaking. "None of it happened the way I expected. You knew it would all fall apart—didn't you?"

Mr. Smith glanced away, as if anything else in this room would be of more interest than the woman before him. "It doesn't matter. There is no way to end the agreement. Any attempt to do so will result in—complications."

Brian's mother shook her head. "More than this?"

Mr. Smith pulled his lips back from his teeth. "You know what will happen."

Even the Chief appeared to be getting uncomfortable with this conversation. "Smith? You didn't tell me anything about—"

Smith glanced at him. The Chief staggered back as if he had been slapped in the face.

Mr. Smith stepped past the stunned policeman, glaring at Officer Porter.

"We need to talk to the boy. You will not stop what needs to be done."

"No." His mother's face caved in on itself. "What have I done?" she whispered. For the first time, Brian saw his mother cry.

"No," Officer Porter said, too. She reached for her gun. Her hand froze half an inch from the grip.

She strained to look over at Brian. It looked like she had trouble even turning her head.

"Brian." It took her forever to even say his name.

"I have had enough of this nonsense. It will be over in a minute." Mr. Smith nodded to Brian, and held out his hand.

Brian took one step forward.

"What is going on here?" A nurse emerged from a cubicle at the far end of the room. "We can't have this kind of disturbance out here."

Brian blinked. Why had he been walking toward Smith?

"Brian!" Officer Porter shouted. "Run!" The policewoman stumbled forward three steps, putting herself between Smith and the teenager.

Brian ran.

He ran back the way he'd come, heading for the stairs rather than the elevator, hoping he could make it out the front door of the hospital. No one stopped him. No one said a word.

It wasn't until he reached the lobby that he realized people weren't moving right. Or maybe it was he that was different.

Time hadn't stopped exactly. But it had gone funny, so that he wasn't moving at the same rate as everybody else. The people around him sauntered about in slow motion, reacting to each other with molasses smiles and handshakes

that moved up and down like seaweed bobbing at the edge
of a beach. No one paid any attention to Brian. He thought
of the monitors back in the ICU. It was like his heart was
running four times faster than everything around him, pushing him into a quicker world all his own.

Karen's place was in one of the large apartment buildings at the center of town. It couldn't be much more than
a mile from here. He'd call when he got close. He wanted
to get as far away from Mr. Smith as he could.

When he moved like this, he wondered if anyone else
could see him. Once, he ducked down a side street to avoid
a police cruiser. In what seemed like only a couple of
minutes, he stood in front of Karen's building.

He decided not to bother with the phone, just ring the
bell in the lobby and see if she was home. He took a deep
breath. His heartbeat slowed.

The city noise came crashing back in on him, the roar
of a truck, an insistent car horn, shouts and laughter, the
back and forth call of a pair of crows. When he had been
in his own hurried world, he hadn't realized how muted the
sound had been.

He pressed the bell. Karen's voice came over the speaker
to ask who it was.

He was so glad to hear her voice. Until this moment, he
hadn't acknowledged to himself how worried he'd been
that something could have happened to her as well.

He called out that it was Brian. She buzzed him up.

By the time he climbed the stairs to the third floor, she
was standing in the doorway. "Brian? I was so worried
about you."

Brian had never seen Karen look so pretty. Brian had
never seen anyone so alive, or so normal.

They kissed, right there in the hallway. Brian tried to
tell her what had happened. He didn't think he made much
sense. He only knew one thing that made sense now.

"This was the only place I could think to go."

Mrs. Mendeck spoke. "Right now, you need to be any-

place but here." She stood directly behind Karen. Brian
wondered how long she had been there. "If you leave now,
they'll have a much harder time finding you."

"What?" Brian began. "What do you—"

The old lady waved him to silence. "Unless they have
some part of you. An item of clothing, hair, fingernail clip-
pings." She frowned as she looked at both youngsters'
hands. "You both have all your fingers, that's the worst."

Brian had no idea what she was talking about. Karen
had often told him about Mrs. Mendeck's crazy ideas. He
turned to his girlfriend, hoping she could explain.

Karen turned back to the old woman.

"Mrs. Mendeck?" she asked.

"Karen, remember all those stories I used to tell you?
About how I came from another world? I'm afraid most of
them were true." She shook her head. "When we have
some time to breathe, we'll make long-term plans. Don't
worry. I work by a different system. No fingers. I'll be able
to find you."

Fingers? Maybe Karen wasn't as confused by all this as
he was. Brian hoped that when they both got away from
here, they could find some quiet moment where they could
make sense out of what was happening.

"I'm sorry," Mrs. Mendeck continued quickly. "This
has caught me by surprise. Maybe I wished it would never
happen. I've been a little foolish, haven't I?"

She pushed a wad of bills into Karen's hand. "Here.
This will have to do." She smiled at both of them then.
"Don't worry. This is only a temporary setback. When we
are ready, we will go and show them all."

. 10 .

AUBRIC STARED AT THE
quilted ceiling. The fabric was the brightest white, laced
through with threads of gold. Gold was everywhere in the
room; candleholders and jewel boxes, doorknobs and window latches, three mirrors and all the picture frames were
made of the bright metal. A painted gold leaf design brightened the grey walls between the tapestries; and the hangings themselves were full of the color with costumes,
chalices, and unicorn horns all of gold; the throw rugs on
the floor were trimmed with golden borders. There seemed
to be nearly as much of the shining metal here as in the
hidden treasure room of the Orange. The effect of the place
was close to overwhelming, but Aubric did not find it at
all surprising. From what he had seen of this chamber and
her actions in the throne room, m'lady surrounded herself
with excess and drama.

Such thoughts did nothing to calm Aubric concerning
his eventual fate. But what else could he expect? He was
a soldier of the Green captured by the enemy. His com-
manders had told him many times what would happen to

him should he be captured alive. Aubric knew his death would not be as simple as that of the man who died instantly from m'lady's playthings. The Grey were famous for their inventive tortures, both physical and magical. But he was resolved to give up nothing. He would keep his silence. He would have a good death.

"Interesting that it would be a human." The lady Karmille's voice broke the silence. "For a long time, I have been detecting unauthorized magicks in the corners of my palace." She laughed, a light, airy sound that Aubric might have found charming under other circumstances. Now he felt a chill in his heart. "Not of course, that my own dabblings are sanctioned by the high and mighty Judges. But people like you and I are not subject to their petty laws."

Now she would put herself and Aubric above the Judges? That went beyond the dramatic, straight to the absurd.

Growing up in the House of Green, Aubric only had to learn one lesson concerning the Judges: you never wanted to see one. Judges did things to people just to show off their sorcery. They could end your life on a whim, or make whatever life they chose to give you full of ridicule and pain. From childhood, Aubric remembered a certain jester who had been indiscreet in the presence of a Judge. That Judge had changed the fool's body so that the jester was no more than a bloated head forced to drag himself from place to place with his distended tongue.

And those were the actions of an even-tempered Judge of the Green! Heaven knew to what extremes the vengeful Judges of the other houses might go.

Aubric felt the woman's cool hand upon his chin. "You will look at me as I address you, or you will soon have no eyes to look at anything." She jerked his head down so that he was staring directly into her pale grey eyes, the first time he had dared to look straight at the face of royalty.

Her face was a perfect oval framed by dark curls. Her skin had that lack of color shared by all the High Lords.

Her lips were painted a deep red brown, like the color of dried blood. She continued to hold his chin as her lips parted in a smile to show very small, very white, very perfect teeth.

"We all have magic inside us, you know," she continued. "Everyone, whether highborn or common. It simply takes a certain ability to discover that magic. That is one of the many things the Judges hide. And who could blame them? What would happen if everyone decided to use their magic?" She released his chin as she laughed again, the sound of crystal bells. "It would be chaos." Her smile grew even broader, as if chaos was her fondest desire.

"But I have a plan." She winked at Aubric. "As no doubt do you, my young magician. Perhaps you would like to share your thoughts on magic." Her hand was at his chin again, but this time the touch was far gentler. "I have always wished to collaborate with the proper man."

Aubric refrained from giving her an answer. Her mouth smiled around her words, but the truth of her feelings could be seen in the anger in her eyes. As much as she asked for his opinions, she seemed to require his silence.

"Listen to me," she continued brightly. "I chase you halfway around the lower kingdom and then I start making plans for the both of us." She laughed again. "I *am* a demanding bitch."

She turned and strode away, continuing her speech. "Our magicks are somewhat different. No doubt you are wondering how you arrived in this room when you should have been miles from here. I may even tell you how I did it, if you share a secret or two with me." She spun about and stared at Aubric. "How did you get by all the protective spells to find the tunnels in the first place?"

Her lips were pressed together, her smile gone, as if this was his one chance to talk. There was no answer that he could give that would satisfy her; no answer that didn't involve the true magician, Summitch.

"You seem fond of that gnarlyman," she said abruptly,

as if she could read his thoughts. "I have never understood how people form these sorts of attachments. That's something else you might show me—someday."

She paused again; her smile returned. "You still don't wish to speak? One would imagine you have some misguided loyalty to the Green. Perhaps we got rid of the gnarlyman too quickly. We can bring him back, you know, and begin the removal right now. Are you not familiar with removals?" Her smile grew as broad as when she had mentioned chaos. "They are very efficient. What do you think he will miss the most, fingers or toes?"

She sighed then, regarding Aubric silently for a long moment. "This is rather tiresome, isn't it? I even tire myself."

She glanced at her guards and nodded once. They moved to either side of Aubric without a word.

"You will need to rest," the lady said as she walked away one more time. "Then we will talk again. Perhaps time will change your mind."

Aubric felt a guard's hand pressing gently against each of his arms, urging him forward. While there was no great pressure there now, he knew that would change if he offered the slightest resistance. He walked forward, and the guards kept pace at either side.

It was almost a relief to be taken to his cell. It would certainly be quieter. *Time will change your mind*, she'd said. No doubt he would be tortured at some length during the night to make him more agreeable. The lady Karmille believed he had information. That at least would keep him alive.

The guards stopped him before they had walked fifty paces.

"Your room for the night," the guard to his right announced. The door was remarkably close to the lady's chambers. No doubt Karmille liked to keep an eye on her prisoners.

Aubric glanced over at the guard. His features—straight,

slightly upturned nose, strong jaw, thin lips, and grey eyes—were so refined, he might have been a member of the royal family himself. The guard pointed to the latch.

"M'lady said that you were to open the door."

"And you never disagree with m'lady?" Aubric asked.

Neither guard replied. Well, he could only die once. Aubric decided to open the door and see what happened.

The door swung open silently, revealing a room that appeared to be a more modest version of Karmille's chambers. While the gold in this room was kept to a minimum, the hangings and furniture were every bit as elegant as those in the room he had just left.

"Inside," the guard on his right ordered.

Aubric took three hesitant steps forward. He had not been expecting anything like this.

The door slammed shut behind him. He heard the sound of metal against metal, like a heavy bolt being thrown into place.

"They will not unlock the door until morning."

Aubric spun about at the sound of the woman's voice. She stood by the side of the bed, a young woman close to Aubric's age, wearing a simple grey gown, perhaps the uniform of the household staff. Or perhaps not. The dress's fabric glittered in the torchlight.

She curtsied ever so slightly. "I am here to see to your needs."

She was a far more attractive jailer than Aubric had any right to expect, with dark hair that fell to her shoulders, dark eyes that looked very large in the candlelight, and a complexion that held more color than the High Ones. This woman was another of those like Aubric.

That meant she was human, too.

"OUT," THE LADY Karmille announced. She looked away from those assembled in the room. When she looked back again, all four were gone, three guards and the royal assassin who had watched from behind the curtains. At another time, their quick response, a lovely sign of their fear, would have brought a smile to her lips. But not today.

The lady Karmille was feeling most dissatisfied. The warrior of the Green had been particularly unresponsive, and, after all the effort it had taken to call in her creatures, she had not had the energy for anything that might cause him any real discomfort. She always found causing the more subtle pains to be by far the most difficult, especially if your subject had some sorcerous means to defend himself.

Karmille shook her head, and, alone at last, allowed herself to sit upon the bed. Sometimes she thought she was too involved with sorcery. She wondered now if this soldier was even a magician. Perhaps there was nothing at all beneath that stolid exterior, and he was exactly what he appeared to be: handsome and silent and stupid. Perhaps there was a third player in all of this, a magician in hiding who used the human and gnarlyman as pawns. She could think of no two creatures who were more expendable. She wondered if someone had concocted this as a joke at her expense. She would like nothing better than to turn this little drama around on the joker.

She stood again. She should be exhausted, but her mind could not stop trying to make sense of her intruders. She needed some way to relax. Well, if the soldier had proved unrewarding, there was always the simpler pleasure of torturing a gnarlyman. She crossed the room and opened the secret way down to the dungeon. She seemed to feel better with every step her slippered foot took on the carpeted stairs. Gnarlymen were so direct. Sometimes they'd start to scream when you were only heating the instruments.

She reached the bottom of the stairs and a section of the wall swung away before her. She stepped out into a recessed space kept always in shadow so that if anyone was watching from the cells, she might appear to be stepping out of nowhere.

The air, always considerably colder than in the castle above, made Karmille's face and hands tingle. She had instructed the guards to place the gnarlyman directly in the torture room, and so proceeded down the corridor past the cramped cells to the larger space at the prison's center, a room large enough to accommodate half a dozen prisoners along with twice as many torturers and perhaps a small audience.

She turned the final corner of the twisting corridor that led to her goal. At first, the torture room appeared empty. There was certainly no gnarlyman chained anywhere along the walls. She heard a faint sound. As she stepped into the room, she realized it was the snoring of a torturer, half-hidden by the iron maiden that he'd curled up behind. If he liked the maiden so much, Karmille thought, perhaps she should grant him a more intimate view.

Not yet, though. She doubted the torturer's sleep was entirely natural. She would simply wake him now and find out if he remembered anything about the spell that freed the gnarlyman; and what signs he might have ignored that allowed him to be overcome by the true magician. The guard would tell her everything—eventually. It would be much more rewarding to kill the torturer in the morning when she had an audience.

Her hidden magician was one step ahead of her. Karmille actually found herself smiling. Perhaps this little duel might be diverting after all.

· 11 ·

ERIC JACOBSEN KNEW HE was in Hell. There was no light and no sound beyond his breathing and the scuffing noise he made with his feet. The air was still and a little cold. By cautiously feeling around him, he discovered two parallel walls of rough-hewn rock with perhaps six feet between them. He could find no intersecting wall in the dozen or so paces he risked in the total dark. The floor was made of dirt; at least it felt, smelled, and tasted like dirt. If there was a ceiling, he couldn't reach it. He guessed he was in some sort of corridor, or at least a very long room. For the first time in years Jacobsen wished he still smoked, and had a lighter in his pocket to take a look at his surroundings.

No such luck. In a last-ditch effort to save his life, Jacobsen had peeled away his vices one by one; smoking first, then drinking. It was the gambling he'd never quite been able to give up. And the gambling had brought him here, right where he belonged.

He kept seeing the face of the girl he had been supposed to kill, Karen Eggleton, not much more than a child, staring

at him from that open door. He was glad he hadn't been
able to pull the trigger. He was even glad the old woman
had waved her arms and made the hallway and young
Karen Eggleton and the whole world go away. At least that
was what Jacobsen thought had happened. Magic, drugs,
hypnosis, trapdoors—Jacobsen had no idea what really
happened; every explanation for his arrival here was as
likely as any other. He knew only one thing. He had made
a devil's bargain, and the devil had brought him here.

The gun had come with him. It sat now, all too solid,
where he had jammed it in his pocket. Jacobsen wondered
what would happen if he pulled the trigger in a place like
this. The flash from the muzzle would be blinding, the explosion of the gunpowder deafening. The bullet might fly
forever, or it might turn around and find the heart of the
man who fired it in the first place.

Maybe the gun wouldn't work at all. Jacobsen stroked
the handle of the gun where it jutted out of his pocket. The
metal felt even colder than the surrounding air. It felt as
cold as death.

What did he want now, anyway? He had no idea how
long he had been here, or how long he would be here. After
a while in the silent dark, he wondered if he could use the
gun on himself.

No. If he wanted to kill himself, he would have done so
already. After all, it was the death threats from the debt
collectors that had driven him to that meeting with Mr.
Smith, the desire not to die so strong that he would consider
murder instead. It was only after everything—job, home,
money, wife—was gone, that Jacobsen really learned how
to survive. Eric Jacobsen might not have much of a life,
but he would go to almost any lengths not to die.

So what should he do now? Just because he had been
left here didn't mean he had to stay. He might be in the
middle of nowhere, but this corridor must lead from one
real place to another.

Jacobsen started to walk. Slowly and carefully, one foot

placed firmly in the dirt in front of the other, his right hand lightly brushing the wall. He could take nothing for granted. Just because there was a floor beneath him now didn't mean it would keep on being there.

He saw the faintest greyness ahead, at first only the suggestion of light seeping into the distance. It grew brighter as he watched, defining itself into a small square of brilliance now, still very far away. The slightest of noises came with it; a whooshing sound, like a distant wind.

What should he do? What could he do? Jacobsen stopped and waited for the light to come to him.

He took a step back when he saw the source of the light and sound. Torches, set high up on the stone walls, were lit one after another, apparently by spontaneous combustion. It was as if some invisible hand were igniting each one in turn, some force rushing down the newly illuminated corridor to meet him.

Jacobsen flinched as the torch above him flared, waiting for something. What? A great wall of wind? The fur and claws of some unseen beast? He felt nothing. There was nothing to feel. He looked behind him. The torches continued to light, one after another, down a corridor that seemed never to end. A hallway that went on forever; that sounded a lot like Hell.

Jacobsen heard another sound beneath the rustle of the torches, a higher sound, delicate and musical. Someone was whistling.

It was a man, or something like a man. Jacobsen could see a figure now, marching toward him beneath the torchlight. He seemed very small in the distance.

Jacobsen stood and waited for his own personal demon.

The newcomer came closer, but remained small. Well, short, really. He couldn't have been more than three feet high. His face was a mass of wrinkles, great folds of skin that might have stretched to cover a man twice his size.

"Ah!" the little fellow called out to him with a wave. "There you are!"

Jacobsen supposed that he was. If he was already damned, an extra question or two couldn't hurt.

"Who are you?" he called. "What are you?"

"At the moment, I look like a gnarlyman, don't I?" The short fellow stopped walking and laughed. "You don't know, do you? You really *are* new here. I'll give you a tour of the tunnels when we have a bit more time." He waved Jacobsen forward. "Come on, we have another of your kind to save. I thought you were him, or he was you, or—" He shook his head. "Sometimes, I wonder why I bother."

The small man leaned against a wall. A door swung open where before there had appeared to be nothing but solid rock. Jacobsen stepped forward. The space beyond the door was as dark as the corridor had been moments before.

"Ah," the little fellow remarked with a nod. "Easily remedied." He clapped his hands, and a new row of torches flamed to life one after another, showing a new passage-way, just as straight and featureless and endless as the one behind them.

"These corridors look like they go on forever," Jacobsen whispered.

The small man nodded at that. "They very well might." He stared up at Jacobsen for a long moment before nodding a second time. "The name's Summitch."

"Jacobsen," he replied quickly. "Eric Jacobsen." Somehow, he was surprised the little man didn't know that already.

"I would expect no less," Summitch replied.

What did that mean? Jacobsen needed some answers. "Do you know—" he began.

But Summitch waved him to silence. "We are all here for a reason. In a place like this, we have to find out what the reason is before we get killed. It is as simple—"

He was interrupted by three clear tones, like the ringing of a gong, that echoed down the hall.

Summitch tensed. Jacobsen found his hand around his

gun. They stood a moment in silence before the small man looked back at Eric.

"That won't do any good down here," Summitch said with a nod at the gun. "We might be able to use it once we make a few modifications—" He sighed. "Modifications that are at the moment beyond my skill. We'd best be on our way."

Summitch marched down the new corridor. Jacobsen hurried to follow. He still wanted some answers.

"Why are you doing this?" he demanded. "Saving me like this?"

Summitch shrugged. "One more to carry the gold."

Gold? Now that was something Eric Jacobsen could understand. He had never had enough of it. His need for it had brought him here. And now it would be thrust in his face all over again.

Perhaps this was a brand new version of Hell. Jacobsen would expect no less.

AUBRIC STARED AT the woman before him.

"I am here to serve you," she repeated when he made no reply. She stared at the floor, her hands folded before her. "As long as you are here, Sir Aubric, it is my duty to see to your every need."

He supposed it would do him no harm to be civil. "I heard you. And I want nothing."

She looked afraid, glancing up into his eyes for the fraction of a second. "You won't send me away?"

Aubric frowned. Until she mentioned it, he didn't know he had the power to send this woman away. If, indeed, he did have that power. There were games being played here, perhaps games within games. Like it or not, the lady Karmille had made him a player. He wondered how much the lady had instructed the woman who stood before him, and how much that woman might tell him of that instruction.

He disliked thinking what would happen to someone in Lady Karmille's employ if they disobeyed.

"Look, what is your name?"

Her eyes were once again on the floor. "Servants are allowed no names."

Aubric couldn't believe this. "You were never called anything?"

She paused for a moment before answering. "When I was young, and helped in the kitchens, they used to call me Runt."

Aubric almost laughed. She was a runt no longer. She had grown close to Aubric's height, with a full head of fire-red hair and a slim but strong form beneath her gown, which on closer inspection was a dress that was both finer and more revealing than one expected to see on servants. She was a beautiful creature. He wished it were a different time and a different place.

But he was in the hands of the enemy. And this beautiful "human," servant or no, was an enemy as well. His superiors had warned him that the Greys might go to any extreme to gain information. The woman before him was simply a sweeter torture than what he had expected.

"All right, then," he said. "I will call you Runt. And if we have to share a room for now, you can take that pile of pillows in the corner. I'm for the bed. I'm afraid I've done my share of walking today."

Runt looked up at him again. This time he saw her eyes were green. "But my lady would expect—"

This was too much. The sight of the bed had been enough to make Aubric realize the totality of his exhaustion. "Your lady expects you to make me happy. And tonight, I will be happy just to be left alone."

"Yes, Sir Aubric." Runt once again studied the floor.

"You can get rid of the light in here," Aubric added after a moment.

"I can?" The young woman smiled. "Thank you, Sir Aubric!" She ran lightly to the wall and made a single motion with her hand. The room was full dark in an instant. Aubric had not wanted to be obeyed quite that quickly. The bed, as he recalled, was to his right. He reached out his hand, and brushed against soft fabric and a naked shoulder. The woman was in front of him again.

"What are you doing here?" he demanded. His voice sounded more upset than angry.

"But, Sir Aubric," she replied softly. "I thought—"

"There will be no thinking tonight," he said more firmly than he felt. This close, the young woman smelled of wildflowers. Her shoulder had been soft and warm. He was glad that he still wore his battered armor to hide what was happening beneath. He turned away from her, taking a quick step to the side. "I'm sleeping in the bed, and you're staying on the other side of the room."

"Oh," Runt replied. A moment later, she added, "Very well." The smell of flowers faded as she moved away. Aubric found himself feeling both greatly relieved and deeply disappointed at the same time. Still, tomorrow, after a good night's sleep, he would be stronger, and he would be able to deal with this. However he decided to deal with this.

He was far too tired. Things would sort themselves out in the morning. Or they wouldn't. At the moment, Green and Grey and Summitch's gold meant far less to him than getting some sleep.

"Sir Aubric?" Runt whispered in his ear. Or maybe it was all a dream.

. 12 .

J OE BEAST DIDN'T LIKE THIS one bit.

As soon as Joe and his cousin Ernie had realized that Uncle Roman was going to let both of them live, they had relaxed a little. That was probably their first mistake.

Yes, Uncle Roman had allowed as how they had screwed up a little bit, and on something that was a special favor to this Mr. Smith. But hey, Roman was willing to give them another chance, especially where Mr. Smith was concerned.

That, Joe realized, was when the alarm bells should have started ringing in his head. They'd screwed up a job, and Roman was smiling? Usually when something went wrong, Uncle Roman at least broke some furniture. Sometimes he ended up breaking heads.

"So, you didn't get the kid," Roman had said, smiling all the time. "The father got in the way. Hey, there's a name for that, right? Human error. Everybody screws up once in a while. Least they do if they're human."

Joe had risked a look at Ernie after that; his cousin had

looked every bit as confused as Joe had felt. Maybe it was the old man's age, maybe it was the botched job, maybe it was the insistent rock and roll beat seeping through the Funland walls, but Uncle Roman was turning into a philosopher.

"But what can we human beings do, huh? Except maybe try again?" The old man's smile seemed a bit strained as he added, "And this time, Joe, get it right?"

Joe had to see if he understood the situation. "So you still want us to go out and snatch the kid?"

"No, no, no, that's old news. There's police crawling all over his place. The kid's too hot." The smile spread back across his face. "We've got another job for you two."

"We?" Ernie asked.

His father grimaced at the sound of Ernie's voice. "Me and Mr. Smith. That's something you don't need to know about. Ernie, when you gonna learn to keep your trap shut?"

Uncle Roman turned back to Joe. Joe guessed it was his turn to talk. "So, this other job?"

"Yeah, this one's downtown. I've got an address." Roman felt in the breast pocket of his suit coat, then in both of the inner pockets. He blinked, then nodded his head.

"Hey, Louse!" he called. "The address!"

Larry the Louse stepped forward, a grimy, folded square of paper in his hand. He handed it to Joe.

"This is the job," Roman explained as Joe unfolded the paper. "Karen Eggleton. Sixteen years old; cute little blond girl. Mr. Smith needs her out of the picture."

Folded inside the paper was a small photo, some high-school yearbook job that showed a thin girl with wire-rimmed glasses. She was cute in that honor-student sort of way. Girls like that never looked twice at Joe when he was a kid. And now he had to snatch her?

It was one thing to grab a teenaged boy; if they were anything like Joe was as a teenager, they should be off the streets anyway. But a young girl? Until now, this was the sort of thing Joe had always stayed away from. People frowned when you snatched girls—Joe could see the headlines now; abduction, kidnapping, maybe even statutory rape, all because he had to grab some sixteen-year-old chick.

But what else could he do? He checked the address written on the paper. The apartment building was on this side of the city. It would be a quick job to drive over, grab her, then maybe ten minutes back here. More than half an hour to Delvecchio's, but that still wouldn't be much of a problem.

After that? Once she was delivered, Joe didn't want to know.

"Karen Eggleton," Uncle Roman continued. "You snatch her, and bring her here, to Funland."

Good, Joe thought. The short trip, then.

"Oh," Uncle Roman added, "if she gives you any trouble, kill her."

Joe stared back down at the photo. Roman Petranova was as much as telling them that the boys were going to whack the girl once they got her here.

"Here's a phone number." Uncle Roman reached back into his suit pocket. This time he pulled out a business card, plain white, the only printing on it seven numbers, without even a dash in the middle. "One of Mr. Smith's associates will answer the phone. Call them once you leave here. They may have some further instructions."

Uncle Roman shifted in his chair. "So you boys understand what you've got to do?"

All too well, Joe thought. He nodded. What else could he do?

"Good," Roman replied. "Over the years, the two of you have been very dependable. You've got a good head on your shoulders, Joe. Use it. And Ernie. Listen to Joe." He waved for Larry the Louse to open the door behind him. "After all, there's only so much human error this organization can tolerate."

Larry the Louse had given them both a gun this time, just before they left. Joe got the feeling that using them was going to get to be a habit.

As Larry closed the door behind them, Joe had looked at the business card in his hand. So they were going to let this Smith character in on every twist and turn of the job? That, Joe thought, was when the alarm bells should have given way to air-raid sirens. But it wasn't until the first time he called the number that he found out how high and deep the shit was piled.

They had left Funland and found a pay phone at the back end of a dying strip mall. Joe got out and told Ernie to park the car in front of one of the many empty storefronts. It was time to give Mr. Smith a call.

"Problems solved," the voice on the other end of the line answered.

What the hell? Joe thought. "I'm looking for Mr. Smith."

"He's not here," the voice replied flatly. "He's never here."

Joe was getting annoyed. "Look, I was given this number by a very important man."

"No doubt." The voice at the other end did not sound impressed. "Mr. Smith knows many important men."

"Mr. Roman Petranova."

That actually made the guy hesitate.

"Mr. Smith has given me some instructions regarding this matter. You are to wait for his signal."

"His signal? What kind of signal?"

"You will know it when it occurs. I'll tell Mr. Smith of your interest."

Joe heard a click and a dial tone. The guy had hung up on him.

Joe went back to the car to tell Ernie what happened.

Ernie hit the steering wheel and swore. "What the fuck are we supposed to do? Sit on our hands?"

Joe thought for a minute. "Let's at least look at the

building. The apartment where we're going to snatch the girl. We could see if there are any problems, double check escape routes, things like that.''

The way Ernie the driver knew the streets of the city, they didn't really need to do that. But they needed to do something.

Ernie kept a cell phone in the car. They never used it for business; there was too much risk of being overheard. But Uncle Roman knew the number, and they could get a message through it. So Mr. Smith could send his signal.

Until then, it was time to sit on their hands.

"Okay," Ernie said. "Get the fuck in." They drove.

But where? Straight into trouble, Joe thought. He could almost hear Ernie's LeSabre whisper those words as the tires hit the pavement: straight into trouble, straight into trouble, straight into trouble. Oh, hell. This job was crazy enough without letting his imagination spook him. One last job; that's what he had to remember. He had told his uncle he'd see this through. One last job and he'd be square.

Maybe after that, Joe thought, it would be time to look for another line of work.

BRIAN HAD NEVER really thought about leaving. Oh, he had dreamed about it often enough, especially on those many occasions when his mother was yelling and his father was trying to blend into the furniture.

But he had never made plans to run away. His escape had always been to spend time with Karen, an afternoon here, an evening there. Now that both of them were together, hopefully for good, he had no idea what to do next.

As soon as they left Karen's building, they knew where they would go first. There was a quiet corner of a park two blocks away, where he and Karen often went to talk, or maybe do a little fooling around. It seemed the obvious place to go and do some planning.

But what were they planning for?

They went to their favorite spot, a small, grassy knoll hidden on one side by a six-foot-high rock and on the other by a great clump of evergreens. They sat side by side as usual, but this time they didn't touch. Karen started out by counting the money. Mrs. Mendeck had given them $268, probably all she had had in her apartment.

"What are we going to do with two hundred sixty-eight dollars?" Brian asked.

Karen looked down at the money in her hands. "I think we'd better do something."

Brian nodded. "Somebody wants to take me away." When they found someplace to hide he'd have to tell her everything that had happened with Smith.

Karen frowned. "With me, I think it's worse than that." She looked at Brian for a minute before going on. Brian remembered how the old lady had acted as if they were both in danger. So these creeps were after Karen, too. He reached out and took her hand.

"It's like a dream I had," Karen said at last. "But I think it really happened. Things get sort of strange around Mrs. Mendeck sometimes. But the more I think about this, the clearer it gets. There was a guy threatening me with a gun." She looked up at Brian. "I think somebody just wants me dead."

Brian hadn't thought about that before. He put an arm around Karen's shoulder. "They may just want me dead, too. They came close to killing my father."

"But why?" Karen asked. "What have we done?"

Brian couldn't think of anything. "You see any drug deals? Notice anybody get shot? Call anybody names?"

Karen frowned at that, snuggling closer. "It would have to be something that both of us had done, wouldn't it?"

But what could they have done that involved other people? Except for the crowds at the occasional movie, Karen and Brian did things by themselves. Their time together was too precious to involve the outside world.

"Something to do with school, maybe?" Karen asked.

That was true; they both had friends at school, and a few people who didn't seem to like them much. But they still needed a reason.

"We're both pretty good students?" Brian put it more as a question than a statement; it sounded lame even before he got it completely out of his mouth.

Karen smiled at that, taking Brian's free hand in her own. "I don't think anybody wants to kill us to get better marks on the curve. But why else would this be happening?"

They held each other in silence for a long moment.

"I don't think we're going to know," Brian said at last. "We'd better just get out of town."

Karen patted the wad of bills she'd shoved into her jeans pocket. "With two hundred sixty-eight dollars, we're not going to get that far. Besides, don't you need a credit card or something if you're going to stay in a motel?"

Yeah, Brian thought, two teenagers, paying cash, with no obvious adult supervision? It sounded like the sort of thing hotel managers reported to the police. And speaking of the police . . .

"We've got another problem." Brian quickly told Karen what happened at the hospital.

"So you can trust this Officer Porter?" Karen asked when he was done.

"I think so. But what good will it do if her boss wants to get rid of me?"

There just weren't any answers. The sun was slanting toward late afternoon. They couldn't stay in the park forever. They sat in silence for another moment. It was quiet here for the middle of the city. You couldn't hear the cars back here, only the occasional truck or bus.

Brian stood abruptly. "I've got an idea." He reached out a hand to help Karen to her feet. "And it's only four blocks away from here."

"What?"

"I just remembered the kind of place where you still pay in cash—the bus station."

Brian loved the idea the minute he thought of it. He realized it was perfect for another reason, too. His mother hated the bus station. It was one of those many, many things she considered beneath her. He remembered, a few years back when he had been in middle school, and he had gone to see a friend off on the bus. His mother wouldn't let him sit down in the house until he'd taken a shower. The bus station? No one who knew Brian would think he'd dare go to a place like that.

Still holding Karen's hand, he led her out of the park.

"So we're going to take a bus?" From the half-smile on Karen's face, she was having trouble taking Brian's idea seriously. "Where are we going?"

Brian thought for a moment before answering. "I don't think it really matters, as long as we get out of here. When we get to the station, let's look at the schedules. We need someplace that's pretty far away from here, so we can stay on the bus all night long. If we can't sleep in a motel, hey, we'll sleep on the bus."

"The bus station is pretty public," Karen pointed out. "What if this police chief has his men looking for us?"

Brian hadn't thought of that. What could they do, if the police really were searching for them? "I guess, then, we run. Let's just hope it doesn't happen."

What would people think of them? Both were tall and skinny. Both wore glasses. He had dark hair and Karen was blond; outside of that, they could almost be related. They just looked like a couple of wimpy teens, the kind of kids who probably walked through the bus station every day. As long as they looked like they belonged there, no one would bother them.

"Just keep calm," Brian whispered as they rounded the final corner across from the bus station. "Look like you know what you're doing. You probably shouldn't pull out the whole wad of bills. We don't want to call attention to ourselves."

They found a deserted alley across the street, where they

quickly split up the money. Brian stuck five twenties in his wallet. A hundred dollars should be enough to get them out of town.

He squeezed Karen's hand, then let go of it as they entered the bus station. It was one of those big, warehouse-type places they built back in the fifties and sixties, full of bright colors and plastic furniture. It had probably looked modern way back then. Now it looked cheap and old. The worn linoleum was clean, though, and the place was almost too brightly lit.

There were a couple hundred people in here, all waiting to go somewhere or meet someone. No one seemed to give more than a glance to Brian and Karen in passing. A cop had his back turned to them as they passed the donut counter. They kept on walking toward a central kiosk that said in large, white letters INFORM TION. There was a large rack with dozens of different brochures, all on bright yellow stock, each one with a bus number and destination printed in bold block letters across the top.

"This is what we need," Brian said as they walked to the rack. "Timetables."

"Does it say what it's going to cost?"

"Let me take a look." He pulled a leaflet from the bottom rack.

GRAVESVILLE LOCAL, the brochure read at the top. According to a line map on the front of the brochure, Gravesville was in the absolute other corner of the state. There were two buses a day, one of which left within the hour. It took almost twelve hours to get there from here, the bus arriving a little after eight in the morning. It was perfect.

Brian looked at the back of the brochure. There was no mention of price.

"Brian!" Karen called. "Look!" She pointed to a banner strung across the far wall of the station. It was bright blue with white letters and bright red stars.

SPECIAL SUMMER SUPER SAVERS! the banner

read. "Go to over one hundred different destinations, round trip, for $29.95!"

Brian grinned. "Hey, this could be our lucky day. Let's find out."

They marched down to a sign reading TICKETS at one end of the banner. A bored ticket seller informed Brian that Gravesville was indeed one of the special round-trip fares. Brian pulled sixty dollars out of his wallet and got two round-trip tickets and a dime. The man behind the counter told them their bus left in thirty-four minutes, gate three.

"Brian?" Karen whispered. She tugged at his sleeve. "Look over there."

A rather disheveled man standing under the Summer Super Savers banner was staring at the both of them. He grinned and shook his head.

Brian had never seen the man before. "I think he's just a bum," he said.

Karen grabbed Brian's arm as the policeman from the donut counter walked right by them. "Benny!" he called to the raggedy man under the banner. "Move along!"

Benny grumbled and shuffled very slowly away from his spot. Technically, Brian supposed he was moving, but at this rate, he probably wouldn't reach the bus station's front door until morning.

The policeman spun about and marched back to his counter. He looked right past Brian and Karen.

Apparently the police chief hadn't sent out Brian's description, at least not yet. Maybe there was something keeping him from doing so. Brian guessed that whatever the Chief was involved in wasn't exactly official business.

"Brian!" Karen cried urgently. She squeezed his hand, hard.

Brian turned. Somehow, Benny had gotten directly in front of them.

"Spare change?" Benny asked.

"Uh, sure." Brian still had the dime in his hand. He reached in his pocket and added a quarter.

"Thanks," Benny said with a grin. "Have a nice day."
He grimaced toward the donut counter and the cop. "Getting so a man can't make an honest living!"

Benny turned and went back to shuffling, walking nowhere in particular.

"I think I'm a little on edge," Karen said once Benny was out of earshot. "Come on." She pointed to their right. "Gate three's over here."

Brian thought they were both more than a little on edge. After all, they were jumping on a bus to keep from getting caught or killed. In a place like this, everything was bound to seem a little strange.

"Maybe we should get something to eat to take along," he suggested.

Karen thought that was a good idea, so they wandered over to the magazine kiosk and picked up some candy bars and chips. Karen bought a big paperback thriller, and Brian chose a movie magazine with an article on "This Summer's Special Effects Blockbusters!" At the moment, this whole bus trip seemed like an adventure.

Karen looked up at him as they started for the gate. "You know anything about Gravesville?"

"Only what I read in the bus schedule," Brian admitted. That, and a couple of half-remembered facts from old social studies courses; something about it being an agricultural center in the eighteenth century. "We'll stop, stay for the day, and come back overnight."

As they crossed the station, heading toward their gate, they noticed that Benny had walked over to a bank of pay phones, where he was staring at them again. Brian wondered if the guy even remembered he'd already hit them up for spare change. Benny nodded and turned away, putting a quarter—maybe the same quarter Brian had given him—into the phone, then punching out a number. Well, Brian supposed, homeless guys had to make phone calls, too.

"How about Mrs. Mendeck?" Brian asked. "She seemed to know an awful lot about this."

"She has a lot of stories," Karen said thoughtfully. "The more I know her, the less I think she makes them up. I'll tell you some of them on the bus. But how is she going to know where we are?"

Brian had been in such a panic trying to figure out what to do, he hadn't really thought about that. Mrs. Mendeck had said she'd be able to find them, but that didn't make sense if she had no idea where they were going. "This bus makes lots of stops. We'll call her from some layover, ask her what to do."

A bored male voice announced that their bus was leaving in fifteen minutes.

Brian took Karen by the arm. "Would you care to join me on a bus ride to nowhere?"

Karen giggled. "I never thought I'd find romance on a bus."

"Stick with me, Karen," Brian said as he waved at the gate before them. "I'll show you the world."

Karen made a face.

"Well," Brian admitted, "maybe I'll show you Gravesville."

They walked straight through the gate and onto the bus. Nobody stopped them, nobody even looked their way.

Maybe they were safe, for a few hours at least.

JOE BEAST COULD see it coming. Ernie Petranova was about to blow.

"C'mon, Joe! We've gotta do something here!"

Joe Beast stared at his cousin across the booth in the coffee shop. Once they'd checked out the place where they were supposed to grab the girl, Joe decided it would be better if they hung out somewhere besides the car. This little coffee shop down the street from the apartment building looked ideal. At least it did until Ernie started on his third cup of coffee. If there was one thing Ernie didn't need at a time like this, it was caffeine.

Joe tapped the Formica table with his spoon. "What would you like to do, Ernie? Your father told us to call these people. The people told us to wait."

"Wait?" Ernie was starting to get that crazy look in his eye that came from sitting too long in one place. "That's totally fucked! The longer we wait, the more chance of something screwing up!"

Joe shifted in his seat, glancing past his cousin at the other patrons in the restaurant. Ernie was making no attempt to keep his voice down. Lots of people were looking their way.

"Look," Joe replied quietly, "it's out of our hands."

"Yeah!" Ernie replied with a harsh laugh. "Yeah! If we screw up again, my father's gonna cut off our balls!"

Joe looked down at his half-full cup. His cousin had finally said something Joe could agree with. Ernie's father, Roman, was cut from the same emotional cloth as his son. Neither one of them was the most rational—or logical—of men.

"What if they can't get in touch with us?" Ernie insisted. "What if the signal's come through and we missed our chance?"

Joe tried to shrug off his cousin's paranoia. "Hey, I just called this guy a half an hour ago." He had gotten up and gone to the phone booth in the back of the shop—a futile attempt to calm his cousin down somewhere in the middle of Ernie's second cup.

"You saw me go and call," Joe continued. He had told Ernie all of this before, but sometimes his cousin needed to hear things twice. "He said two things: 'Problems solved,' when he picked up the phone. And 'I'll tell Mr. Smith of your interest,' the minute I tried to squeeze some information from him. And then he hung up! What else do you want me to do?"

Ernie pulled out the cell phone he'd stuck in his pocket.

"What's the number? I'll call him. I'll get him to tell us something!"

"Ernie," Joe urged, spreading his hands.

Ernie stood, waving the phone above his head. "My father gave us a direct order! If he thinks we're jerking off here—"

There was only one way to put an end to this. "All right. I'll call." Joe got up, too. He threw ten dollars on the table; twice what they owed. "Why don't you go out and wait in the car?"

Ernie looked confused, like he wasn't used to people agreeing with him. "Uh, okay." He held out the cell phone. "You want to use this?"

"No, I think I'll call from next door." On their way in here, they had passed a pay phone in front of a pharmacy. Joe liked to vary the places he called from; it made it more difficult for the authorities to establish any pattern from the calls. Not that—most of the time—he was involved in anything the authorities would think to look at—at least until now.

He especially didn't want to make another call from the coffee shop with the way Ernie had been calling attention to himself. It was bad enough they had to snatch somebody half a block away. Now they probably had half a dozen people who could give a great description of these two guys who had been sitting in the coffee shop for hours.

Ernie calmed down as soon as he got on his feet; once he was walking, he had somewhere for the energy to go. Joe knew from past experience that this calm was only temporary. Unless Ernie thought they were taking this to the next level, he'd start shouting all over again.

They walked out of the coffee shop together.

"You gonna make the fucking call?" Ernie demanded as soon as they were out the door.

Joe had had enough of his cousin bouncing off the walls. "As soon as you climb in the car."

Ernie thumped his chest with his balled fist. He was

pumped and ready. "Why don't you let me do it? I know
how to get fucking results!"

"Remember what your father said." That still managed
to quiet Ernie down. He headed for the car, and Joe walked
over to the phone by the pharmacy. If he was going to keep
Ernie quiet for long, he had to find a way to get more
information. Half of their jobs ended up this way, with Joe
playing nursemaid to Ernie's pain-in-the-ass. Well, Joe
guessed it worked for Ernie, probably in more ways than
one.

He put a quarter in the slot and dialed. Maybe he would
do it Ernie's way. If Joe could be enough of a pain-in-the-
ass himself, he could accomplish something too.

The voice answered after the first ring.

"Problems solved."

"You're not doing anything for my problem," Joe replied.

"Oh, it's you again."

"That's right. And I'm going to tie up the line here until
I get some answers."

"You can't—"

"Yeah, I'll keep on calling, over and over. Got more
than one line? I'll get my cousin to call you, too. I bet the
way Mr. Smith works, he likes the lines open all the time."

There was a moment's silence before the voice replied.
"What do you wish me to do?"

Joe grinned. Jackpot first time. He might as well go for
the gold. "I need to know more about this job. And this
Mr. Smith. Call me when he comes back. Tell me something about him."

"No, I cannot," the man on the other end said hurriedly.
"Do you know what he'll do? What he can do?" He
laughed, a high, brittle sound. "He already made sure I'd
be around to answer the phone!" He took a ragged breath
and when he spoke again, his voice was calm. "I'll tell Mr.
Smith of your interest."

He hung up. Joe got a dial tone. He decided against

calling again. There was something in the other man's voice
that told Joe it wouldn't be worth it. At the very least, the
guy was frightened out of his mind. Or maybe he was just
plain crazy.

Well, if they couldn't solve this one way, they'd go the
other. Joe walked out to where Ernie waited in the Buick.

"We gotta see your father again."

Ernie gripped the steering wheel with both hands, his
wildness completely drained by the prospect of going back
in front of Roman Petranova. "No easy way out, huh?"

They drove back to the pay phone at the strip mall. Ernie
made the call this time. The call was very short; his father
and his lieutenants never let him say more than five words.

Ernie walked back to the car. "Johnny T says he's back
at the restaurant."

Good. People usually didn't get killed at Delvecchio's.
Ernie drove, and Joe stared out at the city. It was getting
dark; that would be better for this kind of job, anyway. Joe
was glad they were moving. The waiting was getting to
him, too.

Larry the Louse was lounging outside the banquet room.
The cigarette hanging from his lip was three-quarters ash.
Larry never moved unless he had to. He raised one eyebrow
as Joe and Ernie approached.

Joe nodded to the muscle. "Tell the boss we've got a
problem."

Larry nodded back. He flicked the cigarette into an ash-
tray stand left there for that purpose and pushed through
the swinging doors into the banquet room. He poked his
head out a second later.

"He says you should come on in."

Joe went first, with Ernie close behind. Roman had three
of his cronies with him at the table today. Joe recognized
their second cousin Sal; all four of them looked like relatives.

Joe stopped six feet from the table. Ernie shuffled up

next to him. Uncle Roman looked at them without expression.

"You have a problem."

Joe explained what was happening. Ernie tried to chime in once or twice, but was stopped each time with a glance from his father.

Uncle Roman let out a long sigh.

"This is my fault, you know, boys? Mr. Smith and I— He calls this an equal partnership. Now the phone calls. Does it sound very equal to you?"

"Not for a minute. It sounds like he's bustin'—"

"Shut up, Ernie. What did I tell you about talking? I was asking Joe, here."

"That's why we came back here, Uncle Roman," Joe replied. "The whole setup didn't seem to make very much sense."

The boss sighed again. "This comes from too many years of sittin' on my ass." He glanced at the other men around the table, then looked back to Joe. "We never moved fast enough. I was always too much of a loner. The last ten, fifteen years, things have changed. Some of the families got involved with the new street gangs. Some of them expanded overseas. A couple of the families got heavily invested in moving money around on Wall Street."

He paused again and looked at the other men at the table as if they, too, were to blame. "But what did the Petranovas do? Oh, I haven't spent the last thirty years just sitting on my kiester. We got a few safe investments, a tribal casino here, a real estate franchise there, but these things are almost legitimate, almost as boring as the shit I get Joe to do every day. No offense, Joe. They're ways to clean your money and keep it, but you're not going to see the kind of profits we got in the old days. And these other families, with these new alliances, they're finding new sources of power, new ways to squeeze us. I tell you, crime isn't what it used to be."

Uncle Roman paused, reached into his left-hand jacket

pocket, and pulled out one of his prize Havanas. All four of the other men at the table leaned forward as he used his cutter to snip off the tip. Roman nodded to Sal. Joe's second cousin pulled out his silver Zippo and did the honors.

Roman drew on his cigar, paused, and slowly exhaled, contemplating the dissipating smoke for a moment before he continued.

"Boys, I should have seen it coming. Somehow, as I got older, I started playing it a little too safe. And the word got around. It sounded like the Petranova family were, hey, just not going to cut it anymore—"

"Pop, anybody says that to my face—"

"Shut up, Ernie." Roman puffed on his Havana. "I heard that stuff about our family, it sounded like a challenge. You get to be an old man, part of you wants to play it safe, but part of you wants to feel like you did as a young man. Cutting deals, making scores, living on the edge. That's what I was missing. And that's when Mr. Smith came along. A very strange fellow, our Mr. Smith, well-connected, but in different ways than you'd expect." He stared at the glowing tip of his cigar. "I needed to feel the fire. And, whatever Mr. Smith is, he smells like danger."

"What do you know about Smith?" Joe asked as his uncle puffed. "The guy on the phone sounds half crazy."

"Can we trust him? Does he have a sense of honor?" Uncle Roman shook his head. "I don't know. But from what my sources tell me, when Mr. Smith makes a bargain, it stays a bargain. This isn't the first time I've dealt with him. We've joined in a couple projects, to our mutual advantage. Small things, mostly to test the waters. And then this business with the kids came up. Whatever's behind it, it made Smith real upset. And when people are upset, they'll part with some serious money."

Ernie rocked back and forth on his heels like a Saturn booster at the end of a countdown. "So we're going to let this guy use us—"

Roman put up his hands. "For now we use each other.

And we learn everything we can about this guy, in case we ever have to take him down.'' He paused, the hard look back in his eyes. He nodded to Joe and Ernie. ''That's why I've put you on the job!

''Joe, you've got a college education. You can think on your feet, and you're family. Ernie's a good kid, my own son; I don't think I could ask for anyone more loyal, but well—'' He puffed on his cigar instead of finishing the sentence. ''Next time Smith arranges a meeting, I'm gonna put Johnny T on him. We need somebody close to him, watching his tail.''

''This guy's quite a mystery man,'' Sal piped up. ''Does he have a tail, too?''

Roman turned to regard him. ''With Smith, who can tell?''

Everybody at the table laughed.

Joe was glad they were all having such a good time. ''So what do we do now?'' he asked.

Roman nodded. He glanced at his burning cigar with half-closed eyes. ''Let's give him one more chance, coming from me personally. I'll have Larry give him a call.''

''Okay.'' Larry went to an old black phone mounted on the wall, a rotary-dial job. He quickly dialed the number, listened, then said maybe a dozen words. He turned back to Roman.

''He didn't want to say nothing.'' Larry told him.

''You said it was me?''

''First thing.''

Uncle Roman contemplated his cigar for another moment before answering. ''There must be some difficulties on the other end. Very well. We'll use Smith's problems to our advantage.'' He waved his cigar at Joe. ''Sooner or later, Smith's going to want this Karen kid. Why don't we snatch the girl and keep her hidden somewhere? We'll say you thought he gave you the signal already. Then Smith will have to come to us.''

"Yeah! Okay!" Ernie grinned. "At least we're doing something."

Higher and deeper was all Joe could think. We're making it higher and deeper.

IT WAS ALMOST TEN P.M. by the time they got back to the apartment building. Ernie jimmied the building lock in ten seconds. He pulled his gun the minute they were inside the door.

"Put that away until we need it," Joe whispered as they quietly climbed the stairs. "We gotta figure the best way to go in."

"Hey, we're talking about some sixteen-year-old girl and her parents. Why don't we ring the doorbell?"

Maybe Ernie had a point. And maybe he didn't. Why did Smith want a teenaged girl taken out, anyway?

They passed the second floor and started climbing for the third. "We've got to be careful," Joe said. "We don't want any more accidents."

Ernie turned his thumb and forefinger into a gun. "Hey. You're the shooter here."

Joe pulled the paper from his pocket to check the apartment number as they reached the third floor. "It's this one over here."

The door opened on the other side of the hall. An old woman stood in the doorway.

"Karen can't come with you, I'm afraid."

"Who are you?" Ernie demanded.

Joe looked at his cousin. "Would you quiet down?"

The old woman calmly shook her head. "I know what you're here for, and it won't do any good. I'm afraid she's already gone."

"How?" Ernie demanded. "Who is this old broad? How could she know we were here to snatch the girl?"

Oh, great, Joe thought. While he was at it, why didn't Ernie just sign a full confession?

Maybe he could keep this from completely falling apart.
"Ma'am, you should go back inside. This is none of your
business."

"Oh, I'm afraid it's very much my business. Her parents, you see, they don't pay much attention to her at all.
So I've appointed myself as a sort of guardian."

Ernie was getting that feverish look again. "Maybe we
should snatch her instead. We gotta show my father something."

This was all going a little too fast for Joe. They didn't
even know if this old lady was telling the truth. Whatever
the truth was.

The old woman smiled sweetly. "I don't feel your hearts
are completely in this. I'll give you young men a chance.
Leave now, and we can forget all about this."

"Do you believe this?" Ernie reached inside his jacket.
"Lady, I've got a fucking gun!"

The old woman sighed. "I was hoping it wouldn't come
to this." She pointed at the floor between them.

A dark spot formed in the middle of the landing, right
where the woman had pointed. As Joe stared at it, the spot
grew.

Joe had a very bad feeling about this. Nothing had gone
right since they started this job. The spot swirled about,
making a whistling noise that seemed to double in volume
with every inch the swirling circle expanded.

Ernie stopped, mesmerized. "Whoa! What's goin' on
here?"

The sound was changing again, now more of a loud,
whooshing roar, like some supercharged industrial vacuum.
The swirling circle kept expanding, rippling out from the
center like an oil spill from Hell. But Joe thought it wasn't
so much covering the floor as, well, it looked like it was
inhaling everything it touched, gum wrappers, loose
change, dust bunnies, linoleum, even the feeble light that
came from the single lightbulb overhead.

Joe backed away from the swirling darkness, maybe as

large as a basketball now, but Ernie seemed glued in place. Didn't his cousin have any sense at all?

"Ernie! Get down those stairs now!"

"No, man," Ernie's eyes were wide with wonder. "Look inside that thing. There's something there."

Joe turned back to the growing mass. It was large enough now, maybe the size of a manhole cover, to see something inside, endless eddies of multicolored lights, far, far away, dancing in a bottomless abyss, like a kaleidoscope in three dimensions. But there was more there, tugging at the edges of Joe's memory, something he should know, something he should recognize. The swirling lights almost formed a pattern. If he looked a little harder, stepped a little closer, they might resolve themselves into . . .

What? Joe had to close his eyes to pull his gaze away. He looked to his cousin, who still stared into the growing maw.

"If you fell in that thing, Ernie, I don't think you'd ever be coming back."

"Good!" the woman called out over the roar. "Leave now. Give this up while you still have a chance to survive!"

The roaring grew louder with every second. Ernie wasn't moving, as if the swirling mist within had already caught him. The spreading darkness had almost reached his Bruno Magli shoes. Joe had to get Ernie out of there.

He grabbed his cousin's arm.

"C'mon, Ernie!"

But his cousin was frozen to the spot.

The darkness lapped against Ernie's left shoe. It anchored him to the spot. But it was worse than that. As Joe tugged on his cousin's unmoving arm, the darkness crept across Ernie's toe, up toward the laces. It started slowly, so slowly that at first Joe thought he might be imagining it, but as he watched, Ernie's shoe, his foot, his leg, all slid slightly toward the abyss.

Ernie's arm, frozen a second before, twisted away from Joe. The darkness would pull Ernie—would pull both of them—down forever. Joe yanked one final time, using every panicked ounce of strength he had in him. He finally felt Ernie budge in his direction—only an inch or two, but it was a start. Joe pulled again, his cousin moving with him now.

"What?" Ernie screamed, as if he had suddenly awakened from a terrible dream.

Joe lost his balance at the top of the staircase, Ernie tumbling after him. They half ran, half fell down the stairs to the landing below. Joe half dragged, half carried his cousin down to the next floor.

Joe had to take a minute to catch his breath. Ernie moaned softly, sagging in Joe's arms. Joe turned both of them around so he could watch the stairs; waiting for—what?—something to follow them? After what had just happened, anything was possible.

The roaring wind was gone. Everything was quiet upstairs.

Joe still wouldn't want to go back up there. He looked over at his cousin. One of Ernie's shoes was gone. The left one, the one caught by the pit.

"Fuck!" Ernie muttered, shaking his head. "That was intense!"

"A little too intense. Can you walk? I think we should get out of here."

Ernie looked down at his feet. "Hey man! How can I walk around with one shoe? Those shoes cost me a fortune!"

Joe couldn't believe this. They were lucky to be alive. "You want to go back up and get it?"

Ernie hesitated for only a second. "Fuck this! I want to go see my father!" He turned, and started across the lobby. Joe hurried after him.

Ernie was almost to the front door when he fell to his

knees. Joe ran to his side. His cousin seemed to be doubled over in pain.

"Not wise," Ernie said from between clenched teeth. "Not wise. From now on, you will wait."

For an instant, Joe thought this might be some after-effect of what had happened upstairs. But only for an instant.

Joe had a very bad feeling that this was Smith's signal.

Ernie looked up at Joe. "Call now!" He groaned. "Jesus, if you don't call . . ."

Ernie howled. This was more than just a signal. Joe wondered if this was some kind of payback for bothering Smith's people, asking too many questions.

It was time to use the cell phone. Joe retrieved it from Ernie's pocket. He quickly dialed the number.

Ernie moaned. The phone rang.

"Problems solved."

Joe's cousin was in agony. Joe was in no mood for bullshit. "I'm supposed to call you?"

"I have a message—"

"And I have to get it like this? You knew how to get me. Why didn't you—"

"Oh, no. I can't call out. Mr. Smith is so very specific about what he will allow."

Joe wouldn't let his anger overwhelm him. He closed his eyes, took a breath. "What are you supposed to tell me?"

"You're working with old information. The girl and the boy are together. They're on a bus to Gravesville."

"What about my cousin—?"

But the man at the other end of the line had already disconnected, without even the usual business about telling Smith.

Ernie groaned from where he knelt on the floor. He no longer clutched at his stomach. His breathing was easier. He looked up at Joe.

"God" was all he could say.

"Let's get out of here."

His cousin nodded, but he could barely stand. Joe had
to help him out to the car.

Joe knew that he would have to drive.

. 13 .

AUBRIC OPENED HIS EYES. Something was wrong.

He was still in that same room, his very well-appointed prison cell. The young woman, Runt, breathed softly at his side, still lost in sleep. He remembered telling her to sleep elsewhere, and then having no strength to enforce his command.

He had fallen asleep as soon as he hit the bed. But the year and more that he'd spent on the battlefield did not leave him so easily. No matter how deep his sleep, how vivid his dreams, some small part of him remained wary, watchful of the night around him. The others in Aubric's battalion had slept in much the same way. It was a skill you perfected if you wished to survive.

He sat up as quietly as possible. He heard it then, the distant tinkling of bells.

He thought of m'lady's creatures. His sword! The guards had taken his sword!

He had to calm himself. He had heard the bells before, in the tunnels below when Summitch and he were attempt-

ing to outrun those horrible things. But the creatures m'lady
sent had attacked those ringing points of light, giving the
two of them a moment more to escape. M'lady's minions
had made a darker sound, a hideous noise that Aubric never
wanted to hear again. The bells had posed no threat, only
a mystery.

He shook his head and peered into the darkness. There,
in the far corner of the room, he could see the faintest
twinkling of lights, a pattern of about a dozen points of
illumination, wavering about like a gathering of fireflies.

He stepped from the bed and heard again the faint,
mournful notes of a flute; the same sound he had heard
when first he'd entered the tunnels, then again when he and
Summitch were on the run. Summitch had claimed it was
all Aubric's imagination. Aubric had never known his
imagination to be quite this vivid. The flute music filled the
room, a simple, mournful tune, repeated over and over.

"Who are you?" Aubric called softly.

The flute music stopped.

He thought of finding something he might use as a
weapon; a candlestick, perhaps. But the room was far too
dark, and he had been too tired to mark where any objects
might be. All he could see were the lights dancing before
him, only at the other end of the room, yet impossibly distant.

He put out a hand and moved slowly forward.

(We knew you were the one.)

He heard the sentence clearly, but it did not come to him
in words. Rather, it came to him in music. The flute was
talking to him.

Perhaps he was still dreaming.

(It is a way we can still talk with the world of men.)

It was the flute again, as though the notes turned to
words inside Aubric's head. The lights in the corner flared.
Were they trying to draw him closer?

"Who are you?" he asked.

(To survive, we have given up so much.)

"Aubric?"

Light flickered behind him. Aubric glanced over his shoulder as Runt lit a candle by the bedside.

"Why are you up?" she asked. "Is something wrong?"

He turned back to look at her. "I thought I heard something."

The flute music stopped.

Runt sat up, letting the bedclothes fall away from her body. Aubric saw that she was naked. "There is nothing that can harm us. The guards will protect us. Why don't you come back to bed with me?"

Aubric almost laughed. And all along, he thought the guards were here to protect others *from* him.

He shook his head. "I don't really feel safe here."

Runt smiled. The candlelight gave her skin a soft golden glow. Her long red hair fell in a wild tangle to her shoulders. Her small breasts cast shadows on her trim stomach. Aubric couldn't remember when he had seen a woman look so inviting.

"As long as you are with me," she said softly, "nothing will happen. M'lady has assured me."

So he was safe for the night. Or so she said. Aubric realized he felt far more than unsafe. He felt vulnerable, exposed. He could not verify a single thing said to him since he had come to this place. And even if Runt was who she said, what of m'lady? What promises did a princess of the Grey need to keep for the sake of a slave? What real purpose was served by putting a prisoner and a slave together? M'lady or one of her servants could even now be watching from one of those hidden passageways that riddled the castle.

He still thought this must all be some sort of trick. A beautiful woman, comfortable surroundings; perhaps they would show him a taste of luxury to make the next morning's torture that much worse.

Aubric knew he could never be comfortable among the Grey. He turned back to where he had seen the glowing

pattern. Whatever these strange new things were, they
promised a way out. He thought for a moment that they
had gone. The lights had crowded even more deeply into
the corner. They were so faint, they were barely visible,
almost overwhelmed by the glow of a single candle flame.

(Sir Aubric.)

The flute sound was low, distant, little more than a melody recalled at the back of his thoughts.

"Yes?" he whispered back.

(We need an answer from you. It hurts us so to be in
this world.)

"Aubric?" Runt called. "Is that music?"

He looked back at the woman in the bed. Why could
she hear it when Summitch could not? Maybe the flute
played only for humans.

Runt frowned, reaching out a hand toward him. She
looked very fragile in the candlelight.

Aubric realized he'd already planned to go with the ringing lights. Whatever they offered would be better than what
waited for him here. But he had not considered Runt. What
would happen to her if he left her behind?

In battle, you must decide quickly.

"Yes," he called back to Runt, "I hear something,
too."

(We have come for only you.)

He whispered again: "She is as much a prisoner here as
I am."

The soft ringing resumed for a moment, then faded as
the flute spoke again.

(Perhaps. Perhaps. She cannot harm us. If you wish her
to join us, we will allow it.)

"Join us?" Aubric asked.

(We need you to help us. We need you in order to survive.)

"Aubric?" Runt climbed out of bed. "Who are you
speaking to?"

(We will take two.)

At least, he would get her out of this place. "If you want to stay with me, put your clothes on. Quickly!"

She hesitated. He walked back toward her. There was no room for doubt. He reached out to take her hands, but stopped before he touched her.

She was missing the little finger from her left hand.

She answered before Aubric could ask the question. "The lady took it for a keepsake. She does it with everyone who enters her service."

How barbaric the Grey were. Aubric was surprised at the intensity of feeling this small act of cruelty produced within him. And Runt simply accepted it. Maybe he could show her a new way of life. Maybe he could rescue her, the way princes did in the ancient tales.

He turned away from the young woman as she climbed quickly into her simple dress. The flute called to him.

(Are you prepared?)

Aubric took Runt's hand and drew her to his side. "Yes."

(Come with us.)

The bells rang far more loudly than Aubric had ever heard them before.

Runt gasped. The wall behind the lights was gone.

(Follow close. We can only transmute matter for a moment.)

They stepped forward together. A chill passed through Aubric as he walked through the space where the wall should have been.

A corridor stretched out before them. They had returned to the tunnels; tunnels that were the same, and yet completely different. Instead of torches, the walls themselves gave off a ghostly glow, a glow that intensified as the bell-creatures floated past, then dimmed back to the palest of pale. Aubric looked at Runt's worried face, then at his own pale hands. There was only one color here, everything the faintest green.

After a few paces, Runt started asking questions.

"Where are we going?"

(Someplace safe.)

"Aubric? Did you say something?" She looked around the endless, featureless tunnel. "Where is that flute music coming from?"

"It wasn't me." How could he explain something that he didn't understand?

Runt frowned. "Why are we running away? What if we're being watched?"

Perhaps Runt had doubts about her mistress after all.

(Nobody watched. We waited until after they were gone.)

"What? What was that?" Runt demanded. "It's like some crazy voice in my head!"

"Listen," was all Aubric could tell her. So Lady Karmille's spies had been watching them. He hoped these ringing lights could give them more of the answers.

(There are many things we want to tell you. That is why we have brought you.)

Runt looked to Aubric.

"Where are we going?"

(Home.) the flute answered.

· 14 ·

K<small>AREN'S</small> WORDS JOLTED Brian awake.

"Maybe we do come from somewhere else."

He opened his eyes. They were still riding on the bus. He looked past Karen to the world outside. The light on the other side of the window was grey and unreal. It must be almost dawn. The trees, bushes, and farmland were all shrouded in a colorless mist. The fields and rolling hills seemed to go on forever; they were virtually the only things they'd seen from the windows of this bus since—had it only been hours? It seemed like days.

Brian stretched as best he could within the confines of his cramped bus seat. "What? What do you mean?"

Karen brushed her hair out of her face, pushed her wire-rimmed glasses back up on her nose. It was like she was stalling until she could figure out what she really wanted to say.

"That was what Mrs. Mendeck said." Karen frowned. "Out of all the weird stories, that was the strangest one of all."

Brian took Karen's hand in his. "Hey. I fell asleep listening to those weird stories. I could probably stand to hear a couple more." He smiled. Mostly he liked to hear the sound of Karen's voice.

After they'd decided that the bus ride through country roads was too bumpy to get any serious reading done, they'd ended up talking most of the night. The bus was crowded at first, and they'd kept their conversation neutral; TV programs, kids at school, that sort of thing. But as they traveled farther from the city, and it got later at night, many more people left the bus than got on at each succeeding stop. After a while, they had the back half of the bus to themselves. That was when Karen began to tell him about Mrs. Mendeck.

Brian had never thought very much about Mrs. Mendeck, besides the fact that she was one of the few adults who treated both him and Karen like thinking human beings. He knew that she'd moved into the apartment across from Karen's maybe ten years ago, and that Karen's always-far-too-busy parents had come to rely on her more and more over the years for watching over their daughter. Ever since he'd known Karen, he'd heard her mention Mrs. Mendeck in passing almost every day. But before tonight, she'd never really talked about what the elderly woman meant to her.

Mrs. Mendeck and Karen had spent a lot of time together. And Mrs. Mendeck had told Karen a lot of stories.

According to Karen, most of the stories were about Mrs. Mendeck growing up in a strange country, running from soldiers. It took Karen a long time to realize that Mrs. Mendeck never said which country or what soldiers, and when Karen finally asked, Mrs. Mendeck changed the subject. Karen said she supposed it didn't matter. There was always someplace where people were being mistreated by soldiers or secret police.

As the night wore on, Karen's reminiscences became more personal, touching on how, with Mrs. Mendeck's help, she'd handled all the bumps and bruises of growing up. If she got lonely with her parents gone, Mrs. Mendeck had a story; if she got upset because the other girls were teasing her, Mrs. Mendeck had a story; if she was scared or confused or sad, Mrs. Mendeck had an all-purpose tale for the occasion.

Brian hardly did any talking, and he didn't care. He felt like he was being let into all the secrets of Karen's life. He had never felt so close to anybody.

The night stretched on and on. It was much harder to sleep on the bus than Brian had imagined. The fact that they had taken a "local" meant that it stopped at a dozen different small towns in the middle of nowhere.

Not that Gravesville was a major metropolis. Brian repeated what he could remember about the place from their state history course. An agricultural center in the bottom corner of the state, it had almost died until the technology revolution moved in with promises of low taxes and relatively cheap labor. Brian shook his head. He realized he was actually using something he'd learned in middle school.

As for the Gravesville Local sign on the front of the bus, what it really meant was that every three-quarters of an hour or so, just as they were drifting off with the rolling motion of the bus, it would pull into another brightly lit depot or main street. The bus doors would open. People would talk, haul their luggage from overhead, walk down the aisle. And both Brian and Karen would jerk awake.

Most of the stops were in front of post offices or gas stations. Once—it might have been at a truck stop—they were assaulted with loud polka music, and the sound of maybe a hundred people trying to be heard at the same time. Most of it was laughter, but Brian thought he heard one woman shrieking. He wondered if he dreamed that one. He was so tired now, he wondered if he was dreaming everything.

Finally, there was a couple hours stretch when they

didn't stop anywhere. Both of them had drifted off to sleep, until now. Dawn. In the middle of nowhere.

"There was only one thing she told me over and over again." Karen gripped Brian's arm. "It always happened when I told her I didn't feel like I belonged."

Brian thought about the way the other kids picked on him at school, the way his mother blamed him for anything that went wrong around the house. "I'm a charter member of that club."

Karen nodded. "Mrs. Mendeck agreed with you."

Brian just stared at her.

"How did she used to put it?" Karen continued. " 'Brian and you are from the same place. So am I. That's why I'm here to watch over you.' "

"What?"

Karen shook her head this time. "When I asked her to explain, she only smiled and said 'Soon.' "

"That was it?"

"Well, I kept at her. I'm good at that."

Brian nodded. Karen never let him keep a secret.

"Mrs. Mendeck wouldn't budge," Karen went on. "She just frowned and said, 'When you're a little older. Have a good time now.' "

Brian felt overwhelmed. This was the story that Karen had wanted to tell all along: that he, and Karen, and maybe Mrs. Mendeck, too, came from somewhere else. What could be so far away, or so secret, that Mrs. Mendeck couldn't talk about it?

Maybe, when he was a little more awake, he could figure out what it meant.

KAREN HAD NEVER seen a deader town in her life. She guessed that was why they called it Gravesville.

Poor Brian kept apologizing. They should have taken a look at more of the bus schedules, gone to a bigger city,

or maybe someplace with a lake. Karen told him he didn't
need to be their social director, but he kept on fretting.

"At least we're away from those people," she said at
last. "And we're together."

She liked the way he had taken control back in Parkdale
and just got them out of there. It didn't matter that they'd
come to a nothing town. This sort of a dead end was the
last place anyone would look, really. It was a good way to
drop out of sight, and a quiet place to figure out what to
do next.

While they were still on the bus, they had decided to
call Mrs. Mendeck collect in the middle of the afternoon.
Then they could figure out what to do next; either take the
return ticket and go home, or take a second bus someplace
else. Maybe they could meet Mrs. Mendeck somewhere
along the way. Karen was sure the older woman would
know exactly what to do.

It was still early morning when they got off the bus.
Almost all the stores in the center of town were boarded
up. Except for a couple of old men on a park bench, the
main street was deserted. There were only two places open
for business on the whole block, a gas station and a small
grocery.

Well, they didn't want to stand around in the middle of
an empty town. They asked a kid at the grocery if there
was a mall nearby. The closest one, he said, was a little
place about a mile outside of town. It wasn't much, but it
was better than downtown.

They had plenty of time. They walked.

"Hey, this is more like it!" Brian called out as they got
to the top of the hill at the edge of town. Ahead of them,
on one side of the road, was a small brick building with a
supermarket at the closer end. On the other side of the street
was a big white sign that said GRAVESVILLE CINEMA.
It only had two screens. But the sign said it had Special
Summer Matinees.

They walked to the mall first. There was a discount de-

partment store at the far end. In between it and the supermarket were a bunch of small shops: bookstore, drugstore,
a combination restaurant/ice cream parlor, beauty salon.
Tucked in one corner was a little store with some beat-up
electronic games and a pinball machine, where they ended
up spending about an hour. After that, they each got a hot
dog at the restaurant. It was barely noon.

Brian wanted to wait to call Mrs. Mendeck until just
before they got on the bus "in case her phone was tapped
or something." Karen thought that Brian might have been
watching too many police shows on TV, but she agreed
they should be careful. It felt strange, the way they had
rushed away from Karen's apartment, only to go someplace
where they could do nothing but wait.

"So how about a movie?" Brian asked.

The air was hot and oppressive when they left the mall
to walk across the street. The movie theater had two matinees. Since one screen was showing a movie they'd just
seen the week before, they went to the other, a cartoon
called *The Magic Princess*. It wasn't doing much business.
Besides Brian and Karen, there were only a couple of moth-
ers with three or four small children apiece.

The movie was only okay. Most of the voices belonged
to actors Karen recognized from TV reruns. The plot had
something to do with a poor farm girl who wasn't appreciated by her wicked stepmother. She was, of course, a
princess in disguise, kept from her heritage by Snardlap,
the Evil King of the Elves.

The animation was pretty stilted. The fairies and their
kingdom were fussily beautiful, while everything else was
drawn for laughs. When they finally got to Elfland, the
characters all sang a slow song about "The Wonder Under
the Hill." Karen had never seen anything so corny. She
nudged Brian, but he had fallen asleep. Actually, Karen
thought, that wasn't such a bad idea.

She must have fallen asleep too, because she had no idea
what happened in the rest of the film. Besides the fact that

they lived happily ever after. That's the way fairy tales always worked, right?

GRAVESVILLE, THE GUY on the phone had said. They'd gotten the word from one of Smith's men at the bus station. The two kids had gotten round-trip tickets and boarded an overnight bus.

Joe Beast realized they could be anywhere in this nothing town. Well, probably not on Main Street, considering that ninety percent of the place was boarded up. But even a dinky town like this had dozens of houses. They had passed a trailer park, too, on their way in. Who knew where else two kids could hide?

He and Ernie had stopped at the bus station in Parkdale first, and gotten a schedule of their own, on the offhand chance they could catch up with the bus, or maybe see if there was a likely stop along the way where the kids might get off. The bus ride to Gravesville took close to twelve hours. Thanks to Ernie's kamikaze driving skills, they'd gotten here in a little over nine, checking out each of the stops along the way.

"Now this is the fucking pits," Ernie remarked from behind the wheel. Joe's cousin had revived a couple hours into the trip, waking up and screaming maybe twenty cuss words in a row. Joe had let him drive after he calmed down. Driving made Ernie happy.

After that, though, Joe's cousin had been unusually quiet, talking a little bit about the family, offering a couple opinions about what was wrong with the local sports teams. The one thing he most definitely wasn't talking about was what had happened to him earlier that evening.

Now that they had stopped, Ernie looked lost. He pressed his fist repeatedly against his forehead, muttering constantly under his breath. Joe realized that even while he'd been driving, his cousin had barely cracked a smile.

Ernie was just not his old self. Whatever happened had

shaken both of them. Joe thought it would be a good idea
to give him something new to do.

"Give a call to your father and let him know where we
are."

Ernie grunted and got out of the car. But now what? Joe
looked up and down the main street. There were thirty parking meters on the street, and theirs was the only car. Joe
had never seen a town this dead. The kids had been here
for at least a couple of hours. They could be anywhere.

Maybe they had relatives in the area. Somehow, though,
Joe felt the mysterious voice on the phone would have told
him that sort of detail. He shook his head. If Smith's flunky
knew that much, they would have caught the kids before
they got out of town.

He walked over to where Ernie was talking on the
phone, first to one of Uncle Roman's flunkies, then to Uncle Roman, mostly just saying, "Yeah, Dad," and "No,
Dad." The phone booth actually still had a phone book in
it. Now Joe really knew they were in the boonies. He
flipped through the thin volume quickly. No Eggletons
listed. There was a Wanda Clark. Ernie finished his usual
brief conversation just as Joe found the name. Joe waved
him out of the way, dialed the number. A recorded voice
told him the line had been disconnected.

So where would two kids go in a strange town? Joe
supposed they could always check the mall, the movie theater, the sort of places kids would go when they wanted to
kill time.

He told Ernie to get back in the car and walked over to
the gas station across the street. A kid maybe sixteen was
pumping gas. When in doubt, Joe thought, ask a teenager.

"Look," he called ahead to the youngster, "I just got
into town, looking for my cousin. Nobody's home. I know
where he'd be, though. What mall around here is the hang-
out?"

"You mean for kids?" The sixteen-year-old grinned.
"It's no contest. There's a big new mall, up toward Hiatts-

ville, about six miles up Route 40." The kid pointed down the road to the right. "This city was dying already. The mall just killed it that much faster."

As much as Joe wanted to talk about dying towns, he thanked the kid and got moving. He jumped back in the car and told Ernie to drive. After everything that happened, maybe they would have some good luck for a change.

IT HAD TAKEN Joe two hours to realize what the kid at the gas station had really been saying.

Before that, he'd been too sure of himself, too full of his own cleverness.

It had taken them maybe ten minutes to get to the mall. Joe was hoping they could wrap it up in ten minutes more. He'd even said, "Let's make this quick" to Ernie as they got out of the car.

But the kids weren't anywhere at the mall. Joe and Ernie checked every screen of the multiplex next door. No Brian. No Karen.

Joe thought about Karen, with her wire rims. She and Brian were just geeky enough to go to the library. But when he and Ernie got there, they found the library was only open three days a week, and this wasn't one of them.

"Where are they?" Joe shouted after they'd gotten back in the car.

"They're probably up in some hayloft, screwing their brains out."

Ernie was starting to sound like his old self.

Maybe his cousin was right. Where else could they be? Had he missed something?

He thought about the gas station attendant's exact words. He had called it the *new* mall.

He jumped out of the car, calling to an old lady walking her dog on the other side of the street. The dog started yapping. But the lady confirmed his worst suspicions.

Sure enough, there were two malls. And the old mall

was just a stone's throw out of town in the other direction.

Christ. What was he thinking? The two teenagers wouldn't walk six miles. They'd go to the one just up the road.

He jumped back in the car.

"C'mon, Ernie. Drive."

Ten minutes later, they had found the old mall. It was a small, rinky-dink place, but it had a movie theater across the street, an old place with two screens.

Joe and Ernie quickly explored the mall. Not only were Brian and Karen not there, except for a couple of salespeople, they didn't see any teenagers at all.

There was still the movie theater. Joe walked up to the ticket booth. It was empty, but there was a black board with white letters that gave the show times.

The place only had one afternoon show, which had started a little over an hour ago. The doors were locked, there was no way in. But they could catch the two kids on the way out. Joe waved for Ernie to join him in the shade at the bottom of the steps leading from the theater.

Three women and eight kids walked out five minutes after they showed up. "That's going to be the cartoon," Joe told Ernie. "I bet they went to see the other movie."

Twenty minutes later, five adults and one kid came out of the other theater. No sign of the two teens.

Still, they should wait a few more minutes. Brian and his girl might be the kind of kids who sat through the closing credits; maybe they were killing time in the bathrooms or had stopped at a video game in the lobby. After all, it wasn't like Joe and Ernie had a lot of options left here.

Except Joe was just plain tired of waiting. He was beginning to feel as hyper as Ernie; like a little voice inside his head was telling him to get the hell out of here.

His cousin hadn't spoken since they left the first mall. When Ernie wasn't driving, he spent most of his time staring off into space or looking down in his lap. Every once in a while, he would just let out a grunt, like he was having a gas pain or something.

Maybe, Joe thought, he was afraid he would end up like Ernie, not just lost in the middle of a rinky-dink town, but lost inside his own head, too.

Hell, whatever was going on here, he wanted to be somewhere else.

"Let's get out of here." He nudged Ernie's shoulder and headed for the car.

Ernie made a noise halfway between a grunt and a groan. Joe turned to his cousin. He hadn't moved.

"Ernie? What's with you?"

Ernie stared out at their car, simmering in the sun. "Joe, I gotta tell you something."

Ernie kept on staring. Except for a single grunt, a minute or two passed in silence.

"What?" Joe prompted at last.

Ernie looked at him at last. "I knew Smith from before."

"What? From where?"

"You remember when I lost that truckload of cigarettes?"

How could Joe forget? He was sure Uncle Roman was going to kill his own son. But then the whole business quieted down and went away. Joe had just assumed Roman had decided to forgive Ernie one more time.

"My goose was cooked," Ernie went on. "If I hadn't gone to Smith, I wouldn't be talkin' to you now. Smith made everything right." Ernie snapped his fingers. "Like that. And he didn't want anything in return. Not then, anyhow." Ernie went back to staring at the Buick.

"He said he'd fuckin' call on me."

"What?" Joe felt like he was ready to explode. "What else don't I know about this?"

Ernie shook his head. "I'm the one who introduced Smith to my father. I'm the one who got us into this shit."

Joe could feel the anger draining out of him, as quickly

as it had come. When his cousin told the truth like this, he actually looked sort of pitiful.

"Oh, hell," Joe said at last. "If it wasn't this, it would be some other pile of shit. Let's grab something quick to eat. Then we'll stake out the bus station. These two don't have anyplace to stay around here. My guess is that they'll take a bus somewhere else."

Ernie looked relieved, and maybe a little less pained. They walked together down to the car.

Joe wished he felt as certain about his plan as he sounded. But it satisfied Ernie. And, who knew, maybe Joe could be right for a change.

"HEY. EXCUSE ME."

Brian woke up with a start. He wasn't on the bus anymore.

They were in the movie theater. But the movie was over, and the lights were on. A kid maybe a year or two older than Brian stared down at him.

Brian sat up. "Oh. Sorry."

The kid, who was carrying a broom, laughed. "Hey. It's no skin off my nose. It's cooler in here than it is outside. It's cheaper for us to keep the air-conditioning going until the evening show."

Karen was awake now, too. She stood up. "I guess we'd better leave."

Brian stood up. Or at least he tried to. His feet didn't want to move.

"What's the matter?" Karen asked. "Your foot fall asleep?"

Brian shook his head. He could feel his heel against the floor, could even wiggle his toes inside his sneaker. He could certainly walk. But a tiny voice inside him was telling him not to.

"No," he answered. "Something's wrong. I can feel it."

Instead of asking another question, Karen frowned and

nodded. "Someone's waiting for us. Someone we don't want to meet."

As soon as the words were out of Karen's mouth, Brian was sure they were true. This was as weird as Mrs. Mendeck's stories.

The kid with the broom grinned at them. "I hear where you're comin' from. My mother and father get into one of their fights, I steer clear of them for days." He glanced up the aisle to the back of the theater, then turned back to Brian and Karen.

"Look." The usher waved for Karen to sit back down, too. "The manager's gone over to district headquarters for the afternoon." He pushed his broom up the aisle. "Stay where you are. I didn't see you."

Karen smiled at Brian and settled in next to him. When she looked at him that way, he knew everything was going to be all right.

"I guess we were supposed to take a nap," she whispered from his shoulder.

"Huh?" Brian asked. "What do you mean?"

"Oh, it's just one of those things Mrs. Mendeck talks about. Sometimes things are just meant to be."

Brian liked that. He and Karen were meant to be.

But he couldn't relax. Not now. They might be safe here for the moment, but what happened when they left the theater?

"Maybe there's some way to get rid of whoever's following us," Karen said, whispering, even though the usher was gone. "Together, we sensed somebody waiting for us. Maybe, together, we can send him away."

Brian grinned at the thought. Well, why not? With Karen around, he felt like he could do anything.

"How do we send him away?" he whispered back.

She grinned at him. "Why not just say it?"

"Say what?"

" 'Leave. There's nothing here.' Something like that."

Brian nodded.

"We need to say it together.

"Leave. There's nothing here." Unsure at first, their voices rose as they spoke in unison. "Leave. There's nothing here." By the third repetition, their voices meshed perfectly; by the fourth it sounded like more than their two voices, as though a crowd were repeating the demand.

"Leave. There's nothing here."

The words echoed around the theater, a room designed with curtains and carpet to have no echoes.

"Leave. There's nothing here."

Brian and Karen stopped together. The words had filled the space around them. That was as loud as the message could get. They could do no more.

Brian felt very tired, as if he hadn't napped at all. He closed his eyes for one more second.

Someone was shaking his shoulder all over again.

"Hey, it's time to leave. The manager will be through here in a minute."

Karen and Brian both stood up this time. "Hey, thanks—" Brian began.

"Hey," the usher replied, "I zonk out myself sometimes when the manager's away."

Brian looked at his watch. They had spent close to four hours in the movie theater. The bus back home left in forty-five minutes.

"We've got to get out of here."

"Let's use the bathrooms," Karen announced, marching toward the ladies' room before Brian could say anything. Hey, it was a good idea.

Brian went into the men's room, splashed some water on his face. They'd grab something quick at the one fast-food place they'd seen on their way from the bus stop.

There was one last thing to do; call Mrs. Mendeck. Brian used the phone in the lobby, and made the call collect.

She didn't answer the phone. After six rings, the operator broke in and told them to try again later.

Karen walked out of the rest room as Brian hung up.

"Mrs. Mendeck wasn't there. Doesn't she have an answering machine?"

Karen shook her head. "I don't think she knows answering machines exist!"

"What do we do?" Brian frowned. All their plans depended on Mrs. Mendeck. "What if it's not safe to go home?"

Karen shrugged. "Why don't we call her later? We're going to stop every forty-five minutes anyway. If we have to, we can get off the bus somewhere and wait."

Brian had to admit she had a point. They'd had a quiet day in a pretty boring town. There was no reason to panic yet.

THIS TIME, WHEN they pulled up to the bus stop, Joe decided to ask the experts.

He walked over to a pair of old men sitting on a bench across the street. Probably did this every night, year in and year out. Joe couldn't think of anybody better equipped to know if there were strangers in town.

"Gentlemen?" he said as he stepped in front of them. "I need your help."

Both of them scowled up at him.

"Really?" one said. "Don't hear that much anymore."

"Not like it used to be," the other chimed in. "Don't know everybody anymore. Not since that SoftTech company moved in."

"Place was dying," his friend agreed. "But it was comfortable."

"Look," Joe interrupted before the conversation got totally out of hand. "I need to know if you've seen someone. A young couple, teenagers. He's my brother. If I don't get him home soon, he's gonna be in a lot of trouble."

"Well," the second oldster said, "I did see a couple of teenaged kids get on the bus just maybe fifteen minutes ago. Don't know if they're the ones you're looking for."

So they'd missed them again. But Joe and Ernie could catch up with a bus that was only fifteen minutes away. "Great. Do you know where the bus was going?"

The first old man nodded. "Buses from Gravesville only go two places, back to Parkdale or out of state."

The second old-timer glanced up at the sky, then down at his wristwatch. "This time of night, that would be Parkdale."

They were on their way back to Parkdale? Joe had to admit, it surprised the hell out of him. Maybe these kids were getting help. Or maybe they were just smarter than he thought and were leading Joe and Eddie on some wild-goose chase.

He thanked the old codgers and ran back across the street. With any luck, they'd catch up with the kids within the hour.

It was time to give a quick call to Uncle Roman and let him know they'd be coming home. Joe turned again and trotted over to the pay phone at the gas station.

Unless, he thought as he dialed the phone, unless none of this—Mr. Smith's demands, Uncle Roman's decision to help, the kids trip to and from a nothing town—none of it tied in together. It was like there was some piece of the puzzle still missing. What if the kids had something else up their sleeves?

The phone was picked up on the first ring.

"Problems solved."

What? Joe almost dropped the phone. How could he have called this number?

"Problems solved," the voice said again.

The voice made him angry all over again. He decided he'd make that doubt that crossed his mind into a real issue. "Well, I have a problem. Those two damned snot-nosed teenagers are doing a pretty good job of staying one step ahead of us."

"What do you want?"

"How about some better information? Some way that will guarantee we can head them off and catch them."

The man on the other end of the phone line hesitated. "Mr. Smith doesn't like to do this sort of thing. Considering the serious nature of your assignment, perhaps we can make some accommodation. Let me warn you that this wasn't part of the original agreement. Every time Mr. Smith makes an extraordinary effort, it comes with a price. You will owe him—"

Joe had had just about enough of this bullshit. "Hey! We're doing a job for him. He owes *us*! Tell your—"

"I'll tell Mr. Smith of your interest."

Joe heard the dial tone. The bastard had hung up on him again. He slammed the phone down and stalked back to the car.

He was so mad he could barely speak. "You wouldn't believe—"

"Right now, I'd believe fuckin' anything." Ernie shook himself violently. "I only know one thing. I want to drive."

Driving did calm Ernie down. Joe handed him the keys.

Just being out on the open road calmed Joe down, too. Maybe he was beginning to feel what Ernie got out of this, the hum of the wheels, the scenery rushing past.

Ernie was pushing it a little. On the straightaways, Ernie was urging the LeSabre up to ninety.

"Careful," Joe cautioned. "We don't want to attract one of the local cops."

"Hell, I could outrun—"

He stopped midsentence, and shook his head.

"It's coming," Ernie announced.

"What's coming?"

"Up ahead." Ernie's arms were starting to shake. "I don't know what's coming, but I do!" He groaned. "I do! I do!"

His eyes were closing, the pupils rolling up so that all Joe could see were the whites of his eyes. Ernie was jerking the wheel back and forth. If they hadn't been the only car on the road, they would have had an accident.

"Pull off the road!" Joe shouted. "Pull off the road!"

Ernie shook himself. He managed to stop the car.

"Oh, God," Ernie moaned.

"What?" Joe demanded.

But Ernie only sat and stared.

Joe heard it then, a heavy engine sound, unmistakable.

The road ahead of them was empty as far as Joe could see.

But from the noise, a bus was coming. And it was almost on top of them.

. 15 .

THE LITTLE MAN FROWNED up at Jacobsen for maybe the hundredth time.

"You aren't much use, are you?"

Jacobsen didn't know what to say. He had tripped twice, and stumbled forward into Summitch once when the tunnel had abruptly opened up into a huge gallery. In these twisting corridors, the torches overhead threw wild shadows on the walls and floor, so that Jacobsen was constantly jumping and whirling about to stare at things that weren't really there. Then he'd turn around again and Summitch would already be twenty feet ahead of him.

"I guess not," Jacobsen replied softly.

The small fellow shook his head. "These tunnels are disorienting to everyone at first. It's simple, really. You'll get used to them or you'll die."

This, Jacobsen thought, was not at all comforting. He already knew from an earlier exchange that Summitch didn't want to hear him complain. If he got to be any more of a burden, he imagined he would get left behind, to starve at the very least, to starve or something worse. Probably it would be something much worse.

"Where are we going?" he asked, doing his best not to whine. All this walking and jumping at shadows had nearly overwhelmed him. He was exhausted.

"Would it make any difference?" his guide cried with passion. "They think they're dealing with a fool. Summitch has resources!"

Jacobsen had given up trying to get the little fellow to explain his rants, too. Even when Summitch did give him a civil answer, it was about people and places that meant nothing to Jacobsen.

So they walked, through tunnels of dirt and tunnels of stone. Once, they came to a place where the floor, walls, and ceiling were all perfect mirrors, so that the world was filled with hundreds of walking Summitchs and Jacobsens. Another time, the sound of running water became so loud that the two couldn't talk, and Jacobsen expected at any second to round a corner and find a waterfall or rushing river. But the mirrored walls ended, the water noise receded, and they were back to walking through stone and dirt. At first, Jacobsen hadn't thought these tunnels could go on forever. Now he wasn't too sure.

Someone screamed.

Jacobsen started. He had fallen into a stupor, following Summitch forever. He might have been dreaming, walking in his sleep.

"What?" he said, shaking his head to get his brain working. "What was that?"

"Somebody screamed," Summitch remarked.

So it wasn't a dream after all. Jacobsen stopped. "There's somebody else down here?"

Summitch kept on walking. "If we walk far enough, no doubt we'll run into somebody sooner or later."

"Don't you know?"

"No one could ever know all these tunnels." Summitch paused, as if Jacobsen had finally asked something that deserved an answer. "I've actually spent most of my time on tunnels closer to the castle than these. However, we need to skirt certain areas. There is a particular unpleasantness that I wish to avoid. But, as I mentioned before, I am not without my resources. Summitch can handle a simple scream.''

"Oh," Jacobsen replied. He actually half understood that. He wondered, if he was down here long enough, if he would be able to actually tell one of these endless passage-ways from another.

A loud banging started up from somewhere ahead; a deep, resonant sound, like people smashing together oil drums.

"I guess someone wants us to know they're there," Summitch said without breaking his stride.

To Jacobsen, the heavy banging sound seemed a bit too ominous to be a simple greeting. "Is that a warning?"

"These tunnels have never been known as social gathering places," Summitch called over his shoulder. If anything, the banging ahead was causing the small fellow to increase his pace. "These noisemakers probably don't want to see us any more than we want to see them. Unfortunately, I only know one way to get to where we want to go, and that's straight ahead."

Jacobsen broke into a trot, using every remaining ounce of energy to get closer to his guide. If Summitch did have a way to protect himself, Jacobsen might need to use him as a shield.

The banging ceased, replaced an instant later by a whistling howl. Jacobsen decided this was no longer ominous. It had graduated to bone-chilling.

He jogged forward so quickly, he almost fell over Summitch for a second time. "Are you *sure* about this?"

The small man didn't even glance back at him. "One cannot be definite about anything, especially in a place like this."

Their exchange was answered by a chorus of howls, half a dozen voices rising and falling not only before them, but behind them in the tunnel.

"What the hell *was* that?" Jacobsen whispered.

Summitch frowned, sniffing the air as if his nose could tell him the answers. "It's not magic-produced, I can tell you that. You don't want to know what can come at you from sorcery. Trust me on this."

Jacobsen didn't see as how he had a choice.

"This is new territory for me," Summitch confessed. "Generally, I stick to the tunnels just below the castle. You run into a better class of unknown adversary up there."

Jacobsen risked a look behind them, but could see nothing beyond a pair of torches they had just passed. Everything beyond that was lost in darkness. When they had first met, Summitch had given a long explanation of how the torches ignited to show you the way so long as you knew the proper magicks. It was one of the many things Jacobsen accepted without understanding. Still, he couldn't remember the torches behind them extinguishing themselves quite so quickly.

He turned as he heard his guide gasp.

"Oh, dear," Summitch remarked.

Jacobsen's first thought was that the banging-and-howling things had chosen to show themselves. But he and Summitch were still all alone. Instead, they'd come to another large spot in the tunnel, a compact chamber that managed to accommodate the openings to four separate tunnels and still feel claustrophobic. In an odd way, it reminded Jacobsen of the studio apartment he'd had in college.

The space was roughly circular, with the tunnel they'd just left immediately behind them. The other three tunnel openings were clustered close together on the far side.

It took Jacobsen an instant to realize that something else had changed.

"What happened to the howling?" he asked.

"Silence?" Summitch nodded his head glumly. "*Now* I would be afraid."

"So now we *really* need to get out of here?" Jacobsen's

sarcasm seemed lost on the small man, who could do nothing but stare at the choices.

"Which way should we go?" Jacobsen asked, trying to urge the other along.

Summitch shook his head. "I'm usually very good at this sort of thing. It's part of my gift, you know."

Jacobsen wasn't in the mood for polite conversation. He thought he saw movement in the tunnel to the left, something creeping toward them through the half-darkness.

An arrow clacked off the stone overhead.

"Summitch!"

"I'm ready!" The small man had a single finger pointed up into the air. What did that mean? Is that where he wanted them to go?

Another shaft flew from the leftmost tunnel. Summitch pointed his finger at the missile, at the same time emitting an ear-piercing whistle. The arrow flashed in midair, disintegrating to powder.

Summitch grinned. "Pretty neat trick, huh? I haven't had to use it in years."

Jacobsen was impressed. "Is there anything you can't do?"

"Most things, I'm afraid," Summitch said with an aw-shucks shrug. "I've managed to master a few of the simpler spells. It's hard, what with the Judges limiting the sources of knowledge."

"Ouch!" Jacobsen cried as he felt a sharp pain in his shoulder.

He turned and saw the source of his pain lying on the ground. Someone had thrown a small rock from somewhere behind them.

"Of course, my powers have limits." Summitch calmly fired another arrow. "We all have our own aptitudes. Mostly, I'm a finder."

Jacobsen dodged another stone thrown from the tunnel from which they'd come. "Can you do anything about rocks?"

"Not a thing, I'm afraid."

Their attackers seemed to realize this as, instead of another arrow, three stones came sailing from the leftmost tunnel.

Jacobsen winced as he barely dodged the missiles. "I think we may need to find a way out of here."

"Yes, certainly, yes." Summitch looked first at one of the two tunnels still free of attackers, then at the others. "Yes. Certainly." He waved his hands in great, ineffectual circles. "My powers seem to desert me in times of crisis!"

He took a single step toward the right, then shook his head. He stared at the central tunnel for an instant, then looked back the way they had come.

"Ow!" Jacobsen cried as another stone hit his shin.

"I can't decide!" Summitch wailed.

"Come on, then!" Jacobsen half dragged, half carried the smaller man forward, into the center tunnel. "All we need to do is get some distance from these things and I bet they'll leave us alone."

"So you say," Summitch whimpered. *This* was the creature who had threatened to leave Jacobsen behind?

They rushed down the passageway, which seemed to be angled slightly downwards. It twisted first to the left, then to the right, then branched into two different tunnels.

Jacobsen stopped abruptly, trying to catch his breath. "Any ideas? This is your world here!"

"I'm not too familiar with this part of it." Summitch looked back the way they had come. "Let's keep moving."

Jacobsen grabbed the small man's arm and dragged him down the left-hand way. This passageway turned into a series of steps, leading farther down.

The steps soon gave way to another chamber, if that word even began to do it justice. If the last chamber they had passed through had been Jacobsen's studio apartment, this one was Grand Central Station.

The ceiling must have risen to well over a hundred feet at the room's center. There were things flitting about in the shadows up there. They were too far away for Jacobsen to tell whether they were birds, or bats, or something else.

The whole huge room was lit by a great vat of fire at the room's center. Silhouetted in the flame was a massive statue, the twenty-foot high-figure of a man seated on a throne, staring upwards, as if he might be able to see through miles of rock to the heavens.

Large rocks littered the floor of the vast room, boulders from three to six feet high, placed in long rows radiating from the fire at the room's center, like spokes of some gigantic wheel. The rocks cast tremendous shadows, throwing perhaps a third of the space into darkness.

Jacobsen noticed that some of the shadows were moving.

"I don't think we should be here," he whispered to Summitch.

The small man nodded his head all too readily. "My guess is that we've probably stumbled on their holy place— probably the very place they were trying to scare us away from."

"Which means?"

"With luck, we've profaned their temple. Our very presence here is forbidden by their gods. That way, death will be quick."

Jacobsen heard a shuffling, scraping noise behind them. He turned and saw his worst fears approaching.

"We've got company."

They poured down the steps Jacobsen and Summitch had taken only a moment before; others emerged from the many shadowy corners of the great chamber. There were thirty or forty of them, in all shapes and sizes. Some of them Jacobsen wouldn't look at twice if he passed them on the street, others looked like nothing he had ever seen before. They wore all manner of clothing, from dented armor to what looked like the remnants of uniforms, to the filthiest of rags tied around their midsections.

"Gontor," one of the ragged folk remarked.

"Gontor," an old woman with a crutch agreed.

"Gontor!" The others repeated the word, seemingly at random, someone calling out from the left side of the chamber, the word echoing from among those who descended the stairs, then again from somewhere beneath the vat of fire.

"Gontor."

But each voice said the word more firmly than the one before.

"Gontor."

Every cry was louder than the one before.

"Gontor!"

It went from being a simple statement to a rallying shout.

"Gontor! Gontor! *Gontor!*"

Jacobsen turned to his guide. "What now?"

Summitch stared at the crowd. "This is quite beyond me, I'm afraid."

"Maybe it's up to me, then." After all, Jacobsen realized, he still had his gun. He hadn't been able to use it on his errand for Mr. Smith, to shoot an adolescent girl. This time, however, he was trying to save his own miserable life. He grabbed the cold metal handle and pulled the .44 from his belt.

"Wait!" Summitch screamed.

Jacobsen looked down, startled that the little man had finally raised his voice.

Summitch waved at the gun. "No, not that! Don't you understand anything?"

Yes, Jacobsen thought, that was exactly his problem. He hadn't understood anything since he'd gotten here. And there was no longer any time to ask questions.

"Speak!"

The deep voice echoed through the chamber. It seemed to come from everywhere. Jacobsen almost dropped the gun.

"Why?" the voice called.

"It's speaking to us," Jacobsen said, realizing. He stuffed the gun back out of sight. "Shouldn't we say something?"

Summitch waved. "Oh, dear. We really didn't—I mean—this is totally—certainly you can see—mistakes happen every day—we never meant—oh, dear." The small man's voice, never strong in the first place, degenerated to a hoarse whisper before failing completely.

There was a moment of the deepest silence Jacobsen had ever experienced. He felt the weight of his gun through his jacket. At this moment, it seemed very reassuring.

The ragged masses shuffled forward.

"Stone them!" one murmured.

"Stab them!" another said.

"We could eat them," a third suggested.

Jacobsen remembered why he'd stuck his hand inside his jacket. He grabbed the pistol one more time.

"Stay back!" he called to the advancing throng. "I have a gun!"

His warning had no effect. The crowd drew closer.

"What's a gun?" asked one of the throng.

"I wouldn't shoot that in here," Summitch whispered. "The consequences could be devastating."

"More devastating than getting eaten?"

"You have a point."

The ragged crowd was closing in around them.

"Maybe some sort of diversion would be in order," the small fellow admitted.

That was it. He'd do more than threaten.

He raised his pistol and shot once at the ceiling.

The noise was deafening.

The ragged masses fell to their knees.

"Sorcery!" an old woman screamed.

"Gontor!" cried one of the men in dented armor.

The whole ragged crowd prostrated themselves before Jacobsen.

"Gontor!" a number of the others agreed.

"There," Jacobsen said with a self-satisfied nod. "That took care of that, with no harm—"

A rumble came from somewhere above. A half dozen small rocks fell from the ceiling in the area Jacobsen had aimed his bullet.

"Now," Summitch said, "I would worry."

But the ceiling didn't fall. Instead, the whole room changed around them, blurring from a place of fire and shadow, then re-forming as someplace much brighter. Rather than a great chamber of fire-blackened stone, they were surrounded by something maybe a dozen times as large overflowing with flowers, trees, and greenery; the colors were so vibrant, they almost hurt Jacobsen's eyes. In fact, the colors looked somehow wrong; something like those too-bright pictures of paradise you'd see in books called *Bible Stories for Children*. The sky—actually, he guessed, a really high ceiling—was a constant robin's egg blue. Above the point where the vat of fire had burned was a bright yellow orb. But none of it looked real. Jacobsen wondered if the glowing yellow globe was painted on the ceiling. The bright blue certainly looked a bit like Rustoleum sprayed over rock. Could you paint a fiercely glowing orb?

The world around them had changed. But their ragged captors still surrounded them. They rose one by one to face Jacobsen and Summitch. In the much better light, Jacobsen saw that many of them held weapons: spears, clubs, even a couple of swords.

"Gontor!" exclaimed one of those in the lead.

"Gontor!" the others chimed in, as they tightened their circle around the pair. "Gontor! Gontor!"

"This is beginning to lose its novelty," Summitch muttered.

Jacobsen looked around. Maybe this bright new world would show them a way to escape. The vat of fire was gone, but the statue remained. It glowed in the odd light.

He still held his gun. He wondered what might happen if he used it again.

"Hold!" the deep voice called out. The ragged throng stopped its shuffling approach.

"Over there!" Summitch whispered. The small man pointed at the statue, which now appeared to be looking straight at them.

The statue raised a hand.

"They have passed the test." Did the voice come from the statue? It still sounded like it came from all around them. The lips on the great metal head did not move.

But the statue stood.

"First, you must find us. Then you must gain access to our secret. No one has done this for over seven hundred years. Until today."

"Gontor!" the ragged cried in unison. "Gontor!"

"Only one other man ever accomplished this, a man I made my brother."

"Gontor!" the crowd roared.

"The war raged above, as it does today. I sent my brother out into the world, to use his newfound strength, to put an end to suffering." The statue shook its gigantic head. "We never heard from him again. He was no match for the destruction above."

The crowd grew silent, as if they, too, might remember that horrible day hundreds of years ago.

"It was too dangerous to risk another. So, we decided to wait for those with power to come to us."

Jacobsen was trying to understand just what they were being told. "So there have been others before us?"

"Others who have failed."

"Failed? How—"

"When they failed, they died."

"Then we must have the power," Jacobsen concluded.

"Good," the voice agreed. "We do not care for false modesty, either. You will be given something to eat, and a place to rest. When you have had time for both, we will discuss your destiny.''

The statue sat, its gaze returning to the heavens.

"Gontor!" the crowd cried a final time in unison. All but a few of them turned away. One man, who wore a dark robe perhaps slightly less tattered than the garments of his fellows, stepped forward.

"Come," he called to the two newcomers. "We will fulfill Gontor's wishes." He turned and walked away. They were obviously supposed to follow.

Jacobsen tugged at Summitch's sleeve. "Let's go." Almost as an afterthought, Jacobsen tucked the gun back in his belt.

Summitch sighed. "So we get to live for a few more hours at least. I wonder what they do with people who fail their test? I'll wager it has something to do with the vat of fire."

Jacobsen decided he'd had enough of his companion's pronouncements of doom. He jogged forward and caught up with their guide.

"What is the name of this place?"

The man in the dark robe glanced at him skeptically, as if no one should even bother asking such a question. "It has no name. It is home."

Jacobsen decided he'd try again. If he could get someone here to speak freely, perhaps he could learn a few things that would help them survive.

"Home? Then you have always lived here?"

That only deepened the guide's frown. "We all come from the castle. Gontor showed us the way. Why do you ask me questions you should already know the answers to?"

Jacobsen figured it was time to smile and retreat. He didn't want to unnecessarily antagonize their newfound hosts. After all, if anything went wrong, he and Summitch could still be Gontor's dinner. He smiled a final time at their guide and dropped back to walk beside Summitch.

Maybe the little fellow had had some time now to make sense of all this.

"Who are these people?" Jacobsen asked in a much softer voice.

"The unwanted of the world." There was a hint of wonder in Summitch's voice. "You can see it in the different armors and uniforms, their monastic robes, even in the different peasant garbs. I think I saw one very colorful outfit that once belonged to a jester." He sighed. "The world above us is not the kindest of places. What if you offend a High One, cross a Judge, run from a battle? Most of those who displease authority die, often very publicly. But some few, apparently, have escaped."

He waved at the bright world around them. Most of the ragged people had disappeared into the vast expanse of the place, and as Summich and Jacobsen walked beyond the circle of boulders, they found themselves passing between long, neat rows of fruit-bearing trees without another person in sight.

"But where could they go?" Summitch continued. "Runaway soldiers, errant household staff, perhaps even the occasional High Lord who has offended someone even higher. There have always been rumors of this sort of place, a paradise on the other side of the world. Now, it appears that paradise is beneath the castle, rather than beyond it."

Their guide turned slightly. The three of them walked beneath a great, spreading tree that seemed to be perfectly symmetrical, fruit hanging from its lower branches at two-foot intervals all the way around.

Jacobsen glanced down at his small companion. "So we could be in worse places than paradise."

Summitch lowered his voice even further. "Paradise for whom? We are still alive, thanks to some very dubious circumstances. I was impressed by your resources."

Jacobsen smiled. No one had ever complimented his resources before. Back in the world he came from, you needed to think quickly to survive. But in this place, his skills paled next to Summitch's.

"Until we came to this—paradise," Jacobsen replied, "we made good use of your—What did you call yourself?"

"A finder." It was only in this too-bright light that Jacobsen could see how lined Summitch's face was. When the little fellow nodded, his wrinkles bounced. "After I'm rested, yes, maybe I can find a way out of here."

If Summitch didn't panic again. If the situation got sticky, Jacobsen would have to depend on his own resources. He reached inside his jacket and felt the cold handle of his gun. The last time he used the gun, he'd changed the nature of the world around them. Who knew what wonders—or terrors—using the gun for a second time would bring.

Their guide led them beyond the trees and across an open meadow. The soft grass was dotted with little, perfect circles of wildflowers, a yellow burst of color to their left, a blue one to their right, circles of red and orange and white in the distance. Jacobsen noticed the painted sky was closer here. They were coming to the edge of the huge room. He saw a number of openings along the wall they approached, but whether they led to rooms or yet more tunnels, Jacobsen couldn't tell.

Their guide motioned for them to follow him through one of the doorways. There was an alcove beyond, the front of which was illuminated by light from the chamber outside, while the near half lay in shadow.

"You may stay here, through Gontor's grace. When you are done resting, Gontor will speak with you."

"How will we let you know we're ready?" Jacobsen asked.

Their guide gave them that odd look one more time. "I'll know." With that, the dark-robed man turned and left.

Jacobsen stared after the retreating guide. "Not the friendliest sort, are they? Maybe they resent not being able to tear us apart."

Summitch wasn't listening. "Don't look now, but they brought us dinner!"

Jacobsen turned and looked where the small man pointed. A multicolored cloth had been spread out at the point that the light began to fade to shadow, a cloth covered by all manner of what appeared to be food.

"Quite a varied spread," Summitch said as he promptly knelt at the side of their feast. "We are indeed honored guests."

Jacobsen for his part had trouble trusting the spread before him, perhaps because the food managed to look both tempting and subtly wrong; the apple-shaped fruits were a delicate purple, the steaming roast of some meat had the slightest tinge of green. He waited and watched what Summitch ate, then picked something similar. He tasted a tart fruit, a salty bit of meat, a pungent piece of cheese. Not the manna from heaven one might expect in paradise, but perfectly edible.

There were two jugs set out on the cloth as well, each filled with a liquid, one clear, one milky. Jacobsen opted for the clear, and was pleased to find it was water.

He was suddenly quite tired. Thoughts of drugs and sorcery flitted through his brain for an instant, but, really, he had no idea when he had either slept or eaten last. It was probably a wonder his adrenaline had supported him this long. He looked to the shadowed area at the back of the room, and saw that Summitch had once again beaten him to it.

"There are some pillows and blankets back here," the small man called. "It looks to be quite comfortable."

Now that Jacobsen looked carefully into the dimness, he could see a pair of softly rounded mounds, with Summitch standing before one of them. He could sleep at last. He took a step into the shadow and marveled for an instant at how quickly it grew dark in the room's center. But he was far too tired to marvel, or think, or to do anything but sleep.

Tomorrow, he would think about escape. Tomorrow, he

would be killed and eaten. Tomorrow, he might even discover he had some special power.

Jacobsen crawled on top of the soft mound of bedding
and closed his eyes.

THEY AWOKE TO find another meal spread out for them,
slightly smaller than the last, but no less varied.

A moment later, their guide reappeared at their door.

"Come. I shall show you where you may relieve yourselves." They followed the robed man to a door three away
from that of their sleeping chamber. Jacobsen was grateful
when the man simply waved them inside.

The small room held a ditch to one side, a running
stream on the other. Quite convenient, and no doubt as
planned as those perfectly symmetrical fruit trees. Jacobsen
pulled down his pants and did what was necessary. Somewhere behind him, he could hear Summitch doing the same.
Jacobsen figured Summitch was either a very odd form of
human, or perhaps not human at all. Still, he was glad the
two of them were allowing for a bit of privacy. Frankly,
when it came to Summitch, Jacobsen didn't want to know
any more than was absolutely necessary.

After they had both cleaned themselves off a bit under
a narrow waterfall at the end of the room—no doubt also
constructed specifically for that purpose—they stepped outside to where their guide was waiting.

"Gontor will see you now," the man said, already walking away. This time, he led Summitch and Jacobsen along
the wall of the great room. Painted the same bright blue as
the ceiling above, the wall was littered with openings, many
of which were small and dark from without; Jacobsen
guessed they were tunnels leading elsewhere. But they also
passed more than a dozen large alcoves filled with objects
that glittered and gleamed in the reflected light from the
great expanse without.

"While it is impolite to stare," Summitch whispered,

"the contents of some of those places look quite valuable."
He grinned. "To call this place paradise is, in a certain
sense, to underestimate it."

Jacobsen didn't think he'd ever seen the small fellow so
happy; now that he thought of it, before this he'd hardly
even seen Summitch smile. Their guide marched along perhaps ten paces before them, apparently oblivious to both
their sightseeing and their conversation.

"This world is a honeycomb of marvels," Summitch
enthused. "I think we've stumbled on one of the great lost
palaces. Who knows what they hide in here? Riches, lost
secrets, perhaps—from what that statue was talking about—
the key to eternal life? I may have to forget about my last
scheme entirely." He chuckled. "Then again, there's no
reason a fellow can't have two schemes."

The robed man turned abruptly to the left, and began to
walk down a lane of golden brick. They turned to follow.
There, in the distance before them, Jacobsen could see the
great statue of Gontor.

"This must be the official route," Jacobsen mused.
"Last time, I think we got the shortcut."

"They may take us by different routes to keep us confused," replied the still-grinning Summitch. "For some
reason, they may not trust us."

Especially if they thought the two of them had this awe-
some power that Jacobsen couldn't begin to understand. He
realized he'd been so overwhelmed by this place that
he hadn't even had time to worry about that small detail.
He just hoped that Gontor wasn't about to ask for any further demonstrations.

Jacobsen looked ahead to the motionless metal man upon
his throne. An even larger crowd than that of the night before
had gathered around the statue. Jacobsen guessed there
might be five hundred people standing in a semicircle before
the huge metal figure. But no one stood on the golden lane
that they now walked with their guide. The path ended just
in front of the statue, between two of the larger standing

stones. Jacobsen imagined that spot had been reserved for them.

Banners flew above the boulders to either side of their path, four multicolored pieces of cloth, each bearing a symbol he had never seen before, each hanging in midair like a kite suspended in a summer breeze. Most of the crowd seemed to be dressed in much better quality robes and armor than they'd sported at their last meeting. Jacobsen wondered if they kept the shabby stuff around for special occasions, like scaring the life out of newcomers.

The crowd noise died as their guide led Jacobsen and Summitch among them.

"Welcome to the world of promise," the everywhere voice said as the guide indicated where they should stand.

"Gontor!" the crowd chorused.

Jacobsen blinked. He half-wanted to shield his eyes. The colors at the center of it all seemed even more brilliant than they had before he'd slept. Too brilliant, really. Sort of like paradise reproduced on a neon sign. Jacobsen had an image of living inside a small glass globe, the kind with a couple of palm trees and a Souvenir of Miami Beach logo.

"Gontor!" the crowd cried in unison.

The statue turned to regard the newcomers as the voice-from-everywhere spoke. "I see you have enjoyed our hospitality, and had a chance to see a bit of my realm."

There was a moment of silence. Some response seemed to be required.

"Thank you," Jacobsen called out. "It was most appreciated." He glanced over at the small man beside him. Summitch seemed to be frozen in place, staring upwards, openmouthed.

"Only what you deserved after your recent demonstration," the voice replied graciously.

The statue pushed itself out of its chair and stood above them.

"Gontor!" the crowd cheered.

The voice continued, "I may, however, need to correct

you on some details. You have found far more than a palace.''

What? Hadn't Summitch just—?

Until then, it had not occurred to Jacobsen that twenty-foot statues that appeared to speak from everywhere might be able to hear everywhere, too.

"You will come to understand in time." The voice's tone was most reassuring. "We will be glad to instruct you as you perform those services that we require of you."

Summitch started at that. He glanced at Jacobsen.

"Uh-oh," Summitch whispered. "That's another thing you'll learn. There's always a catch."

No, Jacobsen thought, that was something he already knew.

"No doubt you've asked yourselves, who or what am I." With that, the statue took a step toward them, ten feet in a single stride. "I am but one more casualty of this most ancient war." The voice sighed. "They could not kill me, so they contained me, for eternity. Eternity?" The statue threw back its head as the voice from everywhere laughed. "It hasn't been more than a few hundred years!"

The bronze head snapped back to regard Jacobsen and Summitch. "Excuse me. I've been so long with my thoughts."

An ancient being of almost infinite power; Jacobsen had read about this sort of thing in dozens of science fiction novels when he was a kid. "Are you the guardian, then? The watchman who protects the—" He couldn't find the word.

"You mean a ring, or a sword, or a staff of power? Something dreary like that?" The statue shook its head. "No, I oversee the force that makes the world."

Whoa! One thing hadn't changed. When Jacobsen stumbled into the middle of something, it was always right when the shit was about to hit the fan.

"So you control—" he began.

"No one controls such a force," the voice interrupted.

"Sometimes, the proper individual may guide it. For I do believe that the power one day will rest within a single individual. It could be anyone." The voice paused as the statue looked down at Jacobsen. "Well, probably not you. Summitch here, well, he has problems too. But who am I to say? I've only studied the problem for some twelve hundred odd years, after all.

"But we must be careful. No power is more corrupt than the ancient power. Whether the individual will seize the power, or the power the individual, who is to say?"

Certainly not Jacobsen. He still wasn't sure why he was standing there.

"The war will never end without outside intervention," the voice went on. "It all has to do with the conservation of magic. The greedy among us try to hoard it. But the only way to control these forces is to harness it everywhere, on each of the three worlds. I don't need to tell you they have already made inroads into the second. At least one of you is from there, after all. Should the second come under their control, the third will not be far behind."

Jacobsen was thoroughly confused. He leaned close to Summitch. "What's he talking about?"

The small fellow shook his head. "I have no idea."

The statue paused to regard them for an instant. "That is the problem with constant war. Knowledge is lost. Dangers reawaken that we thought were past. Perhaps you are here to shift the balance."

The statue made a fist. "The forces have already begun, we only need to speed them up a bit. The reason this war began was the insularity of our world. We are here to end the war, and find our rightful place in the world. We need to reconnect with the other worlds. One could not do it before. Ah, but three beings of power?" He raised his fist high in the air. "Who could stand before might like that?"

"Gontor!" the crowd agreed.

The voice paused as the statue regarded Summitch. "But

you have questions, primary among them, if I deduce it properly, 'What's in it for me?' ''

Summitch shuffled uncomfortably from one foot to the other. "Well, uh, I don't know if I'd—well, yes."

"There are two worlds beyond the castle. Someone, perhaps, will soon rule them both. Those who control the power and those who rule are often quite different."

"Oh joy," Summitch muttered dourly so that only Jacobsen should hear. "An enigma. I so love enigmas."

"But you are about to ask why I brought you here. There are certain things you don't realize about yourselves. Isn't that always the way?"

Now the statue would have Jacobsen believe he really did have special powers. And what did the voice mean when it said they were *brought* here? Didn't they stumble on this place by accident?

"We will save that for later." The statue nodded at Jacobsen and Summitch. "We are here, of course, to save the world."

Summitch frowned as he softly added: "Isn't that always the way? You go looking to make a few bucks and you end up having to save the universe."

"We are here to fulfill our destiny!"

"Gontor!" the crowd concurred.

Jacobsen had had just about enough of this. It seemed the statue was convinced they were the saviors of all these different worlds no matter what. "Wait a moment! What's my destiny got to do with anything?"

"How did you get here?"

The directness of the question so startled Jacobsen, he ended up giving an honest answer. "There was this girl I was supposed to shoot, but then I couldn't—so I ended up getting pulled into this whirlpool of darkness, which dumped me—well, pretty close to here."

"Sounds like destiny to me!" the voice replied triumphantly.

"You know," Summitch said, "it sort of does."

"Gontor!" the crowd cheered for all of them.

AUBRIC AND THE lady Karmille's maidservant had vanished. They had gone before Karmille was ready. She had let her other task take far too long. She might regret such indulgence, if she ever chose to regret.

Karmille sighed as she thought of the last few hours. If only it were not such a pure enjoyment. It gave the torturers a little recreation. They always became inspired when they worked on one of their own, and it provided a valuable object lesson besides. It grew time-consuming, though, when she became involved. And she always had to become involved. She was simply enthusiastic about pain.

As so often occurred, it had gotten very messy at the end. She so enjoyed removing parts of her victims while they were still alive and conscious. But such pleasure could not last forever; such indulgence never came without its price. She had, of course, ruined another of her gowns. She licked the last remnants of dried blood from her fingers.

She stood now in the empty room where she had left the soldier and the maid. The bed had been slept in, some food had been eaten, but nothing was broken or out of place. There was no sign of how they had escaped. Karmille sighed again. She supposed she should feel more alarmed, but the aftermath of a good death was one of the few times she felt truly sated.

She could have had the pair watched constantly, could even have watched them herself. But what had she really missed? A moment or two of intimacy? Intimacy was never as good as pain.

So they were gone. As long as her maidservant was with Aubric, there would be no secrets. Lady Karmille was so pleased that at least this would work as planned.

Only the manner of their escape was surprising. She had planned their flight for early morning; an unlocked door after breakfast, an open entrance to the tunnels behind a hanging in the hall. The human soldier—if that was indeed all he was—might have seen through such a transparent ruse, but she expected Aubric to take the chance anyway, looking upon it as a challenge.

But the escape had been taken from her hands. First the disappearance of the gnarlyman, now this. There were forces working secretly in their High Keep, forces with as much or more power than the Grey. It was a threat to everything they held dear.

How wonderful! She smiled at the possibilities.

Her father had denied Karmille her rightful place for far too long. Now, with her brothers involved elsewhere in this never-ending war, there would be no one else to turn to.

She was so pleased. Now, she had ample reason to go to her father and request the services of a Judge.

He would be outraged at this intrusion. But she would make him see the wisdom of it. It was a part of their special bond, after all.

She stopped by her room to clean herself and change, ordering her handmaidens to fetch one of her most revealing costumes; one her father had commented favorably upon in the past.

Two of her closest maids undressed her, undoing the many buckles and untying the dozens of bows on her ruined gown. But their fingers fumbled at the laces, tugged too long at stubborn fastenings. What was taking them so long? She cursed her servants for lazy sluggards. They couldn't dawdle today. She had to hurry so she might catch her father in that time between his breakfast and the morning meetings with his councilors. Long enough to provoke interest, but not so long as to promote undue complications.

Oh, to be joined on the hunt by a Judge! She could save her special magics for emergencies. And if the court magician proved disagreeable? Maybe she could even kill a Judge. She so enjoyed new sensations.

A third maid brought the gown of grey and flaming red.

Karmille took a series of deep breaths as all three servants tightened the form-fitting gown around her. It would not do to be too giddy upon greeting her father; he would take such an attitude as too open an invitation.

Ready at last, she hurried from her room. It would help to exert herself; the slightest of flushes would make her father find her even more attractive. She walked quickly down the corridors, causing the guards to step aside with the slightest glance. In a moment, she stood before the High Lord's chambers.

"Stand aside!" she commanded her father's personal guard.

The two men glanced at each other but made no further move.

She forced her voice back to a conversational tone. "Lady Karmille has urgent personal business with her father. Step aside, or I will have you killed."

That provoked the proper response. All within the Grey Court knew how the High Lord liked to indulge his daughter with the occasional death.

"Father!" she called once they had opened the doors.

"What?" her father screamed from the inner chamber. "Who dares?" She heard him walk heavily toward her, the door between the chambers slammed noisily aside.

"I will have you—"

The High Lord's rage died in his throat when he stepped through the door.

"Oh. It is you."

"I am glad you may find time to see me." Karmille curtsied, careful to angle her chest forward so that her father might admire the way her dress accented her cleavage.

The slightest of smiles curled her father's upper lip. "I always have time for my princess."

Karmille thought for an instant of the true meaning of his words.

There was always one princess in the house, but never more than one. There were elders who kept track of these things, and were more than happy to share them with her, a member of the royal family.

In the hundreds of years of her father's reign, there had been close to three hundred children produced by the royal lineage. The many sons always seemed to die in the war. And the daughters? In the early days, they were married off to form alliances. Now—once they reached a certain age, they simply disappeared.

Karmille imagined they were disposed of. There were rumors that their blood was put to certain arcane uses, one of the more drastic steps the Judges used to assure her father's longevity.

She knew of only one certainty. She would surely die, unless she found a way to kill her father first.

Until that day, though, the High Lord gave her free rein, within the confines of the Keep of the Grey. But how could she kill him? Up close, his parchment hands were crossed with a hundred tiny wrinkles. His form was so infused with the Judge's art that he could not die in any traditional sense. One day, he would simply cease to exist, his form crumbling to dust.

Her father nodded to a pair of servants who always hovered in the shadows.

"Leave us now. We will talk alone."

He smiled at his daughter. As old as he was, his mind was on things other than conversation. She depended on it.

He ran his hand up her thigh. Karmille did her best not to flinch at his touch. She smiled and caressed his cheek. Now that he was older, simple fondling would often be enough.

Procreation was always kept within the family. Her father had often explained it was the price the High Ones paid for their power. Once the later stages of the war caused the crumbling of the last alliances and put an end to the diplomatic coupling, it was the best way to keep the bloodlines pure.

She whispered her discoveries in his ear.

"What?" he demanded, pulling away; the very reaction she had hoped for. "Spies! They must be spies!"

She thought they might be that and more, but she didn't want to share her suspicions quite yet.

"I will inform the Judges immediately."

"Do you wish to entrust this entirely to the Judges?" she cooed, moving forward to rest a hand on his knee. "Judges have been known to change allegiances."

"You know that business with the Purple?" Her father shook his head. "None of my children has ever had such a sense of history."

None of your children has wanted so much to survive, Karmille thought. No, to survive and conquer. "You need someone to accompany the Judge, to give him guidance," she whispered, her lips close to his neck.

Her father's voice was growing husky. "I have no time to recall any of my sons."

"You do not need your sons." Her teeth delicately nipped at his ear. "Use me."

"Yes." Her father managed a ragged breath. "Yes I could."

She ran a hand across his chest. "Give me a Judge."

A gong rang faintly in the distance. In a few minutes, the business of the Court would begin. In an instant, the Council would be at the door to escort their lord.

Her father sighed and pulled away. "We will have to continue this later. Tonight."

Karmille gripped the front of his shirt. "Give me a name."

Her father regarded her for a moment, his ancient grey eyes mere slits in his face of weathered parchment.

"I will offer you the assistance of one of the best."

He rang a bell, spoke briefly with a servant who silently appeared. The servant only nodded. To ensure secrecy within the High Lord's inner chambers, most of them performed their duties without their tongues.

Her father stood, adjusting his clothing more decorously. "You will consult with Judge Sasseen."

She could not have hoped for better.

Sasseen was second in ascension in the Court, directly beneath Judge Basoff. Basoff was a ruthless man who would never relinquish his power—until the day he died. Sasseen, too, had a need for power, a need that would serve Karmille well. Perhaps they could form an understanding. Perhaps she could help him to destroy his superior.

"I hope he will be of some assistance," her father prompted when she did not respond.

She gave the standard reply, "The Judges live to serve the Court." It was a lie, like so much else here, but a useful lie. The Judges and the Court constantly struggled for power. It was another reason the High Ones so jealously guarded their bloodlines.

If the High Lord's blood was sufficiently pure, the Judges' magicks would be turned against the Judge's themselves. No Judge had tried such a rebellion against the Court in close to a thousand years. But the ancient tales were enough of a deterrent, at least for now.

Karmille curtsied low before her father and withdrew, her head already full of plans. She would use the Judge, as she used all those who came before her. She would kill those who tried to escape her. And she would lead all of the Grey.

Her needs were simple, really.

She would be Queen of the Grey, the first woman to rule in seven hundred years. And no one would get in her way.

· 16 ·

JOE BEAST WAS GETTING RE-
ally pissed. First, they'd heard the noise. Then Ernie had
jumped from the car, fallen on the ground, shouting words
that Joe couldn't understand, twisting and humping around
on the pavement like some holy roller from a country
church. For a moment, Joe felt like the world was ending.

Now the world didn't seem in any danger at all.

The bus would never get here. Oh, sure, they could hear
it, the noise coming from who knew where. But what had
been really spooky for the first minute or two was getting
less scary now that the noise had kept on going for close
to a quarter of an hour. The invisible bus kept climbing up
that invisible hill, never to reach its destination.

At least, after a moment or two of gibberish coming out
of his mouth, Ernie had turned out to be his normal self.
He had gotten up, dusted himself off, and smiled a little
sheepishly. Since then, the two of them had stood there,
waiting for the bus that would never come.

Maybe this Smith guy couldn't do everything after all.

Mystery buses, his cousin talking in tongues, old ladies

who could make vacuums that would suck you straight to Hell; there was only one thing Joe was sure about. One way or another, this was all Smith's fault.

What was it with this Smith character, anyway? He wouldn't be surprised if a minute from now Smith dropped down from a UFO. Or maybe he would burst out of the ground sporting a tail and belching brimstone.

And the damned thing was, Ernie and Joe's uncle Roman were already in bed with this guy! If Smith could do everything Joe suspected, why did he even need Joe and his family?

But Joe knew the answer as soon as he thought of the question. People had ruled through fear throughout history. Fear was Uncle Roman's specialty. Smith wasn't any different. By co-opting Joe's uncle and cousin, the Petranova family supplied Smith with an instant organization.

But there was a difference; everybody in Joe's family always lived by a code. In the past, at the very least, kids and old ladies had always been off limits. There were certain things you just had to respect. Smith practiced fear without honor. His ambitions seemed to know no limits.

He could see it in the way Ernie turned into a zombie at Smith's command, relaying Smith's messages while he clutched his stomach in pain. Sure, Ernie had got himself in trouble, and Smith had done him a favor, whatever it was. Frankly, Joe didn't want to know. But Ernie never asked for this. Whether Smith did this mind-control shit through some scientific brain wave device or old-fashioned, garden-variety voodoo, it didn't matter.

And while Uncle Roman hadn't quite hit zombie-land, he'd been acting pretty strange himself, almost like he was afraid of this Smith. Joe had never known Roman Petranova to be scared of anything. But Uncle Roman was getting old. Maybe he was losing his edge. And this Smith guy could pull some pretty frightening shit.

On one level, Joe admitted, you had to respect someone with that kind of power. But, if the opportunity presented

itself, no amount of respect would prevent Joe from
blowing the sucker away.

For all Joe knew, he was the only one in his whole
family that wasn't under Smith's control. If he and Ernie
got through this little encounter in one piece, he wanted to
go in front of his uncle and his cronies and find out exactly
how deep this ran. Maybe they could cut their losses and
get away from Smith before it got any worse. Or maybe
Joe would have to leave town, or the state, or the country,
while all of this blew over. Because if things kept on like
this, Joe had the feeling a lot of people, including a lot of
Petranovas, were going to die.

Mostly, Joe decided, he was tired of all this cosmic shit.

Right now, besides those bus noises, the evening sky
was fading in and out, full of stars one minute, empty the
next. And the bus noise would get louder, then fade again.
It was like whoever was trying to make this happen didn't
quite have the hang of it.

Ernie's wildness was back in full force, too. After he'd
gotten back on his feet, Joe's cousin had seemed agitated,
his arms and legs twitching like they didn't want him to
keep still.

Now Ernie was pacing back and forth across the highway, as if he never expected any more traffic to come down
the interstate. There certainly hadn't been anybody else
since the phantom bus had started up. The way things were
going, Joe thought, maybe his cousin was right.

Ernie stopped and stared at Joe. "There's a better place
for this. I gotta drive."

"What?" Joe asked. "What do you mean?" But Ernie
had already gotten into the car. This sounded like Smith's
doing all over again. Joe jumped in the passenger side.
Whatever happened, he didn't want to be left behind.

Ernie floored it as soon as Joe had slammed the door.
They didn't go very far, just over the hilltop. There, just
off the next exit, was a huge truck stop.

It didn't look real. All the flashing lights and neon signs

made it appear like some strange cross between a traveling circus and a fairy tale; a too-bright oasis in a world of darkness. It was a big place, too, with a motel, a restaurant, a gas station, and a convenience store, each structure outlined in great strands of multicolored Christmas lights.

Ernie swung into the parking lot and slammed on the brakes so quickly, Joe had to throw out his hands against the dashboard so he wouldn't go through the windshield.

"What's the matter with you?" Joe yelled at his cousin. But Ernie was already out the door.

He heard music wafting their way from the bar, a syncopated tune, led by a wildly pumping accordion.

Polka music?

Joe got out of the car. Ernie had already disappeared. Joe was out here all by himself. He turned around so that the parking lot was behind him. The strange light changes he had seen on the last hill, bright to dark to bright again, were gone. Instead, a vast bank of fog was rolling in beyond the neon, as if the truck stop's asphalt boundaries were the ends of the world.

The music was the only sound, like the accordions and oompah horns were trying to hold back the deepest darkness of this unnatural night.

He spun as he heard footsteps running across the asphalt parking lot.

It was Ernie. "It's coming!" his cousin called. "Now it's coming!"

The engine noise was back. This time, the bus sounded like it was going to run them over. Joe heard the loud squeal of air brakes—then nothing.

The polka music—which, Joe realized, had vanished for a moment—took its place.

"Whoa!" His cousin shook himself.

"Ernie?"

Ernie grinned at him, the agitation replaced by a great excitement. He looked like nothing so much as a kid on Christmas morning.

"We got a minute. Let's go get a beer."

.   .   .

ONE MINUTE, BRIAN and Karen had been looking at the
first pink tinges of dusk. The next, the bus was overtaken
by some kind of fog; a thick greyness that seemed to blot
out everything outside, even the last rays of the sun. Brian
and Karen looked at each other. Neither knew what to say.

The bus was still running, but the motor sounded muffled and far away. At least they were moving.

Brian hoped against hope that this was something natural. He wished again that Mrs. Mendeck had been home
when they called. Karen said Mrs. M was the only person
she knew who didn't have an answering machine.

The driver pressed down on the brakes.

"We're gonna have to slow down for a minute here,
folks," he called over his shoulder. "Sometimes you get
some really weird weather out in the boonies."

The air brakes wailed as the bus rapidly decelerated.
Brian was jolted forward as the bus came to a full stop.

The bus driver stood and peered back into the bus's dark
interior. "Everybody all right back here?" He walked
slowly back the length of the bus, glancing first to one side,
then to the other.

He nodded to Brian and Karen. His light brown skin
glistened brightly in the odd light that filtered through the
fog outside. "You're the only two folks who are awake."
He grinned, showing a single silver tooth among a field of
white. "Nobody else is gonna know anything's happened."

"It's awfully early for everybody to be sleeping on a
bus, isn't it?" Karen asked with a frown.

The bus driver pushed his hat back off his balding head.
"Maybe, maybe not. There's only one thing you can depend on. Every bus ride is different." He smiled again,
pointed at the golden badge on his lapel.

"Vern's the name."

Brian and Karen introduced themselves.

Vern looked back out the windows. "This sure is strange

weather. I can't even see the road from the front of the bus. Thickest fog I've ever seen." He shook his head. "Maybe we should go outside and take a look around."

"I don't think that's such a good idea," Brian quickly replied.

Vern looked sharply at Brian. "You see something out there?"

Brian hesitated for an instant, trying to think of a way to explain everything that had happened. Finally, he said, "Only that some really strange things have been happening wherever we go. We think there's someone after us."

Vern nodded like he heard that sort of thing every day. He waved at the fog. "This is surely strange. We'd best be careful."

Karen laughed. "You mean, you really believe us?"

"Been having a hard time with that, huh?" Vern grinned again. "Let's just say I allow for different points of view. You drive a bus as long as I have, you'll accept just about anything."

"You sound a little like Mrs. Mendeck," Karen said. "She's pretty open-minded, too. Vern, do you believe in destiny?"

It was the bus driver's turn to hesitate. He nodded after a moment's thought.

"I think everybody believes they're destined for some-thing. Maybe not greatness exactly. But something spe-cial." He grinned again. "Sometimes, that something special can just be driving a bus."

Brian heard the hiss of escaping air. Vern turned around as the forward door of the bus swung open.

"Now that," Vern said, "is one thing that shouldn't happen."

The fog was starting to clear some. They could see an odd, pink light through the mist.

Karen squeezed Brian's hand.

"What the hell?" the driver exclaimed.

A neon sign loomed out of the fog.

SHADY REST TRUCK STOP: Open All the Time.

Vern looked to Brian and Karen. "This is miles ahead of where we're supposed to be."

Brian knew then that they'd been found. Smith had done this, transporting the whole bus to this otherworldly place.

Brian doubted very much if they'd be able to contact Mrs. Mendeck now.

They were on their own.

WEARING A BLUE waitress's uniform and a dazzling smile, she walked across the restaurant toward Joe and Ernie with a full pot of coffee.

"Florence," her nametag read. Around forty, she was a handsome woman, with high cheekbones and clear green eyes. Her hair was maybe a bit too bright a shade of red, but that could have been the lighting in this place.

"Why's the music so loud?" Joe had to shout to make himself heard.

Florence laughed. "Hey, if we're all going to Hell, we may as well have an entertaining time along the way."

They had a pretty good speaker system in the restaurant. Accordions were all around. In heaven there is no beer. *Oompahpah.*

"It cheers me up." Florence waved her coffeepot over at a half dozen men sitting at the counter. "Those guys would listen to country and western all the time. I've had enough of cheatin' men and broken hearts. Some days you got to push the dark clouds away."

"Well, we came in for a beer—" Joe began.

The polka music stopped abruptly. Florence looked up with a frown.

"The bus is here," Ernie announced.

"The bus is here," four other men at the counter agreed in unison.

Ernie got out of his seat, as did the four who had spoken. The five turned as one, then began to walk single file across the room, their feet falling so softly on the linoleum that they made no sound.

"Your friend, too?" Florence shook her head, as if this was one more trial she had to bear. "Excuse me, honey." She walked quickly over to the counter and fetched a large pitcher of water. The five men in single file were walking slowly toward the door.

"That one with the red checkered shirt is my husband," Florence continued in a conversational tone. "He's been like this ever since a run-in we had with this really strange man."

"Somebody named Smith?" Joe asked.

"So he says. As if that would be his name. You ever see the fellow?" She frowned. "Sounds to me like the man's got no imagination." Florence hurried behind her husband, lifted the pitcher of water above her head, then quickly upended it, pouring the contents over her husband's head.

The man stopped and sputtered.

He turned and looked at his wife. "Flo! What the hell's going on?"

Flo nodded at the other four. "Looks like Smith's got work for you."

Her husband looked crestfallen. "Flo! I had no idea."

"I know, I know," she replied wearily. "Save it for when this is all over."

"You want me to lock myself up in the shed?" her husband asked.

"No. Get me some more water. Let's see if we can help the others."

"Just water?" Joe asked.

Florence shrugged. "Hey, it seems to work, at least until they dry off again. It helps if there's some ice in it." She nodded toward Ernie. "Try it on that friend of yours."

"He's my cousin," Joe admitted.

"Even better." She handed him a full pitcher and waved

him forward. "Seems the closer you are to the person, the easier it is to break the trance. Try it."

Florence's husband looked around. "We've got to stop this."

"A lot of stuff has been happening at this truck stop lately," Flo continued as Joe ran across the room to fetch some water. Flo nodded at the remaining men, who seemed to be picking up speed as they neared the door. "Smith came here first. After he left, his—people—started showing up." She sighed. "The more of them that get together, the worse it gets. Sort of like the people are radio-controlled." She paused and frowned. "No, it's worse than that. It's more like they're batteries for Smith to channel his power."

"Flo!" her husband called. "There's more of them outside. Maybe half a dozen."

"Well, they're not going to take my family and friends!" the waitress announced as she upended another pitcher.

Joe caught up with his cousin as he was about to walk out the door.

"What the hell?" Ernie roared as the water drenched his head. "Hey! Where the hell are we?"

"Just a truck stop, honey," the waitress answered. "At least for now."

Joe looked out the window. The bus was out there, and so were half a dozen men, most of them with guns.

"Excuse me a sec," Flo said as she walked back to the jukebox. "I think we need a little music." She banged the side of the big old machine. Lights flashed across the top of the jukebox as another polka tune rumbled forth. Flo looked up and smiled. "Heck, I know *I* need a little music."

Joe walked back to the door, his right hand resting on his shoulder holster. Flo's husband offered him a fresh pitcher of water. He took it with his left hand, and kicked open the door.

Okay, then. He'd had just about enough of this. Smith and his zombies were going to pay.

VERN INSISTED ON going first. Brian and Karen stayed close behind.

At first, Brian could see nothing but the fog. Then the grey seemed to vanish, as if a blanket had been pulled away, and he was surrounded by neon and a dark night sky.

Half a dozen men strode toward them. They made no sound as they approached, as silent as cats. Two of them held rifles, while another hoisted a shotgun.

"Now wait a minute, here!" Vern called. "What have these kids done to you?"

No one replied; just the silent approach, like this was all a movie that had lost its sound. More people came running from the open door of a restaurant. One of them threw a pitcher of water into a gunman's face.

The gunman kept on walking.

"It didn't work!" the man called. Brian recognized that voice. It was one of the men who had shot his father.

"The spell may be too strong!" a woman called back. "It may be too late!"

"To hell with that!" The man who had shot Brian's father pulled a handgun from inside his jacket, and shot the nearest of the walking gunmen in the leg.

The gunman dropped his shotgun. He fell to the ground, screaming.

"I've had enough of this shit!" the shooter yelled. "I will not take this anymore. You understand me, Smith?"

The woman who had spoken before ran over to the fallen man. "Les? Is that you?"

The shooter looked from one of the remaining gunmen to the other. Both of them were raising their rifles toward the two teens.

"Brian!" the shooter called. "Karen! We don't have to

take this." He shook his gun up at the sky. "You understand me, Smith? I'm not going to take any more of this.
I'm going to get them out of here!"

What? Brian and Karen looked at each other.

"Look out!" Vern shouted. He pushed both of them
down to the ground as at least a couple of gunshots rang
out above.

"Ernie!" the shooter called. "Give me a hand!"

There were three more gunshots, then silence.

"Okay, you kids can get up now." It was the woman's
voice this time. "You're safe, at least for the moment."

Brian looked up from where he had pressed his face into
the dirt.

What the hell was going on?

IT WAS HAPPENING all too soon.

Mrs. Mendeck sighed. No matter when it finally began,
she knew she would feel that way. She would never be
ready for what Brian and Karen would have to go through.

From the moment they were born, both Brian and Karen
were destined to be a part of this. She had hoped, once they
were of age, to fully instruct them on the mysteries, as she
herself had been instructed at the end of her childhood.
Karen had seemed mature for her age, and Mrs. Mendeck
had already laid the groundwork, casually telling her stories
about another world, giving her the background for what
would become her life's work. But she had told Karen so
little of the truth!

Brian and Karen. They were so much like Mrs. Mendeck, but they were so much more.

She had known from the day she discovered the twin
auras in this small city, that something special was happening. Even as infants, their power was evident. Within their
small forms, they held as much potential as the Strangers
of old. That there was more than one meant it was truly

time for the transformation. So she had settled in the city herself, and waited to Begin.

She had hoped, perhaps, that she could simply shepherd them into the tradition. They had kept the secrets for a hundred generations or more. What was one more?

The world had shifted a thousand years ago, and it was shifting again. Until now, all they had to do was survive, and pass down the knowledge. With the new shift, they would have to act. And she had not told the children some of the most basic facts, who they truly were, and what they could truly do.

Once, when humans still believed in magic, there was a name for these children. Changelings. A simple name that had meant so much more.

They called themselves the Strangers. For a thousand times a thousand years, they had been placed here by those on another world in exchange for human children; an ancient pact that maintained the balance between the worlds, a balance that all but a few had forgotten.

From a very young age, the Strangers would always know that they were different. They would often be shunned by their peers. In ancient days, the young Strangers would often die or go mad. But those who survived adolescence would develop certain talents. Increasingly in the modern age, these talents steadily diminished, until those few Strangers who survived exhibited powers that were little better than parlor tricks. Mrs. Mendeck's greatest gift was that she could send; that she could open a way between the worlds. She had used her gift to protect Karen twice; in both instances against ignorant human adversaries. What good would her gift be against the High Ones?

The same cause that allowed Mrs. Mendeck and others like her to survive for these last thousand years would doom Brian and Karen to a life of turmoil. And they were still children. That no doubt was why Smith rushed the Beginning; to catch them before they were ready. He only needed one; the one he could bend most easily to his will. So he would capture Brian and kill Karen.

And all because of a war on another world.

It was Mrs. Mendeck's task to keep Brian and Karen free of Smith for as long as possible; free to learn and grow and change, even though her protection might very possibly mean her own death.

She thought again of the ancient human word for her kind: Changelings. It was oddly appropriate. She only needed to protect them, to teach them, until the moment their true powers became evident.

From that moment forward, if they were properly used, either one of the Changelings would be enough to change everything.

Book Two

---

*"In all the land, there was no greater seat of learning
than the Library of Orange. And, for well over a hundred years, the Judges and High Council of the Orange
used the teachings of the library to help them devise
tactics to defeat their much more numerous and better
equipped enemies.*

*"But tactics could prevail for only so long without
the resources to properly support them. In those days,
the Grey, the Blue, and the treacherous Purple had all
allied to destroy the lesser kingdoms, and had already
placed a puppet government to rule the White.*

*"The Orange would never surrender. The allied ar-
mies had laid a siege upon their kingdom; a siege that
lasted three years, seven months, and one day. At the
last, their supplies gone, their army depleted, the High
Lord of Orange realized invasion of the Keep itself was
imminent. However, even in defeat, he believed that the
Orange could rise again, if they but had the means.*

*"So it was that the High Lord ordered half of the
remaining army to transport all that was left of the great
wealth of Orange to a secret place, so they might use it
to rebuild, once the war was past.*

*"Members of the High Council tried to prevail upon
their lord to add another form of wealth as well, and to
perhaps secrete a few of the great books. But there was*

no time, and the exhausted army of Orange was already overburdened. Legend maintains that the High Lord himself brought to the hiding place three books of his own choosing, which he managed to tuck within his armor. Legend does not tell us the names of the books.

"But, while the High Lord was secreting his wealth, the allied forces had attacked from three points, then driven their largest force through the only corner of the Keep that the Orange had thought safe. With so many transporting the gold, their divided forces had not been able to turn back the onslaught. The High Lord's forces were attacked as well upon their return, and half the remaining army of Orange was quickly slaughtered.

"The lord fought his way back to the library steps, but found only a smoking ruin, where he and the remainder of his personal guard were killed. Some few of the fierce fighters were rumored to survive, but without a home, they quickly disappeared from the forefront of battle. The Keep of Orange was gone, along with all its great learning.

"Soon, the Purple would show their true nature, and the greatest alliance of the war would crumble.

"Thus did all of the castle truly learn to suffer from the war."

—from *The Castle: Its Unfolding History*
(a work in progress)

. 17 .

AUBRIC AND RUNT FOL-
lowed the bells in silence through the glowing dark. The
lights before them danced through the gloom, pirouetting
among themselves in elaborate formation, bobbing and
weaving to a delicate ringing that rose and fell with their
every move. Aubric noticed a number of different tones as
they danced, as if each tiny bell had a voice of its own.

Runt held tight to Aubric's sleeve as they walked. She
had been startled on first entering the tunnels. Apparently
she had not even known of their existence. A day or two
before, Aubric realized, he had been the same. He shared
with her what he could about these underground mazes,
repeating what he could remember from Summitch's ram-
bling speeches. As he spoke, Aubric wondered where the
small man had gone, and whether he was in any danger.
Perhaps, when Aubric truly understood why the dancing
lights had rescued him, he might get them to help rescue
his former guide.

Runt had asked few questions and, after a while, Aubric
ran out of things to say. He also found himself putting

certain limits on his explanations. He thought it best not to relate his experience with m'lady's creatures. Runt seemed frightened enough already.

"What's that?" Runt whispered.

Aubric started. He realized the mournful flute music had returned. The notes stirred at the edge of his thoughts, then were gone, like a waking dream.

"What?" he asked.

The flute responded, stronger now, as if it could only play when truly invited.

(We have seen you before.)

He remembered how Summitch and he had rushed by the flying lights in their mad dash to escape. The tiny, shining bells had hung in the air, waiting for the terror that followed. He thought about the horrible sounds that had echoed down the corridor, and how the bells had delayed m'lady's creatures.

"Before," he agreed. "When you were decimated by those creatures."

(Some were forfeit.)

"Why didn't you protect yourselves?"

(We could only stop them by revealing our true natures. We could not be sure of your companion.)

So they had sacrificed themselves. But that reference to Summitch—what had they detected? Perhaps Aubric would be unable to get their help in the small man's rescue after all.

"What are you talking about?" Runt asked.

"How I got here," Aubric said, still not wanting to share his peril. Was he protecting Runt? Or was he afraid Runt was not the innocent he imagined, and knew all about m'lady's schemes?

"This is all so strange." Runt looked like she wanted to smile, but her face showed too much pain. "At times I can understand; at other times, it seems only sweet, sad music."

(She is too much of the world above.)

"Only music," she whispered, "but it is a beautiful song."

"What does that mean?" Aubric asked the bells.

(We all have a chance for redemption.)

"Do things always need to have meaning?" Runt answered as well.

Aubric still failed to understand. As a soldier, every day had been a simple matter of life and death. Now he was faced with a world full of choices offered by creatures that were themselves beyond belief.

(We are close.)

"I heard that," Runt whispered back. "Close to what?"

(That place where we dwell.)

"Your home?" she asked.

(Our exile. The castle is our home. The world is our domain.)

"I don't understand."

"I think that's why they've brought us here," Aubric answered. "To understand."

(We all must understand. Everyone on this world is involved. On this world, and on the others.)

Aubric hoped he could help. He was grateful to these creatures for rescuing him twice. But it was still his first duty to return to the Green.

(We are almost there.)

Runt gasped.

They stood at the edge of a great darkness. Aubric could hear the wind, far below him. The void seemed to stretch beneath them forever. Was this some other part of the same chasm he and Summitch had crossed earlier? Aubric had a vision of a chasm that circled the globe; a great crack that split their world.

(We go down.)

They stood at the edge of the abyss. The tunnel ended abruptly before the great, yawning dark. The lights danced over the edge.

(Follow us.)

"Are you crazy?" Runt asked.

(We will let no harm come to you. Why else would we have rescued you?)

Aubric could see no other choice. He took Runt's hand in his own. "Close your eyes and walk with me."

Runt looked up at him, then out at the emptiness. She closed her eyes. Aubric closed his eyes as well as he stepped forward. The sensation beneath his feet changed, from the hardness of rock to the softness of a field full of summer grass. He took a second step, and a third.

He opened his eyes. The walls still glowed before and after them. But there was nothing beneath them but the dancing lights.

They were halfway across the abyss. They were walking across the air.

(We will show you the way.)

The darkness below them melted away as a jagged line of green stretched down into the depths. Aubric looked down, and saw that the lights had gathered beneath them, a swirling cloud of brightness that never quite touched their feet.

The music gently urged them to relax. Buoyed by the cushioning lights, they floated downwards, following the path of light.

When he was a child, Aubric and his friends had built a raft to sail one of the gentle streams that cut through their kingdom. This somehow reminded him of that time on the slow river, twisting and turning away from the safety of shore. He and his friends had lost their only pole in the muck at the river's bottom, and had to give themselves over to the whims of the water, the current pulling them out midstream, then pushing their raft into a shallow bend on the opposite shore. He had the same feeling now, perilously free, not on the water, but on the currents and eddies of the open air.

The sound of a flute rose from below.

(We know every tunnel.)

(We were once the builders.)

Aubric noticed differences in the music; changes in the tone and tempo. There were many voices rather than one.

(Patience.)

(We are almost there.)

They settled again on a stone floor. He heard Runt gasp again. She had opened her eyes. He looked as well.

The new tunnel opened up before them, widening to reveal six equally spaced stone columns above six carved stone steps; a stairway that stretched the entire length of the opening, perhaps a hundred feet. Beyond the columns, he could see openings that led to great halls and rooms; Aubric felt he was looking at a palace carved out of solid rock.

The flutes spoke quickly now, their music overlapping.

(We built this refuge a thousand years ago.)

(We began this when we still had bodies.)

(Something like yours.)

(At most, we imagined it would be a temporary hiding place.)

(We will never truly leave here until we can walk again.)

Aubric and Runt walked toward the palace. The dancing lights swarmed around the columns, clustered in the rooms beyond. A dozen flutes called out to them, and then a hundred, their voices colliding with each other, turning first from a sad song to wild, frenetic music, proceeding from there to sheer cacophony.

(This has gone on for far too long.)

(There are too many dead, too many fighting.)

(In order to survive, some must be destroyed.)

Runt clutched Aubric's arm so hard it hurt. "It's too much," she whispered.

(If we do not, others will destroy us.)

(You will help us, or you will die.)

"Aubric?" she asked. "What's happening?"

(We will all die, and we can no longer save you.)

Aubric tried to cut through the confusion, to understand

what the voices were trying to tell him. Runt stumbled. The
overlapping noise was making him dizzy, too, filling his
ears with dissonance. He had to get the uproar to slow, or
they would be overwhelmed.

The voices needed him to do something. Or perhaps they
demanded that he do something. Nothing was clear. Now
that he had accepted the hospitality of these strange, bell
creatures, he might never be able to leave them behind.

Runt stopped at the bottom of the steps. She stared at
the ground, frozen in place.

(Perhaps it was an error to bring her here.)

(There are no errors, only choices.)

"It hurts!" She let go of Aubric to clap her hands over
her ears. "I can't listen anymore."

(All decisions have a cost.)

(He has joined us.)

(He needed to escape. We provided the means.)

(He cannot leave. We have waited too long.)

(You may leave whenever you want.)

(You are our guest.)

(You have a responsibility.)

(You are our only hope!)

Runt moaned.

(Enough!)

The music stopped. After a moment's silence, Aubric
heard the low notes of a single flute.

(They need to rest. Then we will consult with them.)

(Nothing is certain. Everything is possible.)

(Enough.)

Aubric saw the palace sink before him. But then he realized he was floating, buoyed aloft again by a cloud of
light. He and Runt were lifted over the steps and past the
columns into one of the inner chambers.

(You may stay in here.)

He tried to get a sense of the space before him, illuminated only by the dancing lights. The room was small and
square and empty.

(Rest. All will be well. Rest.)

(Enough.)

They set Runt gently down upon the ground in a corner of the room. She whimpered softly.

(Rest.)

She seemed to fall asleep in an instant.

(We will have to talk to you at length.)

The flutes spoke only to Aubric now.

(They will try to kill you, one way or another. You challenge the existing system. In union there is strength.)

(You will benefit. We will all benefit. The war will end. And we will be masters of the castle once more.)

(The High Ones stole their magic from us. We simply want it back.)

(They tried to kill us, but we were too strong. So they denied us the world of light.)

(You will be our sword.)

Aubric was still confused. "But how? No matter what potential you may think I have, I am only one man."

(Bring us Judges.)

(The Judges deprived us of the ability to accept the light. We will once again rejoin the flesh.)

(Bring us Judges and we will help you in any way you wish.)

Aubric looked down at the sleeping Runt. He had no idea what he truly wanted. To see the Green victorious. To bring back his friends. Perhaps, more than anything else, he never wanted to have to fight again.

(When you know your true wishes, we will be there.)

Aubric felt his eyelids grow heavy.

(Enough.)

ERIC JACOBSEN WAS never very good in groups; especially happy groups. How could you be an outsider when everyone accepted you?

But Gontor had announced that their arrival was a Great

Event, perhaps the first of many Great Events to come. People actually talked to them during the celebration that followed. It mostly concerned things Jacobsen knew nothing about, except that it often seemed to involve some color or other. Without Summitch to act as his go-between, Jacobsen found himself completely out of his depth.

Aside from their few hours of sleep, he and Summitch had had no quiet time at all. Not that it much mattered. Jacobsen still wasn't sure why the small man had asked him to tag along. It was a partnership of convenience. Jacobsen needed Summitch to survive, Summitch needed Jacobsen for—what? Up until now, Jacobsen had been afraid to ask.

Now there was food and music and celebration. "At last!" smiling faces would cry as they stood before Jacobsen. People hugged him and slapped him on the shoulder. A couple of young women looked at him like they might want to do a lot more. At least at the front end, fulfilling a prophecy seemed like nothing but gravy. Jacobsen decided to enjoy it while he could. He'd find out the catch soon enough.

"Gontor!"

The statue was standing again. "We need to plan our futures."

Jacobsen never thought about his future. He was always too busy trying to get away from his past. Two ex-wives, bill collectors beyond counting, some gambling-debt collectors who didn't take bankruptcy as an excuse. And speaking of those who didn't take excuses, there was Mr. Smith. A number of the others in this crowd shared Smith's extremely pale complexion, but there was none of the coldness and cruelty that Smith held in his eyes. Jacobsen was very happy to have Smith out of his life. Right now, hiding in tunnels listening to a giant bronze statue seemed like a very good career choice.

The statue turned to that part of the crowd that included Jacobsen and Summitch and spread its arms wide. "I have hidden too long in the lower depths of our world. It is not your powers I demand so much as your personalities.''

The well-wishers stepped back a respectful distance from Jacobsen. He guessed it was time for some more mumbo jumbo.

The voice-from-everywhere spoke again, ''You do not believe me, Eric Jacobsen.''

He had never told the statue his name. Interesting that he would find this creepier than anything else.

''What do you want from me?'' Jacobsen asked.

''We always need a fool.''

''Gontor!'' the crowd agreed.

''It is a noble cause.'' The statue placed a bronze hand upon its chest. ''He who sees.''

The statue waved at Summitch, currently stuffing his face with food from one of the many banquet tables. ''He who schemes.''

The statue nodded at an open space immediately before the great throne on which he sat. There stood a large man dressed all in white save for a bright orange sash around his waist. The man held a sword so massive it would take two hands to lift.

''He who fights,'' Gontor continued, then waved to Jacobsen, ''and the noble fool. Together, we are a single entity. Should we remain together, we will persevere.''

So Jacobsen was the fool? He was surprised he didn't feel more insulted. At best in his life, he had played the fool a hundred times or more; it was how he got himself tied up with Smith in the first place. Yet it was the first time he'd ever been called a fool to his face. To be called a noble fool? In some ways, he supposed it was a promotion.

The statue waved its arms at the whole assemblage. ''And now I must make my final preparations to go forth into the world.''

''Gontor! Gontor! Gontor!'' the crowd chanted.

The musicians who had wandered through the crowd

started up again, flutes and strings and hand-held drums, all slightly atonal. Jacobsen thought they sounded sort of Chinese, but then he realized he had no idea what real Chinese instruments would sound like. The music was simply different, like so much else in this place.

Whatever they called the music, the new tune appeared to be an excuse for a wild dance. The music shifted from fast to slow to fast, causing the crowd to stomp wildly about one minute, then break off in couples to hold each other close the next. And Jacobsen was in the middle of it. He was swung around from partner to partner.

He found himself across from one attractive young woman whom he had spoken with before. Her gaze caught his own. She would not look away. She smiled. The music slowed, and the two gripped each other's shoulders, swinging about to something like a waltz.

The tempo shifted, and so did Jacobsen's partner. An older woman jumped up and down before him, kicking her heels first to one side and then the other. The music stopped, replaced by the drummer, drumming alone, and Jacobsen's new partner spun away. He looked to the next dancer in line.

The same pretty woman smiled up at him again. She had forced her way back in to be his partner again. When the tempo slowed, she held him more tightly than before. So this was what it was like to be favored by the local god? The day looked very promising.

Still he danced, faster now, step, kick, step, kick, fast and simple and exhilarating.

"Watch out!"

Jacobsen jerked away from his partner. He almost stumbled over Summitch! The small man frowned up at him. "Something is going to happen!"

Jacobsen had to shout to be heard over the music. "What do you mean?"

"The statue is gone," Summitch remarked.

Jacobsen looked over to the place of honor at the cavern's center. The great throne was still there, but the metal man was gone. Still, that could mean anything. Jacobsen smiled at his beautiful partner. Right this minute, he had other concerns.

"Good!" he called down to Summitch as he danced his partner away. Perhaps he could find some quiet corner of this place where he and this young lovely could become better acquainted.

The music stopped abruptly. The crowd was laughing and clapping. The young woman smiled up at him, her face radiant in the unnatural light.

The crowd grew quiet. She looked away from him for the first time. He glanced around, and saw that the crowd had parted behind him.

"Gontor!" the crowd called.

JACOBSEN TURNED BACK to his partner. The young woman no longer smiled at him. The expression on her face was one of regret. She took a step away.

"No!" he called. His fingers bunched into fists. He looked accusingly out at the now-quiet crowd. He had had so few moments of happiness in his life. True, this one was in no way earned, but he had so looked forward to leaving his cares behind if for only a few minutes. Perhaps there was still a way. He looked back to the woman, but she was gone. The crowd had pulled away from him and Summitch as well, so that they now stood a dozen feet away from any of the others.

"Gontor!" the crowd cheered again.

"There!" Summitch pointed behind Jacobsen.

Two men strode toward them through the opening in the crowd. One was the large warrior in white. The other was dressed in a heavy black robe complete with a cowl that hid most of his face in shadow. The robed man's face shown strangely where it did catch the light.

It took Jacobsen a minute to recognize the Great Gontor.

He pulled back his hood as he approached. Gontor still appeared made of bronze, but now he was only six feet tall.

"Do not be alarmed," the voice-from-everywhere remarked. Gontor still did not move his lips. "This is merely another one of my aspects."

"Believe me, I know all about that sort of thing," Summitch said.

Gontor nodded. "It is the only way the tunnels will accommodate me."

Jacobsen thought he was finally beginning to understand. The statue, or what was once the statue, would be physically accompanying them. Until now, he had thought all of Gontor's pronouncements were highly theoretical, taking place on some kind of astral plane or something. One of his ex-wives had been very involved in New Age crystals and stuff. Thanks to that, he guessed, when he heard certain things he had learned not to listen.

"So this destiny will be served by your traveling with us?" he asked.

Gontor nodded again. "More than one path can lead to the same destination."

"You call that an answer?" Summitch scowled. "This is why I hate traveling with enigmas."

The now six-foot-high statue chose to ignore the small man's remark. "This is Tsang," Gontor began with a nod at his companion. "He is a direct descendant of the House of Orange. He has no love of the war, or any of the ruling families. He lives only to hone his fighting skills. He listens, but will not speak. He has taken a vow of silence until his House is restored."

"Until his House is restored?" Summitch looked up to where the heavens might be if they were not obscured by miles of rock. "I am being tested."

"All of our abilities will be tested," Gontor agreed.

Tsang reached over his shoulder and pulled forth his great blade from a scabbard he wore strapped to his back.

As the sword whistled through the air, the blade burst into scarlet flame, carving brilliant figures in the air.

He returned the sword to its scabbard too quickly to see. But then, Jacobsen's eyes were still dazzled by the flames.

"I think I'll let the big fellow take the lead," Summitch said with an appreciative whistle.

Tsang only stared in return.

Gontor nodded. "Where others talk, he acts."

Jacobsen thought, seriously for the first time, about Gontor's earlier explanation. "So there will only be four of us?"

"While there is a certain strength in numbers, there is a greater strength in stealth."

Well, that sort of answered his question. Jacobsen decided to be even more direct. "So what are we going to do?"

"We will discover your talents along the way." Gontor nodded toward Jacobsen, then to each of the other two. "If we are to win, we are all indispensable."

Tsang folded his great, muscled arms across his equally impressive chest. Summitch continued to scowl. Jacobsen shrugged. At the very least, this was a lot more interesting than his last day job. It was a shame about that dancing partner, though.

"Now we leave." Gontor placed the hood back over his head. He waved the others forward. "We have the power. But the power does little good unless it in engaged with the world above. Our quest is not for the power. Our quest is for the world."

. 18 .

THE LADY KARMILLE DID NOT
stop until she was in the safety of her room. She had gotten
exactly what she wanted: permission from her father to
leave the Keep and to seek the assistance of a Judge.

She had gotten exactly what she wanted. She never
wanted anything again. Her father had not touched her, but
she could taste him in her mouth. She could barely think.
She needed a quiet place where she could gather her
thoughts and calm her heart. She dismissed all but her two
most trusted maids, and sat down to examine herself in her
favorite mirror.

She looked no different than she had an hour before.
Her skin was the pale, almost translucent color so favored
by the High Lords, her hair a dark mass of curls uncut for
the past five years. She would be deemed highly desirable,
if others were allowed to touch her.

None would touch her again!

She would make others suffer as her father had caused
her to suffer. When she closed her eyes, she saw his shaking hands tearing her undergarments, felt his quivering lips

slobbering against her cheek, her neck, her breast. She'd been so careful this time, getting her way without having to succumb. It made no difference. Her father's touch was always with her.

The lady Karmille prided herself on her control. She was respected and feared by most in the palace; all but her father and his close advisors. The less the advisors knew about her, the better. But she could not keep that distance with her father, the High Lord, the all powerful—

She shuddered. It was only after time with her father that her emotions threatened to overwhelm her.

Her first desire, as always, was to kill him. But she rejected that desire, as she had a thousand times before. The penalty for patricide was death, even for a member of the royal family; a law formulated by others like her father, others who wished to rule both bodies and minds.

But she did have other options. After all, her father was changing, and to her advantage.

She could see his vitality slipping away as the years finally tested the limits of the Judges' arts. He might be of too much use as a doddering, easily manipulated fool, with her positioned in the eyes of the royal court as the dutiful daughter, sacrificing herself for the good of the kingdom. She actually smiled as she thought of her father, so weak, perhaps, that he could no longer control his bodily functions, so that he might befoul himself and be forced to lie in it for hours, unable to speak, perhaps so weak he could barely move, but still aware of how his daughter laughed at him.

Under such circumstances, it might be worth letting him live for a very long time. She looked forward to her first meeting with Judge Sasseen. Perhaps she could arrange the Judge's assistance in ensuring her father's fate.

Such flights of fancy only raised her spirits for an instant. If she could not kill him, she could take out her anger on others. Sometimes, though, even that was not convenient.

She cursed her father as she stared at the pale face in the mirror. There was no place for the anger to go. There was only one way she might calm herself quickly. She quietly told her maids it was time. Quietly and efficiently, they hurt her in places where it would not show.

FEELING RESTORED, THE lady Karmille changed her costume again, choosing something more modest, in keeping with her first audience with a Judge.

She certainly did not want to wait about her room, or anywhere in the castle long enough for her father to make an appearance. She left her excuses behind as she fled her quarters. These were perilous times. She would use all haste to pursue her mission. Her father's needs would have to wait.

She told her maids not to be alarmed if she was gone for a while. Her mission was so urgent that, if possible, she and the Judge would leave immediately. If that were so, she doubted she would return for some time.

And then she was on her way. Every step away from her rooms, away from her father, raised her spirits. The lady Karmille was leaving her father's court behind.

She walked down the long corridors of the Royal Quarter of the Keep, past rooms once filled with her siblings, now empty, every one, their occupants dead or lost somewhere in the war. She realized a part of her had not expected her father to agree to her proposal. That he had, meant the war went very badly indeed.

Now she made haste to—escape. The word surprised her as she thought of it, but it was the only word that fit. She was using her father's authority to escape from her father's power. Her haste in seeking out the Judge meant that she herself had had no time to prepare.

Then again, how did you prepare to meet a Judge?

While they mingled every day at Court, the Judges kept very much to themselves when not conducting official business. There had been women Judges in the past, but today all seven of the Judges of the Grey were men. Beyond that, even Karmille's spies knew very little.

Very few entered a Judge's chambers and returned alive. She had had an elder cousin, Lila, a minor hanger-on at the royal court, but a beautiful woman, and one of the few who had been kind to Karmille as a child. But Lila had the misfortune to have caught the fancy of one of the younger Judges; a double misfortune, for she was not of a high enough position in the Court to turn that fancy aside.

Karmille remembered how Lila had changed over the months that the Judge pursued her. First, all the joy was drained from her, replaced by a nervous energy that seemed to keep her constantly in motion. Then the energy was drained from Lila as well, and she became still and secretive, favoring the shadows in her room.

The last time Karmille had seen her, Lila seemed so pale as to be almost transparent, as if she would become one more white figure on the dramatic tapestries that covered the halls. And then she was gone. No one knew where. No one dared to speak of it. Sometimes, in the months that followed, Karmille thought she could hear her cousin calling in the halls looking for a way to be free of the Judge, but Karmille never saw her again.

She walked quickly from the Royal Quarters to the Judges' Quarters. The two castes had always kept separate quarters on opposite sides of the Keep, for mutual safety, she imagined, or through mutual distrust.

She skirted the public rooms at the Keep's center, careful to stay away from any of the places where she might encounter her father. At the far end of the public space was another corridor, which led to the suites of the Judges. She took a deep breath as she stepped beyond her father's realm. Before her she saw twin doors, a dozen feet across and equally high, made from beaten silver, the only metal rumored to be impervious to the Judges' magicks. A pair of the High Lord's guards stood before the doorway, barring her way.

"Lady Karmille," she announced in the firmest voice she could muster, "to see the Judges with permission of the High Lord."

The guards bowed briefly and opened the two great doors that separated one world from the other. The doors closed behind Karmille as soon as she had stepped within. The hallway here was a mirror image of that in the Royal Quarters, a broad, high, straight corridor that continued for hundreds of feet. But the royal hallway was crowded with tapestries and statues, live guards and ornamental suits of armor. This hall was bare stone, without a soul in sight.

Karmille's footsteps rang hollowly in the great empty hall. She glanced back at the entryway. There were no guards at all on this side of the door. With the power of the Judges, none were needed.

As was appropriate to his station, Sasseen's suite would be the second largest, and the second from the great doors. She passed the resplendent door of the High Judge, a plate of gold ten feet high on which was beaten a roaring lion, then moved quickly down the hall toward the second. Sasseen's door was a complicated design of gold and wood, showing a bolt of lightning crashing into a mountain range. Though quite ornate, it was not nearly so grand as that of his superior. All was rank and privilege in the Court, even among the Judges.

The door opened as she arrived, even though there was no footman or other servant visible to open it. It was a trick to humble her. Judge Sasseen, then, didn't know her very well at all. Beyond her father, she was the only one in the court of the Grey who would not be humbled.

The door opened to another great hallway, but a hall like none Karmille had ever seen. The walls of the corridor were made of smoke, a dark, roiling barrier to either side. The smoke bulged in places, pushing against the spell that held it in place, as if it hid darker things eager to escape. Kar-

mille had to admit it was a very effective introduction to
the Judge. She walked quickly down the passageway between the undulating walls, wondering if Sasseen's apartments might ever become more substantial.

Then the smoke simply vanished to reveal the great expanse beyond.

Even Karmille was surprised. It seemed not so much a
room as a great cavern, a space far too large to be contained
within the Judges' Quarters of the palace, a space perhaps
as large as the palace itself. Karmille almost smiled. So that
was what the smoke had been about, a screen to mask the
Judge's true intentions. While she had been distracted by
the billowing walls, Sasseen had brought her someplace
else, no doubt to one of those chambers immediately beneath the Grey Keep proper. Well, Karmille, too, had mas-
tered some simple transport spells. Indeed, she had even
used them to bring Aubric and the gnarlyman to her chambers. The Judge would have to do better than this.

She stepped forward into the great chamber, walking
between twin pools of fire. Great gouts of flame roared out
toward the ceiling, first from one pool, then the other. She
had no reaction at all, at least outwardly. All this spectacle
was beginning to try her patience.

"Sasseen?" she called. There was no response. She approached a third pool of a different nature.

A haze formed before her, as if this newest pool contained nothing but fog. She could almost make out shapes
within the mists, faces perhaps, the eyes wide, the lips
curled back in terror. She heard a sound now, distant and
low, disturbing nonetheless, the sound of pain. Perhaps
these were the voices of all those who had caused Sasseen
displeasure.

She thought, for an instant, that she saw her cousin's
face in the mist. Was one of the voices Lila's?

"You are the one who wished to see me."

Karmille turned at the sound of the new voice. There,
standing next to the pool of pain, was the Judge, dressed

in a tight-fitting suit of black crossed with threads of a deep
red—the color of blood. One sleeve bore a band of Grey,
symbol of his allegiance to the House of her father. His
features were regular. His face might be considered handsome, the unwrinkled visage of a young man barely Karmille's age. His face was a lie. His eyes were not those of
a young man. When he looked at her, his gaze seemed far
older than even her father's.

It was Karmille's turn to bow. "Judge Sasseen. I have
come to ask your help in a matter of some importance."

"I have been instructed to aid you in all ways," Sasseen
replied. From the lack of interest in his voice, it was obviously not his wish to do so.

She would not be deterred, either by fire or by lack of
interest. "There are unauthorized magicks at work in this
court," she began.

He stared at her with those aged, colorless eyes. "Yours
among them."

She felt the slightest moment of shock at his knowledge.
He knew of her little spells, which she had tried to hide.
But then, why would he not know? She was a rank beginner
compared to someone of Sasseen's skill. What would he
do with this information?

The Judge, having now shown his superior position, allowed himself the slightest of smiles, the teasing grin of a
young man at play. "This is not the time to discipline anyone. The laws on magic are old and strict and not very
realistic in a world embroiled in never-ending war. Conflict,
if allowed to continued unchecked, will eventually destroy
everything."

It was Karmille's turn to smile. "It seems to me that
conflict may also lead to opportunity."

Sasseen nodded graciously, as if truly acknowledging
Karmille for the first time. "No doubt the reason that both
of us are here."

"I wish to gain more control over my life," she admitted. "The honor of killing spies and traitors will certainly help my position."

"I wish a control outside the walls of the Grey Keep. In this we have similar purposes. That is why you are here."

He acted as if he had a choice in the matter! This Judge's attitude was beginning to disturb Karmille. No one, with the exception of her father, ever talked to her in such a tone. "You are still obliged to obey royalty."

The Judge actually laughed at that! "There are ways to avoid that. Forgetfulness is the simplest of spells. Our whole lives are made up of forgetting; the magic just nudges it along. If I wished it, your father would forget whatever you told him. You yourself would never remember your plans. And I would get away with it. The High Judge might detect some tampering in your father, if he knew just what to look for, and would take the time away from his own machinations; a very doubtful proposition. You, of course, have already alienated most of the Court. No one would bother to look for it in you."

"We are the High Ones!" Karmille insisted. "Our blood is too pure for your magic!"

"The lady knows her history," the Judge acknowledged. "So it was established at the beginning of this war, a thousand years ago. The Judges could not kill the High Lords. Their sorcery would turn on them and kill the Judges instead."

Karmille still sensed a certain mockery in his tone. "And is that not true today?"

"You have lived in the High Court long enough to know that there are many versions of the truth. The High Lords themselves commended us to find new ways that we might attack their enemies, who are High Lords themselves. Many discoveries might be made in a thousand years."

Karmille regarded the Judge silently. His talk skirted treason. If he wanted to enjoy his superiority, she would let him, for now. Every man had his weak points, Judges

included. Sooner or later, she would find them, and she
would control him.

"And what are we to do with your father, my lady?"
the Judge continued. "He is a very foolish man for one so
clever, and his folly will be his downfall."

What was he talking about? Karmille did not come here
to discuss her father. Still, she found herself asking, "What
folly?"

The Judge leaned forward in the slightest of bows, a
mockery of manners.

"You, my lady, are his folly."

She felt the first tinges of panic. What did this Judge
know of her father's secrets? She had always controlled the
world around her; but that world was very small, only a
corner of the castle. Only now did she realize this Judge
was a step beyond that control.

"I understand that my knowledge might upset you,"
Judge Sasseen continued graciously. "Do not look so
alarmed. It is only recently that I have turned my attentions
to you. I assure you that usually I have other concerns that
occupy my time."

Karmille was outraged. She was so angry that she could
not speak. What was this man doing to her? She had not
let her guard down since she was a child, even before her
father began to share his favors.

"I also understand why you told your father you had to
come here; all that business about the infiltration of the
Grey. The threat is very real, and probably far greater than
you have presented."

This fellow would constantly surprise her. Now that the
talk turned away from her, Karmille found her heart calming, her breathing restored. She decided on a continued silence.

"Allow me to speak for a moment. Some of this, you
no doubt know." The Judge watched her as he spoke.
"This war would not continue if the High Lords did not
find it to their advantage. Still, even they are finding their

resources tried. The Judges have much to do with the continuing battle, for their arts are most tried, and most rewarded, during times of conflict. But even the Judges cannot control the worlds forever. It was inevitable that we will enter a new age. The war will end. Even the Judges cannot prevent that. But the war must end in the proper High Lord's favor.''

Karmille decided a polite question might be in order. "So you already know a great deal of what is happening?"

Sasseen sighed. "Only when you are a Judge do you realize how little you truly know."

He regarded Karmille for a moment in silence.

"You are the important one here. You are the High Lord's daughter."

He smiled again, ever so slightly.

"It is only through an alliance like this that I might act. Without the protection of the royal family, the moment I absent myself from the Circle of Judges, the others of my profession would most likely destroy me. As I would do to them under most circumstances. An absent Judge is not to be trusted—unless his movements may be accounted for. And I will be serving the High Lord himself!" He chuckled, as though he found the whole thing incredibly droll.

The lady Karmille paused again to assess her situation. She looked at the smiling Sasseen, and wished to hurt him deeply, for his lack of respect, his mockery, his audacity at delving into her deepest secrets. But even killing the Judge would give her only a moment's pleasure. Her own self-interest directed her elsewhere. She had long ago learned the patience to survive the attentions of her father. Patience would serve her with Judge Sasseen as well.

She was happy, at least, that the Judge could see some advantages to their alliance. The extent of his knowledge about her had made her feel much more vulnerable than she would have liked, although she noticed he had followed none of his early surprises with details. Perhaps he was merely feeling out her most vulnerable points. She reas-

sured herself again that, over time, she would discover his
weaknesses as well.

She had had enough of talk. Her father would be done
with his Court business soon.

"So, we go then?" she prompted.

"Not quite yet." Sasseen studied the grey band on his
sleeve. "Sometimes, we become too involved in our
games."

She noticed that he had phrased it in such a way that
she might be included as well.

"I understand you had one of the soldiers of the Green,"
he went on.

So the conversation turned to Aubric. Unlike the other
surprises, she had expected something like this. The Judges
had spies and methods of their own.

"Do not be surprised," he added. So perhaps he
couldn't read her every expression after all. "I will explain
my motives. It is best, I think, that we do not keep secrets
about the job at hand.

"There were three soldiers in all who had wandered too
close to the edge of our territory. I suspect they had no idea
exactly where they were. Our own forces caught them completely off guard. Delightful, really. It is so rare these days
that I am able to acquire fresh specimens.

"The liveliest of the three escaped, at least for a time,
until you caught him with your naughty little magic. Then
he escaped again, I understand." The Judge laughed very
softly, flexing his fingers as if waiting to grab something.
"Won't we have fun with him when we finally catch him?

"I told you there were three. I kept the others for my
own purposes. One of them is quite dead; the other—"
The Judge smiled. "—not quite."

Now that the shock was wearing off, Karmille noticed
her impatience was returning. "Why do you tell me all
this?"

"They will be coming along."

"Both of them?" She would have to contend not only

with the Judge, but a menagerie of his creatures as well? Whether or not this Judge was loyal to the House of Grey, the lady Karmille was feeling in need of some protection. She wondered if she might bring some of those loyal to herself simply to tip back the scales.

"Well," the Judge continued quickly, almost as if in apology, "neither one of them will be under their own control. Consider it a little surprise when we find your escaped soldier. Their presence may lead him into error."

The Judge grinned at the thought.

"One or two members of your personal guard might be useful as well," he went on, as if he read her mind. "Magic cannot accomplish everything."

"My father—" Karmille began.

Sasseen shook his head. "Your father will be delayed for as long as necessary. Again, I must be subtle here. There are others involved. But none will know of your final trip to your private quarters." The grin again. "I may even be able to provide you with a shortcut."

"And then what?" Karmille asked.

"As you no doubt already know, we are some distance beneath your father's castle already. Once you have obtained your bodyguard, we will leave immediately. We have much to discover, and very little time."

So Karmille would get everything she wanted. She wished she could be happier about it.

"Hurry now, my lady!" Sasseen called after her as she turned to go. "Who knows? Perhaps we can turn our whole world upside down!"

She was surrounded by the walls of smoke and the laughter of Judge Sasseen.

Very well. He could feel important in this little world of his own making. Just as she had left the safety of her small kingdom, the Judge would be doing the same, both of them traveling far from the power of the Grey.

Karmille smiled as the laughter faded away. If the world turns upside down, who knows who will end up on top?

"U H—BOSS?"

There was no peace in this world. Roman Petranova looked up from his card game to see Larry the Louse hovering over him.

Now he couldn't even play cards. What was it, Tuesday night? What the hell ever happened on a Tuesday? Just the time for a little friendly family game. He looked from his cousin Sal to his nephew Vinnie to his second cousin Mike, shaking his head with weariness of the world. He even looked over to the corner of the banquet room where Johnny T and Roman's no good brother-in-law, Earl, were watching the ball game. Except that right now everyone's eyes were on the Louse. Roman decided to join the club. He looked back to Larry.

"What is it now?"

Larry rubbed at a pimple on his neck. "Mr. Smith wants to see you."

He felt the annoyance stirring deep down in his gut. "What you bothering me for? Roman Petranova don't go anywhere for anyone."

But Larry didn't go away.

"No. Smith is here."

Roman put down his cards. "Really?" He didn't know whether to be outraged or honored. Before this, he'd never known Smith to go anywhere for anybody, either. But to just show up outside his private room at Delvecchio's, to interrupt his card game without any notice, showed a certain lack of respect.

Roman looked around at the others in the room.

"How'd he even know I would be here?"

Everybody got that it-wasn't-me expression. Everybody but Johnny T, that is, who like usual had no expression at all. It didn't matter. They all looked guilty as sin.

It was no big secret where he spent his time. Hell, Roman Petranova had his ways to find out things; he was sure Smith did, too. It was this sort of thing that proved Smith had balls. If you wanted to play with the big boys, you always had to know the score.

"Boss, I need to do something here!"

Larry had broken out in a sweat. It wasn't even that hot. Smith had that effect on some people.

Roman Petranova had made a decision. Smith needed to know who was running the show, at least at Delvecchio's. "Smith can wait. It wasn't like he was invited."

That just made Larry more antsy. "I don't think—"

Johnny T stepped forward. "I'll handle him."

Roman Petranova nodded. "Tell him to wait a few minutes, then I'll see him." He took a long puff on his cigar, then added, "If he gives you any trouble, don't break anything permanent. We may still have to work with the guy."

"You will see me now."

Roman didn't even have to turn around to know that Smith was in the room. He didn't bother pulling his own gun either, since six others in the room had already drawn theirs. He gave it a beat, then turned around slowly.

Smith was standing just inside the door.

Roman sighed. "What do you think you're doing?"

Smith's pale eyes glared at him from under the shadow of his hat brim. "I have business that cannot wait."

That was another thing, Roman thought. "Do you think you can remove your hat? Show some respect. We have a way of doing business here, you know." He nodded to the six others with their weapons drawn; handguns mostly, except for Johnny T, who favored a sawed-off shotgun. "You do business our way, or else."

Smith still didn't take off his hat.

"I had a connection with your son, Ernest," he said instead.

Ernest? Nobody called Ernie that. It couldn't have been much of a connection. Still, Roman didn't like this guy making deals behind his back.

"I didn't give you permission to do that."

"I do not need permission."

His nephew Vinnie jumped up from the table and started waving his gun around. "Let me shoot him, Uncle Roman."

Vinnie was almost as much of a hothead as Roman's son. Out of all that generation, only Joe really had a calm head on his shoulders. It was a shame he was Roman's sister's boy, what with Ernie next in line to take over should anything ever happen to Roman. Which was why Roman Petranova had to live forever—if he could ever figure out how.

Roman sighed. "Not yet, Vinnie."

"It has become more difficult to make contact," Smith continued. "Some times, my connections can be dangerous."

Roman wasn't going to admit he didn't understand that; the words at least. The threatening undertone came through loud and clear. So this guy was going to come here and threaten all of them?

"I'll show him dangerous!" Vinnie clicked off the safety as he swung his .44 around to point at Smith's chest.

"I think not," Smith said softly.

Vinnie's arms started to shake. He seemed to be having a problem pointing his gun.

"I do not like to exert this kind of control," Smith added. Even though the stranger was staring at his nephew, Roman knew Smith was talking to him.

Things definitely weren't right with Vinnie. His whole body was shaking. He didn't look too happy about it, either. Gun still in both hands, he jerked away from Smith, back toward the table piled high with cards and chips.

"Uncle Roman?" Vinnie asked doubtfully. Roman noticed that his nephew's gun was now trained on his uncle.

"He cannot help but pull the trigger." Smith's lips pulled back from his teeth in something like a smile.

If there was one thing Roman Petranova hated more than two-timing bastards, it was smug two-timing bastards. Smith qualified on both counts.

"Take it easy, Vinnie," he said softly.

"Uncle Roman!" Vinnie shouted, his whole body one continuous spasm. "I can't hold it back!"

Roman glanced at the others in the room. All of them still had their guns on Smith. With any luck, his nephew would be shaking so wildly he wouldn't be able to hit anything. Still, this approach to Smith may not have been one of his best decisions.

"If I increase my control," Smith said softly, "he won't shake at all." He took a step closer to Vinnie. The kid's spasms were already decreasing. Vinnie moaned as his gun pointed straight at Roman's heart.

"Sorry, Vinnie." Roman could see no way out of it. "You gotta shoot him, Johnny."

Johnny raised his shotgun.

"Use your Luger," Roman told him.

"I gotta pull the trigger!" Vinnie wailed. Every muscle in Vinnie's body was tight with tension. He looked like his arms were going to snap.

Johnny dropped the rifle and pulled the gleaming Luger

from his shoulder holster. The weapon was one of his father's war souvenirs, and Johnny only used it for special
occasions. He pointed it right at Vinnie's heart.

"In the leg!" Roman added hastily. "I kill him, his
mother would never forgive me."

"I can take you over one by one," Smith replied.

"The rest of you shoot Smith." Roman tried to puff on
his cigar, but the damn thing had gone out. He stared at
their visitor. "We ain't big on mumbo jumbo here. Nobody's dead yet." He waved at Vinnie. "So you kill me,
we kill you and Vinnie. What the hell's that gonna prove?"

Smith continued to stare at Vinnie. "You have let down
your side of the bargain."

"What do you mean?"

"Your nephew, Joseph, has not followed instructions."

"How do you know what the hell Joe is doing?"

"My methods, while not yet perfect, are very thorough."

"Uncle Roman!" Vinnie wailed.

Roman had had enough of this. "Can Vinnie put down
the gun?"

Smith's eyes flicked away from Roman's nephew for an
instant. "If your men do the same."

It was the best way out. "You can let him go now, and
we'll forget this happened. If not . . ." He let the threat
hang in the air.

Smith looked away from Vinnie. Roman's nephew
groaned and sank to his knees. His gun fell to the carpet.

Roman Petranova nodded. Guns came down all around.

He exhaled slowly. It had been a long time since he'd
been involved in an old-fashioned pissing contest. And he
didn't like it any more now than he had back then.

When he was younger, Roman Petranova would have
pulled out his own gun and shot Smith between the eyes,
just for the way the Pale Man had made him look in front
of his men. But with age came diplomacy. There were still
a few things he could get out of Smith before he shot him.

"Joe is very dependable, very levelheaded," he said instead. "Whatever he did, he has a reason."

"I do not care about reasons. I care about results. I am involved in something you will never understand."

Smith would be surprised exactly what Roman Petranova might understand. He'd gotten an advantage over cops, judges, and other crooks by playing stupid and acting smart. He could do it with Smith just as well.

Everybody else in the room either still held on to their guns or had dumped them on a table close at hand. They were all waiting for any excuse to shoot.

Roman needed something to ease the tension. "I understand that you come from someplace pretty far away."

He figured it had to be Russia or someplace. Organized crime was showing up everywhere.

"Farther than you will ever know," Smith replied.

That mystery shit again. He decided to let it pass.

"All right. I've been willing to cut you a little slack. But no more. My men work for me. No more of this hypnosis, voodoo, whatever it is. If we do something, it's because we both want to."

Smith hesitated a moment before answering. "Very well. But no one cheats me and lives."

"I'll talk to Joe. We'll work this out."

"If you follow my orders, you could find this very rewarding. If you don't, and I lose everything"—Smith looked at all those around the room—"you will be very sorry."

Smith pulled his hat brim down so that his eyes were hidden and walked backwards from the room.

No one spoke until the swinging doors had shut behind him.

Vinnie started. "Uncle Roman! What did he do to me?"

"Are you going to let him get away with that?" Vinnie's father, Earl, spoke up for the first time.

"For now." Uncle Roman looked at everybody in the

room. "Put your guns away. We're having a friendly game of cards."

He waited for all the guns to disappear before he continued.

"Sure, we could have gotten Smith. But he's into some weird shit. I didn't want anybody here getting hurt. The Petranova family only gets burned once. As long as he behaves, we'll play along. It's worth a lot of money. But the next time he tries something—" Roman Petranova made a gun with his thumb and forefinger and fired.

"Do you think we can really kill the guy?" Sal asked.

Roman actually allowed himself a smile. "Everybody can be killed. Smith included. Why else would he have backed down?"

"So what do we do now?" Johnny T sat back down near the TV, but Roman noted he was keeping the shotgun nearby.

"Joe will call in," Roman replied. "He always does. We'll check out what happened."

"What about Smith?" Vinnie asked. "What if Joe has double-crossed him?"

Roman Petranova sighed. There might be no way around it. "We may have to let Joe go."

JACKIE PORTER HAD left the hospital rather than talk to the Chief again. That whole scene up in the intensive care unit had really shaken her.

What had the Chief been thinking? Even a totally green rookie like Jackie could tell the mystery man had been calling the shots. Then the kid Brian had run from the ICU, and, as far as Jackie could tell, completely disappeared. Not that a kid could disappear for long. But what would happen when the mystery man caught up with Brian?

Jackie Porter missed her traffic grids and charts. She was used to a different sort of problem; the way you figured out an accident. You talked to people, got their stories. You checked for mechanical damage, studied hospital reports. Speed, road conditions, time of day, blood alcohol levels; these things could be codified.

She knew it was the details that kept her sane. The details let her put up with all the inane crap she got from the other deputies, the jokes, the ignorance, even the constant demands for coffee. It didn't matter what the other guys on the force thought as long as she got to do her little problems.

Now, though, she had lost a boy and couldn't trust a man. She felt like she'd been in an accident herself.

She sat at her desk in the station. After the hospital, she hadn't known where else to go. She had opened her top drawer, but she couldn't even look at the forms. What paperwork did you fill out when your boss was working for the wrong side of the law?

She saw movement out of the corner of her eye. She looked up. The Chief was standing in front of her.

"Porter. I need to see you. Now."

Everybody else in the room was suddenly very busy doing something else. This was it then. She'd be looking for a new job tomorrow. It would be easier that way, really—if only she knew that Brian was safe.

She followed the Chief quickly into his office. He waved her to a seat across from his desk and closed the door.

He sat heavily and looked not at her but at a picture on his desk; the wife and kids. He kept it there even though his wife had left him and the kids had both grown up. Maybe, Porter thought, it reminded him of happier, simpler times.

He glanced over at her at last. She had never seen him looking so tired.

"You don't have to say anything." His voice was low, with none of the usual bluster. "I'm the one who's wrong."

This was a side of the Chief she'd never seen before.

"You don't always do things the way you should. I thought I had a chance to get back some of—" He shook

his head. "You don't need to hear this." He rested his
upper arms on the desk, both his hands balled into fists.
"You want to do something that would make you big in
town. Make your ex-wife sorry she left you, let your kids
know they can be proud of you." His eyes had wandered
back to the photo. "Suddenly, you're sitting there over your
head."

He paused, then added, "You never make enough on a
cop's wages. Never listen to a guy like Smith."

The Chief looked up at Porter. "You got a couple days
vacation coming to you. By the time you're back, this will
all have blown over."

She had forgotten. Three months ago she had put in to
take her first long weekend since joining the force. She had
been busy making plans until this thing with Brian had
come up. She looked at her watch. Had it only been a few
hours? It felt like a month.

The Chief looked at a paper on his desk. "I know it
starts the day after tomorrow, but you have my permission
to take off early."

She couldn't let it go that easily. "I'd like to know what
happened to Brian Clark."

The Chief leaned back in his chair. "He's with his girlfriend. They're on a bus, going to Gravesville. Don't ask
me how I know." He stopped, and shrugged. "I think
Smith has people working for him in the bus station. He
probably has people working for him everywhere."

He sighed. "There's things I can't tell you. Things that
are probably going to come out anyways. I made a mistake.
A big mistake. I thought I could handle it easy. I'm going
to take care of it, no matter what it takes."

He took the photo of his family and placed it, picture
side down, on his desk. He looked up at Porter.

"You've got to get away from all this. Get out of here,
now."

•   •   •

"OH, JESUS," ERNIE kept saying over and over again. "Oh, Jesus!"

Joe Beast would get this situation under control. Ernie would never stop moaning. Brian and Karen looked like they were going to bolt at any second. But nobody else could do anything as long as Joe was driving ninety miles an hour. For now, the only thing that kept them together was that they were getting away from something worse.

The truck stop was out of sight, and this looked like a normal stretch of the interstate. Joe would feel much better, though, as soon as he passed another car.

He looked in the rearview mirror, past the two kids huddled on one side of the backseat. The road was empty. At least no one was following them.

That whole thing back at the truck stop had totally creeped him out. The way those people had jerked around like puppets; if Joe hadn't shown up, they would have killed the kids for sure.

It was funny. Until that moment, he wasn't even sure he was going to help Brian and Karen. But, hell. He still had a sense of honor. Not Uncle Roman's honor, or his cousin's honor, and certainly not that creep Smith's honor. It was his own personal code. That was the one thing that he needed to survive.

The biggest problem had been the bus driver, Vern. He had claimed the two kids were his responsibility. Flo's husband had called out that another car had shown up on the far side of the restaurant. From the way it careened into the parking lot, he was sure it was driven by one of Smith's zombies. Flo had said they might be showing up for hours. Apparently, this sort of thing had happened before at the truck stop. Polka music had blared from the open restaurant door. Roll out the barrel, we'll have a barrel of fun.

Karen was the one who'd made the final decision. She had looked straight at Joe and said, "We can trust them." It was like she could see something inside Joe that even he wasn't aware of.

"Well, then," Flo had said, "you'd best get the hell out of here."

Vern had relented then, and Joe had gotten Ernie and the teens in the car, and taken Flo's advice.

And no one had followed them, at least not so far. Apparently, Smith's loony powers only threatened you if you stayed put.

Right this minute, Joe felt like driving forever.

"Where are you taking us?" Brian asked from the backseat, his voice so quiet Joe could barely hear him.

Joe had no idea. But he had to say something. He'd try to keep it light, and figure it out as they went along.

"Hey, we non-zombies have to stick together."

Brian frowned and pointed at Joe's cousin. "How about him?"

Brian had a point. "Ernie? He's only a zombie part-time. I'm hoping to get him to retire." Joe shook his head. Even he thought he sounded lame. "Look, Brian. Karen. I was sent to find you, but nobody told me anything about those creeps—"

"Oh, Jesus!" Ernie moaned.

Joe glanced over at his cousin. Enough was enough. "Will you just shut the fuck up!" He glanced back into the rearview mirror. "Sorry kids. Things were out of control back there. Things were happening that I never would have agreed to. We had to do something. No matter what this Smith guy wants, we're not going to hurt you."

"You shot my father."

"Well, yeah. But I didn't mean to. He surprised me and grabbed for the gun. It was a pretty gutsy thing to do for some guy from the suburbs." It was also a stupid thing to do, but Joe didn't think the kid would appreciate hearing that right now.

"Sometimes my father surprises me, too," Brian admitted.

"Yeah." Joe glanced over at Ernie. "Families are like that."

Karen spoke up for the first time since they'd gotten into the car. "What about Smith?"

"Do you know why he wants us?" Brian asked.

Joe shook his head. "I don't have a clue. When they gave me this job, they tossed the reasons out with the trash."

They drove in silence for a couple of minutes.

"My name's Joe," he said to fill the space. Back at the truck stop, there hadn't been time for introductions.

"Oh, Jesus," Ernie repeated.

"This is my cousin Ernie. He's a little upset."

That started Ernie going. "I got no idea what I was doing back there. What if I do it again? How do I stop it?"

"It's like sleepwalking or something. You stopped when I drenched you with water." Joe found himself smiling at the thought. "I don't think it was the water so much as the surprise. That Smith guy isn't going to control you so long as I can shock you out of it."

"I always thought you were never supposed to wake a sleepwalker," Brian piped up from the backseat.

Kids. Joe shook his head. "That's in a normal world, Brian. I think we left normal a long time ago."

"Well, we're away from that place now," Brain said. "You can let us off someplace, and we'll disappear."

"Do you really think you can get away from Smith?" Karen asked.

Frankly, Joe was surprised that they had made it this far. But what did he really know about Smith? Only that he had this posthypnotic suggestion thing that he kept working on Ernie. And, from what had happened back at the truck stop, Ernie wasn't the only one Smith was jerking around. But Smith couldn't do everything. Otherwise he would never have hooked up with Roman Petranova in the first place. Joe was beginning to suspect Smith was a one-trick pony. It was a pretty good trick, but Joe bet Smith could be beaten.

"Are we your prisoners?" Brian asked.

Joe was wondering when it would get around to this.

"I don't think so," he answered frankly. "Right now, I don't think I'm working for anyone."

"Joe? When my dad hears about this, he's gonna kill us. Oh, Jesus!"

Joe wished he could pour water on Ernie all over again. Smith didn't play by the rules. Uncle Roman would have to understand.

"Who is this Smith guy anyways?" Ernie whined.

"I think I know," the girl, Karen, piped up. "Mrs. Mendeck would talk about this all the time."

"Mrs. Mendeck?" Joe asked.

"She lives across the hall from me."

Joe realized they were talking about the old lady with the black hole. "Oh yeah, I think we met Mrs. Mendeck."

"Anyway, Mrs. Mendeck said she knew all about where he came from. She says he wants to control the world. But he's overreaching himself. He comes from somewhere else. He doesn't know the rules around here. That's how we're going to beat him."

"The rules? What rules?" Ernie wailed. "Somewhere else? Oh, Jesus."

Maybe, Joe thought, if he just ignored him. "So where is this somewhere else?"

"Mrs. M never told me. She's real good at telling stories. She's not so good at answering questions."

It seemed to Joe that nobody seemed very fond of answering questions these days. This whole thing was really beginning to piss him off.

"Well, if I have my way, Smith isn't going to do anything to anybody! As long as you kids are with us, you're going to be safe. You have my word. I'm going to get my uncle Roman to give his word, too."

"How are you going to do that?" Ernie put his fist in his mouth and moaned.

Joe waved at the man in the seat next to him. "All he has to do is take one look at Ernie, here. Ernie's his son.

And, in case you haven't noticed, Ernie isn't feeling too good. Once Roman Petranova knows that Smith was screwing with his own flesh and blood, the deal's off.''

Even Ernie nodded at that. ''That sounds okay. But how do we handle Smith?''

Wait a moment. Maybe Joe had an even better idea.

''You weren't just riding the bus. I saw you using the phone. You were trying to get in touch with somebody, right?''

''Yeah,'' Karen agreed. ''Mrs. Mendeck.''

''Well,'' Joe suggested, ''why not try calling Mrs. Mendeck again?''

· 20 ·

AUBRIC HAD WITNESSED THE scene before him far too many times.

Two once-great armies faced each other on opposite hills. Who would triumph, the Green or the Grey?

Usually, he had been on the winning side. He had always lived to fight another day. For what? To stand here, day after day, until the day his luck deserted him?

He studied the ranks of soldiers on the opposite hill, knowing that his own decimated army looked much the same. Where once there might have been thousands, now there were only hundreds. Nearly all were seasoned soldiers who had cheated death a dozen times. Scattered among them were a few raw recruits, conscripted too young, insufficiently trained. Most would be the first to die. A few would survive the battle and leave their youth behind.

How many battles had Aubric seen? So many that he had lost count. He had spent little more than a year on the battlefield. It felt to him like at least ten lifetimes.

He turned and looked to where the Green Command conferred above him and his fellow foot soldiers, high up on the ridge. One man held everybody else's attention. Aubric could not see his face clearly at this distance, but could tell from the forceful movements that the one in the center was Etton, first son of the High Lord.

Aubric had played with Etton as a child. Because of that, some of the others said, Aubric had received special treatment. At first he'd resented such accusations. Now he was too weary to care. Anything that would keep him alive, from special treatment to pure dumb luck, was fine with him.

The High Ones who directed the battle were the sons of each lord, many only a few years older than the youngest recruits. They were each flanked by their personal Judges, who countered each other's sorcerous strategies, trying to give each side some advantage. Aubric and the other soldiers had been trained early on not to watch the fantastic swirls of color and light mixing overhead, a second battle raging above their own.

There was always a war, but it ran hot and cold. These days there were more skirmishes than battles, and Tevvard believed that even these smaller engagements would soon be over. The remaining powers needed to regroup; not so much a truce as a resting period, as the different factions rebuilt their strength.

Aubric had no time for theories. He lived to fight, his two closest companions, Lepp and Savignon, by his side, closer than brothers. Somehow, he felt they would always survive. He was charmed. All of the Green were charmed. They would prevail.

And if they did not?

There was no surrender, only death.

The signal came from above to close ranks.

They started down the hill with a roar, and an answering roar echoed from the other side. Aubric ran forward, Lepp to his left, Savignon his right, one eye on the battle ahead, the other on his footing, careful not to trip over a rock or a hidden root. He looked up, and they were face to face with the enemy. Did it take an hour or the blink of an eye?

His sword sliced beneath his opponent's guard. He kicked the dying man away as he parried another blow. His opponent staggered forward, sliced between the ribs by another man of the Green. Aubric nodded his thanks and was on to his next contest. He faced someone years younger, barely a boy. He shook as Aubric approached him and dropped his sword, falling to his knees and begging for mercy. Aubric hit the back of the boy's head with the hilt of his sword. The boy fell face forward to the earth. Perhaps he would live, perhaps he would not. There was no time for mercy in the middle of battle.

Aubric found himself in a minute of calm in the midst of chaos. He glanced to either side. Where were his comrades?

He had become separated from the rest of the Green.

The Grey were all around him. He would be overwhelmed.

He was surrounded by darkness.

Aubric opened his eyes. It was a dream. He was in a tunnel deep underground. Though he had been away from battle since he had come into these tunnels, the battle was always with him.

He closed his eyes again. This time, he dreamed of light.

He had been too long in the tunnels. Now he'd even lost the sputtering torches to the eerie green glow of the dancing lights. He longed for open space, and the delicate blue of the real sky, or a thousand stars looking like a field of wildflowers in the cloudless sky of night.

So he dreamed. He was aware of colors and shapes just out of sight, as if he were frozen in that moment between when the eye sees a thing and the mind puts a name to it. And beyond that obscure wash of shape and form was something else, an illumination so great it could turn the darkness of the tunnels into day, a single point of light no larger than his thumb, but as bright as the sun.

He opened his eyes. This was where he was going, to find the light.

Runt stood above him, silhouetted by the strange half-light of the tunnel creatures. "Aubric? They say we have to go."

He sat up. The creatures of light had been reluctant to let them rest in the first place, arguing among themselves about the time, very long ago, when they, too, had bodies.

Runt held a pair of bowls in her hands. "They've given us something to eat."

The exact nature of these creatures still eluded Aubric. They seemed to exist only partly in this world. Through a great deal of effort, they were able to transport physical objects for short distances. A cup of water had appeared in the sleeping chamber at the creatures' palace. They had somehow managed to rattle a bag full of utensils so that Runt could find it before they began their journey. The dancing lights had indicated that Aubric and Runt should each take a sack and a waterskin. One of the sacks held bowls and utensils, the other a few provisions.

Now Runt presented him with a bowl filled with a thick, steaming liquid, no doubt prepared from those supplies. It looked to Aubric like a kind of porridge.

"As far as I can tell, it's made of mushrooms," Runt explained. "That and—other things."

He looked down at the bowl before him. "I assume you asked our hosts?"

"For what good it did."

They both smiled at that. Their hosts' power of description was sometimes lacking.

Flutes sounded nearby.

(Please finish your meal.)

(It costs us. We feed on different things.)

Aubric picked up the ladle Runt had given him and took a sip. The creamy liquid was warm and reasonably tasty. It could have used a little salt.

"Must we rush?" Runt complained after eating a bit of the goo herself. "Why are we in such a hurry?"

The lights flew about each other in a tight formation. Four flutes played at once.

(He is important. She—)

(She is beyond our understanding.)

(Portions of the prophecy are obscure.)

(If he wishes it, it will be so.)

The lights swarmed around Aubric, purposely avoiding the space close to Runt.

(The world is changing. We must be gone.)

With that, they swarmed away again, hovering farther down the tunnel they'd been traveling before they slept.

Runt finished her porridge and sighed. "They turn away from me, too?" She looked after the dancing lights, so beautiful and cold. "I was never meant to do anything but serve m'lady."

Aubric spent a quiet moment finishing his meal as well. These creatures were so impatient, he had no idea when they would eat or sleep again.

Aubric had a number of questions. Beyond staying alive, his fondest hope was to help the Green. Where were these things taking them? He wondered if he would ever see his home again.

Their past hours were a study in contrasts. At first, things had happened so quickly. With the arrival of the lights, their escape from m'lady, their descent through the air, there had not been time for thought. Now it appeared that thought was all they had. Even though the tunnels would change their nature from time to time, from mud to rock to fitted stone and even something like blackened brick, even these lost their novelty with repetition, and a sameness descended upon their travels. Aubric and Runt had talked for a time, sharing superficial details of their lives, not all so different in the castles of the Grey and the Green. But there was much about the army that Aubric didn't wish to share. And when he asked Runt for certain details about m'lady's life and habits, she would give the most general of replies or not answer at all. They had been thrown together by circumstance. Every step they took showed how far they had to go before they found mutual friendship and trust.

The meal done, Aubric stood, every muscle still complaining of fatigue. There was no way to tell the passing of time in these tunnels. Surely, they had been walking for hours. Now, after far too short a rest, they had to do more of the same.

He turned to look at Runt, who stared after the buzzing lights.

"Are you sad that you've come?" he asked.

She looked back at him. "It's so different. Mostly I'm afraid. I've always been afraid." She smiled wistfully. "It was much simpler in the palace."

"What would happen if you returned to the lady Karmille?"

"I disobeyed her. And I took something from her." She looked at Aubric for a long moment before she continued. "I imagine she would kill me. She did the same to many others who had done far less. My mistress truly loves to watch the approach of death."

During the long stretches of silence on their earlier march, Aubric had wondered why they were not pursued. He thought about how m'lady's creatures had devoured the guard. Why hadn't Karmille sent them out again?

Runt's observation had explained something Aubric had not understood. The only reason those creatures didn't pursue them now was that the lady wanted to watch her captives die.

He took Runt's arm. Together, they walked toward the lights.

(Quickly!) the somber flute called. (To the heart!)

"We can only move so fast!" Runt complained.

(Sometimes we forget. We want so much to remember.)

(This will help everyone. If we don't rise above our petty differences, we will all be destroyed.)

"Where are we going?"

(Only one may gain the light.)

(No. To gain the light, we must go deeper.)

(There are others.)

(We do not need to fear. They are the ones who fear.)

(We have kept our distance.)

(Surely they have forgotten.)

(It will change soon.)

(Everything will change.)

Promises, promises, Aubric thought. The farther he walked, the more he only wanted to find home.

THE HALLS WERE oddly empty, and very quiet, as Karmille returned to her rooms. Even those guards still in the hall only glanced at her briefly before looking away. This, Karmille realized, was the result of the Judge's promise. They would see her, but they were to pay no attention to her.

So she would be given a few moments' peace to consider her next move. Sasseen had suggested she bring a pair of guards, and so she would—almost. She had considered all those who served her, and decided she would bring two, but only one would be a member of her regular guard.

She was pleased that the one she had chosen was one of the pair who currently guarded her quarters. "I will need to see you within. Find a replacement, then join me." Her guard of choice was a tall man who had nearly died once in defending her. Some nonsense about the relatives of someone she had killed seeking revenge; as if the daughter of the High Lord wasn't above the law.

Her servants rose as she entered her room, ready to meet her every need.

She waved away their attentions.

"Have Flik brought to me."

A pair of her handmaidens ran off to obey.

Flik. She smiled at the name, so appropriate to the man. Although once a slave like all the others who served her, he had earned both Karmille's respect and his right to a name. When you had a position in the High Court, a private assassin of Flik's ability was a necessity.

The door behind her opened, and her guard entered; the tallest of the tall, a man as loyal as any. He bowed slightly, then stood before her without expression. He was very good at doing that, no matter what she might try. He had no sense of humor; in his position, he could not afford one.

"Guard, I have a special duty for you."

"M'lady," he replied.

"I am to go on a special mission, and I will take two to protect me. You are one of those."

"An honor, m'lady."

"You will protect me from any and all. When you see who else I am bringing, you will better understand."

"M'lady?"

Another voice interrupted.

"Are you saying that you don't trust me?"

It was Flik. His black-clad form leapt from the shadows at the corner of the room, making no sound as he ran. She noticed how her guard's hand was already on his sword. Yes, she thought. These two should counterbalance each other nicely.

Flik managed to do a bit of a dance as he landed before her, his short, wiry form twisting about as he tossed his black hat in the air and caught it again at the end of his pirouette.

"No, my Flik," she replied. "I was simply becoming impatient for you to announce your presence."

The assassin bowed again. "M'lady knows my needs like no other." He looked up with a grin, as quick as his every move. "I understand you have a new task for me? Idleness chafes at me like a noose. I eagerly await your every desire."

"No doubt." She allowed herself a smile in reply. In this, Judge Sasseen was correct. She did feel so much better when surrounded by her own people. "But you say you chafe from idleness? Someone of your talents could seek his fortune anywhere.''

Flik flipped his hat again, pulling a tiny silver dagger from within the lining. ''It is true that I have certain talents, but those talents need a certain atmosphere in which to flower.'' He glanced idly at the guard by Karmille's side as he opened and closed his hand. The dagger, held between two of his fingers an instant before, had disappeared. ''I am the instrument of your will and your imagination.'' He leapt forward to the guard's side. The guard grabbed his sword, but hesitated as a dagger fell out of the assassin's sleeve. Flik retrieved the tiny blade and jumped back beyond the reach of the guard's sword before the other man could recover. Flik nodded to Karmille. ''And your imagination in these areas is unsurpassed. I can aspire to no higher goal.''

She raised a hand to stay any retaliation from her guard. ''That was our Flik's idea of a demonstration.'' She nodded to the assassin. ''I trust you have made your point.''

Not only did Flik have ability, but he would cheer her on her trip. He moved quickly, and, should you look away for an instant, he was no longer where you expected him to be. She wondered how Judge Sasseen would deal with that. So long as the assassin was in her service, it amused her. Of course, as with all her servants, she held a little bit of Flik as well to ensure his loyalty.

The time for comfort had passed. ''Come,'' she called. ''We need to leave here as quickly as possible.'' She instructed her servants to gather a small number of items she might find useful in the hunt. While they acted, she retired to the next room with a pair of maidservants to change into one of her riding outfits. Out of all her many costumes, she decided this would be the best for hiking and climbing, and whatever other activity she might find herself engaged in. She had one of her servants pack a second, identical set of clothes, then placed that parcel with the other items gathered at her command. She entrusted all her belongings to her tall guard. She thought it best for the time being if Flik could move about unencumbered.

When all was ready, she turned a final time to the rest of her staff. "We had best leave now. I expect my father to visit shortly. Please make my excuses."

The servants bowed as she turned to leave.

The two guards preceded Karmille out of her rooms.

"What?" Flik called.

They were swallowed by smoke.

She heard a dry chuckle. Judge Sasseen was playing with her again. She found his need to show his superiority increasingly annoying. She would find some way to use it against him.

"Behind me, m'lady!" her tall guard called.

They were back in the Judge's cavern.

Sasseen coughed delicately. "Excuse my abruptness, but we have no more time to waste. Other forces are on the move." He nodded to Karmille's entourage. "I see you have brought members of your staff. May I introduce you to our guests from the Green?"

A doorway opened in the smoke. Two men strode from the darkness, both with military bearing. Their skin was pale, their cheekbones pronounced. Both were of royal blood. But their faces showed no expression, their eyes stared off into space.

One had a great rip in his clothing. Beneath the rip, Karmille could see a scar that had been hastily sewn together with bloodred thread. His face was the more haggard of the two, though neither of them would have been described as robust. They both had the look of prisoners held too long, with most of their life beaten from them. The one with the scar looked like he had been beaten even beneath his skin.

"This is the one who is dead." Sasseen pointed to the man with the scar. "The other is at least technically alive. The dead one is Lepp, the other Sav. They will respond to their names." Each man nodded as his name was called.

"I suppose we might as well be introduced all around," Sasseen said with a charming smile. "Will you give me your names?

"We already know the lady Karmille. But her two companions?" He paused to stare at Flik and the lady's tall guard. "As is usual with servants, they are without identity? But they are stepping out beyond the Grey Keep." He smiled at the two. "Perhaps it is time to give them names as well."

How could Karmille tell him that one was named already? What good would it serve, except to reveal Flik's true identity. Better that the assassin might have a second name for the duration of their journey. Unless, of course, Karmille might be able to name him all over again.

"So, how should we choose—?" she began.

The Judge shook his head. "If you were going to name them, you would have done so already."

He stood first before the tall guard. "You are good with your hands, quick with a weapon. I think I shall name you Blade. And you?" The Judge stared at the small man for a moment. "Why, you're Flik, aren't you?" He grinned as he glanced back at Karmille. "The name just came to me."

He so enjoyed playing with her. Karmille reminded herself again that it did not serve her purpose to let the Judge anger her. She would remain quiet and observe. She had already reached much of her goal in the palace. There would be a way to be the mistress here as well.

"I have one final thing to show you."

He clapped his hands, and something took shape above his fingers. Something dark that leapt and sputtered like a roaring fire, but was in fact a flame that absorbed light rather than giving it off.

"This will be the final member of our party."

What? Karmille had thought they would both be accompanied by two apiece; her guards, his soldiers. The Judge had said nothing about bringing magical beings.

"I did not say I was bringing only two as well," Sasseen

reminded her before she could say a word. "Besides, this little fellow is of small importance." The black flame flared above the Judge's fingertips. "In some cultures, they would refer to this as a spirit, a soul, a life energy. None of those descriptions are truly precise. No matter. The body of this fellow has long since ceased to exist. And I have, of course, made some further adjustments to this spirit, to suit my purposes."

The Judge thrust his hand upward, as if he were tossing a ball. The black flame leapt into the air high above their heads. "Today is a day for naming. Let's call our latest friend Imp, shall we?" The flame spun in a circle overhead. Sasseen laughed. "How beautifully he soars. Of the four elements, my favorite is the air. All Judges specialize, you know."

The newly named Imp rose even higher in the great chamber, darting now among the stalactites that hung from the naturally vaulted ceiling. But even as the dark flame flew through the most shadowed recesses above, Karmille could still see it, a hint of blue here, a flash of red, a trace of deepest green. The flame was not the absence of color, it was all colors together, flashing in the darkness.

"Enough!" the Judge called.

Imp ceased its darting course, falling back to hover a few inches above Sasseen's outstretched hand. Karmille was reminded of a falcon returning to its master's gloved fist.

Sasseen smiled at his pet. "I keep it on a tight leash. It has learned to obey." He turned to Karmille. "Enough of introductions. You are the mistress here. How do we begin?"

Karmille was as surprised by this sudden admission as she was by the mockery that preceded it. Unless, of course, Sasseen calling her mistress was another form of mockery. Still, she would show him she could lead.

"I have something that will help show us the way."

She reached into the pocket of her riding jacket and

pulled forth a small object wrapped in silk. She unwrapped it for all to see: her maidservant's little finger.

Even Judge Sasseen looked impressed.

"Your reputation for preparedness is apparently well-founded. With this to guide us, we should find the two of them in no time." He waved to the others. "Come now! We must be off. My soldiers wait for a reunion with their comrade, who ran off, leaving them to die—or worse." He pointed to a couple of sacks piled in a corner. The two soldiers quickly walked over and picked them up. "It was—and is—far worse."

"So we should catch them soon?" Karmille called.

"Not too soon. What's the fun in that? We will have to walk. My spells will be reserved for counteracting other magic. And I know that they are not headed upwards toward the castle, but deeper into the tunnels below. No doubt they seek something far more interesting. Interesting enough that we might seek it as well."

This, at least, sounded promising. Anything that piqued a Judge's interest must be powerful indeed. Karmille gestured for her two servants to follow Sasseen's soldiers. They would work together to catch Aubric and her maid, then take from them anything of value they might have found.

By that time, Karmille should have devised a plan to defeat Sasseen and keep the power for herself.

. 21 .

JACOBSEN HADN'T EXPECTED
to spend the rest of his life walking around underground.
Still, it was better than some things—say a painful death
at the hands of Mr. Smith. Jacobsen was surprised at the
strength of the reaction he'd had to his pretty dancing partner back in the cavern. Lately, he'd been so busy running
and hiding and desperately trying to make ends meet that
he had forgotten how wonderful it could be to have somebody look at you and smile.

He found the young woman's face in his thoughts a lot
as he trudged along after the others: the silent warrior Tsang
in the lead, then the metal man Gontor, followed by Summitch, who spent much of the trek grumbling quietly to
himself. Jacobsen took up the rear, the spot where no one
paid much attention to him, which was fine with him. He
could spend some time with his thoughts, or at least as
much of his thoughts as he could manage in between Gontor's lectures.

Jacobsen wasn't at all surprised at the lectures. As he'd
already seen in the vast cavern they left behind, Gontor

really liked to talk. He wondered if that was another reason the warrior whom Gontor had chosen to bring with him was one who had taken a vow of silence.

In a way, Jacobsen was glad for the diversion as they walked through the endless tunnels. It was sort of like books-on-tape; it helped to pass the time. And once in a while, when he decided to pay attention, he could even figure out what Gontor was talking about.

"There is a seat of power, at the heart of the world," the disembodied voice boomed throughout the tunnel. "It is our ultimate goal, but, like all worthwhile goals, very difficult to obtain. The makers wished to protect their secrets. The paths themselves wish to turn you aside. Observe."

Tsang stopped abruptly, as if Gontor had given him some silent signal, and stepped to one side for the metal man to pass. The warrior hefted the long spear with the elaborate blade that he had used as a walking stick, now holding it before him with both hands, his feet spread wide apart, ready for any danger.

Gontor walked up to one of the tunnel walls. He pulled back the sleeve of his robe, and balled his metal hand into a fist. The fist passed through the wall without resistance, as if there wasn't a wall there at all.

"Is this supposed to impress us?" Summitch laughed. "There are secret doorways everywhere underground."

"Perhaps," Gontor's voice allowed. "Above, they were placed to help with court intrigue. Casual spying, secret assignations, escape routes, that sort of thing. Here, though, they have an entirely different purpose. Nearly all the paths within the castle were created with the aid of magic, largely by the Earth Judges, back in those days when the Judges were more independent of the monarchy. But, unlike the tunnels above, these still retain traces of the spells used to create them, spells that would cause the person without knowledge to choose the wrong way, to travel in circles, to perhaps even stumble all the way back to the surface before they realized that the tunnels had turned them aside. Without a true sense of destination, we might wander around forever.''

Gontor's hands rang as he clapped them together and shouted a quick string of words. A hole formed in the wall before them, widening like the iris of a lens, until it revealed a brand-new tunnel.

Even Summitch appeared impressed. "It's different. I'll admit it.''

"We enter the secret ways," Gontor's voice boomed. "It will get more difficult before we reach our goal.''

It figured, Jacobsen said to himself. He might be free of Smith for the moment, and traveling with a couple of guys who looked like they could handle themselves—but no matter where he ended up, his life always got difficult.

Tsang entered the new tunnel first, followed by Gontor and Summitch. As usual, Jacobsen took up the rear. So no one saw him when he stopped in surprise.

This new passageway was different from anything they'd come across before. The walls, floor, and ceiling were all a smooth white, cool to the touch. Instead of a line of torches, the ceiling itself glowed faintly. It was more the hallway of a hospital or office building. Or maybe a space-ship. It seemed a thousand years removed from the rock-walled tunnels they had walked through only moments ago. The whole setup made Jacobsen nervous. He hurried to catch up to the others.

Summitch whistled.

"The builders saw no reason to imitate the caves," Gontor was saying. "If you have reached this level, you know some portion of the truth. The illusion is no longer necessary.''

"Okay," Summitch admitted. "You've impressed me.''

"Good, because all four of us will have an important part if we are going to succeed.''

For all the information Gontor had passed onto them, Jacobsen realized, there was very little specific to their purpose here. "You still haven't told us what you expect us to do," he said.

"No, I haven't," Gontor agreed. He and Tsang marched forward at the same steady pace, with Summitch grumbling in their wake. The next few minutes were spent in an uncharacteristic silence.

The passageway appeared to stretch on forever. The walls, ceiling, and floor were beyond white, featureless, with no doors, windows, or ornamentation of any kind to break the monotony. Jacobsen imagined there were doors here somewhere, hidden like the entryway to this place. No doubt Gontor was aware of every one; maybe Tsang and Summitch could see them, too. No doubt everyone knew far more about this place than Eric Jacobsen.

He wondered if his companions found this place any less boring.

"Hold!" Gontor called. Jacobsen looked up to see that Tsang had raised an arm in a gesture of caution. Just ahead, this corridor intersected with another, the two passageways bisecting each other at perfect right angles.

Noise echoed back from somewhere up ahead.

"What was that?" Jacobsen asked.

"Others," Gontor replied.

Jacobsen stared into the never-ending whiteness. "There are others here? Other people have passed through that barrier?" This place looked so antiseptic, he couldn't imagine anyone living here.

Gontor nodded. "All manner of creatures have passed this way. This part of the tunnel may be a secret, but it is a badly kept one. Some prefer to live within this place. The hidden entry gives them extra protection." He looked down the corridor to either side, then waved for the others to follow. "We continue."

They continued to walk in a straight line, ignoring the passageway to either side, which, so far as Jacobsen could tell, was every bit as featureless as their current path. He noticed that Tsang once again held his spear as a weapon rather than as a walking stick.

It was a few moments before he heard the noise again, more like the howling of an animal than the call of a human being.

"It's closer," Summitch observed.

"They're waiting for us," Gontor said.

"What?" Jacobsen demanded, surprised and maybe a little offended by the matter-of-fact tone of Gontor's booming voice. "Do we just come and announce ourselves?"

"They guard the place jealously," Gontor replied. "It is best if we do not give ourselves away any sooner than we have to." He looked up the corridor, then back to his three companions. "My silence now may serve us better. This voice projects well to crowds. Perhaps too well. I was not made for stealth."

"They guard this place?" Summitch mumbled a bit louder than usual. "This could be interesting after all."

Jacobsen didn't like where this was going. It sounded like they were headed straight for danger. Now, he supposed, instead of being killed on his own, he'd be killed as a part of a group. Well, he would try to pay a bit more attention to his surroundings, so at least he could see it coming.

Tsang held up his hand again. A band of metal, perhaps a foot high and three feet from the floor, stretched from one wall to the other.

"That's new," Gontor said.

"What do you mean?" Jacobsen asked.

"I've been here before. Actually, I lived in this place for a time." Gontor shook his head. "Well, it has been a few hundred years. I tried to get away, you know. Then, of course, there was my long imprisonment, followed by my miraculous recovery. But I'm talking again, aren't I?"

Summitch snorted. "Sounds to me like you're trying to make up for hundreds of years of silence."

"Really?" Gontor nodded. "I've felt that way myself."

Tsang prodded at the metal band with his spear. Or at least he tried to prod it. As soon as either the metal tip or the wooden staff came within an inch of the metal band, it bounced back as if he had hit some invisible rubber wall.

Gontor stared at the metal bar for a long moment. "Somebody is still practicing magic down here."

"You can't get past this?" Jacobsen half-hoped they couldn't. The longer he spent in this vast empty nothingness, the more those dark, torchlit tunnels seemed like home.

"No, this is simple. Our complications lie ahead." Gontor studied the obstacle intently. "This is Earth magic again; a spell not too different from the one that would lead you on paths away from your goal. A diversion spell, I guess you would call it. They have placed this bar elsewhere, so that we cannot reach our destination through conventional means. But when you are Gontor, well—" He did not need to finish the sentence. Instead, he pulled back the sleeve of his robe to reveal his lower arm up past the elbow. He pushed his hand to one side of the bar so that it disappeared into the right-hand wall.

"I just have to find this—"

A metal hand, Gontor's hand, Jacobsen assumed, appeared behind and slightly above the metal bar, another 90-degree angle away from where the metal man's arm entered the wall. There was no way his arm could reach that far or twist to that angle. Well, Jacobsen thought, it was magic.

Gontor's arm flailed about for a bit before he knocked it against the bar, metal clanging against metal. "There's a knack to this. Sort of like shaving with a mirror."

What would a metal man know about shaving?

"There!" the great voice boomed.

The bar swung aside.

"Now just let me put myself back together." The metal man pulled his arm from the wall and shook the sleeve of his robe back into place.

Jacobsen was ready to throw up his hands. Whether it

was arms emerging from solid rock or metal men with whiskers, he wasn't sure exactly what physical laws were being violated. He wasn't sure what physical laws still even existed. As they went deeper and deeper into the tunnels, they seemed to be going farther and farther away from reality. If he ever got separated from the others, he'd be truly lost.

"Ah. Here we go," Gontor announced as the distance between the walls began to grow. Tsang swung his great spear back and forth, perhaps as a warning, perhaps searching for invisible barriers or enemies. With the warrior's continued silence, Jacobsen had no idea of the true purpose of any of Tsang's actions.

The passageway widened into a good-sized room, perhaps twenty feet by thirty. After the closeness of the tunnels, the place felt huge. But everything was still the same unrelenting white.

Gontor looked around the room, studying the ceiling and floor and, as far as Jacobsen could tell, three completely arbitrary points on the surrounding walls.

"They're gone?" the metal man said at last, as if he couldn't believe the evidence before him.

"Is that good?" Summitch asked.

"We'll find out soon enough." Gontor waved his companions forward. "When we find the second room."

It seemed to Jacobsen that there was an awful lot of speculation going on here. Shouldn't a god know more of this stuff?

"This is only the first room, after all," Gontor said, "what we seek is beyond the three rooms entirely." The way Gontor was talking now, Jacobsen got the idea he was trying to reassure himself as much as his followers. "Last time, they caught me in the second one, and imprisoned me for close to a thousand years. I've been looking forward to going back and finishing the job."

"How do you plan to do that?" Summitch asked.

"Last time, I tried to do it by myself. I won't make that mistake again."

Summitch glanced sourly back at Jacobsen; the little fellow looked like he was about to begin muttering again. Jacobsen had noticed it, too: Gontor answered most questions by hardly answering them at all. This might be the real reason he was the leader of all those in the painted chamber. He might be an imperfect god but he was one heck of a politician.

Jacobsen decided it was his turn to try. "So you need all of us? Then don't you think you should answer some of our questions?"

"I thought I was—" The great voice hesitated for a moment before answering. "Well, not all of them, I'll admit that."

Well, that was a step in the right direction. "We are looking for some power," Jacobsen prompted.

Gontor nodded. "In the broadest outline, that is correct. We seek power. But then, doesn't everybody?"

Maybe, Jacobsen thought, it would help if his questions got more specific. "How does the power manifest itself?"

Gontor studied the walls for a long moment, then looked to the ceiling, and the floor, before regarding Jacobsen again.

"I'm not exactly sure." The metal man lifted his hooded shoulders in a gesture of helplessness. "I imagine that power might take physical form for a time."

"Sounds like a ring to me," Summitch remarked. "Or a staff. Or a sword."

The voice sighed, a sound like wind through the high trees. "I don't really know. Mostly, it is a secret. But I held part of that power, if only for an instant." He held up his metal hands. "How do you think I became as I am today?"

So the power had something to do with Gontor becoming a metal being who could change his size at will. Beyond that, what had he shown that was in any way extraordinary? Well, there was that thing with the wall, but Jacobsen wasn't all that impressed. Perhaps the metal man was so evasive because his answers weren't really all that spectacular.

Tsang turned to the others, and placed a finger upon his lips, a sign for silence. Without Gontor's booming voice filling the room, Jacobsen could hear it, too.

The howling was faint, but it came from both the tunnel they had emerged from and the tunnel that continued on the far side of the room. A low, moaning sound came from the way behind them, followed by a higher-pitched wail from the way ahead.

The warrior shook his head, pointing his spear first at one tunnel, then the other.

"Tsang is right," Gontor explained. "They know exactly where we are."

Another howl drifted from the tunnel behind them, somewhere in pitch between the first two. A series of short noises, like the yips of a dog, followed.

"They are discussing their strategy."

Tsang waved his spear toward the wall to his right, one of the two without a tunnel entrance.

"I agree," Gontor said. "This is as good as anyplace to take a stand. If we form a semicircle with the wall to protect our backs, perhaps we will live a few minutes longer."

"So we're going to die?" Jacobsen demanded. "I thought you were some sort of deity."

The sigh again. "Life as a deity is highly overrated."

"So you're not a god after all."

Gontor's metal face turned to regard Jacobsen. The expressionless mouth, high cheekbones, clear forehead, and unmoving eyes were all carved in bronze, and yet Jacobsen felt the anger in the other's gaze.

"I can do anything I set my mind to." Gontor's voice seemed even louder than before. "Anything. That's a little like being a god, isn't it?"

The warrior jerked his spear again.

"We must prepare for the worst." Gontor nodded to the

warrior in white. "Tsang is different. He has a purpose. Those with a purpose can be both useful and dangerous. I trust that Tsang will be both." Gontor and the warrior walked to the right-hand wall. Jacobsen and Summitch quickly followed.

The howling was getting closer, the same four voices, or maybe more. It was hard to tell, exactly. As the sounds grew louder, Jacobsen could hear the echoes of their cries reverberating down the tunnels to either side. It felt as though Jacobsen and the others were surrounded by wolves, closing in for the kill.

Jacobsen pressed his back against the white wall. It was cool to the touch and totally smooth, without flaw or feature. It was odd to have to face the unknown in a place as bright as this. This sort of stalking was supposed to take place in darkness, not unrelenting light.

"How do we defend ourselves?" he asked.

"That depends on what they want," the booming voice replied. "Tsang has that nasty-looking pole and a sword at his waist. I myself carry a sword that until today was ornamental."

Jacobsen didn't find this reassuring. "What am I supposed to use, my fists?"

"We may be able to defend ourselves with words. If not, why not borrow a knife from your short friend? He has a number of them."

Summitch looked at the bronze man as if he had been betrayed. He shook his head, then glanced somewhat guiltily at Jacobsen. "I suppose I have to."

Gontor nodded. "We need every pair of hands. All four of us together."

Summitch sidled over to Jacobsen and handed over a nasty-looking blade that he fetched from somewhere under his jerkin. "Be careful. I want it back. You can never have enough knives."

Jacobsen looked at the knife in his hand. The blade was short, about six inches, but had a sharp point and a ragged cutting edge. He had carried a switchblade when he was a kid, mostly to make himself feel better, but he'd never once used it. Holding a knife now mostly made him think of the possibility that he could get cut himself.

He had another weapon. He still had his gun, with seven bullets left, tucked in his belt. If, in this place, the gun could really be called a weapon.

Last time he had used it, he wasn't sure if it had helped or hurt him. Summitch was dead set against him using it again. And Gontor, who had seen him use the piece, and somehow knew about Summitch's hidden knives, hadn't even mentioned it. The cold metal still felt reassuring beneath the palm of Jacobsen's hand. A gun here was out of place, a magical device without rules. There appeared to be dire consequences in using such a thing. If he used the gun again, he could kill any or all of them.

But if he was going to die anyway, why the hell not?

Summitch looked to Jacobsen. "I've spent much of my last few years underground," the little fellow said.

"As a finder," Jacobsen replied quickly, glad to have something to do besides wait. "Yes, I remember."

"But much of my talent has been used in finding ways out of places." Summitch's wrinkles quivered as he shook his head. "Finding treasure is a wonderful talent, but it does you no good if you are not alive to spend it."

"Is there a way out of here?" Jacobsen asked.

"The cries are meant to disorient us, the featureless walls to confuse us. Why spend all this energy diverting our attention unless there is something they don't want us to see?"

The howling outside redoubled. Perhaps Summitch was right. Otherwise, why hadn't their enemy simply attacked?

"If we're afraid," Gontor said, "we'll make mistakes. I made mistakes, the last time I was here."

"You've met the things down here before?" Jacobsen asked.

Gontor nodded, looking at the corridor beyond the room

before turning back to Jacobsen. Jacobsen could feel another lecture coming on.

"I've told you before that these tunnels are far from empty. My followers, the simplest of refugees, occupy that space above, far enough below the castle proper to discourage unwanted strangers, but not so far that those in need can't find us. Here, however, we are more than likely to meet some darker things. The discarded, the rejected, the lost, the desperate.

"You remember our first meeting, when my followers attempted to scare you away?" Gontor nodded, as if answering for all of them. "We patterned some of our behavior on that of the others we had found—deeper in the bowels of the world. As you discovered, we have no bite. I have firsthand knowledge of the others—they bite first."

Well, Jacobsen thought, that was nice and alarming, and not at all helpful. "But what about what Summitch said, that there are other ways out of here?"

Gontor hesitated, then nodded. "There is more than one way to get to the center of the world. It could be either within this place or the other hidden regions. Who knows if even I know them all?"

Tsang held up his hand. The howling had stopped.

"Perhaps," Gontor added, "this is the attack."

They waited in silence for a long moment.

"Where are they?" Summitch whispered. Jacobsen noticed the small man clutched a knife in either hand.

"Something has taken their attention away from us," Gontor said after another moment had passed. "I'm not sure if that's good news."

"You mean," Jacobsen asked, "those things might have been done in by something worse?"

He was answered by a distant scream.

Tsang pointed his spear at the tunnel they had come from.

"Whatever it was, it's behind us," Gontor explained.

Tsang left his place against the wall and turned toward

the tunnel leading deeper, waving for the others to follow.

"It appears we are free to pursue our destiny," Gontor said as he followed the silent warrior.

"Whether we want to or not," Summitch added.

. 22 .

KAREN HELD BRIAN TIGHT as the Buick sped through the darkness. Funny how quickly her life could change. Brian was the only person left from her life of yesterday.

Yesterday at this time she'd been worried about going back to school for her senior year. She had had her courses and activities all laid out, even called a couple of girls she had gotten close with the year before. Things seemed to be turning around for her, ever since she met Brian and knew she didn't have to be alone.

It wasn't always like this. Especially back in middle school, every new semester had been a nightmare, with Karen singled out as a nerd and a loser. School had gotten easier when she'd hit junior year. Most of the bullies and with-it kids chose to ignore her now, happy to go off in their own little cliques. Mostly, with Brian, she had a clique of two.

It was so different to have someone who really cared about you. Her own parents might not yell at her, at least not in the same way Brian's mother would always give him a hard time. They simply ignored her, always complaining about their busy lives. Most of the time, they just made her feel like one more problem. She wondered what they thought of their missing daughter now. She imagined they might not even know she was gone.

She had been glad, too, to find someone like Mrs. Mendeck to fill the hole her parents left in her life. The old woman might be slightly dotty, but she made up for it by caring, for Karen and Brian both.

But how could Mrs. Mendeck be just a phone call away when she was never around to answer the phone?

Brian glanced back at her from where he stared out the window. Not that there was much to see; mile after mile of dark trees between the exits, occasionally an abandoned car at the side of the road, a pair of rest stops, one every thirty miles or so. Nobody thought about stopping. Now that they were on a road with real traffic, they all just wanted to get away.

Karen thought it was funny how she and Brian had accepted the help of the men in the front seat. Their lives at the moment seemed dependent on these two gangsters. Just because Joe and Ernie had saved them from whatever craziness was behind them didn't mean they were going to help them now; they might even deliver the two of them straight to that Mr. Smith.

But there was a part of her that didn't think so. She had seen that honesty in the driver's eyes. Karen knew from high school who to trust. That was one advantage of being an outcast. You had to develop a social radar to survive. Back there, it was laughter and derision; here it was life and death.

So the world was falling apart, and a couple of half crazy guys had saved them; guys who had been involved in the shooting of Brian's father, guys who now sent them speeding away from a truck stop full of creepy people and too-bright polka music. Brian was as helpless as she was. Even though they were moving, they all seemed helpless.

Sooner or later, Karen knew, they were going to need Mrs. Mendeck to make it right.

"So should I make the call?" she shouted to the front seat. Joe, the driver, glanced at her in the rearview mirror. It was Joe who had suggested calling Mrs. Mendeck in the first place.

He nodded. "I think we've gone far enough. I'm going to get off here so we can find a phone."

They pulled off the interstate, but Joe didn't slow down. They were out in the country somewhere, houses and buildings widely spaced, flat farmland stretching off into the distance in between. They still sped by twenty homes or more, some dark, some with a single light in a bedroom or living room, one or two blazing with lights in every room of the house. She glanced up at Brian. The world was full of so many different people, so many different lives. Why had this happened to them?

She saw a stoplight ahead, the first one she'd seen in close to twenty minutes.

"This'll do," Joe said. He opened the glove compartment, pulled out a roll of quarters. "I think these will be safer than using a calling card. You never know."

Karen reached over the front seat and he put the roll of quarters in her hand.

"We'll make sure nobody bothers you," Joe added. She realized he was holding a gun.

Joe had stopped the car in a small town, at a pay phone sitting outside a combination post office and general store. Karen got out of the car quickly and made the call.

This time, Mrs. Mendeck answered the phone.

"Oh, dear, I'm glad it's you. I've been worried about you."

Karen felt a rush of emotion as she heard Mrs. Mendeck's voice. She was just so glad to hear the old woman's voice that all her fear and anger was forgotten.

"It's all my fault that we haven't been in touch," Mrs. Mendeck went on in that hurried way she had, like she had a minute's worth of information she had to relay in half a minute's time. "I've been busier than I thought I would be. Things are moving at a much faster clip than I had at first imagined." Karen could picture Mrs. Mendeck shaking her head as she made a *tsking* sound. "But that's no excuse. I imagine you were worried. How are you, dear?"

Right now, Karen didn't need to tell the whole story. She tried to hit the important points.

"Smith has been after us, but we got away. Some people are helping us, we're heading toward home—it's awfully complicated."

"Yes, it is, isn't it? Smith has found you already? His resources extend farther than I had imagined. We'll have to do something about that."

"So do we come home?"

Mrs. Mendeck hesitated. "Our Mr. Smith is likely to concentrate his energy on recapturing you once you return here. So you should not return. I'll meet you on your way."

"You'll meet us?" Karen asked. "How will you know where to find us?"

"My dear, I always know. As do you."

She did? Know what? Sometimes, Mrs. Mendeck made Karen want to throw things.

"I imagine you're at a pay phone somewhere. Leave now. You said people are helping you. Do they have a car?"

"Yes," Karen began, "but—"

"Good. That means you can travel some distance. Until we're together, we don't want to stay too long in one place. I'll see you soon."

Mrs. Mendeck broke the connection. Karen hung up the phone and went back out to the car. Brian had gotten out and was leaning against the trunk.

"She says she'll meet us!" she called.

"Where?" Brian asked.

Karen didn't know what to say.

"She says she'll find us."

"How?"

"She's Mrs. Mendeck."

"Why are you having problems?" Joe leaned out of the driver's side window. "I only met the old lady once, and I'd bet she could do anything. I'm just glad that this time she's on our side."

He started up the car. "She wants us to keep on driving? We'll keep on driving."

"Mrs. Mendeck said that would be best." Karen agreed as she and Brian climbed into the backseat. "I think maybe, when we're moving, the creep Smith has a harder time finding us."

Joe's cousin Ernie groaned, the first noise she'd heard him make in over an hour. "I know how he found us." He glanced over at Joe. "I think it was me."

Joe looked like he wanted to strangle him. "What do you mean, you think it was you?"

Ernie stared out at the road as he replied. "I just didn't call my uncle. I called Smith, too."

"He told you where to go?" Joe demanded.

Ernie nodded.

"He said something to me that made it even worse. Something that made me—" His voice trailed off, like he had forgotten the words.

"What?" Joe demanded.

Ernie shook his head violently. "Fuck it—sorry, kids—I can't remember."

Joe sighed. "Probably just as well. The farther we get away from Smith, the better." He pulled the car away from the general store. "This Mrs. Mendeck. She didn't make any suggestions on where to go?"

"No," Karen replied. "She just said if we drive, she'll find us."

"I can accept that," Joe agreed. "Right now, I can accept anything." He stomped on the accelerator, speeding down the country road.

Ernie stretched and yawned.

"My head's clearing up. Maybe I can drive after a while?"

Joe looked skeptically at his cousin. "Maybe. I want to make sure you're over this thing with Smith."

Ernie stared at Joe for a long moment before replying. "I don't think I'll ever be over Smith."

"That depends," Joe replied. "I think you'll get over Smith pretty fast if we kill him."

OFFICER JACKIE PORTER was dead tired. She sat at her kitchen table and stared at the chair where she'd hung her holster and gun. She'd never had to use it, but it was always there; both a privilege and a responsibility; a cold, compact symbol of law enforcement. Law enforcement—being a police officer had seemed so straightforward once, before she started the job. Now, with those kids in trouble, the Chief involved in some way that didn't seem completely legal, and that mystery man Smith, pulling strings behind it all, the deeper she got into this, the more complicated it became. She was supposed to use the gun to keep the peace, to stop criminals. What if the Chief was a criminal, too?

Officer Porter sighed. Part of her never wanted to strap that gun on again.

She remembered, just the other day, how much she was looking forward to a few days off the job. To get away from the routine, dump the paperwork, take some time to think. She had found that she liked some parts of her new job, but it wasn't everything she expected. She remembered the incident with the fender-bender involving the mayor's son; how her accident report placing the blame on the young man had disappeared. Politics were everywhere.

She wished now all she had to worry about was politics.

She knew what she had to do. It was why she'd become an accident specialist in the first place. There was a flip side to her problem-solving. If she found something she couldn't worry to a solution, she couldn't get it off her mind. Unless she acted on it, this whole thing with Brian Clark was looking to be a problem that would haunt her for a long time.

It put a whole new spin on her free time. Before, she had vacillated between getting out of town for some serious sightseeing up by the lakes or just holing up in her apartment and resting for four days straight. Now it looked as though she was headed for Gravesville. Good, flat, boring farm country.

Unless—what if Brian had gone back home? Jackie had asked both the hospital nursing staff and Brian's mother to let her know if the boy turned up. The nursing staff she could count on. Brian's mother seemed to need all her energy to nurse personal grudges.

Jackie quickly looked up the number of Brian's house and dialed.

"Hello?" an acidic voice answered after the first ring. Brian's mother made even a salutation sound negative.

"Mrs. Clark? This is Officer Porter. I met you today at Parkdale Memorial—"

"I remember you," the other woman snapped. "You're the one who let Brian get away."

Jackie was a bit surprised by the attack. "Mrs. Clark. I didn't—"

"Oh, I know where he's gone," the other woman interrupted again. "After that horrible Karen girl. He never gives a thought to me."

"Karen?" Who was that? Did Brian mention a girlfriend?

"I know he's there. I need him twice as much to help me around here now. How can I expect to get anything done after what happened? Her parents don't even answer the phone. I know it. They're trying to avoid me."

Jackie saw an opening. "Well, they can't avoid the police. Why don't you let me try?"

Mrs. Clark paused for a minute before replying. "Well—

why not? You tell Brian to get right home. I'm going to give him a piece of my mind!''

"Mrs. Clark. You'll have to give me the phone number.''

"What? Oh yes. Her name's Karen. Karen Eggleton. They live over in those apartments on Washington.'' She rattled off a phone number. "You make sure my son gets back here, and soon!''

Jackie said she would do her best and hung up. It was no wonder Brian would take as long as possible to go home. With a mother like that, it was a wonder that Brian could cope at all.

She needed to call Karen's parents. Maybe they would have some clue as to Brian's whereabouts.

She called the number. There was no answer, no answering machine, the phone just rang and rang. She got up and pulled the phone book out of the kitchen cabinet. The number she'd called was indeed for an Eggleton on Washington. She knew where the apartment building was, less than half a mile away. Maybe she'd go over there, take a look around, leave a note if nobody was home.

It was worth a trip. Jackie decided to take the gun, just in case. She'd take her own car, though. Might as well keep this as low profile as possible.

It took less than five minutes to reach the place, a non-descript four-story building made of yellow brick, the sort of "modern" architecture so popular in the early sixties. Now the brick looked dirty and old. She walked into the lobby. The name Eggleton was typed next to an apartment on the third floor. Now, though, she had to get past the inside security door. She wondered if she should go and see the building super and make it all official.

The buzzer sounded on the glass door before her. She reached out and pulled on the metal handle. It opened easily. Someone had just let her in. Was someone waiting for her?

She was glad now that she had brought the gun. She climbed the stairs quickly and quietly.

An old lady stood in the hallway on the third floor.

"It's about time," the old woman said as Jackie reached the landing. "We've got a job to do."

Jackie frowned. "We do?"

"Karen and Brian need us, as soon as possible."

Jackie stopped herself from reaching for her gun. The old lady might be strange, but she didn't appear to be dangerous.

"Who are you?"

"I'm Mrs. Mendeck. I live across the hall from Karen. I take care of her. And you?"

"Oh. Jackie Porter." She kept right on frowning. What was happening here?

Mrs. Mendeck nodded. "Since I was expecting you, you expected me to know your name?" She sighed. "I wish I did. Know everything, that is. It would make everything so much easier. But we can't waste any time."

The old lady hurried past her down the stairs, waving for the policewoman to follow.

"And where are we going?" Jackie asked.

"I'll explain as we drive."

Porter was surprised how willing she was to accept the old woman and her explanation. She turned around and followed Mrs. Mendeck down the stairs.

· 23 ·

At first, Aubric had thought he might still be lost in a dream. One minute, he and Runt were walking through endless corridors filled with spectral light. The next—

The world dissolved.

Aubric could think of no other word for it. They had left their resting place only a few moments before, to follow the dancing lights and the green glow they produced within the tunnel. The tunnel was unremarkable, save perhaps that it was unusually straight and had a more noticeable than usual downward slope, so that Aubric's feet wanted to hurry forward. As quickly as they now trotted down the slope, the lights urged them to go faster. There was a point up ahead where the passageway veered sharply to the right. If he and Runt didn't slow their descent, they'd run into the wall.

(Prepare,) the flute called. The lights, which had buzzed about each other, formed a single straight line before them, pointing arrowlike toward the wall they so rapidly approached.

"Prepare for what?" Runt had whispered.

The tunnels had changed. The tunnels were no more. They were surrounded by light so bright they could see nothing else. The flute songs piled one atop the other, perhaps a dozen different voices striving to be heard.

Aubric could still feel the deep slope of the tunnel beneath his feet. Runt cried out and stumbled against him, sending him forward even faster than before.

(We approach the heart of the world.)

(We are deep within the world.)

(Those who guard the way have changed the nature of things.)

(Too much light!)

Even as they cried about it, the nature of the brightness changed, shifting away from white to yellow, green, and blue. Aubric managed to regain his balance without falling, and grabbed Runt's arm before she could stumble past.

(Bright light pains us.)

(It is the curse visited upon us. The curse we will remove.)

(It pains us, but we are with you.)

The light shifted again, to a deep red, the color of sunsets. The air around them was bathed in a crimson glow. Aubric blinked, trying to adjust his eyes. Runt still stood by his side. The dancing lights swirled about before him, their red-tinged light like glowing embers. Aubric could once again see a floor beneath them, and walls to either side. The tunnel once again led straight ahead. Aubric had no idea what happened to the wall.

(They wish to stop us with tricks.)

(But we can change anything. We were the builders.)

(We will be builders again.)

The lights formed a line before them again.

(Let us guide you.)

They were like a signpost, pointing the way.

(Nothing will happen to you.)

(We need you to fulfill our destiny.)

Aubric was beginning to wish that the lights did not feel the need to reassure them quite so often. If he could believe these strange and beautiful creatures, he and Runt were safe until the light beings fulfilled their destinies. But what happened then? These creatures had given them some information, but it had been a decidedly one-sided conversation, and, after their initial decision to flee the lady Karmille's guest chamber, the lights had offered them no further choices.

The tunnel turned again, this time to the left, but the creatures flew straight ahead. The lights were leading them through another wall.

"Where are they taking us?" Runt asked.

Aubric tightened his grip on her arm. "We've done it before."

Another brief flash of light, and they passed from the tunnel into—somewhere else. Every step took them farther away from the world they knew. The air was full of colors, translucent patterns that were never still, swirling shapes of such complexity that Aubric could stare at them forever. He felt they might be passing straight through the rock, the solid made insubstantial. If what he suspected was true, the dancing lights could change the very nature of things.

The red of the tunnel was joined by strains of purple and blue, an interlocking swirling pattern of light that the embers would pass through, causing the pattern to burst, shards of color exploding outward like flower petals carried by the wind.

They mustn't dawdle. If what Aubric suspected was true and he and Runt were left behind, the rock would become solid once more, crushing them where they stood.

"Look." Runt's voice sounded faint, very far away. He looked over to her, and saw the colors swirling about her face, stroking her arms, ruffling her clothing like some mischievous breeze.

She pointed behind them.

The exploded shards were rejoining, shaping themselves once again into their former patterns.

The change the lights brought was temporary. Whatever they truly passed through, there would be no lasting sign of their passing.

Aubric wondered if they were seeing the world in the same way their guides did, a world not of physical objects and sounds, but of pure light and music.

(Hurry.)

(We cannot contain the forces forever.)

(We near our destination.)

(We will find rewards.)

(All of us will be rewarded when we are done.)

The world around them was once again sunset-red.

(Hurry. We come to air and light.)

(Prepare.)

Aubric blinked.

They were suddenly back in the world of the flesh. This time, though, the tunnel was white, and there was another person, turned away from them, perhaps fifty feet ahead.

(A scout.) The flute played very softly. (Hurry.)

The scout, who did not seem to be aware of their approach, had the pale, high-cheekboned look of a High One, save that his hair was matted and his clothes dirty and torn. He was turned away from them, his hands cupped to his mouth, making a high, wailing sound.

The lights rushed ahead of Aubric and Runt, now only a dozen feet away from the scout.

He spun suddenly. "Who? Where did you come from? This tunnel leads nowhere. How—"

The lights descended upon him.

(A scout!)

(We are not without power.)

The lights swarmed over the scout. He screamed as his flesh turned bright red. His skin was soon lost beneath the lights, his whole form glowing white. The screams had stopped.

The lights drifted away. Where the scout had stood was now only a pile of pale grey ash, which fell as soon as the lights had left it.

The lights danced back toward Aubric and Runt.

(Renewed!)

(Do not fear.)

(We only swarm on our enemies.)

(There are others.)

(We must act quickly.)

(They are surprised.)

(They will not be able to counter.)

(Hurry.)

Runt was shivering at his side. Neither one of them spoke.

(It is our destiny.)

(You must join us.)

Aubric no longer saw the music as an entreaty, but as a command. If they did not join the lights, would he and Runt be consumed like the scout?

He urged Runt forward as they heard another scream somewhere ahead.

KARMILLE KNEW THE theory behind the tunnels, had even explored some of those passageways close by the Grey Keep. Beyond that, though, she knew few details. There was very little written about these places, even in the forbidden texts. The secret network of passageways that she now walked was the one place beyond recorded knowledge.

She was beyond the royal court, with all its expectations and responsibilities; beyond all but one of the Judges, with their twin cloaks of mystery and terror. Most important of all, she was beyond her father, both his commands and his person.

She walked through a whole new world, the only world that held the possibility of safety. Maybe, Karmille thought, this was where she could be truly free.

But she had left behind her own personal court as well. What would she do without her influence, and her underlings? There were times when only destroying lives made her truly happy.

She would have to build her influence, and her control, all over again.

The Judge consulted a small stone he had withdrawn from a pouch that hung at his belt.

"Others have passed this way before us. That is good."

"Is it those we seek?"

"Most likely. Whoever it is, it is they who will spring the hidden traps, or be waylaid by those who choose to dwell down here. They allow us to move more quickly in pursuit."

There was a whole new set of dangers in the tunnels as well; unknown and exciting. Karmille smiled at the thought. That was a freedom of a different sort.

They traveled through these passageways in three groups of two: Sasseen's soldiers first, then the Judge and the lady, finally her guard and her assassin.

As they walked through the torchlit tunnels, Karmille found herself staring at the soldiers in the lead. She did not know the exact nature of the spell over them, or even their exact definition of life.

"Can they talk?"

The Judge nodded. "If they did so before, they may do so now. My work is very thorough." He sounded slightly offended that she would even think to ask such a question.

The guard whom Sasseen had dubbed the Blade stepped forward to speak.

"They come from the enemy, m'lady. If they were dangerous before, might they not be dangerous now?"

"Ah," the Judge purred, "that is not to say I haven't put certain limits on their activities." He pointed to the one on the left. "This one is quite aware that my magic is the only thing that gives him life, if you wish to call it that. And his fellow soldier is quite aware that I could place him in an equally precarious predicament at a moment's notice.''

"So you would not mind killing the second one?'' Karmille asked.

"It would be entirely within reason. They are much more controllable after they are dead. The only unfortunate side effect is that no matter how potent the magic, after a time they begin to rot.'' He waved Karmille forward. "Why not go and satisfy your curiosity? We are in no danger at present, and it will help to pass the time.''

Karmille decided she would do just that. She hurried forward so that she was directly behind the marching pair.

She addressed the dead one first. His highborn skin shone paler than pale, as if he might be made of wax.

"You are Lepp?''

"That was my name in life.'' His voice was even, but without emotion.

She turned to the other. His noble face was the one that showed pain. "And you—''

"Must I?'' He grimaced, clutching at his stomach. "Savignon.'' His words came slowly, as if he fought against even using his voice. "I—live—to serve—the Judge Sasseen.''

Lady Karmille laughed softly. "This one appears to have a bit of fire still in him.''

"This control is a delicate thing,'' the Judge called from behind her. "One does not wish to drain away their energy entirely. This sort of—fire, as you call it—will show through from time to time.''

"And you seek Aubric?'' she asked the soldiers.

"He was our friend,'' Lepp replied flatly.

Savignon joined in. "We must make sure—that he joins us.''

"The Judge commands us,'' Lepp put in.

Karmille clapped her hands and laughed. "It is a wonderful irony.''

"And properly cruel,'' the Judge agreed. "I knew you

would approve. Consider this method of capture my gift.''

Karmille spun about to smile at Sasseen. Now he wished to curry her favor? Perhaps there was hope for this Judge after all. She slowed her pace so that Sasseen once again walked beside her.

"So, what do we do when we capture Aubric?"

"Ah. Capturing your errant soldier is only the beginning. We will enlist him in our service as well. And there is a maidservant, too, I believe? We may have a different use for her. Bait, I believe it is called."

"So Aubric will be mine, to do with whatever I want?"

"If you so desire. But, so long as your father has seen fit to free us from the castle, it would be a shame for us not to explore certain other regions down here, regions that might give us the means to do the things we've always wanted."

"Always wanted? What do you mean by that?"

"You are far more transparent than you believe, m'lady. To begin with, I believe we will topple your father from his throne. In the end, everything will change."

So it shall.

Karmille found that she was not in the least upset that Sasseen knew that particular fact about her. If she had her way, everything would change.

That, she realized, was another definition of freedom.

· 24 ·

F EAR COULD ONLY TAKE A
person so far. Jacobsen just wasn't used to running.

Tsang and Gontor had not simply left the first room
behind. As soon as they entered the next stark-white corridor, they left in a hurry. Tsang had started running and
Gontor had followed, loping along easily behind the warrior. Jacobsen was surprised that Gontor's body made no
noise as he ran. He guessed he had expected it to clank like
the Tin Man in *The Wizard of Oz*.

By the speed of their flight, Jacobsen guessed the two
in the lead might know a bit more about what was following them than they were willing to explain. Summitch managed to keep up with them, too, pumping his short legs up
and down with astonishing speed. And Jacobsen? He managed to keep up for a couple of minutes. He hadn't really
run like this since back in college. His legs grew tired. His
ribs ached. His lungs were burning. He didn't think he'd
be able to run another step.

"Stop," Jacobsen managed. "No more."

"Hold!" Gontor boomed. "Friend Jacobsen is correct."

He was? Jacobsen leaned against a wall, trying to get air back into his lungs.

"We could be running into a trap," Gontor explained. "No matter what manner of beast might be following us, we need to find the second room. We have put some distance between ourselves and, well—it is time for more cautious exploration."

Tsang nodded, turned again, and marched off at a steady pace. Jacobsen had hoped for more of a rest period. He was so winded, he could barely keep up with a steady walk. Still, he didn't dare get left behind.

"I have met some things down here that I would rather avoid myself," Summitch said. "There was a certain set of creatures controlled by the lady Karmille, dark things that moved so fast they couldn't clearly be seen; things that would not be satisfied until they consumed somebody's soul."

"Nasty things," Gontor agreed. "But rather primitive, really. I would imagine, this deep in the tunnels, there would be protections set up against that sort of spell. The Judges were very thorough in erecting safeguards, especially since a disagreement soon erupted over who had true ownership of this place. Now, looking at that displacement spell we ran into before the first room, I imagine those spells are still firmly in place."

"Primitive?" Summitch shivered. "I suppose that is one thing you can call those creatures. But then whatever is now killing the other occupants of the tunnel is—what—more sophisticated?"

Gontor nodded. "These tunnels hold many secrets."

"That didn't answer the little guy's question at all!" Jacobsen was getting annoyed with the metal man's non-answers. "Do you just like sounding mysterious?"

Gontor considered the new question for a minute. "Why, yes, yes I do. Good of you to point that out, too."

Tsang pounded his staff on the hard white floor to attract his companions' attention. Jacobsen looked beyond Gontor, and saw they had reached another intersection, with another all-white corridor again intersecting their present passageway at exact right angles.

Gontor considered their options for a minute before speaking.

"Straight has served us well so far. Unless either of you fellows have another idea?"

Jacobsen could feel his frustration rise. "So you have no idea where you are going?"

"As I said, much can change in a thousand years."

Gontor stared down the tunnel again. Perhaps, if he looked long enough, he would indeed be able to see everything. "I always find I get to where I want to go, eventually. Perhaps it is a gift, perhaps it is simple perseverance."

Jacobsen still wasn't satisfied. "What if whatever is killing things behind us catches up with us before we reach our goal?"

"That will not happen if we are the chosen."

Jacobsen decided not to pursue what would happen if they were not the chosen.

Gontor waved them forward. "Even though we exercise caution, we should not dawdle."

Summitch spoke up as Tsang led them forward. "What exactly are we trying to avoid?"

"Avoid?" Gontor pondered this for a moment as well. "We'd just as soon avoid any unpleasantness. Primarily, however, we wish to avoid the Judges."

"Judges?" Summitch asked. "Down here?"

"They were the ones who first created these tunnels, with the aid of certain other entities, which the Judges then summarily banished. Even in those days when they worked together as a caste, the Judges were not to be trusted."

Summitch frowned at the walls around him. "I did not know we would be confronting Judges."

"Only if we have to." Gontor pounded his metal chest with his fist. It rang hollowly, as though there was nothing inside. "Remember, I do have certain powers and abilities.

However, I don't like to test them any more than necessary. It is astonishing how much farther you can get on mystery and innuendo than you can on brute force."

The small man shook his head. "Summitch never goes anywhere that has Judges," he said, his voice sliding back into mutter mode.

Gontor shook his head as well. "It is only through challenging ourselves that we might achieve our aims. The time is come at last. But I'm not the only one aware of this.

"Nothing is ever simple in these things. In the end, many of us will be dead, a few will have found glory, and all three worlds will be changed forever."

So Jacobsen was stuck in the middle of it? He sighed. All he had ever wanted was a little peace and quiet.

Gontor turned to Jacobsen and nodded. "Sometimes we are moved by forces greater than ourselves, or our desires."

There he went again. Jacobsen suppressed a shiver. Could this being read his mind? Gontor seemed to be half god, half confidence man. Sometimes, he reminded Jacobsen of no one so much as the last guy to sell him a car.

Jacobsen had no other options. He had to see this through. After all, he could have been saddled with a far less clever leader than one with the soul of a used car salesman.

"I will tell you," Gontor went on, "as succinctly as I know, what we need to achieve for now." He looked, in turn, at each of his three companions. "We need to possess three keys. Whether or not they will look like keys is, of course, entirely another matter.

"Once, each of the three rooms held a key to the power. At least one of the keys has been moved. It's a problem." Gontor shook his head once more. "You're imprisoned for a thousand years, things change."

The metal man did like to go on about that, as if his imprisonment gave him his identity. Jacobsen had done a couple of nights in jail himself, and found it a strange mix of boredom and depression, broken by the odd moment of total fear. He supposed doing a thousand years of that might be enough to drive anybody off their rocker.

Tsang pointed with his staff down the left-hand side of the intersecting tunnel. Gontor stepped forward to take a closer look and Summitch and Jacobsen crowded after him. There appeared, at some distance, to be some variation in the light, as if there were some change in the perfectly straight tunnel.

Gontor confirmed what Jacobsen was thinking. "That could be the second room. Or it could be a trap. Why don't we go and see?"

Oh, Jacobsen thought, why the hell not?

AUBRIC HAD BEEN through many battles, but this was the first time he had witnessed a slaughter.

The first man's screams had drawn half a dozen others, all with weapons drawn. But none of their swords or knives or spears or arrows were any match for the dancing lights. One by one, the newcomers were stripped of their blood, their flesh, their lives. The floor was littered with pale grey ash, so light it drifted away even in what small breeze the tunnels had to offer.

The death dance always began in the same way, with the singing lights swirling above their enemies' heads like halos. Most of their victims were too surprised by the glowing creatures to put up much of a fight; one or two hardly moved at all.

All Aubric could do was stay well out of the way, wary of any attack from the other end of the tunnel. Runt stood silently beside him. They did not touch.

There were more lights than before, the tunnel above the ash aglow with a hundred dancing flames, as though feeding on flesh caused their numbers to double, then double again.

The flutes trumpeted ever louder as well, gaining a hard

percussive edge that turned the tunes from melancholy
pleas to marching demands.

(We grow in strength.)

(We grow in number.)

(We will be reborn!)

(You are the one.)

(We have wanted this for so long.)

(Finding you was the sign.)

(You gave us courage.)

(We will consume all our enemies!)

(They will pay for their treachery.)

(We will rule again.)

(When the time is right, you must do as you are bid.)

Aubric watched it all in numb silence. He had fought in
the war for a year and more. He had seen death, but never
like this. What was he supposed to do? He had killed, but
they destroyed.

Runt hugged her arms close to her chest and silently
observed the carnage. After an initial moment of shock, she
simply watched, as if she could become used to anything.

Once, in a moment of silence between deaths, she remarked, "The most beautiful of serpents are often the most
deadly. It is something that my mother used to say."

Kitchen wisdom. Aubric had heard similar sayings himself. It was also something, he reflected, that might equally
apply to High Ones such as the lady Karmille.

The lights wavered toward them, giddy in their power,
drunk on destruction.

(We are strong.)

(We will be free.)

(Give us more.)

"I think this will stop now."

Aubric turned at the sound of a man's voice. Three individuals stood in the middle of the tunnels; two men, one
woman, dressed all in black. Aubric had not seen or heard
them approach. They were simply there.

(No.)

(We are too strong.)

(We are too many.)

The lights swarmed back toward the newcomers. The three in black moved their arms in unison, first lifting their right arms, then their left, then both at once, their hands describing fantastic shapes in the air, a silent dance of sorcery.

The lights darted away, their music gaining a desperate rhythm.

(It is time, Sir Aubric.)

(You will help us.)

(Quickly!)

(You must help us!)

The lights were swarming toward him. Runt screamed. Was it their turn to be consumed?

One of the men in black stepped forward. "That will never do." He clapped his hands and spoke four words. "Judges must be obeyed," he added.

The dancing creatures stopped abruptly.

The Judge smiled. "These lights are frozen in place. Quite literally. I have frozen the moisture in the air around them. They will not move for quite a while. It is a temporary solution, but it will suffice for now."

"Are you surprised that we defeated them so easily?" the second male Judge asked. "We've been waiting for them. We knew they would be coming back." He studied Aubric and Runt. "We didn't know they would have human accomplices."

"They may be innocent," the first Judge remarked.

The second Judge pointed to the frozen lights. "Nothing tainted by those things is ever innocent."

"Tainted?" Runt complained. "We don't even know what those creatures are!"

The first Judge considered her remark a moment before replying.

"They are both beautiful and powerful. So powerful they could not be destroyed. Once they had bodies, much

like you or I. When we could not take their power, we took
away their physical form.''

"Should they regain the castle," the second Judge
added, "there would be disaster."

Aubric didn't speak. He could still hear the sound of
flutes, very far away.

(We will destroy all of you!)

(We will have our rightful place.)

(We will have our revenge.)

The first Judge sighed. "They did beautiful work. It is
a shame they are so unstable." He glanced at Runt and
smiled. "Of course, we added a thing or two to the tunnels
as well. Fire Judges gave us the torches, for those who need
an external source of light."

"Do you really think they know nothing?" the second
Judge demanded. "We have innocents in our midst?"

The woman spoke then, "I think they may be *too* innocent." She smiled at Aubric and Runt. "There are methods to determine innocence and guilt. And they are
nowhere as severe as rumored. Even some of the guilty
survive."

Runt cowered like a cornered animal. "What do you
want to know? We'll tell you anything!"

The woman in black renewed her smile. "Apparently
they still know the power of Judges." She walked closer
to Runt. "Why are you here?"

"I came with Aubric. He followed the lights when they
came into our chamber."

"It does indeed sound innocent," the female Judge acknowledged. "But you have not really answered my question, telling me instead only how you came here, not why."

"I came because my lady told me to do so. 'Whatever
the soldier desires, that you will fulfill.' Those were her
exact words!"

"Your lady?"

Runt nodded, eager to please. "The lady Karmille, princess of the Grey."

The first Judge spoke up then, "You work for a lady of the Grey? Now we may need to have you killed."

"We have managed to stay far away from the Colors of the castle," the second said. "It was inevitable that some-day the Colors would come to us."

"We do not acknowledge the lords above," the first added. "The Judges are the true masters of the castle. Soon, we will reassert our right to rule."

Even someone as unskilled as Aubric knew that, for good or ill, most Judges' spells would not affect a High One from within the royal court. The pure-blooded lords of the castle could only be harmed through indirect action. The High Ones would not hesitate to destroy a renegade Judge. How could this small band of rebel Judges hope to prevail in a direct confrontation with the powers above?

"We have been waiting for the proper moment," the first Judge continued. "This lady's kind shall no longer be a problem. They will destroy themselves, after they have destroyed each other. There will be no end to war until all of the old order is dead."

"Or until a new order takes its place," added the woman among them.

The second Judge looked straight at Aubric. "Your sol-dier does not speak."

Aubric had indeed maintained a cautious silence. All Runt's words had gained her was the likelihood of an early death. He was no doubt overdue for death as well, probably in some macabre, painful, Judge-inspired way. Why not speak, then, if only to confound their superior captors? "You seem very sure of your plan, even though you have spent a thousand years underground. These creatures spoke of a prophecy as well; a prophecy quite different from your plans for the future."

His statement only caused the Judges to smile.

"I would think it would have to be, the first said.

"It always happens in times of strife," the second added. "Perhaps a dozen prophecies will rise from the chaos. All too mortal a response, anything to give the people hope."

"And I believe that nothing happens completely by chance," the third remarked. "The possibility exists that one of these prophecies might actually be true." It was the woman's turn to study Aubric. "No doubt you were told that you were a part of these prophecies." She smiled. "What better way to ensure your cooperation. At least until our little blood-sucking embers grew hungry. You should be glad that these things found other sustenance."

"But we are now burdened with these innocents," put in the second Judge. "What should we do with our discovery?"

"Kill them and move on," the woman advised.

The first Judge raised his hand to quiet his fellows. "I think we should not limit our options. Let them stay alive for now. Others are coming soon, the wait will be over. This only makes the wait more interesting."

He turned to their captives. "So you will be our guests." The first Judge bowed slightly in a mockery of manners. "You know we could do whatever we wished with you. Why not come with us under your own power? It's decidedly more pleasant that way."

Runt stepped forward; Aubric could see no alternative but to follow.

"Oh, yes," the first Judge added. "Bring our blood-sucking friends as well."

The female Judge clapped her hands. The shimmering cloud of light followed them down the hallway. Music still came from within the cloud, but it was discordant and held no meaning.

The creatures were only frozen; not defeated. Even the Judges had said this was only a temporary measure. The creatures had wanted to use Aubric before. Perhaps he could use them in turn.

Since this adventure began, Aubric had wanted nothing so much as to return to the Green. Now, he found himself in the midst of a secret society of Judges, a society that appeared to hold great knowledge of the world and the war above. If he listened carefully, he might be able to discover information helpful to the Green's cause. Until then, he only had to remember two things:

He would use anything he needed to survive and return to the Green.

While he was still alive, he had not lost.

. 25 .

"MY LORD."

Kedrik, High Lord of the Grey, looked up from his reverie to see First Judge Basoff standing by his side.

Kedrik had been expecting the Judge. He had sent all his servants away and locked himself alone in his most private quarters, the one room where no one but the High Lord of the Grey was allowed to enter.

Or so the others of the Court assumed. Basoff had sought him out here before. Basoff and Kedrik had an understanding. The Judge knew what the High Lord truly needed.

As Basoff knew when Kedrik truly needed him.

The Judge bowed low before his lord, his wrinkled face inclined toward the rich grey carpet of the royal suite.

"You have summoned me," the Judge intoned.

Kedrik raised a single eyebrow. Had he summoned the Judge? Not through any command; not, indeed, through any spoken words. But he had desired Basoff's presence in his thoughts. And now Basoff was here. Had they grown that close?

"I suppose I have," the High Lord agreed. "Arise, Basoff."

Basoff lifted his head to look at his lord.

Basoff was almost as old as Kedrik, his face a mass of fine lines, defeating the visage of perpetual youth most of the Judges maintained. Basoff and Kedrik were by far the oldest within the Keep. Together, their years were greater than even the length of the great war.

"The honored Judge Sasseen is gone," Basoff stated.

"With the last of my daughters," Kedrik added. Basoff would know it all already.

"It is an audacious move."

Kedrik nodded slightly, accepting the compliment. "Only when they realize their predicament will they be willing to accept our assistance."

Basoff considered this a moment before replying. "Even then, Sasseen may resist. But we may find other enticements. But by inserting them within the inner seat of power, the battle will come back to us, straight to the Inner Keep of the Grey."

Kedrik smiled when he thought of it. "It is only through taking great risks that we might win our greatest victory."

"Still, my lord, I do wish you had consulted me before you set out upon this course. No one knows the renegade Judges better than myself."

"No, Basoff. I wanted to be sure that Sasseen and the other Judges had no inkling of my plan—our plan, now." He looked down at his hands, the dark spots once again appearing beneath his knuckles. "Even with all your knowledge, I can feel my life begin to slip away. We must act now, while we still have the strength."

"But to bring such power here—"

"If we win, we gain it all. And if we lose?" Kedrik chuckled. "After all, if we are dead, who cares what happens to the rest?"

Kedrik shook his head, almost overwhelmed by the sheer cleverness of his own plan. "It will happen, Basoff.

My dear daughter has been directed toward this every day of her life. Even now, she puts the wheels in motion that will bring the power straight to our door, and under our control." Kedrik sighed at the pleasantness of the thought. "And then, Basoff, we will live forever."

Basoff smiled at last. "Perhaps we shall, my lord. Such a plan deserves a celebration."

Kedrik did his best not to sound too eager. "I was hoping you would offer."

"No, you were expecting it. You know I can deny my lord nothing."

So they played out their small charade. Ever since a dozen years before, when Basoff had first introduced Kedrik to the sprites, they had repeated this sort of conversation perhaps a thousand times. It was all so casual, as if what they spoke of mattered little.

When he first began to use Bosoff's gift, Kedrik supposed it was casual, another diversion to help him forget for an hour or two the weight of leadership in time of war. He would go months without contact. But then the war went badly, and Kedrik found he needed the reassurance every few weeks. People seemed to be plotting against him within his own court! Perhaps he needed to relax every few days.

The war quieted a bit. Immediate court intrigues were settled. But Kedrik had fallen into a routine. He needed these visits to sustain himself, to give him the strength to carry on.

Life would not be worth living without his little pretties. They would let him do most anything. And what they would do to him in return—Kedrik shuddered in anticipation.

Until he met the sprites, the High Lord had been reluctant to waste his seed. He jealously guarded his vitality, careful to keep pure the bloodlines of the House of Grey. So his daughter Karmille was of course his granddaughter, his great-granddaughter, and his great-great-granddaughter as well; and, if he had his way, the mother and grandmother of future sons and daughters. And he should soon use Karmille to produce a new generation. Except that, lately, he could not find the enthusiasm. He had to marshal his energies for what was important: these special evenings with his pretties.

But he was High Lord. His saying was law. If his daughter survived, perhaps he could add her to the game. The way they excited him, melding with his skin as he entered them, caressing his thoughts, setting every aged nerve ablaze with passion. No single woman, even of his own flesh, could satisfy his passion this way.

Perhaps the pretties could prepare Karmille, emotionally, physically, sensually. As, even now, he could feel their touch upon his extremities.

Kedrik looked up to realize that Judge Basoff had departed. When had he gone? Not that it mattered.

Kedrik shuddered with anticipation. Nothing mattered now, save what happened next.

THE JUDGE STOPPED abruptly.

"Danger," Sasseen announced.

Lady Karmille saw no difference in the tunnels whatsoever. She lacked the senses and the skills. This, after all, was why she had brought a Judge along.

"There are spells here, but they have already been violated," the Judge explained. "The damage makes them easy to find." He pointed to a rock wall to their left. "Here."

The single word from the Judge seemed to change the wall before them. A small hole formed about three feet from the ground, then grew until it reached from floor to ceiling, revealing a new tunnel before them.

Karmille took a step forward. The boundaries here were white and smooth, altogether more civilized than the earlier tunnels. "These walls are much finer than the others we have passed through," she observed. "It's almost a palace underground."

Sasseen glanced at their new surroundings as he waved for his soldiers to lead the way. "There are indeed palaces built within these tunnels. This is something else." He entered the new, almost blindingly white tunnel himself.

Karmille quickly followed. "You said something—*disturbed* this place before. Was it Aubric and the girl?" She glanced back to see her guard and her assassin both close behind, both frowning at their new surroundings.

Sasseen frowned, too, as he looked about. "It may be, in part. I am sorry I cannot be more specific. I am surprised by the complexity of the currents. These lower tunnels have spent hundreds of years empty, virtually without use. But, only within the last few hours, all that has changed. There are a number of others nearby." Before Karmille could ask a question, he added, "The air tells me."

"Does the—air tell you who else has passed this way?" she asked.

"Not so much who," Sasseen replied, "as what."

Karmille frowned. She did not like these complications. Who else would want to search these places? Perhaps the plan she had put before her father had been too convincing. He would not dare to leave the palace, but he could have sent his agents.

"I sensed traces of other things before," Sasseen replied. He raised his hand, feeling the space before him as one might feel for cracks in a wall. "They are quite strong here."

"Before?" she asked.

"I detected them upon your clothing when we first met. Do not be alarmed. I don't believe you had any direct contact. But you, or someone close to you, has encountered them recently. I think they may have even been in your chambers in the palace."

Then this plot against her had gone further than she imagined! She felt an instant's alarm that she had not been safe even in her own quarters, even thought again of her father and his plans, but dismissed those emotions as unimportant to her present task. That life was behind her for now. Her life in the palace would never be the same again. But she would make those who plotted against her—Aubric and the gnarlyman and whoever controlled them—suffer for a very long time.

The Judge ordered his soldiers to slow their march. At this slower speed, the movements of their arms and legs grew herky-jerky; they looked less like thinking beings and more like six-foot marionettes with a Judge pulling their strings.

Sasseen looked back to Karmille. "I will tell you a little story to pass the time." The casualness of his tone was in marked contrast to the care with which he took every step.

"The tunnels have not changed greatly for hundreds of years," Sasseen continued, "harkening back to a time when all Judges attempted to act in unity; when they tried to find some place far away from the castles of the High Lords. Such an effort was doomed to failure. Magic is far too individual an art to lend itself to a group. The four great magicks, earth, air, fire, and water, each at times finds itself in opposition to the others, and the practitioners discovered, in times of strife, that their spells controlled their actions, rather than that they controlled their spells."

A hundred paces down the hall, they came to a place where the corridor intersected with another. Sasseen called for his soldiers to halt as he strode forward to study the situation.

"We are once again in the Judges' domain," he said. "It becomes difficult to find our way. The air shows traces of a hundred different sorceries." He pulled the servant's finger that Karmille had given him from some inner pocket of his robes, and held it in the center of his palm, murmuring a finding spell just under his breath. The mummified finger rose from his hand and pointed down the tunnel to the left.

Sasseen smiled. "The simple spells are always the best." He snatched the finger from the air and returned it to his pocket. "We are shown the way to follow those we seek." He sniffed the air. "I believe them to be quite close."

He barked a quick command, and his two soldiers marched heavily down the hallway to their left. This newest tunnel was no different from the one they had just left; white, and featureless.

Karmille realized that the Judges had constructed this maze of tunnels as one huge trap. They certainly would have the means to identify their location; no doubt there were mystical symbols here which only they could read. Sasseen said the place reeked of sorcery. As ordinary as the tunnels appeared, she doubted they even stayed fixed in place, but were full of hidden entryways and treacherous turns that might change at a Judge's whim. And anyone not thoroughly versed in the Judges' art would become instantly lost, until such time as they were captured or died of starvation.

This had only one practical result. The farther down the tunnels they journeyed, the more she needed Judge Sasseen.

Karmille did not enjoy feeling dependent. She wanted to smash something, to hear someone cry out in pain. She would have to find a way to express her anger. Perhaps she would be inspired when they finally caught up with Aubric and the maid.

"What?" Sasseen's angry outburst made her look ahead.

The soldiers stopped, their feet moved up and down, but they made no forward progress, as if they had come up against an invisible wall. Their arms flailed and their heads bobbed as they bounced repeatedly off the unseen barrier. It made them look even more like spastic puppets.

Sasseen hesitated. "Perhaps those we seek have not come this way at all."

Karmille could hear her heart beating. "Is it a trap?"

"Or a warning. If we turn around now and they let us leave—"

"Is there no way to defend ourselves?"

"I am only one Judge. They are many."

A single, clear tone filled the hall before them, like a sustained note from a crystal gong. As the note surrounded them, Karmille noticed the air shimmer in the tunnel, the white of the walls shifting to reds, yellows, and blues, so that for an instant the place was full of rainbows, as if a single clear tone might change everything.

The tone faded, replaced by silence; the walls returned to relentless white.

Sasseen nodded. "I believe that was an announcement. Others approach us. I do not have the power to turn them away. It could be that we should turn back."

But Karmille did not have a choice.

"I can never go back to the palace the way it was."

Her father had done her a favor. He would expect much in return. She could never go back to the palace without a means to kill him.

"Nor can I," Sasseen agreed. "Whatever influence I had in Court disappeared with my departure. But I, like you, seek bigger things. You are a clever woman, and I maintain some small skills. Perhaps we can be more determined in our desperation."

He sniffed the air. "They will be here in a moment."

Sasseen called his soldiers back to his side. They turned from the barrier and began to march the twenty-five paces that separated them.

The clear gong sounded for a second time, followed by another wave of color. Sasseen nodded.

Four figures dressed in heavy black robes stepped through the barrier the soldiers had been unable to pass. From their dress, they all looked like Judges, but Karmille could tell no more about them, for none of the figures had faces. After looking at the four again, she realized that while she could study every detail of their robes, or the

ornate staffs of obsidian and gold that two of the four carried, it was impossible for her to focus her gaze on those
spaces where their faces should be.

"Hold!" one of them called. "Make no move!"

Blade and Flik stepped forward, undaunted by the newcomers' strange appearance.

"Behind us, m'lady," Blade said.

"It is foolish to threaten us," remarked one of the faceless four; Karmille found it impossible to discern which one
it was that had spoken. "We could destroy you with a gesture."

"All too true," Sasseen agreed from where he stood at
Karmille's side. "But we have far too much to offer for
you to resort to violence."

What was Sasseen doing? He had not spoken previously
of alliances. Would he turn against her to join a band of
renegade Judges?

"He is Air." This time, the Judge's voice was that of a
woman.

"Judge Sasseen of the House of Grey," the man's voice
agreed. The voice carried a sarcasm the equal of Karmille's
father's.

"At least one of them is a Water Judge." Sasseen turned
to speak to Karmille as if the others didn't matter. "He
reads my identity within my blood." He looked back to the
four, who still approached. "Why won't you do me the
same courtesy and identify yourselves?"

"Does such a question even merit a response?" the
woman's voice asked.

"The House of Grey was a place of treachery when last
we were in contact," answered a second man's voice,
somewhat lower than the first. "We doubt that seven hundred years of constant warfare have made your court any
more benign."

"You will know only what we choose to tell you," the
first Judge added. "Until such a time as we reach an agree-

ment, we will continue to employ every tactical advantage."

The woman Judge spoke next, her voice even cooler than before. "And this is the lady Karmille."

Karmille's own guards stiffened at the mention of her name.

"A direct descendant of Kedrik?" The slightest of the four Judges raised her staff and shook it at the Judge by Karmille's side. "You did not tell us, Sasseen, that you brought us a gift."

"I did not tell you anything," Sasseen replied dryly.

"Perhaps even too direct a descendant," the woman's voice purred. "A magnificent example of inbreeding."

"A High One from the court of the Grey," the second Judge agreed. Karmille believed the voice was coming from the Judge to the woman's right. Even without faces, she was beginning to be able to tell them apart. "Now she can be of some use."

"As a sacrifice?" the woman mused.

"Quite possibly. But first she might serve us best as a hostage."

"I believe I have heard enough," Sasseen replied. "We didn't come here simply to die, nor for your amusement. After all, you are the ones who've chosen to hide yourselves away for a thousand years."

The Judges continued to approach, passing to either side of the soldiers frozen mid-stride. Karmille was aware of her guard and her assassin, one to either side of her, both breathing shallowly, preparing for a battle that they could not win. Neither, she noticed, had drawn a weapon. It was a prudent decision on their part. Had they appeared more of a threat, no doubt they would be as frozen as Sasseen's puppets.

"Animating the dead, are we?" a male Judge asked.

Karmille wondered if that was supposed to be a joke. Sasseen's soldiers couldn't move at all.

Three of the four faceless ones stopped next to the fro-

zen soldiers. One bypassed the pair, walking forward until
he was directly facing Sasseen. Not that Karmille could
discern any of this Judge's features. Trying to look at his
face this close up made her short of breath. Light seemed
to bounce away from the Judge's features, causing her eyes
to want to look up or down or side to side, in a dozen
different directions away from his face. It was making her
nauseous.

"You are not unaware of the risk in coming here," the
Judge said to Sasseen.

"Indeed I am quite aware. But it is not the only risk in
my life." Sasseen waved to those around him. "I did not
bring an army, only a few individuals for personal protection. I never planned to fight with you."

"A prudent course," the Judge agreed.

The woman laughed. "Because you could not win, unless, of course, you found a way to attack us by surprise."

"One Judge, perhaps," Sasseen agreed. "A group of
Judges—"

"Impossible?" The Judge with the deeper voice spat out
the word. "Yet someone manages it."

The Judge who had stepped forward looked back to the
others. "Do you think he knows?"

The deeper-voiced Judge laughed. "I doubt it."

The woman added, "Yet looking for that deeper mystery
is what brought you to our attention."

Sasseen stared at her. "Are you saying I was beneath
your notice?"

"Oh, we would have dealt with you eventually," the
woman assured him. "We simply did not perceive you as
much of a threat."

The Judge in the lead turned to regard Karmille.

"We should kill her," the woman remarked.

"If you feel it necessary," Sasseen hurriedly replied.
"However, a High One like this would be of use to you in
a changing world."

"It is true," the first Judge agreed. "In setting the lords

one against the other, she might make an attractive pawn.''

"It is not for us to decide anyway," the deeper voice interjected. "We need to take them elsewhere to decide their fate."

"Time to move on," the woman agreed. "You are only worth so much attention."

"For now"—the last of the Judges, another woman, finally spoke—"you will join us."

"A moment," Judge Sasseen said. He walked quickly over to the spot where his two soldiers still stood frozen mid-stride. He spoke sharply, and the dead one, Lepp, jerked into motion. He said something once, then again, finally clapping his hands in front of the other, before the still-living one responded. It was the first time Karmille had seen her Judge falter during a sorcerous act. Perhaps it betrayed a certain nervousness with the other Judges, or perhaps the Judges' spell was difficult for Sasseen to overcome. Either way, Karmille did not find the spectacle reassuring.

Sasseen stepped away from his reanimated soldiers. "Now I am ready."

"By custom," the first Judge explained, "you will get a review before the assembly. But it does seem a bit of a shame we can't dispose of all of you now." He waved for Sasseen to precede him.

The soldiers turned to follow.

Blade and Flik both glanced at Karmille, looking for direction.

"Now is not the time," she said softly. Both of her personal guards fell back a step behind her.

The Judges fell into step on either side of Sasseen. Like went with like, she guessed.

"And the rest of my party?" Sasseen asked.

"They will follow us," the second, mostly silent, woman ordered. Karmille guessed that she was the true leader.

With that, the five Judges turned back to that passageway from which the four had emerged a moment before. No one urged Karmille or the others in Sasseen's party to keep up with the Judges, no one even checked to see if she was walking in the same direction; as if Karmille was beneath their notice. They were Judges; escape was out of the question. Perhaps they wished her to try. Perhaps they were still looking for an excuse to kill her.

She walked forward in her own small group of five, the soldiers before her, her guards behind.

"Sasseen!" The first Judge who had spoken seemed to want to chat. "You are the first Judge from the High Ones that we have seen in close to three hundred years."

"Who was the last one we let live?" the first woman asked a bit too cheerfully.

The one with the deep voice explained. "One hundred and sixteen years after the beginning of the great war, we accepted seven Judges from above into our midst. We were most naive. They almost destroyed us. The experience left us with a certain skepticism."

"So we have not let a Judge live since—how long has it been?" the first woman added all too enthusiastically. "Perhaps three times as long as that."

"There have been one or two who have survived our tests," the first Judge added. "But for the most part? You know as well as we do that Judges are not to be trusted."

From the way the faceless ones laughed, they all found that quite amusing. Even Sasseen attempted a smile.

The second woman's voice cut through the merriment. "This is not for us to decide. Their fate rests with all of us."

Karmille had no illusions that Sasseen might sacrifice himself for her. Maybe these Judges knew of spells that might destroy even a High One.

Her guards would die for her. And she would die before being humiliated by a Judge.

She would survive, even triumph, if she could find the way. And if not?

The lady Karmille would not go gently.

• • •

IT MOVED BECAUSE it was told to, marching down the tunnel next to its dead companion.

They said it was still alive.

Once it had had a name. It had trouble recalling. Its master reminded it from time to time. When it heard its name, it could remember; not a lot, little things mostly, moments from another life.

It reached for those flashes from its past, as if the memories could save it from its servitude. Marching from a castle, the sun through the trees, swallowing cool water, a sword swinging through the air, a woman's fingers caressing a cheek.

It remembered, but it could not translate its memories into action. It could wish for movement, but it could not get its muscles to obey. There was no escape.

Yet still it remembered.

He remembered.

He was Savignon, a soldier of the Green.

He remembered when he was taken. Lepp had already been stabbed, his life nearly gone. Aubric had been farthest from the attack. He had moved more quickly than his companions. They had been confronted by an overwhelming force. Aubric had run.

Perhaps Aubric was still free.

Perhaps Aubric could get revenge for all of them. Savignon knew he would do the same if he could.

If he could.

His memories were all he had.

Perhaps he could hide these glimmers of consciousness, hoard his memories, gather his willpower together until he could act on his own. Perhaps he could learn to move a finger, then a hand, then a fist.

It might not be much, but it would have meaning. Perhaps it could lead to the death of a Judge, or the great lady of the Grey who traveled with them.

His life might be draining away by slow degrees, almost beyond his control, but, if he could have that final moment, it would not end in vain!

"Wait a moment." It was his master's voice. "One of my playthings will not follow."

No! His master knew something was wrong. He had given something away. His master said something, words Savignon could almost understand.

His eyes lost their focus; his thoughts—his thoughts—had to keep his—

Everything was slipping away.

He would remember!

The master turned to him.

He would . . .

The master raised his hand.

He . . .

The master snapped his fingers, then nodded.

"That's better."

It followed its master deeper within the passageway.

. 26 .

"IT WILL BE VERY SOON now," Mrs. Mendeck announced. "Take the next left."

Jackie Porter did what she was told, just as she had for the last hour and a half. Once the old woman had climbed into her car, she had immediately begun giving Jackie directions, taking her out of town in the general direction of Gravesville, though not on the interstate or any other major road. Conversation beyond that had been kept to a minimum. Mrs. Mendeck claimed she had to concentrate.

In a matter of minutes, Jackie and Mrs. Mendeck were driving down back country roads. It was remarkable how quickly they'd left even the suburbs behind. They were in a part of the state that Jackie had never driven through. Mrs. Mendeck acted like she knew exactly where she was going, directing Jackie to zigzag along state roads that seemed to pass through only the smallest towns. She was so sure of every sudden turn. Maybe when she was younger she liked to explore. Maybe she really was on some supernatural wavelength, proving that all those ads for psychics on cable TV were really true.

Perhaps, Jackie thought, the old lady was really taking her on some wild-goose chase. Brian would show up safe at home, his father would recover from his coma, and everyone at the station would start treating her as a human being.

She sighed. If the woman next to her wouldn't talk, Jackie could at least lead a rich fantasy life. Whatever happened, she had decided to see it through to the end.

"We are very close now." The old lady seemed to relax a bit. She sighed. "Forgive me for not being more sociable. It is not my primary skill. Without your help, both Brian and Karen might be lost to us. And that could lead to something much worse."

"Something worse?" Jackie prompted.

"Much worse," Mrs. Mendeck said. She frowned and peered out the window.

Apparently, the older woman didn't want to be drawn into conversation. Or maybe Jackie was just too tired to come up with the right thing to say. It was the middle of the night. She was awake thanks to a combination of caffeine and nerves, and her reaction time wasn't what it should be.

"So what do we do when we get there?" she asked instead.

"Why, save them, of course."

Jackie was beginning to find this annoying. "Excuse me, but I think I have the right to know," she said, doing her best to keep her voice even. "Save them, exactly, from what?"

Mrs. Mendeck sighed again. "Oh, dear. Some times I just assume everyone knows. Part of my background, I suppose. Well, we don't need to go into that now. What are we saving them from?" She sighed once again. "Well, he's known as Mr. Smith. He is a very bad man, Officer, except he isn't exactly a man. Both Karen and Brian pose a threat to him. No doubt he's behind the wounding of Brian's father. He's been after Karen, too. Even I can't guess at his exact plan."

So they were after some sort of child abductor? Maybe Jackie shouldn't be out on her own like this. Maybe she should call in the staties, or even the FBI.

"Do you have any proof of this?"

The old woman nodded her head. "Oh, I believe it completely. And, when this is over, I imagine you'll agree with me."

In other words, Mrs. Mendeck didn't have any proof; at least nothing that could be verified in a court of law. Jackie could still just be listening to the rantings of a crazy old lady. She'd have to look into this a little bit further before she brought in anybody else. But what if this Smith was some sort of molester or procurer or something else just as bad?

Jackie would have to approach this cautiously, and call in the big guns at the first sign of real trouble. Maybe she could do some good here after all.

She looked up in the night sky as the car climbed a hill. The stars had been blotted out by extremely dark clouds, illuminated by distant flashes and rumblings. Heat lightning, maybe, lighting up one corner of the sky, then another.

The old lady shifted in her seat. "Oh, dear, I don't like the look of that at all."

"I wouldn't worry, Mrs. Mendeck. I'm out in the squad car in all kinds of weather. I'm used to driving in the rain."

"It wasn't the weather I was worried about. This sort of thing, it isn't quite natural, you see." She paused a moment before she added, "When we reach Brian and Karen—it means Mr. Smith will be there, too."

It did? She almost asked the old woman how she was so sure this child snatcher would be waiting for them. But she was sure if she did that Mrs. Mendeck would launch into a whole new round of vague explanations which would be more confusing than not knowing at all.

"It will be very soon," Mrs. Mendeck assured her.

Jackie nodded. She'd have to concentrate on driving, and leave the puzzles for later.

JOE SAW THE headlights in the distance. It was the first car they'd seen in over an hour. He supposed, if you lived in the boonies, you didn't do much driving after three A.M. There was something about the dark sky and the weird lightning that made him want to pull the LeSabre off on some hidden dirt road and not even get close to another car.

Brian leaned forward from the backseat. "Who's that?"

Joe wondered if Brian felt it, too.

"Probably nothing," Joe replied, searching for some logical explanation. "Some guy going out to do the milk deliveries."

"Milk deliveries?" Karen asked.

Wow, Joe thought. These kids had probably never seen a milkman. That's what living in the city would do for you. "All right, so maybe he's delivering the newspapers. They do things like that out in the country. At least I think they do."

The lights kept on coming.

Ernie sat up in the front passenger seat and stared at the oncoming car.

"Uh-uh," he muttered.

"What?" Joe demanded. Not that he got a reasoned reply from his cousin at the best of times. But Joe was just looking for something, anything, to help him figure out what was going on here.

Ernie moaned. "We can't do this anymore! My head is gonna explode!"

"We're going home," Joe replied evenly. "You'll feel better when we're back in the city."

Ernie shook his head violently. "You gotta pull over!"

"What?" Joe hadn't heard this much emotion in his cousin's voice in a long time. "You're gonna be sick?"

Ernie lurched over and grabbed for the wheel. "Pull over! Now!"

The car swerved for an instant before Joe got it back under control. He pushed his cousin away with his free hand. "What? You want to get us all killed?"

"Pull over!" Ernie shrieked like some demented two-year-old. "Pull over! Pull over!"

"What's gotten into you, man?"

"We can't go there!" Ernie rocked back and forth in his seat. "We have to wait! If we don't wait, oh, what he's gonna do to us!"

Now Ernie was really scaring him. This had something to do with the Smith guy again.

"You don't stop this, I'm throwing you out on the road."

"We can't let them go! He needs them!" Ernie grabbed for the wheel again, but this time Joe was ready. He threw his elbow in Ernie's path, so that his cousin caught it on the chin. Ernie made a whuffing sound and fell back in his seat. It was a good thing Ernie was still a little out-of-it from that stuff back at the truck stop. He didn't seem to have much fight in him.

But his cousin wasn't done yet. "More than one way . . . one way to stop a car." Ernie opened the glove compartment.

He always kept a .44 in there. Maybe, Joe thought, his cousin was groggy for another reason. Maybe Ernie wasn't Ernie anymore. Maybe he was being controlled again by someone else. Maybe he was going to try to kill all of them.

Joe knew he'd strapped on his own .38 for a reason. He pulled it quickly from the holster under his jacket, and pressed the muzzle into his cousin's neck. "You make a move toward that gun, I'm going to blow your head off!"

"More than one way." Ernie kept fumbling for the gun. "More than one way."

"Oh, hell," Joe muttered. He pulled the gun back from Ernie's neck.

"Aha!" Ernie called as he laid both his hands on top of the .44.

Joe swung the hand with the gun down hard on the back of Ernie's head. Ernie slumped down, unconscious.

Joe shook his head. He glanced up at the road. The headlights were maybe a hundred feet away. He looked down at Ernie. "Your dad's going to have to have a long talk with you when we get home." If they ever got home.

"Watch out!" Brian called from the backseat.

Joe looked up. A man in a trench coat was standing right in the middle of the road.

Joe swerved to the shoulder, then back on the road. He was barely able to keep the car from plowing into a six-foot ditch just beyond the shoulder. He had to thank his cousin for that. The fight with Ernie had forced him to slow down. The car couldn't have been doing much more than thirty when the guy appeared.

"That was Mr. Smith!" Brian announced.

So the guy after the kids was out here, waiting for them? But if he was out in the middle of the road, who was in the other car?

Joe looked in the rearview mirror. The man in the trench coat was nowhere to be seen.

The other car honked its horn as it approached. It pulled off to the side of the road just ahead.

Oh, what the hell. Joe slowed down to get a look at the occupants of the other vehicle. The passenger door opened and an old lady stepped out; an old lady Joe had seen before.

"It's Mrs. Mendeck!" Karen called.

"Okay," Joe said. He stopped the car. He felt an immense sense of relief, although he realized that—beyond what Karen and Brian had told him—he had no concrete reason to feel that way.

Hey, why would Brian and Karen lie?

For that matter, why would Ernie try to kill him?

Enough of that. Joe climbed out of the car.

He hoped this was what they were looking for.

· 27 ·

"Is there any doubt that we are the chosen?" Gontor cheered. "Look what has happened here! The moment we are about to be discovered, the forces of darkness are turned aside!"

Well, Jacobsen thought, if the metal guy said so. It sounded to him more like the so-called forces of darkness were out there fighting other forces of darkness. If anything, it made him think their situation was even more dangerous than it was before.

"And the second room is just before us," Gontor continued. "We'll easily find the second key, which of course, won't look like a key at all."

"Of course." Summitch looked toward the ceiling. "What else could we expect?"

Tsang quickly strode ahead of them. "We are certainly among the chosen!" Gontor exclaimed.

Jacobsen turned to follow the others, staring at Tsang's form, which rippled as he marched ahead, as if Jacobsen were seeing the warrior through a pane of ancient glass.

"We pass through another spell!" Gontor announced in case they hadn't noticed.

It tingled. It felt rather soothing, if Jacobsen could believe this particular spell was benign. He almost laughed.

Were *any* of the spells benign?

"Hold!" Perhaps the warrior and the metal man could communicate in some way that was beyond Jacobsen.

Tsang plunged the spear ahead of him.

"What have you found?" Gontor's chuckle echoed off their surroundings.

Their surroundings answered for the silent warrior. The walls shifted. Spaces grew. They were already in the room. It formed around them.

Tsang's actions had caused a transformation. Where once there was a featureless white corridor, now there was a space the equal of the room they had recently left. But this room was full of color. A hundred different objects vied for their attention: a silver globe, a rod of crimson light, a pile of ancient books stacked against a wall, a tapestry that appeared to move as you walked across the room, a multicolored bird perched far overhead, singing a simple, repetitive song. Everywhere Jacobsen looked there was more; too much color for the eyes to hold.

With all those other things around him, Jacobsen still could not take his eyes away from the bowl on the table in the center of the room. There in the bowl was an assortment of fruit quite similar to what had been served with their meal back in Gontor's cavern; similar, but better. A few of the shapes seemed more familiar than his last breakfast. Jacobsen thought he saw apples and a banana. The closer he came, the more of the fruit he thought he recognized. A pear peeked out toward the bottom, an orange showed itself near the top. But these were more than simple apples and pears and bananas. The reds and greens and yellows were vibrant. They caught the light just so, inviting him to run his fingers across their shiny skin, to feel their cool weight in his hand. Their delicate aroma made his stomach rumble. How long had it been since he'd eaten, anyway? He wanted to bite into one, to taste the sweet pulp on his tongue.

Jacobsen stepped over to the bowl for a closer look.

"I wouldn't eat any of that," Summitch cautioned. "In a place like this, if it looks too good to be true, then it is."

"Obviously a man who knows the world underground." Gontor agreed.

Jacobsen yelped in surprise as a great purple spider nearly the size of his fist crawled atop the very apple he was reaching for. The creature hissed at him, the sound of air escaping a punctured tire. If he had touched the fruit, he would have found the spider, too.

Gontor's laughter echoed through the room. Jacobsen realized he had jumped when the spider had shown itself.

He was feeling more than a bit annoyed. What would a spider be doing in this most antiseptic of environments? Until now, these unnatural tunnels had been free of insects and vermin.

What would be the last thing in the world Jacobsen would want to touch? He looked closely at the great hairy thing. Its multifaceted eyes were black and foreboding, its fangs dripping something the color of blood. This was no ordinary hideous purple spider. Its hideousness was here to serve a very definite purpose.

Jacobsen turned to the small fellow at his side. "Summitch, I think I finally have a use for your knife."

Summitch looked less than pleased at the prospect. "Careful! You can't replace those around here!"

"And you only have seven more secreted about your person," Gontor boomed. "Or is it eight?"

Summitch looked most uncomfortable. "It depends upon your exact definition of knife."

Jacobsen had already pulled the blade from where he had tucked it in his belt. Something about this spider wasn't right, and he would find out exactly what it was.

The spider hissed again as Jacobsen slowly lowered the blade toward its body, but it made no move to escape or defend itself. The spider clanked as the blade bounced off it, the sound of metal striking metal.

Jacobsen winced as Gontor laughed again. He didn't like being the butt of even a minor deity's derision.

"Jacobsen," the metal man's voice boomed, "you are indispensable!" He stepped forward, reaching out for the bowl of fruit. "The noble fool will show them the way. Gentlemen, we have found the key."

The spider crawled up the bronze man's fingers and sat upon his palm.

"What better place to hide your most prized possession than by making it the last thing you would touch?"

Tsang beat his staff against the wall to gain the others' attention. He pointed toward the tunnel that they had just left behind.

"We have visitors again." Gontor glanced down at the spider in his hand. "I suppose we could continue to avoid them, but why bother? With the possession of one of the keys, our position has changed."

Tsang looked most upset at that decision. Summitch began to mutter.

Gontor threw his arms open. "Follow my thinking. One of the keys has gone elsewhere. Either they have moved it, or they know who has taken it. And I've seen the third key in their Council chamber. We must confront them sooner or later. And, with luck, we can prevent them from killing us long enough to gain the information."

There Gontor was, talking about death again. Jacobsen stuck the knife back in his belt. He doubted it would be of much use against the kind of forces Gontor spoke of. Maybe it was time for the gun.

The colors swirled about them as a dozen men in black strode into the room from what appeared to be a dozen different points.

None of the men had faces, or at least faces that Jacobsen could see. The light played tricks in the space before their hoods, so that Jacobsen's eyes couldn't focus properly, seeing only a blur of light and shadow as he looked away.

"Not that old trick!" Gontor roared. "What kind of welcoming committee doesn't show their true nature? I think we should be on a more equal footing than that, don't you?"

The metal man clapped his hands. A great ringing filled the room as all twelve of the newcomers cried out at once.

Suddenly, Jacobsen could see the faces of all the men in black; faces wincing in surprise and pain. Wisps of smoke rose from a couple of the robes.

"You'll have to forgive the crudeness of my remedy," Gontor announced. "I admit that wasn't the most exact of spells. But at most you've only lost your outermost layer of skin. You won't have any trouble growing it back, so long as you stay out of the sun." The man of metal chuckled. "Sorry. I did find that amusing."

"We will be able to counteract anything you attempt!" one of the men in black shouted angrily. "We are united, a hundred Judges strong. You will come with us *now*."

"I suppose I will," Gontor agreed. "We all will. After all, there are one or two things in your possession that we need."

"You seek to infuriate us." The man in black who'd spoken before—a Judge?—seemed calmer now. "We are ready for your tactics. It will not be so easy to escape us this time."

Gontor nodded. "As I recall, it wasn't so easy the last time, either."

"We have studied your escape long and hard," the Judge continued. "The weaknesses you exploited before no longer exist."

Gontor's voice sighed from everywhere. "No doubt you will find a way to do everything eventually. It's a problem with immortality, you know. Sooner or later, the impossible becomes the everyday."

The twelve Judges formed a circle around the four intruders.

"You can say what you will," the Judge said, "but you will come with us."

So they were to be taken prisoner. The Judges kept their distance; the circle drew no closer. An opening formed before Jacobsen as two of the Judges stepped aside.

Tsang led the way. Summitch followed. Jacobsen went third this time. He felt like they were being herded.

Jacobsen felt the reassuring weight of the gun beneath his coat as he walked past the Judges. He wondered, Do herded sheep ever bite?

The metal man strode by his side.

"Do not do anything foolish," Gontor warned.

Foolish? But, Jacobsen wondered, if he was the fool, wasn't that his very nature?

"At least," Gontor amended, "until we allow our guests to escort us to their innermost chambers. After all, there are still those items we seek."

Surrounded by Judges, they walked from the room. Jacobsen noted that no one had asked Gontor for the return of the key. He wasn't sure who was in control here. From the behavior of both Gontor and the Judges, he guessed they didn't really know either.

The Judge who was the spokesman walked immediately behind them. "We will take you directly to the inner chamber. You will stand before the Grand Council."

"Sounds good to me," Gontor said amiably. "Even a deity needs the occasional change of pace."

Jacobsen kept his arms close to his sides, pressing the gun between his elbow and his rib cage. He might need to do something very foolish very soon.

. 28 .

AUBRIC HAD NEVER EX-
pected to find this great an open space so far beneath the
earth. The three Judges guided them down a corridor that
grew wider and higher with every step they took. Rocks
and grass and bushes appeared near to either wall, the way
between them defining itself into a path. The ceiling grew
more distant, too, as if they might leave the tunnels behind
forever.

Trees began to appear on either side of the widening
path. They passed a small building made of stone. Aubric
saw dozens of trees before them, as if the path were entering a forest. But, once they reached the woods, they passed
only another ten or twelve trees before the path turned
abruptly, showing a great vista spread out below as their
course angled sharply downward. Before them were a hundred buildings or more, a small village laid out at the bottom of a valley that stretched for miles in either direction.

As they began their descent toward the hamlet below,
Aubric once more looked above. They might almost be in
the world outside, save that the grey far overhead was not
cloud cover but a rock ceiling.

It was as bright as day in this place, but the light didn't come from anywhere. It simply was. Aubric noticed that he cast no shadow. Perhaps it was only because he was once again a captive, but Aubric found the whole place to be a bit depressing.

Runt clung to his arm. Ever since they had been captured by the Judges, she seemed to be attached to his side.

"What will they do with us?" she whispered as they climbed down the path, one Judge before them, the two others behind. Between the two Judges who followed, the cloud of once-ringing lights floated through the air.

"I can't see that they would have any quarrel with us," Aubric replied. "Certainly none with you."

He knew he was only speaking in an attempt to calm her. He hoped their captors' words from before, when they had threatened to kill Runt simply because she was a servant of the Grey, were only meant to frighten them into submission. Judges were capable of any excess, even in the courts upon the surface of their world, where each Judge had to answer to a High Lord. He didn't want to think what they might do without the restraints of the High Court.

The slope of the hill grew less pronounced, and small buildings of mud and stone appeared on either side of the path. They were entering the outskirts of the village. It was larger than it had looked from the hill above; over a hundred of the smaller structures spread around them, with perhaps a score of larger structures directly before them. They saw other people in the distance on the path leading down, men and women dressed in the plain brown clothing of peasants, but as they approached, these folk scurried out of the way, rushing into or behind the small homes on either side, as if they wanted no part of those descending the hill. How long had it been since any of these people had seen strangers? Aubric wondered if they were more scared of the Judges' captives or the Judges themselves.

The Judge who led their party glanced back at Aubric and Runt.

"Judges require many others to serve them. These dwellings around us house a few of those who do our bidding. Depending upon the Council's decision, you may become our servants, or our prisoners."

Aubric's hand automatically reached for his sword, the sword already taken by M'lady's guards. The Judges regarded him with a mixture of amusement and contempt. They obviously did not consider him a threat.

The first Judge seemed genuinely amused by Aubric's reaction. "You act as though you could affect your destiny; as though you once had control." He waved to the man and woman behind Aubric and Runt. "Only Judges have control. All else is illusion."

"You are fortunate," the woman Judge said from behind them. "The others have been captured, and are being brought here even now. The Council has already convened. You will not need to wait long to learn your fate."

Others? Was Aubric supposed to know who she was referring to? It seemed the Judges already assumed his guilt. But for what crime? He recalled again how quickly the Judges seemed to condemn Runt when she revealed she was employed by the House of Grey. He again resolved to say nothing.

The buildings to either side of them grew taller, one after another, as Aubric and Runt were led into the village center. The path they walked had widened to a broad avenue as they left the hillside, with market stalls to either side. But there were no buyers and sellers in this market; all had fled when they saw Aubric and the Judges approaching.

They walked past dozens of low buildings made of mud and dark stone and a pair of cross streets full of buildings much the same. All were silent and empty. At most, Aubric glimpsed a fleeing figure in the distance or heard a slamming door. They passed no children or animals, no colorful signs or market displays. Life here seemed always hidden. There was no joy in this place, only fear.

The street opened into a plaza with a grand structure at its center; a high, circular building made all of stone.

The first Judge stopped half a dozen feet before the entrance. "We've reached our final destination." He stepped aside and indicated a stone archway before them. "You will go first now. Others will follow."

Aubric and Runt passed beneath the arch. They found themselves on a path of fitted stone, which led to a set of seven steps leading down, then opened up into the floor of a large amphitheater; an amphitheater with every surrounding seat filled by hundreds of individuals in black. The place was full of Judges.

"Wait," a deep voice rumbled overhead. "Others will join us."

Aubric looked around for the source of the voice, and saw a great, dark shape hovering in the air, like a shadow in a place that held no shadows. The shape spun about and Aubric realized it held the form of a gigantic head, with the outline of eyes and nose and mouth sketched in a brighter grey. The shape's mouth moved as Aubric heard the voice again.

"I am the Great Judge, voice of the Council, voice of the Unfettered. We wait for others of your kind. If you wish to declare your guilt now, it will make the proceedings simpler."

Runt looked up at the shadow. "We haven't done anything!"

"Trespass, spying, deceit, plans to overthrow the Unfettered," the Great Judge replied. "But those are the merest sample of your crimes. Only you may confess to the true enormity of your actions."

The shadow paused, waiting for them to speak. But even Runt was silent now. Perhaps she realized as Aubric did, that to speak would be to incriminate themselves.

Runt moved close to Aubric's ear.

"Everyone's sleeping," she whispered.

Aubric looked down from the huge face that dominated the amphitheater and turned his attention to the seats beyond. All the Judges who sat in the theater around them appeared to be in a trance.

"They are my mind," the Great Judge rumbled. "They are my power. I am their voice. Individually, we might fail. But I hold the strength of the multitude."

The cloud of light creatures had floated in behind Aubric and Runt, but there was no sign of their escort of Judges. Aubric guessed the three had joined the others, to add to the great shadow's power.

"Others approach," the Great Judge advised.

"My lady," Runt whispered.

Aubric turned back to the entryway to see the lady Karmille, accompanied by a Judge with a band of grey upon his sleeve. Aubric was startled by who was in her company. Not the Judge, or the pair of men who, from their similar grey garb, appeared to be part of Karmille's personal guard. No, it was the two ragged soldiers who moved stiffly at the rear.

"Sav!" he called. "Lepp!"

The two acted as though they had not heard him. At first Aubric thought they might be angry. He had fled rather than fight by their side. But then he noted their pale faces and blank expressions. No doubt Karmille's Judge had them trapped in a spell.

Runt had turned toward Karmille and prostrated herself upon the theater floor. With all the Judges surrounding them, this woman was the one Runt truly feared.

"M'lady!" she cried. "Do not judge me harshly."

The lady Karmille nodded at her servant and smiled. "You have nothing to fear from me. You were only doing what I asked."

What exactly might that be? Aubric wondered. Not that it mattered here, where the lady had no power.

The lady Karmille smiled at him. "I was hoping to meet you again in different circumstances."

Aubric had little patience for her now. He looked to the Judge by her side.

"What have you done to them?" Aubric demanded.

The Judge raised his eyebrows in overdramatic surprise. "Ah. You would be talking about your friends. I simply inducted them into my service. No small task, considering one of them is dead."

Aubric's hands tightened into fists. When he had left the two soldiers, they had been fighting for their lives. Now they were puppets for the lady Karmille's pleasure. Aubric felt a great anger grow within him; an anger the Judges might never let him express.

The light in the amphitheater flickered for the merest of instants. The Great Judge moaned. The Judge at Karmille's side gasped and staggered back a step.

"Judge Sasseen," the great shadow rumbled. "To test our power is to test our patience. Do not do so again."

The Judge at Karmille's side bowed low. "I only wish to—"

"Silence," the shadow commanded. "We have no use for a Judge's lies."

(We will.)

Aubric blinked. He heard the words inside his head; the first coherent thought to come from the frozen mass. Was he the only one to notice? He hoped he hadn't looked too surprised. The Great Judge, distracted perhaps by Sasseen's trickery, seemed not to realize the ringing lights were pulling free of their frozen spell.

"You will be judged," the great shadow announced to Sasseen

"Judged?" Sasseen demanded. "On what evidence?"

"We know all we need to know."

(You must.)

(Only one.)

"There are others," the Great Judge continued. "We will render the final judgment when all are present."

(We will not.)

(You must help.)

"We have sent search parties throughout our domain," the shadow explained. "There is no way they can escape."

(Only one chance.)

(We will not be.)

The shadow head quivered in the air. "Something is interfering with our concentration. Sasseen, we have warned you."

Sasseen seemed greatly offended. "What if I were to tell you that it was not me?"

"There are others." The Great Judge paused. "Others who have given us difficulty. They are coming to join us." The shadow head swung from side to side, as if searching for trickery. "Soon we will know the truth. Soon we will end our exile underground."

(You must help us.)

(We will not be defeated.)

Aubric wished he knew what the lights wanted. If only they would show him the way.

His arms began to tingle. The tips of his fingers felt as though they were on fire.

(It will be soon.)

(We only await the proper moment.)

The great shadow laughed. "The others arrive! Soon we will have everything!"

(Soon.) The ringing lights agreed.

IMP KNEW.

Sasseen had set him free in the last moment that he dared, so Imp could fly. He was gone in an instant from that place choked with magic, gone from the village of a thousand frightened souls, gone through the tunnels that pierced the rock, then gone through the rock itself.

Sasseen had created him for this moment. Now he would be fulfilled.

Joyfully, Imp flew toward home.

· 29 ·

It was all a matter of belief; belief that had been gone from this world for a thousand years.

Mr. Smith—or the being who in this world called himself Smith—would now have to gather all his power. He had never expected it would come to this so soon.

At first, it had been absurdly easy. When they no longer believed in you, they no longer had any defenses. They accepted Smith's bargains easily, not realizing the true price. More humans fell under his sway every day; more pawns to be used in the coming game.

But there were those few who were not human.

They were an annoyance, almost beneath his notice. He would never have thought that eliminating a nuisance could become so much trouble. He should have seen to the problem himself. But it had become so easy for him to remain in the background and allow others to take the risks.

The others made mistakes. The nuisance grew.

And then he noticed other cracks in his perfect plan. Again, it was a matter of belief. He even had difficulty with those who accepted his bargains. In the old days, they would have immediately known they were damned. Now they fought him. They would fight for their freedom. They would fight for their pride. They would lose of course, but the conflict was distracting. It drained resources not yet fully formed, diverted spells already shaken by the physical laws of this new reality.

And the nuisance grew. It was such a small matter, a bargain that was a remnant of ancient times, the exchange of humans for Changelings. Changelings, put upon this hostile world where, if they did not die, they would never realize any more than a small part of their potential. The High Ones gained human servants, and disposed of those who might prove dangerous were they allowed to remain in the realm.

They were more than a nuisance, then. They could be a danger.

Much could happen in a thousand years. A few of the Changelings had survived, had even gained a certain knowledge. They helped each other, and, as they survived, they grew stronger. The key told him there were those growing among them who might approach the ancient strength, before they had been brought under control in that most ancient bargain. The thought of Changelings regaining that much power was most troubling. It was only prudent to eliminate them before they reached their potential.

Humans had traditionally sensed the difference in the Changelings, and had always hated them for it. But many of the old ways had been lost, replaced by the worship of science. Most in this modern world would deny the very existence of these beings from elsewhere. And the Change-lings had used this ignorance to their advantage, leading invisible lives among them. The key whispered that a few of the Changelings had managed to join with the humans, to marry and produce offspring, a mingling of bloodlines.

When he first devised his plan, Mr. Smith had not considered the changes wrought by a thousand years. Perhaps, in this place, the differences were not so great as before.

It was a matter of belief.

This whole world conspired against him.

JOE BEAST COULD hear nothing but the wind. And he could see nothing at all.

He could feel the car behind him. He leaned against it, reassured by its reality. The air before him was impenetrable, dark beyond the blackness of a cloudless night, except for occasional flashes of blinding light. If it wasn't for the car at his back and the asphalt beneath his feet, he might think he was floating in a cloud in the middle of a thunderstorm. He shook his head, and saw glimmers of light at the edges of his vision. He shut his eyes tight, then opened them to slits to see a hazy view of the highway and farmers' fields. It was gone as soon as he opened his eyes again; the world—or his sight—plunged back into darkness.

That bastard Smith was playing with his mind. If he was this overwhelmed by his surroundings, he hated to think what was happening to Ernie.

"Jesus." He heard his cousin's moan from somewhere nearby.

"Ernie!" he called. "Stay close to the car!"

"Joe. Don't know. Can't think. Jesus. Joey."

He hadn't called him Joey since the two of them were kids. Ernie was always a little slow, but right now he sounded pitiful.

"Ernest!" another voice rasped nearby, almost the sound of branches tossed by the wind. "Come to me, Ernest."

"Jesus, Joey!" his cousin moaned again.

"Ernie!" Joe yelled back. What could he do for his cousin if he couldn't see?

Smith was going to win.

No. Joe Beast wasn't the kind of guy who panicked,

even now. Smith wouldn't win if he refused to play by Smith's rules.

"Smith! I know you're out there! And I'm not letting you get away with this!" He had pulled his gun from its shoulder holster. But where should he point it in the darkness? The world flashed white for an instant, too bright to see. The wind redoubled, pushing him back against the LeSabre.

Joe shouted and pointed the gun over his head. He pulled the trigger.

The gunshot sounded like thunder.

FOR ONE VERY long moment, Brian Clark felt very much alone. The world was shrouded in an unnatural darkness. He felt like he would never see the sun again.

Brian had always been alone. His parents had never wanted him. Whatever he did—or failed to do—made his mother angry, his father embarrassed. His father had gotten shot because of him. And now? Brian couldn't even run away right. Smith had them right where he wanted. Brian would get them all killed: Karen, and Mrs. Mendeck, and the two men who—

"Brian!"

Brian blinked, pulling himself out of his thoughts.

Karen's voice called out of the darkness. "Mrs. Mendeck is here. She wants us all together."

Together? Yes. That's why they were here, to be together. Brian shook his head. The despair had been overwhelming, as deep as the darkness. Everything hadn't been lost yet. There were still choices to be made.

"Together," Mrs. Mendeck said, "we can push this aside."

He felt two hands take one of his.

"We're here, Brian," Karen said into his left ear. "Together."

"All three of us need only one thought," Mrs. Mendeck added on the right. "Stop."

"Stop?" Brian asked.

"That's it," the older woman said. "Think it as hard as you can."

That was it? But how did you think *hard*? Brian recognized doubt, creeping back in. He would have to concentrate. That was what Mrs. Mendeck meant, after all.

Stop, he thought.

"Again. When I squeeze your hand, squeeze Karen's in turn. All together now. Stop."

He felt Mrs. Mendeck squeeze his right hand. He squeezed Karen's hand a second later.

Stop.

Brian heard a gunshot.

The darkness was gone. He blinked, trying to adjust to the daylight, focusing on an ordinary stretch of road. Smith stood fifty feet away. Joe's cousin Ernie stumbled toward the Pale Man. Ernie was holding his head. He looked like he was in pain.

Over by the car, six feet away, Joe held a revolver pointed into the air. He lowered it to aim at Smith.

"Ernest!" Smith cried hoarsely.

Ernie's head jerked up to look at the Pale Man.

"You must protect me!"

Ernie stopped and stared at Smith.

Smith smiled back at him.

"There are some people here who need to die."

ERNIE'S HEAD HURT.

Mr. Smith was smiling his death's-head grin. He held out his hand as if he expected Ernie to join him.

Ernie walked toward the Pale Man. He couldn't help himself. He could see nothing but that grin.

"Ernest. I need you."

He couldn't do anything but walk.

"Jesus," Ernie moaned.

"Not exactly," Mr. Smith replied. "Didn't you hear me, Ernest? I need you to protect me."

"Protect." Only after he heard the word did Ernie realize it had come from his own mouth.

"Do you see the man with the gun?"

Ernie spun around. There. There was the man with the gun, pointing it past Ernie at Mr. Smith.

Ernie recognized the man.

"Joey?" he asked weakly.

"Take out your gun, Ernest," Smith called from behind him, "and shoot him."

Take out his gun?

Yes.

Ernie felt his fingers curl around the handle, felt the weight of the piece as he freed it from the holster.

"Shoot," his voice demanded from somewhere far away.

He had to do it.

Didn't he?

JOE WONDERED IF it was too late. Smith had gotten to his cousin. Ernie was pointing his gun straight at Joe's chest.

"Ernie!" Joe called. "What are you doing? Don't you know me?"

Ernie's gun hand shook. He moaned.

"Shoot," he said.

Smith was going to have cousin kill cousin.

Not if Joe Beast could help it. He looked away from Ernie, back at his real target. He was going to rid the world of Mr. Smith. That way, only one cousin had to die.

"Shoot, Ernest!" Smith demanded. "If you do not shoot, I will make you very sorry."

"Joey!" The word started out as a moan in Ernie's throat, and ended up a scream.

Joe pulled the trigger.

Ernie shut up. But behind him came a sound that was half the scream of an animal, half the howl of the wind.

Smith clutched his shoulder. He twisted around, falling to the pavement.

THIS COULDN'T BE.

The Changelings had ripped away Smith's magic. The human had used his primitive projectile weapon to shoot him. Shoot him!

Smith felt pain.

Blood flowed from the wound in his shoulder. He needed to retreat to a more familiar place, where he might be able to speed the healing.

He needed only a moment to get away; a simple disorientation. Simple? Nothing was simple anymore. It was hard for him to gather the strength through the pain.

"Ernest!" he called.

His lumbering servant spun to face Smith, the gun still in his hand. "No more! You wanted me to kill Joey! No more!"

He pointed the gun at his master.

Smith still had enough strength to handle this.

. 30 .

WELL, JACOBSEN THOUGHT, *now* we're in fantasyland.

The dozen Judges led Jacobsen and his companions into an open space far beneath the ground; sort of a world out of time, filled with stone cottages straight from the Middle Ages. The empty village had been suitably rustic, and, despite its lack of occupants, had an oddly lived-in look. The market square they passed through was full of fruit and vegetables and freshly slaughtered game. They passed a tiny horse on wheels, a child's plaything, discarded in the street. A fire roared beneath a cauldron at the market's center. It all felt as if the townspeople had disappeared only an instant before.

The Judges had not stopped until they marched the four of them into this huge open amphitheater, the sort of place you always saw in gladiator movies. Every seat had been filled by somebody in black. The severity of their robes emphasized the paleness of their faces, their skin like carved ivory. It looked like these people never saw the sun.

But then, Jacobsen thought, the sun wasn't much in

evidence this far underground. He sighed. Perhaps he was the noble fool after all.

There were others waiting for them at the center of the amphitheater. It looked like Gontor's group was late to the party. They'd been beaten here by eight people and— what?—a couple of odd looking *clouds,* both hanging about six feet above the ground. One of them glittered prettily in the air, like a large balloon made of Christmas lights. The other cloud was all blacks and dirty greys, looking like nothing so much as an escaped puff of industrial pollution.

These two floating things were particularly noticeable because one of the clouds—the dark one—was talking.

"Our final guests arrive," the dark cloud boomed. Its voice, imposing as it was, was no match for Gontor's. "I see they bring something that doesn't belong to them."

What was the cloud talking about? The spider key?

"And I suppose it belongs to you?" Gontor's voice boomed back.

The cloud spun about to regard them. Yes, regard them, for on this side the smoky blacks and greys formed the outline of a face.

"It has for a thousand years," the cloud replied.

"A thousand years of war," Gontor pointed out. "Quite a legacy."

The cloud glowered at the man of bronze. "We were too lenient the last time you were our guest. We will not repeat the mistake."

Gontor laughed at that. "Last time I was your guest, you nearly killed me."

The cloud did not appreciate the humor. "This time, we will complete the job."

Gontor clapped his metal hands. "And all this time, I thought I was immortal." The ringing filled the amphitheater.

The great black cloud paused for a moment at this. "If you do not surrender the item, we will kill your companions."

Summitch shook his head and muttered. He took a step forward. "Um—Why do you only speak to him?" he called in an uncertain but much louder voice. "Others here may have valuable information."

Before the cloud could respond, the small fellow turned to another of those standing in the circle.

"It is good to see you again, Aubric. After all, we have not concluded our bargain."

"You speak from a position of power, you Judge of Judges," Gontor's voice boomed. "You must have the keys."

"We make no such claims," the cloud replied.

"They don't seem to be saying much of anything," Summitch commented.

Gontor turned to regard the others in the room. "They have had the keys in the past. They generally keep one with them at all times."

"We will hear no more of this!" The cloud was growing angry. "You will give us what we want!"

Jacobsen didn't know how an emotionless bronze statue could look bored, but Gontor managed it. "You don't push around someone who has entered into godhood."

(Now!)

What was that? Jacobsen looked around to see if some-one else had spoken. He could have sworn he'd heard that last voice inside his head.

"So you'll kill us without a fair hearing?" Summitch asked.

"Fair?" the Great Judge replied. "This word holds no meaning."

"It appears," Gontor remarked, "this overstuffed cloud could improve its vocabulary."

"The Great Judge is the greatest power in the world! The Great Judge will not be mocked!"

Gontor glanced at Summitch. "I guess the Great Judge doesn't like us pointing out his character flaws."

The smoky edges of the cloud roiled about, turning

darker still. If this cloud was anything near ordinary, it would be looking a lot like rain.

"Silence, or we will kill you!" the cloud rumbled. The smoky mass made another sound, halfway between a cough and thunder. "There are some things the Great Judge cannot do. We will pick a representative from among us who will choose who is the first to die."

Great, Jacobsen thought. Gontor and Summitch were actively annoying this supernatural being. Between them, they seemed to be hatching a plan. Not that they'd tell Jacobsen anything about it.

All he knew was that something unpleasant—pain, death, even more magic—was very near. And if he was going to be involved, maybe he could take one or two of these black-garbed creeps with him.

Jacobsen had had just about enough *attitude* in his life. Maybe, he thought, it was time for the gun.

AUBRIC FELT ALL his senses were heightened. As strange as the world seemed before, now it felt far stranger. He was surrounded by pieces of his history.

His two closest friends in battle, or what was left of them, stood only a few feet away. Aubric was not sure which was the greater abomination: Lepp, reanimated from beyond the grave, or Sav, still alive but helpless to control his actions.

Summitch had sidled up and spoken to him with a knowing wink. It was as if the little fellow had expected him to be here all along. And the lady Karmille; she had been so deadly in the kingdom of the Grey. Now, even with her entourage, she stood in silence before the all-powerful Judges, no more than a shade of her former self.

All those Aubric had encountered in the past few days were together now, as though, from the moment he and his friends were attacked in the sunny field above, everything had been leading to this moment.

(Now,) the lights announced.

"Now," remarked the single Judge, who had stepped down into the amphitheater. "We begin to remove the players from the game. Who will be the first to die?" He glanced first at Summitch. "Perhaps the gnarlyman who spoke with surprising eloquence. He should be reminded how little Judges like to be spoken to out of turn." He turned to Aubric, who stood above the still prostrate Runt. "Or one of those who accompanied our ancient enemy. We will show what happens to those who turn against us."

He walked a few more paces until he stood before the lady's entourage. "Or perhaps we may best make a statement by killing Karmille." The lady stared back at him, as if his words had no effect. "Rarely have we seen a High One so full of pride." He shook his head. "In this world, only the Judges are allowed pride."

He paused before Sasseen. "Unless, of course, a Judge would turn against his peers. There are so many that have to die. I should thank you for the amusement you will provide."

He strode back at last before Summitch and the three who accompanied him.

"Um—" Summitch said. "Perhaps I spoke out of turn."

"Surely you can find a better victim than a gnarlyman!" came the booming voice that seemed to originate everywhere. Aubric figured it had something to do with the metal man.

The lone Judge ignored them. "Our real business is with Gontor, and the three who have the misfortune to accompany him. If we wish to save the gnarlyman to hear him plead for mercy, what of the other, silent two?" He looked past Summitch to a tall man in white, then shook his head again. "Oh, not the warrior. He will die much too stoically for any real amusement."

He smiled as he looked at the oddly dressed man standing behind the others. "What of this nervous fellow in the very strange clothes? Yes, I imagine we can make his death both noisy and unpleasant.''

The nervous man spoke for the first time. ''You're threatening me?''

The Judge laughed. ''This is far more than a threat.''

''Mister, I've been threatened by far better than you.'' He glanced forward at the metal man. ''Gontor, I think it's time.''

''We await your signal,'' a booming voice called from everywhere.

''Allllrrright!'' the nervous man screamed. He pulled something silver from within his clothes. ''Die, fantasy scum!''

A loud explosion shook the air. The lone Judge fell back as the dark cloud shivered overhead.

(Now!)

Aubric could feel the voices in his blood.

(Now! Now! Now!)

He spun around. The loud noise seemed to have disturbed more than one of the Judges' spells. The ringing lights were no longer bound together. Hundreds of tiny points of brightness streamed forward, all swarming toward Aubric.

(We are fulfilled!)

Aubric screamed.

LAST TIME JACOBSEN fired the gun, the sky had fallen. This time, it was a real catastrophe.

He was pretty sure he'd killed the man who was taunting him. At least the gun could still do that. But that was only the beginning. The weird cloud with a face had started screaming. And the second cloud dissolved into what looked like a thousand fireflies, all of them streaming toward the man Summitch had called Aubric.

The people in black were stirring in the stands. Some appeared disoriented, and a few were obviously unconscious, but a dozen or more rushed down toward the floor of the amphitheater.

"Stop him!" they called.

"Stop Aubric! Kill him before they can bond!"

Aubric was screaming, too. His whole body was covered by the tiny lights, glowing bright red where they met his skin.

"Sasseen!" the highborn lady called. "What's happening?"

"Whatever that fool did disrupted all the spells," replied the Judge by her side. "Nothing's working right!"

One of the soldiers had a knife at the Judge's throat. "You have no more control over Savignon, soldier of the Green."

"We may have ill-used you," the lady called to him, "but we are not your greatest enemy." She pulled a short blade from her belt. "It is time to kill a few Judges. I need a little sport!"

"We need to protect Aubric!" Sasseen called. "He is the one who will save us!"

"Flik! Blade!" the lady called. "Let us form a circle around our glowing soldier, and let this process reach an end."

Three soldiers, the lady, and Sasseen gathered around the glowing man. The lady pulled a second woman to her feet as she jabbed her sword at the approaching Judges.

Aubric moaned. The lights appeared to be sinking within his skin. The glow faded to a rosy pink, then vanished altogether as Aubric fell to his knees.

Aubric opened his eyes. There were no pupils in the sockets. Instead, his eyes were full of light.

"We will leave this place!" he called with a voice as loud as Gontor's. "But there will be a reckoning!"

A wind sprang up in the amphitheater, almost pushing Jacobsen to the ground.

"We can't leave without the key!" Gontor's voice called over the gale.

"Where would they hide something that valuable?" Summitch asked. "We can't let it blow away!"

The warrior clanged the blade end of his spear against the stone steps leading to the seats.

"Where, Tsang?" Gontor's voice boomed.

The warrior in white thrust his spear into what remained of the Great Judge.

"In the cloud, of course!" Gontor rushed forward.

A small black box fell into his hands.

Jacobsen decided it was his turn to urge them on. "So we got what we came for!" he shouted. "What say we get out of here?"

"This is far from the end," Gontor exclaimed. "But it is a glorious beginning!"

"No Judge will stand before me!" Aubric's voice rang out. "You will all fall! We shall be triumphant!"

"I think it's time for a change of scene!" Summitch remarked.

Jacobsen felt an abrupt shift. The wind was gone. Instead, the four of them were surrounded by blue sky, and sun, and grass, and trees. They had found their way back into the outside world.

"Wow," Jacobsen admitted.

"I've had enough of tunnels," Summitch agreed.

Gontor nodded. "The third key is elsewhere, but the four of us will find it."

It was all quite beyond Jacobsen. At least he was still alive. Alive and impressed.

All this from one simple gunshot.

· 31 ·

KEDRIK FOUND HIMSELF TORN from the embrace of his lovelies, the spell that surrounded him shattering into a thousand pieces, piercing his ecstasy, destroying his calm, ruining his love.

"Who dares?" he demanded. He found he was shivering. The spell was over far too soon; he had not had time to properly withdraw. He could still taste them on his lips, feel them in his loins. He took a deep breath. Whoever had done this to him would pay dearly.

The world of the castle swam back into focus.

The voice was far away at first, but grew louder with every word. "Forgive me, my lord, for this most improper intrusion."

It was Basoff, the Judge who had first given him this joy, first shown him this fulfillment. How could he, of all people, disturb—

Basoff still spoke. "We have important news, courtesy of Sasseen."

"Sasseen?" Kedrik had to struggle to place one word after another. "I thought he worked against us."

"No. My junior Judge simply pursues his own interests. For the time, his interests and those of the Grey intertwine. He has sent a messenger. He has found what we seek."

What they sought. Words swam into Kedrik's foggy brain.

"The seat of power?" he whispered.

Basoff nodded. "And at least some of the instruments."

Kedrik's wits abruptly returned. This was tremendous news.

"He asks for our aid," Basoff continued. "A bit forward of him, considering the circumstances. However, with such important dividends, I suggest that we give it."

"Very well," Kedrik agreed. He climbed from his bed, pulling his robe tight around him. "What do you wish of me?"

"I will need your seal on a couple of items," Basoff replied with a smile. "And it may be wise to issue a proclamation. The quicker we act, the better our chances of success."

"By all means." Kedrik led Basoff from the royal bedchamber and into the study beyond. He was eager to hear the Judge's plans. Together, they would bring the power to the High Court of the Grey. And once they had the power?

Kedrik cackled with delight.

His lovelies were almost forgotten. He could stand to be denied a moment of pleasure when he could have that pleasure for all eternity.

JOE FELT LIKE he'd been in the middle of a whirlwind. There had been a final moment's darkness after he'd shot Smith; then the world had returned to midday.

Ernie had turned on Smith in the end. Joe had heard a final gunshot. He guessed it came from Ernie's gun. He hadn't been able to tell, because, with that noise, the world was once again thrown into darkness.

The sky turned bright again. Smith was nowhere to be seen, but Ernie lay huddled on the ground.

"Are you all right?"

He turned at the sound of the voice and saw an attractive young woman with close-cropped hair. She was carrying a gun, too.

She nodded to Joe. "Jackie Porter. I drove Mrs. Mendeck here. I never got the chance to get out of the car."

"Don't worry, Officer Porter," Mrs. Mendeck called. "You've been more than helpful. And you'll get plenty of other chances—very soon."

Officer Porter? Then this woman was a cop.

He must have looked alarmed, because she said, "Don't worry. I'm not going to arrest you for anything. Frankly, I don't know what I'd arrest you for."

He stuck his own piece back in the shoulder holster, and turned back to look at the road. This whole scene had left him a little woozy. Ernie was flat on his back. Brian and Karen and the old lady had gathered around him.

"Is Ernie all right?" he called to the others.

"He's breathing," Mrs. Mendeck replied with a frown. "I don't see any blood."

Joe guessed that was good news. Ernie was a pretty hearty guy. Joe hoped his cousin was hearty enough to survive what had just happened.

"Is Smith gone?" Officer Porter asked.

Mrs. Mendeck paused before answering this time. "I'm afraid so. And I think he took part of Ernie with him."

What? Joe started walking quickly toward his fallen cousin.

"What do you mean?" he demanded.

"Ernie's body is here," the old woman replied. "But I don't sense his spirit."

Took his spirit? Well, Joe guessed Mrs. Mendeck was the authority.

"So what happens here?" he asked.

"To his body?" She shook her head. "I imagine it will

stay alive—for a while, like he's in a coma. But without the spirit, sooner or later the body will die."

So his cousin was as good as dead? Uncle Roman wasn't going to like this.

"How do we fix this?"

"I don't know if we can, unless someone goes after him."

Joe sighed. Wouldn't you just know it would end this way?

"Then I have to go." He shrugged. "It's a family thing."

Mrs. Mendeck considered this for a moment. "You'll need help. One of the two children. They're untrained, but very powerful."

Brian stepped forward. "I'll go."

"But—" the lady cop began.

"Officer Porter," Mrs. Mendeck chided. "We're going to need you here. Simply because Smith is gone for now doesn't mean that he, or someone else just as bad, couldn't pop back up on a moment's notice." She nodded at Joe. "I need to send you to an associate. Summitch is his name. He can see to Brian's training as well as I."

It was Brian's turn to frown. "How do you know he'll help us?"

"He has to. He owes me too many favors."

Joe almost panicked. What had he just agreed to do? What was he doing, going to enter a world full of Smiths?

Well, Uncle Roman would kill him, anyway.

"If you want to save your cousin," Mrs. Mendeck continued, "you'd best be going now." She lifted both her arms over her head. "This is my gift. I'm a sender, and I will send you straight to Summitch."

A tiny hole appeared half a dozen feet before Mrs. Mendeck, a hole that grew just like the other one had back in the apartment building, the first time he and Ernie ran into the old lady. It was accompanied by the usual wind, too. This time, Joe hoped he was ready for it.

"You ready?" Joe called.

"I guess so," Brian agreed.

Joe breathed deeply and took his first step into adventure.

Damn his cousin, anyway.